The
Jillian
Factor

B. A. Mealer

Copyright

BAM Publishing
P.O. Box 748
296 W., Grand Bvld.
Ash Fork, AZ 86320
bamealer@bamealer.com

First Printing, 2018
ISBN 978-1-970130-06-5 Paperback
ISBN 978-1-970130-05-8 Mobi
ISBN 978-1-970130-04-1 Epub
ISBN 978-1-970130-07-2 Hardcover

Acknowledgments

I would like to take this opportunity to commend the Lake County Sheriff's Department, which is composed of a wonderful group of men and women who work extremely hard to protect the people of Lake County. They put their lives on the line and do a fantastic job. I apologize in advance to them for my using their department and wish to let them know it was due to the resort being in their jurisdiction, so I really didn't have much choice. The situations in this book are from my imagination and does not reflect on their honesty and dedication to upholding the law and protecting the people of their county.

The idea for this novel came from a visit to the Vacation Village Resort on the shores of Lake Louisa. It is a beautiful area to go and relax, but me being me, I could imagine a murder, intrigue, and a few other things happening there. Hence, murder, impropriety, intrigue, mayhem, and a romance. All characters contained in this novel are figments of my imagination. Any relation to real situations or people is by chance only.

Chapter 1

MURDER 101

Jill's evening had become unbearable after spending the day listening to the continuous bickering among her family members. Without Brad, her oldest brother, being here with her, she couldn't stop her family's normal interaction, which was done loudly, using language most people don't use in public. Prior to her slipping out the front door into the peaceful night, her parents and two siblings had been engaged in a high-volume exchange over what to watch on TV for the evening. This was only one of the myriad of reasons she avoided spending time in their company. She could only imagine what the people on either side of the rented vacation villa were thinking.

Enjoying the peace of the night, Jill meandered along the semi-deserted winding resort road toward Lake Louisa, putting distance between herself, the villa, and her noisy family. This was her only vacation for this year, and she was wasting it staying here, unable to relax. After her arrival at the resort, the pleasant start swiftly decayed into a turbulent free-for-all. The family claimed it was a discussion, but to her, it wasn't a discussion. It was a grating, continuous, noisy confrontation with everyone screaming and no one listening, lasting from the time they got out of bed in the morning until going to sleep at night.

Resigned to the inevitable, she blinked back tears of pain from the pounding headache caused by the ongoing chaos. Upon reaching Lake Louisa Road, Jill stood for a few seconds surveying the area before continuing across the road to the sloping bank of the lake. Approximately halfway down the incline, she veered to the right to find a seat in the shadows of the trees, wanting to be alone. Until her headache eased, she didn't want to hear anything louder than the soft hum of insects and the sounds of the water.

The reflection of the rising moon shimmering on the surface of the water was beautiful and calming. A gentle breeze set the leaves to rustling, adding to the rhythmic soft lapping of the water against the shore. She took a deep breath, inhaling the scent of water and damp vegetation, wishing she could stay in this peaceful spot for the rest of the week. Eventually, she would need to return to the villa and her family. With luck, everyone would be passed out before then. There was no way she could withstand any more of their chaos before becoming nonfunctional.

The raised root of a cypress tree provided a seat off the damp ground and a perfect view of the lake. Leaning against the rough trunk of the tree, hidden in the shadow of the bush beside her, Jill released a big breath, allowing a few tears of self-pity to escape. This was a totally wasted vacation. Tomorrow, she would tell her parents she was summoned back to work. It was a lie, but it wasn't as if her parents or siblings would miss her. The prospect of spending the rest of the week at home, hiding from her boss was more enticing than enduring the chaos here.

After spending almost twenty years avoiding them, you'd think her parents would understand why she didn't visit. Two days was all she could endure of their ceaseless conflict. Each time they started, she developed a massive headache and transformed into a puddle of nonfunctioning protoplasm. Over the years she had explained the problem to them more than once, but to no avail.

It wasn't only her intolerance of the noise which set her apart in her family. There was no way to miss that she was the oddball. Her appearance was totally different from the rest of them. While her family members were these enormous giants, she was a diminutive five-five. Even her mother and sister were close to six feet tall, furthering the illusion of her not belonging with them.

Whereas the rest of the family had brown or green

eyes, she had inherited the columbine blue eyes of her grandmother. She had also inherited her grandmother's elfin facial features and stature. The only physical things she had inherited from her parents were their freckles and auburn hair. Again, she had taken after her grandmother with silky curls she kept to earlobe length. Meanwhile, her mother and sister left their coarse tightly curled hair long and untamed. While they were striking, she was a cute elf, appearing childlike even though she was in her twenties.

Being the family elf, or according to her grandfather, fairy, wasn't always pleasant. Rick and Belinda, and occasionally her father, would do things like patting her on the head, calling her shorty, twerp, imp, baby, and so forth while treating her as a child. Brad and Ryan, her oldest brothers, were the only two who treated her as an intelligent adult and helped her with the family dynamics. They were aware of her inability to handle the chaos and were quick to stop the others when at home. Yes, it was her problem, but a little consideration from the rest of her family for a week would have been nice.

A quick mental shake stopped her from dwelling further on her family problems. Her attention shifted to the full moon sitting on the horizon, silhouetting the trees and reflecting on the lake. The rhythmical sounds of the night soothed her pounding headache. As she relaxed against the tree, her eyelids fluttered shut, the small sparkling waves lulling her into a doze.

After spending close to three hours doing nothing but dozing and permitting the peacefulness of the night to seep into her, her headache had abated. From her left came the soft plop of a fish jumping to catch its evening meal. At the sound, she opened her eyes to the serene scene of the lake. With no noticeable ripples on the water, she presumed the jumping fish was farther away than it appeared from the sound. The moon, now high above the trees, indicated it was time to return to the villa and her family.

A movement to her left held her in place. The shadowy figure of a man rushing along the shore emerged from the brush and trees. He turned to his right and climbed the bank toward the road, his labored breathing harsh in the silence of the night. A few seconds later a woman dashed along the same course as the man, closing the distance between them as she ran up the bank, also breathing hard. The sounds of a low heated discussion reached Jill as the duo moved away across the road, proving her family weren't the only people with issues in the resort.

With seeing the couple, Jill decided to wait before leaving, not wanting to risk the possibility of running into anyone on her way back. After another half hour, she moved from her hiding spot, hoping her family would be in bed. Carefully working her way along the uneven ground in the moonlight, she searched for the faint path to the road in the dark.

Less than a minute later, Jill realized she had missed

the path when she reached a marshy inlet on her right. No big deal. If she followed the shore to the resort's cabin on the lake, a left at the driveway would take her to Lake Louisa Road. The extra distance would allow time to ensure the family would be in bed. Confident her two days of exploring the resort would enable her to find her way along the shore after missing the path to the road, Jill picked her way through the cypress and brush.

She passed the dock of the brown cottage located before the resort cabin before moving inland to avoid another marshy inlet. After stumbling over what she assumed was some roots, Jill moved closer to the lakeshore where the trees let more light from the moon in, enabling her to see obstacles on the ground. A rustling of leaves in the tall brush near several trees brought her to a halt. The noises sent her heart into overdrive. Something was there, stopping the normal sounds of the bugs and frogs as it moved through the brush.

Jill peered into the murky shadows, but there was no further movement seen or heard. When the normal night sounds returned, she relaxed. With a shrug, she continued toward the cabin, assuming the disturbance was caused by the wild cats scurrying around the complex.

The ghostly glow in the moonlight of the white resort cabin gave her a point of reference as she wended her way through the large cypress trees. The driveway to the dock was hidden by a dense patch of brush at the back of the cabin. Working her way around the obstructing plants, she kept to the shore where the moonlight filtered through the tall trees. After rounding a tall bush, she halted, staring at the scene before her.

There was someone prone on the ground in an open space a short distance from the shore. Casting her gaze around the immediate area, she noticed nothing unusual. The only sounds she heard were the typical night noises and a car moving slowly along the road. With a pounding heart and extreme caution, she moved to the person, careful not to disturb the immediate area.

It was a man, and he wasn't moving. Jill squatted beside him, checking for a pulse and breathing before spotting the gun in the man's right hand. There was a dark fluid oozing from under the shoulder near her foot, seeping into the dirt. From the coppery scent, it was fresh blood.

A man's voice from the dark commanded, "Freeze where you are," sending fear zinging through her.

Swiveling her head toward the disembodied voice, Jill studied the man standing in the shadows, a pistol aimed at her. While she didn't move, she tracked him as he approached, uncertain if he was the murderer or the police. From what little she had learned during the cursory examination of the man on the ground, he was dead.

"Stand up slowly. Hands on top of your head." The rich baritone voice held a melodic element, yet had a threat woven into it. She wanted him to continue speaking, but for now, there was no way to ignore his commands while looking down the barrel of the large caliber pistol, held with a finger on the trigger.

Jill stood up, her hands laced on top of her head, watching the gun. A slight shiver passed through her. Whether it was from fear or the coolness of the night breeze was a toss-up. She probably should have put on something warmer than her shorts, T-shirt, normal vest, and sandals. Flashing lights lit up the night from multiple vehicles pulling off the road into the driveway to the dock.

"Take two steps backward," was the next command. As she did as he requested, her eyes didn't move from the barrel of the gun. The last thing she needed was to get shot for finding a dead man.

Multiple police officers rushed past where they were standing, flashlights in their hands. She remained still while monitoring the officers surrounding the corpse on the ground. Jill caught her bottom lip between her teeth, aware the man with the gun, who was with the police, believed she was connected to the death of the person on the ground. First her family, now this. Some vacation!

After releasing a deep breath, she waited for the next orders from the gun-wielding man, concerned about her boss's reaction to her involvement in a homicide. He wouldn't be thrilled, to say the least, when he discovered she was a primary suspect. She was his best detective, and he had complained loud and long when she requested the vacation time to be with her family. He was correct. She should have stayed home for the week.

Jill continued to watch the officers surrounding the body, her hands on her head. An officer came to her and performed a quick frisk for weapons while Jill followed what the others were doing without moving. The only indication of what she was thinking was a tightening around her mouth and a slight shake of her head. The crime scene was now contaminated and useless for any evidence they may find.

"You can put your hands down," the man stated, his voice softer than before.

Jill lowered her arms. The multiple officers surrounding the dead body had destroyed what she had preserved. Why? Who had notified them of the man shooting?

The man advanced closer to her after holstering his gun. "Your name," he demanded, drawing her attention to him.

After she glowered in his direction, her gaze reverted to the dead body and the officers, lips pulled down in disgust. "Jillian Potter," she replied, readying herself for the question-and-answer session with a deep breath.

"Why are you here?"

His voice had changed to friendly, bringing her attention back to him, a crease between her eyebrows. That shift in his tone of voice after hearing her name confused her. Did he recognize her name? Until she discovered more about what had transpired here and the man beside her, the most viable option was to answer only the question asked if she wanted to stay out of jail.

"I was returning to my villa, when I rounded those bushes and trees and found him on the ground. I was checking for a pulse when you told me to freeze." Her waving hand had indicated the trees and brush she was referring to in her answer.

"What were you doing out here this time of night?"

"Avoiding my family." There was no reason to conceal the truth. Without an alibi, she was the primary suspect until proven differently. The man on the ground was dead, and she was found beside him.

"Why?"

Jill took another deep breath and let it out. "They were in one of their regular disagreements, and I didn't wish to be there."

"Where do you live?"

"Fort Lauderdale." It was the exact answer to his question.

Her gaze followed the officers by the body, waiting for the next question. He needed to ask for specific information, not generalities.

There was a pause of several seconds before he said, "Address, please."

Jill hid a smile behind the hand she raised to scratch

her nose, then gave him the mailing address to the Hollywood condo where she lived.

"Telephone number."

"954-735-2692." It was the landline number. The cellphone she carried was registered to the agency where she worked, not her. It was a perk of the job but not something he needed to know just yet.

The detective was quiet for a few seconds, then inquired, "Okay, why are you here in Clermont?"

"For a vacation."

"You mentioned a family. Are you here with them?"

"Yes." She glanced at him. Her responses were frustrating him. Too bad. He should be aware that not every person was stupid enough to ramble and give incriminating evidence.

His jaw muscles jumped from clenching his teeth. He took a few seconds before asking, "Do you recognize the victim?"

Jill wanted to grin at the annoyance she heard in his voice, but kept her expression neutral. "Probably not."

"I need a more precise answer, Ms. Potter," he sharply requested, revealing his growing exasperation with her short answers.

"I've only seen the back of his head," she informed him, crossing her forearms and facing him. "Until I see his face, I can't be more specific."

Jill had to look up at the man whose height was six-foot-plus or minus an inch or two. There was a badge on his belt, but she couldn't read it in the diffuse light from the flashlights and moon. Since he was in jeans and a T-shirt, she presumed he was a detective. With the way the others deferred to him, he was of sufficient rank to run a crime scene. The shadowy light hid his facial features, but he had that nice voice, which drew her to him. From what she could see, he was young, indicating he was very good at his job to be the detective in charge.

From his stance, he was studying her, attempting to figure her out from her answers. Jill quirked an eyebrow, her lips pursed to hide a grin, waiting for the next question. There was a slight upturning of his lips before he shook his head.

"I see you aren't the normal suspect," he observed, scanning the scene before his gaze shifted back to her.

"You're right, I'm not," she agreed.

"In that case, tell me what happened in your own words, starting from when you left your family. I need what you heard, observed, and who you talked to or met until I found you over the body." He had finally figured out how to get the information he wanted.

"Do you mind if we sit while doing this? I know you'll hold me for questioning, and I don't want to stand for the next couple of hours."

He let out a soft chuckle before escorting her to a stump from a recently cut tree. A crime scene van had arrived, and the team was setting up spotlights to start their investigation. Jill shook her head, mouth twisted in disgust. The original officers had destroyed the footprints, plus any other evidence around the body, making the crime scene unit unnecessary. Idiots!

Before imparting the information requested, she released a long breath. It wasn't easy to talk about her private life. The few seconds gave her time to get the pertinent facts in order.

"My family is dysfunctional. They love to argue and drink in that order. When there were no signs of them winding down this evening, I left to get away from the yelling and screaming. That was somewhere between nine and ten.

"I started walking and ended up at the lake, back toward the resort from here. I knew I would be hidden under the trees, so I found a place to sit and enjoy the moon on the water, allowing the headache I had to ease up.

"The moon was about three fingers above the horizon when a man came from this direction. He was walking fast before turning to go up the bank to the road to the resort. It wasn't but a few seconds later, a woman followed the man. She apparently caught up to him near the road, because I could hear them talking, but I couldn't distinguish the words. It sounded like they were having a disagreement as they continued moving toward the resort.

"Around twenty minutes later, I headed in this

direction looking for the path to the road. I missed it in the dark so decided to come to the cabin here by the dock, planning on using the driveway to get to the road. On the other side of those two trees, something moved in the bushes. I looked around, but there weren't any further sounds or movements, so I continued on toward the cabin."

This time her hand pointed to the specific bushes and trees, which had concealed the shore, the body, and the cabin from her.

"I walked around the trees and saw the victim lying there, not moving. I scanned the area, but didn't see anyone. When you saw me, I was checking to see if he needed help. I noted the gun near his hand and blood oozing from under him before you told me to freeze."

She stared at the lake before remarking, "I hope you realize they destroyed the crime scene."

"And how do you know that?" he asked without emotion.

"You're the detective. You tell me." Her blue eyes engaged his shadowed ones with her challenge. If he was any good at his job, he would ask questions to find out how she knew about crime scene procedures.

"Ms. Potter, you're in serious trouble right now. Don't play games with me."

"Call me Jill. I'm not my mother," she instructed before adding, "I can help you or be your worst nightmare in investigating this case. Your choice."

"You're our number one suspect, and so far, you haven't given me any reason to believe differently."

She sucked on her teeth at his being so dense. With sarcasm dripping from every word, she asked, "What did I use to kill him? Why was I still here? Someone had to have called you at least five to ten minutes ago, if not longer, before you arrived, so this murder didn't take place a few seconds ago. I've seen no one, and no, I don't know who the man is or what happened to him. I may have seen him around, but I can't say for sure until I see his face."

Jill watched as he rubbed his chin, contemplating what she had said. A "humph" told her he recognized the problem of her remaining a suspect. She had preserved the crime scene, but the initial police on the scene hadn't. Why?

She was curious about the couple who had passed by earlier. They had been in a hurry. The absence of gunshots made her question how the man had died. If he had been shot, as she presumed, they had used a silencer, but she hadn't heard any gunshots, with or without a silencer . . . or had she?

The detective finally asked the question which would give him the information he required. "What's your occupation?"

"I'm a private investigator," she answered, then pursed her lips, speculating if he would follow up on that piece of information.

She sensed his scrutiny. "Not very many private investigators walk around without a weapon on them."

Okay. He had picked up on one point, but it hadn't led to the question she had been expecting. Time to prevaricate. "I'm on vacation, several hundred miles from where I work. There's no reason to carry a weapon in a resort. Besides, I wouldn't have one where my family could find it. They'd use it on each other. My piece is in my car, secured and hidden so the idiots, who are my family, can't find it."

"Are they aware of what you do for a living?"

Jill grabbed her lower lip between her teeth for several seconds to quell the fear. It was the last question she had expected. "No. It's none of their business. I have a job, and that's all they need to know. My credentials are in my car with the gun, so they're not likely to find them."

"If your family is such a mess, why are you vacationing with them?" The question threw her. Why was he asking for information on her family? What the hell was he seeking?

"I needed a change of scenery. It also reinforced why I seldom visit them." It was only a partial truth of why she had come here.

"What sort of cases do you work for your agency?"

The change in topic was a common tactic to extract information, only the man was slow at picking up on the important points. It had taken him this long to ask one crucial question. "Mostly criminal for several private law firms who defend guilty and innocent people."

"Hmm, explains the comment concerning destroying the crime scene."

Duh! He finally got something right!

"So, I assume you work with the police?"

Jill wanted to let off a string of profanities, but instead said, "Let's just say I have an excellent working relationship with them."

"What sort of response would I get if I spoke to your employer?" he queried, scrutinizing her with an elevated eyebrow.

Jill grinned and leaned forward, her hands on the stump, her right foot moving back and forth in a smooth rhythm. "Be prepared for an earful of colorful words telling you what an idiot you are and how he expects me to return to work in a timely manner. I'll give you his number. I'm *positive* he'd just *love* a call in the middle of the night with you telling him I'm a suspect in a murder case."

"Okay. Give me the number so I can get it out of the way." There was a chuckle in his voice.

She reeled off the agency number as he dialed. When the phone started to ring, he put the call on speaker, allowing her to listen to her boss when he answered.

"Wyatt Detective Agency. How may I help you?" the gruff voice growled through the speaker. From his voice, Jill could tell he had been sound asleep and was trying to wake

up.

"This is Detective Thomas Wellington of the Lake County Sheriff's Department. I need to obtain some information on a Jillian Potter."

It was easy to imagine Wyatt bolting to a sitting position in the large bed, a scowl on his face at Tom's words.

"*What?*" Wyatt asked, his voice sharp. "*Is she okay?*"

Jill sucked in a sharp breath at the hint of fear in the words, before gnawing on her bottom lip again. She froze, waiting on what the detective would say next.

"Well, she's a suspect in a murder investigation," Thomas informed Wyatt as he observed her with a slight upturn of his lips as if he was having fun.

"*What the fuck?*" Wyatt roared. "*You motherfucking cocksucker. I don't know where you pricks got your fucking training, but she's my best fucking operative. You had better get your fucking heads out of your cocksucking asses. Jill is fucking better than the most experienced fucking detective you fuckers have. If I have to fucking come up there, you cocksuckers will regret it. She's a highly respected investigator and works with the fucking police. I want to fucking talk to her, you fucking moron.*"

His tirade was more intense than she anticipated, but that could be partly due to the relief that she wasn't hurt or missing.

"I'm here, Wyatt," she stated before he went off the deep end. A glimpse at the man she now knew was Thomas

Wellington, detective of LCSD, surprised her. He was grinning, enjoying the conversation.

"What the fuck, Jill?" Wyatt bellowed.

She cut him off before he could continue. "I found a body on the shore of the lake. Because I was the only person around, I'm the primary suspect. It's the normal drill."

"Fucking idiotic morons," he growled, having gained control of himself during her explanation. There was a hesitation before he asked, *"Were you packing?"*

"No, I'm not stupid. I'm with my crazy family."

"Fuck!" Wyatt exclaimed. She knew where he was coming from when he said, *"Jill, get your fucking ass back here. I have three fucking cases I need you to work and that fucking court case next month."*

"Well, darling, you need to convince the nice detective here I'm not a murderess."

Thomas was pleasant when he said, "Mr. Wyatt, I take it you know Jill well enough to vouch for her."

"Cocksucker. What the fuck do you think? She's been working for me for five fucking years." Jill sucked on her cheeks to keep from chuckling. If Detective Wellington wanted to have Wyatt blow, he only needed to ask how good she was at her job.

"So, I take it, you're positive she's not likely to have killed a man." Tom glanced at her, grinning. He *was* having fun with this conversation at her and Wyatt's expense.

As expected, Wyatt went ballistic. *"You're the stupidest cocksucking asshole in the state if you even consider her a fucking suspect. She may be a fucking bitch, but she ain't no fucking killer. You mother fucking sons of a bitch had better get your fucking heads out of your cocksucking asses. She's due in fucking court next month, and I don't need this fucking crap messing up a fucking murder case."*

She knew what he wasn't saying. Time to reinforce this was a routine to be endured. "Chill, Wyatt. I'll be there. He needed to verify I wasn't trying to pull a fast one on him."

"Jill, you had better get your fucking ass back here as soon as the fucking assholes clear you to leave there. Don't you ever ask for a fucking vacation with your fucking family again."

She reiterated, "Wyatt, I'll be back in time for the court case."

Thomas, with a grin, stated, "Mr. Wyatt, we'll be taking a formal statement from her. At the moment, there's minimal evidence to hold her, but we'll need her to stick around for several days until the preliminary investigation is completed."

"You had better keep me posted, Jill. I don't trust the fucking cocksuckers to not try and pin this on you."

"I'll keep you posted. If I need your help, I'll call."

"You fucking better. I'll be there in less than three fucking hours."

"Thank you, Mr. Wyatt," Thomas replied. "I'm positive she'll call you if she isn't released."

Wyatt broke the connection. Her foot continued the

rhythmic back-and-forth movement, lips pursed, cheeks sucked in, waiting for Thomas's commentary on Wyatt. He was crude, but was an expert private investigator, having worked as a police detective for ten years before opening his own agency. Also, he would be the one to show up if they arrested her, not some underling.

What she wasn't telling Thomas was how Wyatt was six four with more muscles than any one human being should have, coupled with a bad attitude if crossed. One run-in with him had many a seasoned police officer or criminal backing down and rethinking challenging him. He was a force to be reckoned with in any situation even though he was at retirement age. Not only that, he had a lot of influence in the legal system, working with many agencies, local and nonlocal. Most of the agents he worked with were in powerful positions.

Thomas's voice drew her back to the situation at hand. "You could have informed me who you worked for instead of waking him up in the middle of the night."

"And miss all the fun?" she asked, holding in a giggle.

"Well, it would have spared our ears, if nothing else. I can see he hasn't changed."

Her gaze locked onto him as she stared at the portion of his face revealed in the dim light. "So, I take it you've met him."

"Oh, yeah. He'll recognize my name, and I'm expecting a callback in less than ten minutes to berate me for being an idiot and a moron."

"If he knows you, I'll give him less than five minutes to remember your name."

The phone rang. It had taken Wyatt less than three minutes to place the detective. Thomas didn't get a word out before Wyatt grated, *"Tom, you cocksucker. You better get my girl off the hook and fucking fast."*

"I'm working on it. It took a few answers before I figured out she knew how to answer my questions without giving me the information I wanted. I've a hunch we'll be using her on this, so don't get too eager to get her back for three or four days to a week at least."

"You'd better let her get back to her fucking job. She's the best I've had since you fucking left." Wyatt was upset with Tom and her involvement in a murder while on vacation. There was still fear in his voice, which concerned her.

"Wyatt, don't go there. I'll have her back before that court case, with no criminal charges."

"You just get her the fuck back to me." Wyatt hung up, not allowing the detective time to respond.

Thomas chuckled. "Okay, I have my orders. Now, getting you off the hook for murder might be problematic until we find out who our victim is and precisely how he died. Let's see if you recognize our corpse."

The crime scene investigators had rolled the body over to his back. She and Thomas joined those in the circle of bright lights shining on the body. The man was shot at close range in the chest, the entry near the heart. Jill stared at the face, attempting to quell the sense of doom washing over her. The dead man was someone she knew from Fort Lauderdale. There was no way to hide the connection to him. Time for enough truth to keep her ass out of jail. Unconsciously, she pushed the curls back from her face and fluffed them, while deciding how much information to give the detective.

What she imparted was minimal. "His name is Charles Knight. Four days ago, he was in Broward County. He's a known drug trafficker, and is suspected of smuggling illegal immigrants. I haven't seen him around here since I arrived on Friday."

"Anything to connect you to him?" Thomas asked, staring at the corpse, his brows knitted together in a frown.

This was where things got tricky. With a sense of dread, she answered the question. "Yes. He's involved in the case I'm currently working. He dropped an illegal who, when picked up, has accused him of kidnapping his sister, then threatening to pimp her if he didn't pay the requested ransom. We were hired to find her. The illegal's concern is his sister, not the charges against him. She's barely seventeen."

Thomas remained silent, studying the body, before asking, "Do you know of any reason for Knight to show up here?"

"Not sure. Maybe I was too close to what he was doing."

It was the truth. He had ties to this area, but did he really know she was here, or was there another reason? No one other than her family and Wyatt knew she was going for the week, so it was a stretch for him to have known she was here.

"Please explain that statement?" Thomas demanded, rotating his head to face her.

She shifted away from him, her hand automatically sweeping the loose curls of her short hair behind her right ear. With a slight twitch of her shoulders, she concluded it wouldn't compromise her case to give him more information.

"He was taking the money for smuggling people into the country, then was delivering all but the younger women. The families had to pay more for him to release them. If they didn't, he sold the women to the highest bidder. He was aware I had evidence he was the one demanding the ransoms. I've been working on discovering where the women are being held. Charles was pond scum. He'd do anything for a buck."

"Anyone you know who would want him dead?" Thomas inquired, guiding her back to the stump.

She glanced back to the body, a scowl on her face. "You'd be better off asking who didn't want him dead. That list is short."

Detective Wellington changed the subject again. "You're still concerned about the man and woman who went toward the resort, aren't you?"

"Of course. My guess is they came along here near the time of the murder. If they didn't do it, they may have seen who did."

A crime scene officer came to where they were sitting. He reported to Thomas, confirming him as the lead homicide detective on this case. "Our corpse was shot at close range with a large caliber pistol with a silencer. There's only one hole. Best guess as to time of death is within the past two hours."

Thomas inclined his head toward the man to indicate he had heard him. "Well, Jill, that means a trip to the station. We need to get your statement on record and do a quick gunpowder check."

"So long as I have a ride back. I'm not paying for a taxi back to here from Tavares."

Thomas ignored her statement. "I'll need your gun."

Jill took one last look at the destroyed crime scene. "Let's go. I need to get my keys without waking up the beasts."

Chapter 2

TRUST AND SECRETS

Tom placed a hand at her waist, walking her to the driveway where the squad cars with flashing lights were parked. She ignored the gathered vacationers awakened by the lights. He guided her to his car, opening the front passenger door, indicating for her to get in. She directed him to the villa where she and her family were staying. He parked in the parking lot around the corner from the building, walking with her to the front of the villa.

"I'll be right back," she declared before unlocking the front door, not wanting him to come in with her for fear of waking up one of the family.

He nodded and took a seat on the low wall to wait, trusting her to return with the keys to her car. It only took a few minutes to retrieve her purse from her room without waking the now-sleeping family. Once the door was closed, she handed the purse to Tom. He went through it, looking for weapons, before lifting out her keys. Jill walked around the side of the building to the parking lot at the rear of the villa, leading him to her beat-up car. She waited until he opened the trunk.

"Allow me to get it," she requested, rather than permitting him to tear the trunk apart to locate where she had hidden the gun case.

When he didn't object, she lifted the wheel-well cover, then the tire, before stepping back for him to remove the compact case from where the jack should have been stored. Tom opened the case, visually examining the Glock and three magazines before removing the two IDs and concealed weapon permit. He didn't touch the gun before closing the case. His hand again returned to her waist, guiding her back to where his car was parked.

Her eyes shifted to his face when he opened the front passenger door again. His hand on her arm indicated she was to get into the car. Swiftly she slid in and fastened her seat belt. He deposited the gun case behind the driver's seat. For her, anything was better than riding in the back of a police car, but this wasn't standard procedure for a murder suspect.

Thomas folded himself into the driver's seat, closed the car door, then faced her in the dim interior. "Jill, I take it one of those cards I took was a concealed weapons permit."

"Yes, it's there along with my police and PI IDs."

"Yet you aren't carrying. Why?"

Jill avoided looking at him. "Like I explained you before, I have a crazy family. There's no way any sane person would have a gun near them. Besides, I'm here on vacation."

She was conscious of him watching her as she stared out the windshield. Yes, she was lying, not wanting to give up the small pistol she was carrying until they arrived at the sheriff's office.

"I know you have one on you. Where is it before you get into serious trouble at the station?" He glared at her, his mouth in a straight line, confident he was correct, which he was.

Reluctantly, she reached behind her and withdrew the pistol from the soft holster around her middle. She was surprised when the officer who searched her hadn't found it. When Thomas put his hand at her waist, almost on top of it, it was all she could do to keep from hyperventilating.

She swiveled her head to face him. He lifted a brow, holding out the evidence bag for her gun. The 380 Glock wasn't all that small, but the officer hadn't done a thorough search. The soft holster had shielded it when the officer had only lightly tapped the area and assumed it was her spine. Reluctantly, she dropped the gun into the bag. Before he could ask, she reached into her pocket and removed a credit card knife, dropping it into the bag with the gun.

"We need to teach our officers how to do a thorough search. He should have found that pistol, and a credit card in your pocket should have made him suspicious," Thomas stated as he studied her, his voice calm.

Jill didn't reply, because working for Wyatt meant you were never off-duty. Since you never knew when you would need it, you didn't go anywhere without your weapon. It was part of the job.

"Do you have anything in your shoes or hidden in the bra?" he probed.

"No. That's it. I wasn't expecting problems up here. I turned off my phone before I left to prevent being traced through it. Wyatt's the only one who knew where I would be, other than my family."

"Jill, I can't help you unless you're honest with me. I understand not leveling with me about the gun. I would have done the same thing. Now, again, any other weapons on you?"

"No."

"Now, why don't I believe you?" His stare backed up his words.

"I've got no other weapons I can give you," she stated, telling him the truth this time.

"Explanation, Jill."

With her head lowered, she clasped her hands in her lap, fingers woven together, before giving him his explanation. "I have advanced martial arts training. If I want to kill someone, I don't need the weapons. In two quick moves, I could kill you without your feeling it. You wouldn't be able to stop me without the same level of training."

Jill shifted in her seat, gaze on the windshield. "I'm the weapon. It's the reason Wyatt wants me back. I can get in and out of places others can't because I'm difficult to stop." She peeked at him, unsure if he believed her. It was the truth as far as she took it. There was another reason Wyatt wanted her back, but that was none of the nice detective's business.

There was silence as he examined her, his expression composed, lips pursed. "So, you could have gotten away with me holding a gun on you," he inquired.

"Easily. There was no reason to leave. I needed to know which side you were on before reacting."

"So, you're going with me voluntarily, knowing you may end up in jail for a murder you didn't commit."

She chuckled at his statement before turning away from him. "Yes. It won't stick, but you can try." Jill sobered then faced him again, wanting to reassure him she wouldn't create a problem. "Detective Wellington, I won't try anything stupid. I would have given the weapons to you before getting out of the car. It's just that I don't like being without the normal defenses. I don't use the other until I have no other viable choice left.

"I'm on your side where this case is concerned. Like you, I want to discover who killed Knight and why. I also want to find our client's sister. Once I have that information, perhaps I can find the others he's held or is still holding. Knight was a minor player, but his operation leads to bigger fish. One or more of them may be in your territory if Knight was here." The last sentence was an understatement. She knew the fish were here, but needed a link to them from Knight.

"Call me Tom," he ordered. "Jill, I hope to God you're telling me the truth. I've worked too damn hard to get to where I am to have it come crashing down around me." His gaze didn't leave hers.

It wasn't difficult to decipher what he hadn't said. "I understand. Undercover sucks sometimes."

He didn't refute her statement, convincing her she had it correct. Even though he was a homicide detective with the police here, he was deep, and she wasn't going to blow his cover. He needed her cooperation.

"Don't worry, Tom. I've been doing this long enough to protect you and what you're doing. It looks like our cases are overlapping. I may be of help to you with what I've discovered, and you can help me with some of the missing links in my case."

Detective Wellington started the car without answering and pulled out of the parking space. Jill felt the tension radiating off him. A primary concern was blowing his cover, then there was Wyatt's orders to clear her of murder. He was young, but he didn't get to where he was without being smart and good at his job.

For clues, all she had was one dead criminal, a missing murder weapon, two mysterious people in a hurry, and an undercover detective who knew her boss. So much for a vacation. The connection appeared to be Wyatt and the case he had her working. Had she finally gotten into a case leading her to the bigger fish she wanted to fry?

Staring out the window, Jill knew there was nothing to do but play by the rules and let the chips fall as they may. Wyatt was her ace in the hole. He'd get her off if they tried to charge her with anything, let alone murder.

Chapter 3

THE PLOT THICKENS

Tom pulled into the secured parking area at the county sheriff's department in Tavares. When he shut off the engine, Jill exited the car and waited on him to join her. With a hand at her waist and the gun case and evidence bag in his other hand, he guided her into the station. They stopped at the duty desk and waited for the officer to process the paperwork for her weapons.

She was instructed to take a seat in one of the plastic chairs bolted to the floor where the duty officer could observe who was sitting there. She wondered what was in store for her when a female officer came and performed a thorough frisk for weapons. When the officer was finished, Jill noticed Tom waiting at the doorway to a hall. He motioned for her to join him. Apparently, her statement wasn't going to be taken in the fishbowl.

In the bright overhead lighting, she noticed he was a decent-looking man, somewhere around thirty to thirty-five, give or take a year or two. The nondescript light brown hair, a face without any distinguishing features, and a physical build, which didn't make him stand out were all pluses if you didn't want to be noticed. He was a person you would initially see, then forget or pass over, unless you noticed his eyes or heard him speak.

The pine green eyes followed her as she advanced toward him. Her heartbeat sped up as she ambled across the large room, imagining the impossible where he was concerned. Even with having met less than three hours ago, there was no way she would forget those eyes or his mesmerizing voice any time soon.

He led her to an interrogation room, then left her alone after saying he would return in a few minutes. The furniture consisted of a metal table and three institutional molded chairs. There was a one-way mirror on the wall to the left of the door. On the other side of the mirror would be Tom's bosses, watching him interview her.

Jill wandered around the small room, attempting to get a handle on the murder. Knight being here raised many questions needing answers. First and foremost was: Why was he here and who had he met on the shore of the lake?

Another question was who, among the large number of suspects who hated Knight, killed him? Was it someone at the resort or a person he met by the lake? The couple who had passed her were still persons of interest. Had they seen who killed Knight, or observed something that led to the heated discussion they engaged in while leaving the area? Since they passed by near the time of the murder, had they murdered Knight?

Damn. Why was this all happening while she was on vacation? Luckily, she hadn't fired a weapon since she had been here. Neither one of her guns had a silencer, nor had they been fired since target practice at the range last week. The quick test shouldn't show enough gunpowder to hold her for Knight's murder. The last thing she needed or wanted was Wyatt to show up, making things worse than they already were with her family.

An officer entered the room, a kit in his hands. After taking samples from her hands, arms, and clothes to run the quick test for gunpowder residue, she was left alone again. Before resuming her pacing, Jill glanced down at what she was wearing. The outfit wasn't the one she had worn to the range, so the residue test would be inconclusive.

She needed to discover why Knight was here. Once she had that information, it should lead to why he was murdered and possibly to the murderer. Shit, the last thing she needed was to sit in jail on a murder charge. This was her case, and she needed those answers!

After a quick scan of the room, she faced the large mirror, letting whoever was back there get a good look at her before moving to the table and chairs. A quick rearrangement of the chairs made it so her back would be to the mirror. Only the officer questioning her needed to observe her reactions as she answered their questions. And yes, *their* was the correct term. Tom would confer with the higher-ups as to what questions to ask her and they would watch through the mirror as he asked those questions. She worked with the police enough to know their routines.

The door opened and Tom, with another officer trailing him, entered the room. Tom stood with a hand on the table as the officer read her rights from the card he held. After answering, "I understand my rights," she asked, "Am I being arrested? If so, for what?"

"You're not under arrest, yet," Tom stated, observing her reaction to the word *yet* before scanning the room. A quick lift of the right eyebrow showed he hadn't missed the rearrangement of the chairs. "Please take a seat," he requested with a straight face, but she noted the merriment in his expression when he faced her.

Taking the chair with her back to the mirror, Jill placed her arms on the table, hands folded together. This was his show, not hers, but that didn't mean she needed to be a passive participant.

"This interview will be recorded. Please recite your full name, date of birth, address, and occupation." Tom placed a portable recorder on the table and flicked the on switch.

After reading her rights to her and now the private interrogation, Jill was positive they were attempting to pin the murder on her. She recited her name, date of birth, address, and occupation then waited. Tom needed to be careful with the questions. She would only answer what he asked. There were several tracks of questioning he could try. It was a tossup as to which way he would go.

"Jillian, in your own words, please tell me what transpired earlier tonight." Okay, so he hadn't forgotten the earlier question-and-answer session. Maybe there was hope for him after all.

Jill repeated her statement at the scene, adding nothing to the recitation while watching Tom's face. She had nothing to hide in finding Knight. The police needed to find something more concrete than minor powder residue to hold her, and that was what this session was all about, finding a way to charge her with murder.

Tom's next question was no surprise. "When did you last fire your weapons?"

"Last week at the firing range. Tuesday to be exact."

"What range?"

"The police range in Broward County."

"Will we be able to verify the day and time you were there?"

"Yes. I have to sign in and out. Plus, I date and initial my targets and leave them there."

"You haven't fired a gun since then?" he questioned, watching her, not missing a thing in her reaction to the questions.

"No, sir."

"When did you last clean your guns?"

"When I got home from the range."

He moved on to what they hoped was enough to hold her for murder. "Prior to today, had you seen the victim?"

"Yes." The short answer resulted in Tom pausing. It was her turn to lift an eyebrow. There was no way she was volunteering information at this time.

"Where had you seen him before today?"

She stifled a grin. "Broward County."

"Did you have any contact with him? If so, please explain that contact."

"Knight was a person of interest in the case I'm currently working." Tom's questions were by the book and her answers weren't those of the normal suspect. That last open-ended question was intended to elicit information as a person rambled through a response.

"No other connection to him?"

"None," she answered, with a frown, wondering where this line of questioning was headed.

"So, you never socialized with him or went to his home?"

Aha. Now it was clear what they were doing, but it wouldn't work. "Yes, I socialized with him, and yes, I've been to his house."

"Work related or personal?"

"Work related."

"You mentioned him as a person of interest in a case you were working on prior to coming here. Why was he under investigation?"

"A client accused him of kidnapping a seventeen-year-old girl and holding her for ransom."

"Who hired the agency for this job?"

"That's confidential information, and you'll need to contact the Wyatt Detective Agency with a subpoena to obtain the person's name."

"Do you know who hired the agency for this job?"

"No."

"No?" His head popped up, a crease between his brows, staring at her.

"I'm not privy to the client's name as it isn't pertinent to my portion of the case." Dunce. As if she was going to release confidential information even if she knew the man's name. Any policeman worth a damn was aware a reputable

PI didn't release a client's name. Even if the operative knew the name, without prior approval from the client or a court order, it was confidential information for the agency and was never disclosed. Like doctors and lawyers, there were rules of confidentiality for private investigators.

Tom darted a glance at the mirror. It was confirmation of someone watching and listening. Not reacting as expected to the questions or his glance, she watched him, waiting for the next question. She had her reasons for moving the chairs so her back was to the mirror, and this was one. The officers watching couldn't see her reactions and she could see the questioning officer's communication with those behind the mirror.

"What are you able to tell us about the person who hired the agency?"

"The man is an illegal alien and hired Knight to bring his family here. His seventeen-year-old sister wasn't delivered with the rest of the family. Knight wanted more money to release her."

"And you don't know who this person is, correct?"

"Correct."

"How often were you and Knight seen together?"

Tom was good at questioning. She knew most suspects would blurt out all sorts of information as their fear increased. She kept her answer short and concise.

"Often enough for people who knew him to assume we were dating."

"How many nights did you spend with him?"

"None."

"Any physical relationship with him?"

"No."

Tom studied her, the green eyes not leaving her face, before asking, "Have you ever engaged in a physical relationship with a person under investigation by you?"

Okay, this was getting way too personal. Her past relationships had nothing to do with this case. Time to pay attention to what other information they wanted to use to discredit her.

"No."

"Jill, I need the truth."

She glared at him. "I have never engaged in a physical relationship with a person under investigation by me or the agency."

"Then explain the relationship with Quinton Harrington?"

She ground her teeth to keep her temper under control before answering the question. Someone had gained access to her personal information and was now using it in an attempt to throw her under the proverbial bus, but they didn't have all the details.

"That relationship was over long before then. Nothing personal happened during the time he was being investigated."

The controlled voice used in answering the question

warned anyone who knew her to be very careful, or be prepared to deal with a miniature Wyatt.

"What was your relationship with Harrington?"

"I met him before going to work for the agency. We were a couple for close to a year. I broke it off after discovering he was using and selling drugs."

"You didn't go over the investigation, Jill."

"Two years ago, there was an agent in deep cover with a group of drug dealers, and my job was to get him out alive while helping the authorities break the ring. I ran into Harrington again on that assignment. My investigation ended up taking down the drug ring. I used our past relationship to get the agent out alive. Harrington got ten years for dealing. He'll verify there was no rekindling of the past relationship."

"And we're to believe a criminal?"

She let out a big breath to calm herself before saying, "Why would he lie to protect me? I put him in jail and he knows it."

Tom's voice and expression were controlled when he commanded, "Tell me about Jason Aldean?"

Damn. How in the hell did these guys get all this information? Was he going to go through her whole past at their request? Her anger cooled. Fear took its place. The past wasn't a place she wanted to go at any time, and during a murder investigation was the worst possible time to delve into the things she kept hidden.

"What about him?" she asked, relaxing against the back of the chair. She wasn't going to let the questions drive her into revealing information they may not have.

"What was your relationship with him?"

"We were close friends." Before Tom could ask, she added, "Yes, I spent the night at his place several times, but I slept in the guest bedroom."

"Yet you investigated him."

"Yes."

"Why were you investigating him?"

"That's confidential information you'll need to obtain from the agency."

Tom tilted his head, lips pursed as he studied her. "So, if I want any information on any other personal relationships with people you investigated, we need to contact the agency?"

"Yes."

The glare she sent in his direction dared him to go after the information they wanted. Asshole! Any more questions concerning any other cases, or her private life would result in that call to Wyatt for a lawyer. It took all her willpower to stay calm as she waited for the next question.

The man was a real piece of work. He could have refused to ask questions that weren't relevant to the murder investigation. Wyatt could expect an interrogation when she got back as to how these people obtained their information, because those cases and her involvement weren't in the public realm.

The officer who had taken the sample earlier entered the room and handed Tom a piece of paper. He studied the report before staring at her.

"I'll return in a few minutes."

He and the other officer left her alone in the room. No doubt he was conferring with whoever was watching the interview. Unable to remain sitting, Jill wandered around the small room, attempting to regain a sense of calm after the unexpected probing into her past.

They didn't have a reason to hold her. The quick test for residue wouldn't have enough residue to prove she fired a gun recently, let alone a few hours ago. The amount of gunpowder revealed by the test on her hands and arms could be explained by contamination from multiple sources. Yes, she knew enough to be dangerous to them if they didn't have an airtight case against her.

Tom reentered the room with the other officer on his heels in less than five minutes. She again took a seat at the table.

"Jill, do you always date criminals?" he asked, raising the question of how much more information these people had concerning her past.

"No," she snapped, scowling at him for asking the ridiculous question which had upped the fear factor for her. Fear of a past that could destroy her career if revealed in the wrong way.

Who she dated, past or present, wasn't anyone else's business. He and his handlers would get nothing further from her. They weren't privy to the whys of her past and weren't likely to be now or in the future. Wyatt had the answers, but it meant obtaining a federal warrant or subpoena to obtain that information.

Tom took the chair opposite her. "We're going to let you go. There isn't enough evidence to hold you, but don't leave the county without clearing it with us first. So far, your story checks out. Now, how may we get in touch with you?"

Okay, reasonable question. He must have figured out that the number she gave earlier wasn't for her cellphone. There was no reason to keep the cellphone off. The people she was hiding from now knew she was here.

"Use my cell. 954-554-2839. It isn't on, but I'll turn it on when I get back to the resort."

Tom turned off the recorder before escorting her to the property desk to complete the paperwork to retrieve her weapons and purse. She put the small gun into the hidden holster. The knife went back into her pocket. She checked her purse and the gun case for missing items. Someone had put her IDs and concealed weapon permit back into the case. After closing the case, she picked it up and let Tom lead her back to his car. He again held the front passenger door for her. She slid into the seat and fastened the seat belt for the trip back to the resort.

Tom took the driver's seat, snapping the seat belt in place, but didn't start the car. Facing straight ahead, his hands on the wheel, he said, "I'm sorry about what went down in there. It seems someone knows you quite well." He rotated his head to face her. "Jill, I'm sure there are good reasons why you're personally connected to criminals who are now in jail. They were trying to connect you to the criminals with those questions. You're lucky there wasn't but minimal residue on your hands or arms or you would be sitting in jail charged with murder."

She turned away and stared out the windshield, anger coursing through her. "My past is none of your fucking business. I'm a damn good detective, and what I do in my private life has no bearing on this or any other case."

"Someone seems to think it does. You may want that lawyer on hold just in case they find a way to put you on the inside looking out."

"I'll have one of the best lawyers in the state with one call. They knew there wasn't enough evidence to hold me, so why waste the time doing the paperwork only to have me released in less than four hours."

"I take it if you were arrested, Wyatt would be here in less than the three hours he promised."

"Fucking right he would!" she snapped before crossing her arms, jaw clamped to keep from saying more. She wasn't sure which side of the law he was working. Until determining who he really worked for, he was the enemy.

"From your language, I take it you're not in the best of moods," he stated with a snicker.

She glared at him before turning back to the windshield. He wouldn't be in a good mood either if someone was trying to frame him for murder.

He observed, "I guess there's just enough red in that hair to give you a nice temper." Her head whipped around, setting her curls to bouncing. The scowl on her face warned him to back off before returning her gaze to the windshield.

With a chuckle, he started the car, then backed out of the parking space as she fumed. Insufferable asshole. He asks her about things not related to the murder and then wonders why she's pissed. Imbecilic moron!

The sun peeked over the horizon as they pulled into the parking lot at the resort. A hand on her arm held her in place before she could open the door.

"Jill, stay in touch with me with what you find. You need to work with me or I can't protect you. Wyatt will hang me out for the vultures if anything happens to you." He waited until she faced him. "You must mean a lot to Wyatt for him to be so upset," he finished, studying her face.

"Now, just what made you think he was upset?" she snidely questioned, wondering if he really knew just how shaken up Wyatt was when he hung up the phone last night.

Tom stared out the windshield and let a smile form on his lips before he rotated his head to face her. "Well, Wyatt's normally crude, but gets more so when pissed. When he didn't let loose with his normal verbiage when I mentioned your name, it made me wonder about your relationship with him. Until I stated why I called, he was panicking. When he stated he would be here in less than three hours, it let me know he feels personally responsible for you. As far as I know, none of the other detectives he has working for him have that type of devotion from him."

Okay. He knew Wyatt better than most of those who worked for him. She would give him a chance to show which side of the law he was working.

"Give me your card. I'll call if I find anything relevant."

He was correct in that Wyatt had a good reason for protecting her. Yes, he also had a reason to be upset. He had offered her the use of his place in the Bahamas or Aruba as an alternative to coming here. She had turned him down to spend time with a family she normally avoided when Brad promised to be here to run interference for her.

Her last vacation had been spent at the villa in Aruba, but that was information Detective Thomas Wellington didn't need for this case. He also didn't need to know she was living in one of Wyatt's penthouses. That was also between her and Wyatt.

Tom handed her a card. She put it in her pocket

without looking at it. If the card didn't have a cellphone number, he'd never get a call from her.

"Thanks for the ride back," she said before opening the car door.

His voice held her in place. "Jill, be careful. They'll kill you now that they know you're working for Wyatt."

"That's my problem, not yours," she snarled before she stepped out of the car and slammed the door. Imbecile. This wasn't her first day on the job!

The trail for Knight led to somewhere in this area. It was only a coincidence she was here on vacation. A lucky coincidence, but a coincidence just the same. Time to go back to work. Her vacation was over, not that it had been much of one up to this point.

Chapter 4

FIRST THERE WAS ONE

After returning her gun case to its hiding place, Jill slipped in the front door of the villa. She entered her room without awakening the family. Exhausted, she collapsed onto the bed, having been up for twenty-three hours.

Prior to agreeing to come for the week, she had insisted on having a private room. There was no way she was sharing sleeping space with Belinda. Along with a private space to retreat to when the constant battling became overwhelming, it enabled her to come and go at will. Hopefully today, no one would awaken until late morning or early afternoon, allowing her to get at least three hours of uninterrupted sleep.

At one fifty in the afternoon, Jill awakened to the smell of food and her brother, Rick, yelling at Belinda. Her parents began bellowing at each other over the plans for the rest of the day after screaming at Rick and Belinda to stop. She had slept for two hours longer than expected after going to bed at daylight.

Once showered and dressed, Jill shoved her cellphone, the key to the villa, and Tom's business card in the pocket of the cargo shorts she had donned. The TV program playing loudly in the living room was punctuated by bursts of accusations hurled between the four family members. The noise allowed her to slip out of her room without being noticed.

She snatched two still-warm hamburgers from the tray on the counter, then snuck out the front door, leaving them to their day. It didn't take long to arrive at the police tape surrounding where Knight's body had lain. It was being guarded by a young police officer. She walked around the cordoned-off crime scene while finishing the last hamburger.

The only evidence inside the tape was the congealed blood. The initial officers at the scene did a good job of destroying the evidence in and around the crime scene. The footprints and any other clues were gone.

There was nothing new to examine, so Jill retraced her steps from last night. At the spot where she had heard the rustling in the bushes, she stopped. A scan of the trees and bushes in the daylight turned up a footprint in the soft dirt near a thicket of brush. There was a recently broken branch on one of the bushes. Someone or something large had recently moved through the dense brush just beyond the footprint. With care, avoiding where the person had passed through the thicket, she eased her way between the bushes. To the right of a small opening in the brush, nestled in tall grass, she saw the unexpected—a gun with a silencer attached.

Not moving from the spot, Jill retrieved her cellphone and Tom's card from her pocket. After dialing the cellphone number, she waited for him to answer. It took only two rings.

"*Jill, what's up?*"

The deep melodic voice sent a wave of warmth through

her, but the use of her name startled her. Then again, how many people with a 954 area code would be calling him today?

"Where are you?" she questioned, hoping he was nearby.

"Just pulling into the parking area by the dock. Why?"

"Meet me by the lake to the right of the crime scene."

"Be there in two minutes."

Jill backed out of the brush and waited for Tom. A few minutes later she spotted him striding toward her. The young detective looked even better in daylight. From his energetic strides, like her, he must have gotten a few hours of sleep.

Today he was dressed in fitted jeans, a black T-shirt stenciled with the sheriff department logo, and tennis shoes. Again, a badge was attached to his belt. The thick short hair was combed, and he had shaved. To her, he was eye candy with the neat, unremarkable appearance.

As he strode toward her, Tom scanned the vicinity, his gaze resting momentarily on the officer guarding the crime scene. The expressive lips turned up in a big smile, then quickly flattened into a grim line upon seeing her. She turned away toward the lake, not sure which expression showed his actual feelings. If it was the smile, she could handle working with him. The way the smile had lit his face made her want to see it again.

Upon reaching where she was standing, he stated, "I

gather you've found something of importance."

"Well, remember I told you I heard something moving in the bushes, right?"

"Yes," he stated, watching her.

Without elaborating, she led the way into the brush, following her previous path to avoid contaminating the scene. When she halted, Tom peered over her shoulder to examine the miniature flat open space in the middle of the brush. It took him only a few seconds to point to the footprint less than a yard from where the pistol with a silencer was lying nestled in the clump of tall grass.

After releasing a big breath, Tom stated, "Let me handle this. Go ahead and disappear. I don't want you around when the crime scene team gets here."

With a slight shrug, she said, "Why not? They'll see my footprints."

He didn't argue with her. "Suit yourself. Do you recognize the gun?"

"If you are asking if I've seen one like it, I have, but haven't handled one for over three years. Before you ask, if I'm handling a piece that isn't mine, I smudge the prints. Even if it's the same gun I handled back then, they'll not be able to lift my prints from it."

His glare was returned with a raised brow and smug grin. "Jill, I hope you know what you're doing. There are some mighty powerful people trying to hang you for this murder."

As if she hadn't already guessed that from the interrogation last night. Her grin widened. "They haven't dealt with me yet. I'm an unknown factor for them, so they need to protect themselves. I'm aware those questions came from whoever wants to neutralize me, so watch your back. I'll watch mine."

Without comment, he backed out of the brush to call the crime scene team. Meanwhile, she examined the footprint. Male. Two hundred pounds, give or take a few pounds. Dress shoes.

Jill moved farther into the brush along the path of the murderer. There was a tiny piece of torn cloth hanging off a branch. From the type of material and color, it was from the lining of a jacket, light brown in color. Not touching the scrap of thin material, she examined how it hung on the branch before following the trajectory of the person through the bushes.

With painstaking care, she moved along the path of the broken twigs, partial footprints, and trampled grass. Once the man left the brush, the prints headed toward the road. At the road, Jill hesitated before crossing and examining the dirt at the edge of the blacktop while moving toward the resort. When she located the print of a dress shoe four or five yards down the road, she deduced the killer parked in the picnic site parking lot at the resort.

At the edge of the parking lot, there was another footprint. A quick examination of the dirt along the edges of the paved lot revealed no more prints matching those from the brush. The killer had parked here to meet Knight. It was anybody's guess as to how Knight had arrived for the meeting. If he landed at the dock, any footprints along the dirt driveway from the dock to the murder scene were gone, thanks to those first officers on the scene.

Tom joined her where she stood by the last print at the edge of the paved lot. Without looking at him, Jill recited a rundown of what she surmised concerning the killer.

"Our killer drove to this lot. He was wearing a light tan sport coat based on the piece of lining he left behind. He wore dress shoes, and from the prints, he weighs somewhere around two hundred pounds."

She glanced up at him. The information was more than he had an hour ago, that is unless he was smarter than he had shown until now.

"Yeah. I got that far. Your showing up scared him or he wouldn't have left such a clear trail."

"That or he wanted me to follow him. I believe whoever it is knew I was here. Also, he may have seen me coming along the shore after killing Knight and recognized me. There's no question in my mind that this murder connects to my case. Somehow, they found out I was here and now want me to follow the trail they left. So, it's a trap of some sort. As I said, watch your back."

Not giving him a chance to respond, Jill walked away along the road, heading to the lake. It didn't take long before she found an occasional print, confirming the couple's path along the shore and behind the two houses. They had come from the vicinity of the resort cabin to where Knight was murdered.

Retracing the path of the couple, Jill crossed the road and found the woman's print at the sand just off the pavement. It headed into the trees to the left of the resort road.

The occasional footprint in the soft soil let her know she was going in the correct direction. The prints led to the left around two tall bushes. Upon rounding the brush, Jill came to a screeching halt. A man and woman were sprawled on the ground. Their bodies were in a sandy spot under the trees near three large rocks at the base of the steep hill below the resort.

Jill surveyed the immediate area. It was hidden from the road and the resort by the trees and brush. There were footprints all around the bodies. Taking her cellphone from her pocket, she pulled up recent calls and tapped the one with Tom's number. If this kept up, she would need to program his number for speed dialing.

He picked up on the first ring. *"Jill?"*

She answered the unspoken question. "There are two more bodies. That couple who passed me last night, well, they either saw or participated in the murder. I'm looking at two bodies and footprints from men in dress shoes all around the scene. My guess is three or more men. I'm across the road left of the picnic area behind some brush at the base of the hill."

"Don't move from that spot. I'll be right there."

He hung up, giving her time to check out the new murder scene as she waited. First, there was one; now there was three. If only she could find the connection between her, Knight, and this couple. This was no coincidence. Three murders on the same night this close together were related. The couple had to have been familiar with Knight and most likely their killers. No, this wasn't a coincidence.

Tom arrived less than five minutes later with a young officer in tow.

"Johnson, keep this scene secured until the forensics team gets here. No one else is to enter this area until the initial investigation is completed. Understood?"

"Yes, sir," the young man responded.

Jill followed Tom around the periphery of the murder scene. Footprints showed where the men milled around near the trees to the left of the concealing brush. There were no footprints of anyone going or coming from the resort. A thorough examination of the surrounding area showed where more than two people had walked around the site.

Tom frowned, studying the murder scene. Jill moved to beside him, not sure what he was seeing. There was a distinct path leading toward the lake along the base of the hill. She rotated to view the couple on the ground, deliberating on what their connection was to Knight and his ventures. The couple weren't anyone she recognized from her investigation of Knight, but the connection was there somewhere. These weren't random murders.

Think, Jill. Unless they had no knowledge of Knight's killer, they might have met with Knight, then came here to meet with whoever was waiting on them before being murdered. But why?

Were there two separate killers working independently? Two different reasons, yet connected? Or were the killers working together and planned to get rid of Knight and the couple before meeting them here? If so, why? Maybe Knight's killing wasn't planned, unlike this one. From the number of people involved, this murder was well planned. Again, why?

The timing was there, pointing to a connection between the murders. The couple either talked to Knight or his killer, or both. Now why, after meeting with Knight, was a second meeting held at this spot with the men who killed them? If she was to venture a guess, this was a planned set of murders to protect whoever was controlling Knight and his operation. She had a good guess as to who that person was, but she needed hard proof.

A hand dropping on her shoulder had her sucking in breath. "Penny for your thoughts," Tom said.

"Not worth sharing yet," she answered before rotating toward him. "Check if the couple had any traceable dealings with Knight. There's a connection somewhere."

The eyebrows rose while he studied her face. "Jill, you've given me two leads. Why aren't you following up on them?"

With a glare, Jill pushed her hair back behind her ear. What had Wyatt ever seen in him? So far, the young detective wasn't appearing all that brilliant.

"I'm a suspect, remember? If I dig into an open murder investigation, the police or sheriff's office will pull me in so quick your head will spin for a month."

Her attention returned to the bodies, noting the mode of death—strangulation by garrote. The killers were up close and personal for this killing. That meant whoever they were, they were trained killers, narrowing the field to police, gang, or military types. By the shoe prints, she was betting cop. There weren't any boot or tennis shoe prints except those of the murdered man.

When Tom didn't comment, Jill pivoted to face him. "Look, I said I'd help you. That means I give you the leads, you check them out, then tell me what you find while I connect the pieces together. That's what I do at home and it works great. I don't get into trouble by messing in an active police investigation. The cops get their collar, nice and neat with the bows in all the right places."

"Okay. Call me if you come up with anything else."

"Will do. I guess Wyatt is paying me for this week as work instead of vacation." Her phone rang. "Speak of the devil," she mumbled after checking the caller ID before tapping answer and saying, "Hi, Wyatt."

"Jill, what the fuck is happening?"

"Well, they turned me loose. No powder from a close-up shot. I found the murder weapon and two more bodies. Put me on the payroll as of two this afternoon."

"Girl, you be careful. I don't need to be arranging a fucking funeral."

"Don't worry, I prefer staying in one piece. Looks like my case led to Lake County and Clermont. Knight didn't know I was here, but someone did."

"Honey, you be real careful. Work with Tom. He's safe and I've worked with him before. If the fucker won't work with you, you fucking call me and I'll come up and help."

With a glance at Tom who was watching her, she said, "He's working with me for now. I'll report in tomorrow. Normal time."

"If you don't call, trust me, I'll be there. I'm not going to lose you again."

"Wyatt, chill. I'll keep you posted. If I need you, I'll call."

"Let me guess, some motherfucking cocksucker knows you and is trying to fuck you over."

That one statement showed how good a detective he was. He had picked up on what she didn't say. With another peek at Tom who was listening to the conversation from her end, she said, "If you get a call from the Lake County Sheriff's Department, make sure there's a viable subpoena before releasing any information."

"It'll need to be fucking federal for them to get anything. Jill, I don't fucking like this. You sure you don't want me to come and help?"

"Not yet. Let's see what transpires in the next couple of days, but if I don't call in, you better come."

"You got it. You better not get yourself fucking hurt."

He loved her and the worry was because he wasn't close enough to assist her if she called for help. "I'll do my best. Bye."

"You tell that fucking dick, Tom, he better take good care of you."

Wyatt hung up, leaving her with a grin and a warm feeling. Yeah, he was concerned enough to have Tom watch over her. It was nice that someone cared enough about her to worry, because her immediate family certainly didn't.

Jill used a soft voice, so Johnson couldn't overhear, to tell Tom, "His words for you were, and I quote, 'Tell that fucking dick, Tom, he better take good care of you.'"

With his brows drawn together, Tom regarded her. She grinned at his glower.

"What hold do you have over Wyatt for him to be so concerned about you?"

With a chuckle, Jill said, "You'll have to ask him. Just be aware, if I miss a call to him, he'll be here in less than three hours to find out why."

She walked away, not caring if he called Wyatt. He

wouldn't tell Tom what made her so important to him. Wyatt left it up to her to decide when and to whom to divulge the secret of why he was so concerned.

Back at the lakeshore, she found confirmation of how the men who murdered the couple had arrived. There were marks of the pontoons from paddleboats and the footprints of someone who had held them off to the right of where she had been sitting. They had gone along the water runoff channel to where the couple were murdered.

She returned to where she had sat last night and took a seat on the same root. Sitting and staring at the lake, she allowed the events starting from when she left the villa last night through today to replay in her mind, picturing what she saw and experienced in minute detail. There had to be something she was missing.

Connections. There was no question that there was a connection between Knight's murder and that of the young couple. It was just a matter of finding that connection, but where did she start?

Men in dress shoes and sports coats should stand out at a resort where bathing suits and shorts were the daily wear. Someone could have seen these men. You don't wander around a resort in a suit without being noticed.

Next question was: what type of men wore dress shoes during a murder at a resort? Businessmen, cops, security men, detectives, or anyone who wanted to make their appearance count. Sports coats. Businessmen, plainclothes cops, and appearance-conscious men. A lot of the high-end criminals also wore dress shoes and sports coats. Think, Jill. There had to be a way of narrowing the field.

The men who killed the couple used the paddle pontoon boats to get to the meeting spot. It meant they came across the lake from the state park. Knight's killer drove to the resort. The likelihood of discovering how Knight and the couple arrived was nil due to the destruction of evidence at the initial murder scene.

It had been late, between 11 and 1 AM. The darkness was their cover, along with an awareness that the resort patrons out that late were most likely tipsy. Because of the drinking, most patrons wouldn't be paying attention to strangers no matter how they were dressed.

Next, how had Knight gotten here? There wasn't any evidence of a boat letting him off on the shore. No new boats were at the dock. No strange cars in the parking lot. Teleportation wasn't a viable option, so he had gotten here in a conventional manner. It was the same with the couple. How did they get here?

The splashing of the small waves on the shore could have hidden the sound of paddleboats if they were going slow. There had been no sounds of a motor-driven boat while she had been sitting here with her eyes closed, half asleep. That meant Knight either walked from the parking lot after riding with his killer, or had come from the dock after being dropped off by the men who murdered the couple. The other scenario was Knight and the couple came together then separated. That meant the couple could have murdered Knight. If that was true, who had been in the bushes with the murder weapon?

The gunshot wasn't heard by anyone due to the silencer. What she believed was a fish flopping in the water last night was most likely the gun being fired. That occurred approximately four to five minutes before the man passed her with the woman following him by less than thirty seconds.

In the dark, it would have taken a good five to ten minutes to traverse the shoreline from the Knight murder scene. That meant the couple could have talked to Knight, then left before someone shot him. They came along the shore and proceeded to the park to meet their killers. Logistically it worked, but why murder the couple? How did they arrive and what was their connection to Knight and the killers?

Why was Knight here? Who was he meeting and why? And who discovered she was here? She smelled a trap, but who was setting it up and why? The attempt to frame her for murder wasn't in the plan, but they had lucked out when Tom found her by the body. Right now, all she had were questions and no answers.

The one thing she was sure of was the presence of a mole in the sheriff's department, highly placed, from what Tom said. Also, the connection to the Broward group she was investigating was proven. If she had to guess as to the connection, it was that the girls they didn't deliver were being kept in this vicinity until ransomed or sold, whichever came first. Five more days before returning home to figure it out.

Luck sometimes played a big part in solving a case. Other times it was grunt work. This time, luck put her in the correct spot at the correct time. She was scaring someone enough to kill Knight and his connections.

The mole in the police department concerned her more than the killers. He had access to Tom's investigation, putting him and her at risk. From what she observed and experienced, there was one or more officers involved in the murders.

To ferret out the mole, it was time to follow the money. These people wanted money and power. With that thought, Jill pulled out her cellphone and tapped the icon for Sam, Wyatt's right-hand man, on the frequent caller list.

"Hi, Jill. What can I do for you?" His greeting put a smile on her face. From working with her, he was aware she needed him to do research.

"Sam, I need your brand of expertise."

"What do you need and when?"

"I need who, in the Lake County Sheriff's office, has money they shouldn't have."

"Let me guess. I can't set off any alarms in finding this information."

"You got it. I'm sure there's more than one. Most likely around five. One should have over five years of payoffs."

"Doll, you aren't making this easy, are you?"

"Hey, with three bodies, I don't want to become the fourth. There's a trap being set for me, and I need to find out by whom."

"Okay, let me get on it. I'll let the old man know I'm getting the permissions and using the system so he doesn't freak out. Want me to update him?"

"Sure. He might want to send an unknown or two for backup. I may need them."

"You got it kid. You're aware . . ."

Jill cut him off. "Yeah, I am. Sam, call me when you find the big ones. I need names. Start at the top and work your way down."

"Sounds like you're getting a handle on this."

"Maybe. It'll depend on what you find."

"Okay. Bye, doll. You be careful."

Okay. Dirty cops. She estimated there were at least five and one wasn't a street guy. Now came the waiting. If her guess was correct, she wouldn't object to Wyatt being close. This was one time she might need his help. These men weren't playing games. They were playing for keeps, and like she told Sam, she didn't want to be the fourth body.

Chapter 5

EENY, MEENY, MINY, MOE. CATCH A COPPER BY HIS TOE.

Jill remained under the tree watching the officers going back and forth between the two murder scenes. The medical examiner arrived and removed the bodies from the wooded park. When there was nothing left to see, the large contingent of spectators dispersed.

What had surprised Jill was how none of the people tramping along the shore, road, and path noticed her sitting under the tree. Several police officers, who had shown up in plain clothes, passed right by her as if she was as insubstantial as a ghost. It was a great spot to observe the coming and going of the officials investigating the murders.

Two groups of four officers each had caught her attention as they headed to the scene of the new murders. The groups came along the shore somewhere around five minutes apart. In the second group, there was one very nervous man who was fidgeting and talking to one of the older officers. Jill wondered why. Was he a new officer, nervous at seeing his first murder, or was there another reason? A more sinister reason.

It was over an hour before the officers trooped back to their cars. The nervous guy was calmer, but he had changed groups and was laughing at something one of the men had said. Whatever had been bothering him seemed to have been handled.

It appeared Tom was going to be among the last to leave, indicating he was the lead detective for all three murders. What she needed were the names of the couple so Sam could look for connections to Knight. Once she had the connection, it would be easy to discover how they fit into the overall picture.

Roughly two hours later, Tom went by, talking to another plainclothes officer. Like the others, they went past without seeing her. She wasn't hiding, but no one looked to the right where she was sitting. Nothing like being in plain sight and not being seen!

Aware Tom's leaving the site indicated the initial investigation was over, she left her seat under the tree and headed to the newest crime scene. The police tape was up, but she wasn't interested in that spot. She walked farther into the trees, scanning the ground for anything out of place. A white object fluttered in the gentle breeze. She stooped and picked up a piece of paper from a clump of grass and put it in her pocket. After searching the locale and finding nothing else, she headed back to where crime scene tape was strung around where the bodies had been.

Tom had returned and stood staring at where the couple had been found. "Jill, where were you?" he asked without looking at her.

"Where I was sitting last night, out in plain sight."

"What did you pick up?" he inquired, facing her, his gaze probing, mouth in a grim line.

Uh-oh. He had returned without her seeing him. She pulled the paper from her pocket and glanced at the writing. It had a series of numbers separated like a combination to a lock. Jill handed the paper to him. After studying the writing, but without comment, he put the slip of paper into the pocket of his jeans. He let out a big breath, turning to the road, avoiding looking at her.

"Jill, you need to get Wyatt here. This is bigger than you realize."

Her weight shifted to her right leg before she crossed her arms and glared at his back, tapping her left foot. "Really? Let's see if I have a few things correct. Knight had connections here. My guess is the couple here were working with the smuggling group. Most likely they were the ones keeping the girls hidden. On top of that, there's a mole in the sheriff's office who's high up. That's how they realized who I was and had my dossier from Broward, which they used to feed you names and suspicions.

"There are four or more dirty cops working with him to protect the smugglers. Whoever the head guy or guys are, they're well placed and respected. I'm too damn close, and they're trying to get me off their tails.

"These murders were to keep me from following the Broward connection to here, but they goofed, unaware I was here. There's a trap being devised to neutralize me and you. I believe one of them knows you aren't who you say you are."

He rotated his head, eyes narrowed, and questioned, "And just how did you come to those conclusions?"

She rolled her eyes and shook her head, still wondering what Wyatt had ever seen in him. "You're the detective. You tell me."

"As I said earlier, this is bigger than you think it is."

"No, it isn't. I've a good idea where it's leading and to whom. I need to connect the rest of the dots so he can't slither away like the snake he is. He's powerful, but not invincible. His bosses are putting on the pressure, so he's stepping up the heat on me. You're going to get caught up in this no matter what you do. I have too much information and they're scared."

Tom kept his back to her. "Get Wyatt here. You'll need him."

She needed to know why he wanted Wyatt here. "What information do you have that I don't?"

"It goes beyond the department."

Her curls bounced as she shook her head in exasperation. He was a total dunce. "I'm aware of that fact. The DA department and a judge or two in several counties, the state, and at least one federal are connected to this syndicate. There's been a lot of money changing hands. A whole lot of money. I'm working on tying it up nice and neat for the appropriate authorities."

Tom whipped around, facing her. "What are you talking about?"

She smiled, enjoying the effect her words had on him. "I work for Wyatt. If you worked for him on any related cases, then you understand exactly what I mean."

The green eyes held her blue ones for the longest time. It appeared he didn't understand who her real target was, making her wonder about him and his connection to her boss. If he knew Wyatt as well as she had assumed with his assessment of her relationship with her boss, he should be aware of the types of cases she handled for the agency.

Jill held back a giggle at his expression. The piece of paper she found had given her more information than just numbers. That paper was the proof there were dirty cops. The sheriff's department phone number was on the paper. With that information, she could uncover who they were and how high in the department the evil reached.

Wyatt had slipped up on Tom. He was either clueless or a damn good actor. Right now, she was betting on clueless.

Tom grated through clenched teeth, "Jill, this isn't a game."

"I know that."

Her phone rang, breaking the tension. It was Sam.

"Sam, what do you have for me?"

"Jill, back off, now."

"Why?"

"Orders from the top. You're in over your head."

"Give me why?"

"There's a double agent. He's not going to wait on the sideline and let you take him down."

"Name."

"Thomas Wellington."

"Uh-huh. Doesn't surprise me. Give me what you have beyond that."

"Jill, back the fuck off and get your fucking ass home!" Wyatt grated over the speaker phone in his office. He wasn't happy, and it showed.

With a calmness she didn't feel, Jill ignored his orders. "Give me the information I asked for, I guessed the other."

"No! Get your fucking ass home."

After taking a deep breath and letting it out, Jill stated, her voice showing a bravado she pretended to possess in the face of his anger, "Wyatt, I'm finishing this, with or without your help. I only need to connect the last few dots."

Wyatt's voice warned her to not argue with him. *"I'll be*

there in three fucking hours. Don't you dare leave that fucking resort until I get there. Stay near your cocksucker of a father. That's a fucking order."

She blew out a noisy breath, quelling the fear his order had sent through her, before saying in a meek voice, "Yes, sir."

Wyatt hung up. He must have something, other than Tom working both sides, which was making him so nervous. With a bowed head, she gnawed on her lower lip and blinked back tears. This was the closest she had been to the men she wanted. There was no way she would walk away from the case. Not now, regardless of the danger. His coming here just complicated things until she had the connections to those above Knight.

"Problems?" Tom questioned, right brow raised.

"Maybe. I'll find out soon enough." She raised her head, then rotated to face him. "Just whose side are you on?" she questioned, not actually expecting an answer.

He crossed his arms, mouth in a tight smile before saying, "Ask Wyatt."

"I did. Appears a simple search turned up several questionable things where you're concerned. So, answer the question."

With a smile, he said, "You're a detective. You figure it out." Pivoting, he strode away, not giving her the requested information. There was something about him that made her believe he wasn't working both sides. She would bet her last dollar, the dirty cops were setting him up, but why?

With a sigh, she scanned the crime scene one last time. So much for the combination on the paper. The evidence from the locker would be gone before Wyatt arrived and got a subpoena. Because she liked him and those green eyes, she prayed he stayed safe until completing his assignment.

Jill trudged back to the villa and her family, afraid of what would happen when Wyatt arrived. There was no way she would disobey his direct order. The last thing she needed was for him to isolate her, preventing her from working. He had done it before, only this time it promised to be greater than a week from what she heard in his voice. Wyatt didn't tolerate disobedience of his direct commands.

The villa was quiet. Her parents were seated in the matching recliners watching TV while Belinda and Rick played a game of gin at the table. To avoid talking to them, she went to her room and flopped onto the bed to wait the three hours until Wyatt arrived.

She imagined the reaction of her father when Wyatt pulled her from the villa. Her father had major differences of opinions with Wyatt for over twenty-plus years concerning his position in the agency and her. Oh well, there was nothing she could do now because he was on his way.

Her headache was worsening from the tension, afraid of Wyatt's reaction when he got here. A little over two hours had passed before she joined the family in the living room to keep watch for his promised arrival. Curled into the corner of the divan, she attempted to come up with an idea to prevent the coming confrontation. Her father wasn't going to be happy when he found out she was working for the agency.

Each minute crept by while her nerves tightened until her head was throbbing. It was late afternoon before she sighted Sam, then Wyatt, marching to the villa's back door. Wow! He never brought Sam unless there was a major problem. Added to that, it had only taken them two hours and twenty-five minutes to get here for a three-plus-hour trip.

Before Wyatt knocked, Jill opened the door and bit her lower lip at his glower. There was an audible gasp from both parents when they saw him and Sam filling the doorway.

"Dad, what are you doing here?" her father questioned, moving behind her, his hands resting on her shoulders.

Wyatt ignored the question. "Jill, come with me. I need to talk to you." The command didn't allow for a refusal.

Her father moved so he could see her face. His worried gaze bounced between her and Wyatt. "What do you need with Jill?" he questioned, his eyes coming to rest on her.

"Nate, she's been working for me for the last five fucking years. I don't fucking understand why you didn't fucking know."

"Jill?" her father questioned, needing verification, the concern on his face not fitting with his actions toward her over the years.

"Dad, you never asked where I was working, so don't get bent," she told him, giving Wyatt a quick sidelong glance before peering up at her father. He was staring at her as if she had grown an extra head.

Breaking eye contact, Jill turned away. "Let's go," she said, squeezing out between Wyatt and Sam, blinking back tears at the shocked expression on her father's face. Returning wouldn't be pleasant. A fight between her father and grandfather wasn't something she wanted.

She strode along the narrow road with Wyatt and Sam following her. An isolated picnic table away from the road became the conference spot. Jill took a seat on the bench, leaning her back against the table as she faced the resort. Sam sat on her left, Wyatt on her right, both leaning on the table and looking at her. With crossed arms, she waited for Wyatt to start, determined to fight him and Sam. No matter what, she was going to complete her case regardless of where it led, with or without their assistance.

"Jill, you need to drop this case," Sam told her without preamble.

"Which fed judge has you scared?" Both men stared at her, mouths agape. In answer to their shocked expressions, she pulled her mouth to the side and lifted her shoulders in a shrug before saying, "It has to be Garrett or Levin. Both are involved."

"How the fuck did you find that out?" Wyatt queried.

"I'm connecting dots. The trail comes to here and they both cover this county. I followed the money trail from Knight's group. Sam, what was found concerning the departments?"

"Tom has had four large deposits to an account in his mother's maiden name over the last six months. The deputy sheriff has an account in his son's name with regular payments over the past ten years. There are six underlings with unexplained deposits to various accounts going from eight years to five months."

"Wyatt, is Tom playing both ends or is he deep?" Jill questioned, staring up at her grandfather.

"He's fucking dead if the cocksuckers get to him."

That statement meant Tom was deep and was one of the good guys. "Okay. That explains your concern. Billings, what did you get on him?"

"Fuck, Jill. You can't go after him."

"I want that girl, and he has her stashed. Three people are dead, and there'll be more if he isn't stopped."

She felt the anger and fear radiating off Wyatt. He was aware he couldn't stop her from finishing what she had started. It was the reason he used her for these cases. She always got her man.

"Jill, baby, please. I'm fucking begging. Let this one

go." His big hand turned her head until she was facing him.

"I can't," she said before lowering her eyelids, letting the tears which had gathered slide over her cheeks. Her head rested on his wide chest, unable to look at him or Sam. This type of case had been the main reason she had gone to work for the agency. She wanted Billings, and every person connected to him.

Wyatt put his arm around her, pulling her next to him as if trying to protect her. She cuddled into him, listening to his voice reverberating in his chest. "Jill, please."

She raised her head and studied him. For the first time in her life, she saw raw fear on his face.

"Give me a good reason to stop, Wyatt," she stated, her eyes locked with his.

"There's a contract out on you."

Okay, that explained the fear, but it wasn't a reason to quit. She was too damn close to taking Billings down.

"I'm not surprised, but it isn't the first one I've had on me."

"This is fucking different, Jill. He's a fucking professional, and he's here."

"Who?" she asked, wondering if it was a local she knew.

"The Snake."

She came close to laughing because her assassin was costing them a cool million. These people had to be raking in millions from their setup to pay that amount to get rid of her, not that it mattered. She wasn't stopping until all of them were behind bars or she was dead.

"Wyatt, if anything happens to me, remember your promise."

"Jill, no. You're fucking coming home. Now." His voice caught and his arm tightened around her. Those little actions showed how scared he was for her.

Sadly, she told him, "I can't leave. I'm still a suspect, and they won't let me go and you know it. Let me do my job. Once I have that girl, I'll be home."

Sam put a hand on her arm, getting her attention. "Jill, he's been here for two days. He knows you on sight. He'll kill you as soon as he sees you."

With a shake of her head, she told him, "Wrong. He's playing a game with me. It's called hide-and-seek. He hides, I seek, then he hides again. I have an idea as to where and when he'll try to get me."

"What are you planning?" Sam questioned.

"To get that girl. Did you find the names for the couple?"

"Yes. Here's the home address. They have a warehouse. That's the address." Sam handed her a piece of paper with the information written on it while Wyatt glowered.

"Okay. Let's go play 'pin the tail on the donkey.'"

"Jill, no," Wyatt half begged, and half commanded.

Jill turned on him, determined to have her way. "You don't have to come. If Tom gets in my way, I'll leave him to hang with the rest of the creeps. I'll not leave that girl to a fate worse than death." That explanation alone gave why she wouldn't quit.

Wyatt didn't attempt to stop her when she stood and started back to the villa, not caring if they followed or not. Time to discover if Snake was honorable or not. He owed her one. This had better be the time he paid her back by letting her go if he missed. But would he miss her on the first shot?

Sam and Wyatt waited outside when she entered the villa, which was eerily quiet. The four were sitting in the living room not talking, the TV off. They watched her walk past to get her purse. On the way out to her car, her father's hand on her arm halted her.

"Jill, do you need help?" he questioned, finally willing to help her, years beyond when she had needed his protection. He worked for his father but out of the north office, so he knew what to do.

"Check with Wyatt," she told him and went out the door with him right behind her.

"Dad?" he inquired, staring at his father.

"You got a fucking gun with you?" Wyatt questioned.

"Yes."

"Then get your fucking ass in gear," Wyatt ordered before following her to her car.

She opened the trunk, not taking long to have the holster, the now-loaded forty-caliber Glock on her hip, and the extra magazines placed in the holders. The Kevlar vest, which was folded in the corner of the trunk, went on next, hidden by a long-sleeved shirt. Jill slammed the trunk closed, then stalked to the driver's side door.

Wyatt's hand on her shoulder held her in place. "Jill, you don't have to do this."

Her eyes met his, the pain of the past reflected there. "Yes, I do, and you know it!"

Pulling away from him, she slid in behind the wheel of the car and turned the key in the ignition. Wyatt glared at her before shutting the door, then heading to where Sam and her father waited for him. He hadn't slammed the door shut, so he wasn't angry, just afraid for her. She pulled out, resisting the urge to speed. Time to discover what they had in store for her.

Chapter 6

GAINS AND LOSSES

The address for the warehouse was in a building of storage bays in Minneola, just north of Clermont off US 27. With it being Sunday, no one was around when Jill pulled into the parking spot for the good-sized bay. After scanning the locale, nothing appeared out of place. Wyatt was parked near the entrance to the complex, keeping watch for anyone entering while she was in the warehouse.

The entry at the side of the large bay door was locked with a padlock. This meant using the kit Jay, an expert at picking locks, had taught her to use. After retrieving the small zippered case from under the front seat, she scanned the buildings again, then proceeded to the door.

After a quick examination of the padlock, she pulled the tool needed from the case. She did another quick scan of her surroundings, then went to work. In less than fifteen seconds, there was a click and the lock popped open. Jay would be proud of her! Jill glanced around the locale again before lifting the lock from the hasp. Sunday was a great day for breaking and entering.

She felt a bullet whiz past her ear and embed in the metal doorframe. A split second later, the report of a rifle broke the silence. Jill shoved the door open, leaping inside out of the line of fire. The door slammed into the wall, then swung partially closed. With the Glock in her hand, she peeked around the doorframe. Another bullet smacked into the doorframe near her head. A second shot split the silence. Jill jerked back inside, her back against the wall, breathing hard, her heart racing in an irregular rhythm like a drummer gone wild.

"Fuck!" she exclaimed, angry at being pinned inside for the moment. Hopefully, no one else was in the vicinity to call the police to report gunshots. If anyone notified the authorities, Wyatt would be providing bail for a charge of breaking and entering.

Jill whipped around at a soft scuffing noise coming from the depths of the bay. Pointing the gun toward the sound, she peered around the corner from the office into the dimness. Three young women were huddled together in the far left corner. They didn't move, their wide eyes staring at her. A cursory scan revealed sleeping bags on the floor and food on a table, but no guard. Jill didn't miss the matching padlocks on both sides of the bay door, locking the women into the warehouse.

"It's okay. I'm here to help," Jill told the women, not sure if they understood English. One gave a quick nod before Jill turned back to the door and the problem of getting rid of the person trying to kill her.

She bent over and peered around the edge of the doorway. Another bullet smacked into the frame of the door, again near her head. She jerked back out of view. With a deep breath, she held the gun in firing position, then moved into the doorway holding a shooting stance. When a head popped up over the false front on the roof of the building across the street, she fired twice, the bullets hitting close to where the man had placed his rifle. The head disappeared, along with the rifle.

A quick move to her right returned her to the safety of the office. Jill moved to the doorway into the bay. The three women were still huddled together, watching her. With a wave of a hand, Jill motioned for them to come to her. She poked her head out to check the false front for the sharpshooter. When no shots were fired, she tugged the closest woman to her nearer to the door.

Jill hoped the young girl spoke English before saying, "Get into the back of the car and stay down."

The woman she had pulled to her ran bent over to the car, opened the backdoor, and piled into the backseat, the other two close behind her. They crouched on the floor as instructed, leaving the backdoor open. Jill waited a few seconds before running to the car, kicking the back door closed before she pulled the driver's side door open and slid behind the wheel.

Her key went into the ignition as she slammed the door closed. When the car roared to life, she rammed the gearshift into reverse and peeled out of the parking space. A quick shift into drive before the car had come to a complete stop had them speeding between the long buildings in the quietness of the early evening, moving away from whoever had fired those shots, past Wyatt's car.

With frequent glances to the rearview mirror, Jill drove the two blocks to US 27 at a high speed, then turned north toward Tavares, slowing to the speed of the traffic. A car pulled in behind her when she turned right onto county road 561. Using her right hand, she put a Bluetooth headset on and said, "Call Wyatt."

On the second ring, his gruff voice answered, "Yeah, Jill."

"I have a tail. They'll try to stop me before I get to the Sheriff's Department in Tavares."

"I'm ahead of you on 19. Don't fucking stop until you're at the fucking Sheriff's Department."

"Got it. I'll meet you there. Thanks."

There was a slight hesitation before Wyatt said, "You be careful, baby girl. Call me if they try to force you off the road."

"You got it. I may need bail for evading them," she said with a chuckle.

"Baby, they may make it so you can't fucking evade them, so you be real fucking careful."

"I'll be there in approximately twenty-five minutes barring having to make a detour or two."

A tap on the headset hung up the phone. Wyatt would be waiting and he had backup, aware there was more than one person in the department who didn't want these girls to talk.

It wasn't until she turned onto Highway 19 north, the tailing car turned on their flashing lights. At the next side street on the right, a marked sheriff's car lights came to life and joined the slow speed chase. With gritted teeth, Jill ignored the blue and red flashing lights, not pulling over as she followed the GPS to the Lake County Sheriff Department parking lot on West Ruby Street.

After pulling into a parking space, Jill turned off the engine and waited for the officers to surround the car, hands on the wheel so they could be seen. A survey of the men surrounding her showed she hadn't been wrong. These were the officers from the two groups she had noticed while sitting under the tree after finding the couple murdered.

"Get out of the car," an officer ordered, a hand on his gun.

Jill complied with the request, standing with her arms crossed, leaning against the car door she had closed, preventing them from entering the car. The deputies moved closer. None had pulled their weapons, but several had hands resting on the grips of their pistols.

Jill glared at the officer who had ordered her out of the car. He shuffled back a half step even though he was twice her size. Her direct stare kept him quiet. She scanned the deputies with distain before saying, "Look, asshole, if I wanted to run, I certainly wouldn't have come here," indicating with a thumb the building behind her.

The officers' eyes rounded when they realized where they were. Four deputies were standing at the doorway, curious as to why they had chased someone to the station. Jill reached over and opened the back door. The women climbed out and stood huddled together, holding onto each other, fear on their faces. Jill slammed the door in anger before she guided the women to the station as the officers from the chase stared at her, not moving.

Wyatt appeared at her side, face grim, his bulk hiding her from the men who were still standing around her car. When the five of them approached the entrance, the group at the door parted and let them enter. It was easy to tell the deputies were confused as to what was happening. She and Wyatt showed their IDs and entered the station lobby without having to give up their guns.

The officer in charge stalked across the lobby and glared up at Wyatt.

"What can I do for you?" he snapped before examining her, the women, then Wyatt.

"Nothing, we're waiting for the feds to show up," Wyatt stated.

"I'm sorry, but you'll need to wait elsewhere."

"No, we're waiting right here with you. They'll be here in a couple of minutes," Wyatt growled keeping his language respectful.

"You can't stay here," the officer stated emphatically.

"Why?" Jill questioned.

"Because you can't. Now leave."

Wyatt plastered a smile on his face, aware the deputy had no authority to make them leave. "Sir, you have no say in us waiting here. Nice try though."

The officer marched to a phone on the wall and made a call. Within seconds the deputies from outside formed a ring around them. Jill raised a brow and glanced up at Wyatt. He was smiling.

"Nice try, but it won't work." Wyatt lifted his phone and tapped it twice, then waited. "Fred, where are you?" He inquired then listened before breaking the connection. Less than thirty seconds later a group of men holding guns entered the lobby and spread out around the officers.

"Drop the weapons," Fred commanded. "Two fingers only unless you want to take a chance we'll miss."

The officers complied, watching Fred, a US Marshal, and the deputy marshals who had entered with him. The weapons hitting the floor rang in the large cavernous room. One deputy marshal picked up the weapons as another frisked the local deputies under the watchful gazes of those who had been at the door when they entered the building. Each deputy had at least one or two hidden weapons. The handcuffs snapped shut on their wrists as the men stood stoically, aware they weren't going to walk away from this.

The deputy sheriff entered the lobby from the elevator. Jill observed the fear on one girl's face when she saw him. Fred hadn't missed her reaction. The officer had made a major mistake by letting the women see him. It was time for him to pay for that error.

"What's going on here?" the deputy sheriff snapped, glaring at Wyatt, then her before turning to Fred, who had a pistol aimed at him.

Fred grinned. "Hands on top of your head, please," he commanded, mocking the man and his rank.

The deputy sheriff complied, albeit slowly. He was frisked, his weapons taken, then cuffed and moved to where the rest of the men stood. One of Fred's men stepped before the group and in a loud clear voice read them their Miranda rights, then waited until each had answered they understood those rights.

"Okay, what's going on?" the deputy sheriff repeated, before adding, "and why are we under arrest?"

"The charges will be given when you get to federal court," Fred informed him. He turned to Wyatt. "Good job. What happened to the contract on our girlie here?"

"Still there. He's playing with her. What about the judges?"

"Arrested. We could use more evidence of their connections to the ring Jill is investigating," he stated, his gaze moving to her.

Wyatt turned to her. "Jill, no fucking way are you going after that cocksucker!"

Fred laughed. "I was getting downright worried, Wyatt. You were being too damn nice and gentlemanly."

She pivoted and started toward the door. Wyatt, not being gentle, grabbed her arm in his large hand, stopping her.

"Jill, no."

"I can't leave him hanging," she told him, her eyes snapping with anger. Wyatt knew who she meant.

"He took the fucking risks, fucking aware of what he was doing. No fucking way you're risking every fucking thing for him."

She jerked away, her mouth in a grim line. "You can't stop me," she grated out and moved toward the door.

He stopped her the second time. "Jill, no."

She whipped around and folded her arms, glaring up at him, standing toe to toe with the big man, not backing down. "Wyatt, this is one time you have no say in what I'm doing. I know you had something to do with him being here. I won't let him go down with the others. I tie up all the loose ends, and Billings and Tom are loose ends."

He glared at her. "Jill . . ."

She cut him off. "No, I won't go home until he's safe and Billings is under arrest."

His glower didn't faze her. She pivoted and marched angrily toward the door. This was her choice, not his. Tom was being set up, and part of her job was ensuring only the bad guys went to prison.

The man in question moved out of the way as she violently shoved the door open, almost knocking him down. Jill grabbed his arm, noting he had changed into dress pants and a dress shirt, before striding to her car with him in tow. He stopped when she got to the car, turning to face her.

"Jill, where are we headed and why?"

She took a big breath and let it out. Time to spill some of what she had learned concerning this mess. "Tom, you're in big trouble. If we can't get to Billings, you'll be arrested as part of the cell here."

"What are you talking about?" Tom asked with a glance behind her. She knew Wyatt and Fred were watching them.

"There's an account set up in your mother's maiden name. It's had four large deposits made to it in the last six months. I'm positive they'll find information on your search at home implicating you in setting up the account."

Not responding, he moved to the passenger side of the car before turning and staring at her over the top of the car. "Why are you telling me this?"

"I don't think you're working both ends. Wyatt doesn't hire or work with someone who hasn't been fully vetted." She paused then asked, "How long have you been working with him?"

Tom didn't avoid her direct stare. "Over ten years. I'm still working with him."

She let out the breath she had been holding. "Fred and Sam are wondering about that bank account. To clear you, we need to get the rest of them. For that, I need your help."

He studied her. "Jill, the Snake is after you. You need to get out of here."

"I'll deal with him later. Right now, I need your help."

He sighed, shaking his head, a tight grin on his lips. "How can one five-foot-five, hundred-and-twenty-pound redhead, with the prettiest blue eyes I've ever seen, sucker me into helping her against my better judgment?"

"Because she likes those pine green eyes and doesn't want them to disappear on her."

He laughed. "Okay. I can't resist that line. Let's go."

He entered the passenger side as she took her seat behind the wheel and started the car. His description of her led her to believe he had noticed her beyond their working relationship. Rotating her head so she could face him, Jill was aware she liked Tom more than she should.

"Tell me where we're going," she requested.

"My place first. I need to pick up a couple of items from the house." He gave her the directions to his place.

As she pulled out, Jill noticed Wyatt's glare following her. She understood what had caused his lowered brows and grim mouth. It wasn't that she wanted to disobey him, but this was something she had to do. At least he would be close when she needed him. Until she had finished what she started, the agency was at her disposal in capturing the men she had been after for the past five years.

Tom glanced back at Wyatt, then turned to her. "What's your hold on him?" he asked again.

With a smirk, she asked, "Do you really want to know?"

"Yes. I've never seen him like this with any other

person, let alone an employee."

With a chuckle, she said, "I'm his granddaughter." Tom's expression was funny, sending her into a fit of giggling. She added, once she sobered, "Tom, he'll be around. There's no way he'll leave me without backup on this case."

"Wyatt's your grandfather?" he queried, surprise in his voice and disbelief on his face.

"Yes. Now you know my secret, so tell me yours. I'm sure there's one concerning which agency employs you."

A glance in his direction showed him withdrawing. He wasn't going to tell her anything she hadn't already discovered. Watching the road, frowning, Jill warned, "Tom, I can still back off and let you extricate yourself. Tell me or I drop you at your place and go home with Wyatt."

"You won't do that."

"Wanna bet?"

"I'd win because you want Billings, and I can give him to you."

Damn man! He was right. She wanted Billings. "I'll ferret it out, eventually," she told him. He didn't know her persistence when she wanted something.

"Wyatt won't tell you."

"What makes you so sure?"

"He'll lose the agency's license if he does."

"Which agency do you work for?"

"Jill, leave it alone."

"Tom, I'm not putting myself out there to only get taken down because I don't have all the facts."

"You're with me, so you'll be okay."

"That gives me so much comfort," she sneered.

Hopefully, he was higher placed than a simple deep-cover operative. If not, she prayed he had pull in the agency where he worked. Not knowing where he fit meant they could end up in big trouble or dead.

Tom directed her to his house. It was a bungalow in an older subdivision. It was a clone of the rest of the houses on the street other than the color and landscaping. The property was well cared for with a manicured lawn and no peeling paint on the building. An old jeep was parked under the carport. After parking behind the jeep, she shut off the engine but made no move to exit the car.

"Come on in. We need to talk," he instructed.

She opened the door and got out. They were standing at the side door when Tom jerked her behind the house. A loud fiery explosion sent debris and heat into the air. Tom placed her next to the house and covered her with his body. The low eaves over the corner protected them from the hot bits of metal and debris raining down around them.

When the debris quit falling, he moved away and grabbed her hand, pulling her behind him across the backyard. With a flick of his hand, the gate in the fence enclosing the yard swung open. They ran down the narrow alley to a main street. She barely kept up with him, breathless from the fear and shock of the explosion.

Slowing to a walk, Tom checked behind them, then tucked her under his arm. Satisfied that her face and hair were hidden, he turned them onto the street. They ambled along the sidewalk as if they were shopping. His six-foot-plus frame hid her from view. Not many people were walking about, but enough so they didn't stand out. He stopped and turned her to a display of jewelry before he pointed out a set of rings in the window. She watched the reflection of the car as it passed them, aware they were hiding in plain sight.

"Don't move yet. They're just around the corner."

"What did you need at your house?" she questioned.

"Nothing they'd recognize. I can get it later." He turned and smiled at her. "Why don't we go in and check out the rings?"

"Huh?" The man was nuts! Rings? She wasn't interested in jewelry right now.

Like a light bulb going on, she realized what he was doing. He wasn't nuts. She was just a bit slow on the uptake after coming within seconds of being blown to bits. This was an excuse to get off the street and hide from those searching for them.

"Sure, why not?" she responded, relaxing when he winked at her, the only indication he was acting.

With a hand on her back, he guided her into the store.

The explosion hadn't dirtied their clothes other than a small black smudge on Tom's right shoulder, so they wouldn't raise any alarms with their appearance. Tom stopped at the wedding ring display.

"What type do you like?" he inquired as if he was her boyfriend and they were shopping for a wedding set.

She shook her head. He was fucking nuts, but it was a game she could play. Jill looked over what she thought of as gaudy rings, not finding anything she liked until noticing a box in the lower corner on her right. Most people would overlook the rings where they were placed. A sharp longing spiked through her as she stared at the set she loved.

The man behind the counter asked, "May I show you something?"

Tom responded when she didn't, "She seems to like the ones in the lower corner there."

The salesperson opened the cabinet and took out the box, placing it on the top of the counter. He lifted the engagement ring out of the box and handed it to her. Her top teeth caught her lower lip as she blinked back tears. This . . .this was her dream ring. None of the stones were large, but it was the design of the ring, not the stones, which had her attention.

The ring was old-fashioned and elegant with a Celtic knot band. There was an Irish rose, completely open, set with a pink-tinged stone in the center. Two smaller roses, set with yellow-tinged stones, flanked the larger rose. The three delicate roses covered the top of the ring, their flower petals appearing velvety against the silvery spun metal of the band. The metal of the band gave the impression of being able to see into the depths of its silvery sheen as it wrapped around in never-ending knots.

Yes, she liked it. This was her dream ring. The wedding ring was a never-ending Celtic knot with alternating pink and yellow tinted stones placed among the silver threads of the knots. It was perfection.

The salesperson and Tom were talking, but she didn't pay attention as she examined the rings. Whoever had made them, their workmanship was flawless. It was so delicate with the roses held in place by the silver threads and knots. Reluctantly, she put it back in the box. There wasn't another ring like this. Even if she managed to find a similar ring, there was the problem of a fiancé. You need one to get engaged, and the likelihood of her ever having a fiancé was nil.

With a sigh, she pulled herself back to reality, turning her back to Tom. If he hadn't been along, she would have bought the set just so she could dream of the man who would have placed the ring on her finger while professing his undying love. It was a dream that wasn't ever going to come true, not now, not ever, but if she had the ring, she could pretend.

Jill blinked back the pending tears and wandered off along the cases, her gaze running over the multitude of items on display. Next to the back wall tucked into the bottom rear of the display case, Jill found the necklace, bracelet, and earrings, which matched the wedding ring set. With longing, she gazed at them, wanting the set more than anything she had ever seen. This set she could have and wear whenever she wanted, unlike the engagement set.

A saleslady hovered behind the counter. Jill requested to examine the set up close. After running the necklace through her fingers, she knew it must have been made by the same jeweler as the ring set. The ring her grandfather had given her came close to matching these, so it was all good.

"How much is the whole set?" she questioned, not actually caring because she was buying it regardless of the price.

"$12,000, but if you pay for it all now, we will give you a $3,000 discount," the lady stated.

Without bargaining, Jill pulled out her credit card. Before she could change her mind, she stated, "Please add on the cost of shipping with insurance. I need to send it home."

"We'll do that for free," the saleslady stated with a smile. When she returned with a receipt, Jill signed it, put the copy in her purse, then gave her grandfather's address, aware there would be someone there to receive the package unlike at her condo.

She rejoined Tom, who smiled at her. He guided her

out to the sidewalk before asking, "What was it that you liked so much about that set?"

His arm came around her shoulders, tugging her close to him. She was next to the buildings so she couldn't easily be seen with the way he was holding her. She leaned into him before saying in a wistful voice, "I'm part Irish and I love Celtic knots and the Irish roses. That set was perfect in the way it was done."

He gave her a gentle squeeze before saying, "That may have been a wasted purchase back there."

"Not really. Wyatt will make sure I'm wearing it if there's enough body parts left," she informed him, not shying from the reality of her possibly getting killed doing her job.

Other than Wyatt, Sam, Billy, and Brad, no one would notice if she disappeared, alleviating further problems where she was concerned. She wasn't afraid of dying, but prior to being eliminated, she wanted to get Billings and the others working with him.

Yes, Wyatt and Brad were aware of her fascination with Irish roses and knots. The first piece of jewelry Wyatt had ever given her was a ring of Celtic knots and roses, which she still wore. It had also been the first time he had ever told her he loved her. He had shown it in many ways prior to then, but had never said it. No one had ever told her they even cared for her, let alone loved her, other than Brad. The love he gave her was one of the reasons she couldn't quit. She had a score to settle with Billings.

They rounded the corner of the street leading to Tom's house. There was the smell of gas, burnt rubber and smoke in the air. There were fire trucks and police cars in front of the house, working on putting out a fire near the street. Across the street, she noticed Wyatt and Sam standing by his car, observing the activity, not having seen her and Tom yet.

Her eyes rounded when they were a house away from his. She stared between the gathered spectators at the scene of the explosion where the mangled remains of a vehicle were still burning. It was covered in foam with multiple firemen watching it.

"Oh no! My car!" Jill exclaimed in a small breathy voice, her hands covering her mouth, attempting to move forward as tears tracked down her cheeks. Tom held her in place as she stared at the remains of her most loved possession. She dropped to the sidewalk, sitting cross-legged, rocking and crying as she stared dejectedly through the legs of those in front of them, at what was now junk.

Tom squatted beside her, his hand on her shoulder. "Jill, it was only a car. We're okay."

With a sob, she turned her tear-stained face to his. "It wasn't just a car. You don't understand," she said before hiding her face in her hands, crying silently. His arms came around her, holding her like Wyatt or Brad would when she was upset.

He couldn't understand because he didn't know the story of the car. It was a reward she had received for saving a life. In return, it had saved her life on more than one occasion. No, he didn't understand her attachment to it and the man whose life she had saved.

Jill gasped when Wyatt's gentle hand stroked her hair, pushing the curls back from her face. She peered up at him, her face wet with tears as he squatted beside her. His big thumb wiped away a tear. He understood what the car meant to her and how it's being destroyed would affect her.

"Honey, it's okay. We'll replace it with a better one. You're safe, and that's all that matters to me."

She turned toward her destroyed car, her lips pulled down, mourning the loss of the car she had treasured. "It won't be the same."

"I know. Let's go. We need to get you out of here," he calmly stated, pulling her to her feet before turning to Tom. "Get what you need from the house. I'm parked across the street."

She leaned into Wyatt, crying as he guided her to the car where Sam was waiting, the backdoor open. Wyatt had her enter the backseat of the car first, then slid in beside her. When Sam closed the door, Wyatt pulled her onto his lap and held her much as he had when she was a child, understanding the tears. He knew it was more than a car to her. It was a tie to the man who had given it to her. A man who loved her regardless of her past. To her, he was a treasured friend. One who would be there for her no matter what happened.

A few minutes later, Tom slid into the front seat. He turned and informed Wyatt, "We were almost in that car when it exploded. It looks like they're stepping up the heat."

Wyatt ran his hand over her hair and pulled her closer to him before kissing the top of her head. His silence and actions had her tilting her head up, facing him.

"I can't quit."

He moved her closer to him before saying, "I know, honey. I know."

She cuddled into the big man who held her, treating her as someone who mattered. He was afraid for her, but recognized he couldn't stop her. Her tears wet the front of his shirt as she clung to him, needing his understanding and love. She didn't ever want to leave the comfort of his embrace. His love was what made her life worth living. He understood and didn't reject her.

It wasn't until Sam stopped the car at the door to a motel that she moved from his arms. She wiped away the tears with his handkerchief before giving him a tenuous smile. Sam came around and opened the passenger door. She exited the car and waited for Wyatt to join her. His size made her look childlike as she walked beside him, his arm around her, keeping her safe. Tom had stayed with Sam, talking to him, intently watching her as she and

Wyatt walked into the motel lobby.

As she had expected, her grandfather had a suite on the top floor. Once they were inside, he told her, "I got the rest of your things from the resort. Why don't you take a shower then a nap?"

She nodded before going to the room he indicated was hers. There was nothing else to be done today. The warehouse could wait. A tiredness settled over her as she showered. After putting on the PJs she had packed, she reclined on the bed, the tears returning. Again, the things she cared about most were being taken from her.

The men's muffled voices brought back the memory of another place and time, sending fear racing through her, speeding up her heart. She pushed the memories back into the compartment where they belonged, willing herself to calm down. She let the tiredness take over, drifting off to sleep.

Chapter 7

WHAT'S NEXT?

A gentle hand pushing the hair off her face woke Jill. It had pulled her from the pleasant dream involving the Irish rose rings. Her eyes fluttered open, surprised to see Tom sitting at the edge of the bed, watching her. His eyes held something she didn't recognize. Something which wasn't there earlier.

His voice broke the spell. "Wyatt sent me to wake you. Supper's here, and you haven't eaten since early this morning."

"I'm not hungry," she stated, turning away, wanting to reenter the dream he had terminated with his touch.

"Jill, you need to eat, plus we need to discuss what's next in this case."

"Leave me alone," she ordered, shrugging his hand off her shoulder, hiding her tears. She needed more time to assimilate the loss of the car and their close call with death.

"No, I'm not leaving you alone."

Gentle hands turned her so she was facing him. Jill buried her head in the pillow, unable to stop the tears, but not wanting him to see her cry again.

"Please, go away," her muffled voice told him.

With a tissue in his hand, he pushed the pillow away and dried her face, the small action of caring creating more tears.

"Jill, staying in bed won't change anything. I understand you're upset. I also know asking why won't get me any answers." He cupped her face with a hand, scrutinizing her. "You need to join us so we have your input in deciding where to go from here. Time for you to get back to work."

He was right. Staying in bed wouldn't change what happened. With reluctance, when he stood, she scooted to the edge of the bed and sat, shoulders slumped, and the sadness washing through her. The bed moved when Tom sat beside her. A hand ran through her hair before he tugged her close to him, no words passing between them. His hand cradled her head on his shoulder while she mourned the loss of her car as he provided a comfort she seldom had, but craved.

The tears slowed, until with a sniff, she reached over and grabbed a Kleenex to mop up the last of them and blow her nose. He peered into her watery eyes, waiting for her to speak.

"I guess I'll get my act together now," she stated, not wanting him to turn her loose but aware it was nothing more than a reaction to her being upset.

"No problem. I've no complaints in holding a beautiful lady while she cries."

The heat rushed up her neck before she hung her head. "I'm not beautiful or a lady."

A hand again brushed her hair, sending a shiver down

her spine. "Now, I'll disagree on both accounts." When she didn't respond, he said, "Let's join Wyatt before he comes to find out what we're doing in here so long."

She giggled, not putting it past her grandfather to do just that. Jill pushed herself off the bed and started toward the door. Tom stopped her with a hand on her arm.

"Jill, we need to have a private talk. It'll wait, but the quicker the better."

"Whatever," she responded and turned away from him.

They didn't need that talk. She had heard it all before, more than once. Yes, she liked him, but held no illusions of a relationship developing beyond working partners. Not only wasn't she his type, but once he discovered her past, he'd hightail it to the proverbial hills. No, she had no delusions concerning a relationship with any man, let alone him. Those riveting eyes, the musical voice, and occasional laughter were something she would enjoy until this case finished. Afterward, it meant returning to being alone and working.

When she and Tom entered the main room, Wyatt was standing with arms crossed and feet spread. He was staring out the window overlooking International Drive. Turning toward them, he searched her face while keeping his from showing any feelings.

"I was beginning to think I'd have to come and check on you two."

She shrugged, glancing at Tom before saying, "Nah. I

needed a prod to pull myself together, that's all."

Jill joined Wyatt at the window, reaching around him, giving him a hug, hoping to alleviate the concern she noted on his face. He bent over, kissing the top of her head. He searched her face again, brows creased with worry when she raised her head to meet his scrutiny.

"It's okay. I'll be together by morning. You know me, I don't let things like no car interfere with my job."

"Fuck it, Jill. Come home. Let Tom do the fucking mop-up."

She lowered her eyelids and shook her head. "I can't. I expected them to attempt to kill me, just not so soon. They're feeling the heat, and I can't back off now. Besides, it's more than mopping up."

Wyatt sucked in a deep breath and let it out, holding her next to him. "You're going to get yourself fucking killed, then what will I do?"

Blinking back the tears at his biggest fear, she told him, "The same as always," remembering Brad's story of what had happened when Wyatt thought he'd never see her again.

A beefy finger under her chin lifted her head so he could see her face. "Jill, you don't have to fucking do this. Just give the fucking information to the fucking feds."

She turned away, standing as he had been earlier, looking out the window, frowning while attempting to stuff the guilt at worrying him back into its box.

"The last time I gave information outside of court, you remember the results. I won't let them get away again."

"Tom, you talk some fucking sense into her. I can't."

"What makes you think I'll do any better?"

Wyatt let off a stream of profanity above and beyond the normal. She stoically stood at the window, aware she held information no one else outside of the syndicate possessed, yet unable to share it due to how she had gotten it.

Tom's hand on her arm drew her attention. "Jill, I can finish this. Share what you have with me, then you can go home with Wyatt. Like you, I want everything tied up in nice neat bows so there's no chance they'll walk."

Her gaze returned to the scene outside the window. "No. It's personal and Wyatt knows it. My case. My bows."

Tom moved so she had to look at him, studying her face. "If this is personal, you shouldn't be working the case."

She lowered her eyelids, unable to meet his direct stare. "This isn't a first for me. I'll finish it like I did the others." A deep sadness washed over her when she turned away, unwilling to explain why it was personal.

Tom caught her arm, turning her to face him. "Why is this case so important to you?"

Fear and anger had her glaring at him. "That's my business, not yours." When he didn't turn her loose, her soft voice, holding an icy warning, commanded, "Take your hand off me."

The restraining hand dropped to his side. Jill strode to the couch, plopping onto it before curling into the corner. She rested her head on its overstuffed arm, her eyes closed to shut out her grandfather's concerned face. No matter what their opinion, she wasn't quitting. Billings needed to learn that not every victim remained a victim.

She opened her eyes when she felt someone moving near her. Wyatt glanced in her direction before he put a chicken leg, a spoonful of green beans, and mashed potatoes on a plate, then placed it in her hands.

"Eat every bite. You're getting too thin again."

With reluctance, she picked up the fork, not willing to fight him. Whether she was hungry or not, she had to stay put until the plate was empty. It was one argument he had won during their butting of heads when she was younger. Wyatt lowered himself into the chair next to her, his elbows resting on the padded arms, his fingers steepled. He grimly monitored her progress while she struggled to swallow each mouthful, his silence saying more to her than any speech he could make.

Her finishing what he put on her plate resulted from a major disagreement he had won when she was twenty and essentially anorexic. There was no way she wanted to go through that again. Tom watched her, but she ignored him, concentrating on completing the meal.

When she had completed half of her meal, the others

filled their plates with food. The three men had finished eating and were talking when Sam took her empty plate in exchange for a bottle of water. She drank a sip, hoping the food stayed down.

When at this point in a case, it wasn't unusual for her to not eat. Nerves kept her on edge, so she lived on coffee and minimal food. In her agreement with Wyatt, her weight had to be at or above a hundred and ten pounds after dropping to eighty pounds during one of her early cases. Wyatt could tell when she was close to the lower weight limit he had set.

Jill shifted, folding her legs to sit Indian style, waiting for Wyatt to start the discussion. After another sip of water, she glanced at him. His hands on the arms of the chair relaxed, showing he was ready.

"Jill, what's your next move?" he asked, his brown eyes watching her. She knew he would know if she was trying to hide information from him.

"Search the warehouse. I didn't do a search because getting the girls out safe was a priority. With the arrest of the deputies and the girls in custody of ICE, I'm not expecting anyone to go there for the next day or two. I want to go through it before someone else does."

Wyatt steepled his fingers, watching her before asking, "What are you hoping to find?"

"Well, information on the women who were there. Then hopefully there will be some paperwork or other evidence on the couple or their handlers."

"If that's a bust, then what?"

She met Wyatt's direct gaze before saying, "Push a few buttons and see who pops out."

Tom leaned forward, studying her with an intensity which made her nervous. "Jill, that's not safe where this group is concerned."

Her shoulders lifted in a quick shrug, the fingers of her right hand tracing the design of the material on the couch. "I'm aware of the risks. Billings isn't doing this on his own. I don't know about you, but I want all of them."

Wyatt's lips thinned before he spat, "Fuck, Jill. I can't fucking protect you if I don't fucking know what cocksucker is coming after you."

"Do you want the list of who's involved now or later?" Her voice hadn't changed, but her glare was icy. Wyatt dropped his gaze, aware of why she didn't share information with anyone, including him.

"You know who they are?" Tom questioned.

Jill warned Wyatt with a flick of her eyes to let her answer. "Of course. I only have minimal evidence on some of them. They'll pop out of the woodwork one or two at a time, attempting to stop me. Oh, before I forget, the Snake gave back the money and negated the contract on me."

"How the fuck did you find that out?" Wyatt grated.

"A little birdie."

"When?" Tom questioned.

"While I was asleep. He didn't connect me with the contract until seeing me at the warehouse. When he missed, and I fired back, he backed off."

"Why?" Tom questioned, his brows lowered, searching her face.

She again sent a silent warning to Wyatt. "He owes me."

"So, he negated the contract because he owes you," Tom stated, his right eyebrow raising, taking a quick peek at Wyatt.

"Something like that."

Wyatt chuckled wryly, aware of her relationships with some questionable characters. "Just drop it, Tom. She has fucking friends in strange fucking places." Wyatt sobered before saying, "I can get a car here for you by morning."

Jill sighed, sending her curls bouncing with a shake of her head. "I'll get one when we go home. You know me, I want to make sure it's got everything I need on it. Tom will have to find something with suitable speed for now."

"How much speed?" he questioned, watching her after a quick glance at Wyatt's pursed lips and merry eyes.

"As much as you can get. The one they blew up could outrun a Porsche and did on several occasions."

He didn't react other than relaxing against the back of the couch after scanning Wyatt, Sam, and her. "Nothing like setting a high standard. I'll see what I can come up with for us to use before morning. Just don't expect a flashy car."

After glancing at Wyatt, she met Tom's scrutiny. "A good muscle car that is beat up suits me fine. Just make sure it has a powerful engine and a transmission able to handle tons of abuse."

"Let me guess. The car you had was a race car disguised as a street car."

Wyatt's bark of laughter drew Tom's attention. "You have the right fucking idea. She can handle it though. I've seen her beat the fucking street racers."

Tom grinned. "I didn't know I was going to be working with a race car driver who has friends in strange places."

Sam chuckled before commenting, "You ain't seen nothing yet. The girl's a fantastic shot, and don't even try to take her down. She'll make you regret it."

Wyatt watched her, adding, "She can also get in and out of places you wouldn't expect. Now if we can keep her fucking alive long enough to get these guys."

Tom turned and faced her, his face sobering. "So, you have marvelous abilities. Care to explain why everyone is so afraid of them killing you."

"Ask them. Not me," she told him, eyeing Wyatt, hoping his explanation wouldn't lead to more questions.

"Because they'll use whatever they can to fucking kill her. They know her on sight." The last statement gave Tom more information than she wanted him to have.

"Care to explain how they know you?"

"Nope." She wasn't telling him, and Wyatt wouldn't without clearing it with her first.

"Wyatt?"

"It's her story to tell, not mine."

Tom questioned, "Jill?"

"None of your fucking business," she snapped, glaring at her grandfather. Why didn't he tell him to mind his own business?

She uncrossed her legs and stood, stating, "I'm going to bed. Be ready to search the warehouse tomorrow morning."

Yes, it was her story to tell, and she wasn't sharing. Sam and Wyatt were privy to part of the story, but they were the only ones other than Brad, one good friend, and her therapist. Tom didn't need her story. Once this case was finished, he'd disappear. Until the trial, the information he got would be on a need-to-know basis.

In her room, she crawled onto the big bed. Yes, she could name or identify everyone involved, and yes, they knew her on sight. She had spent enough time with them. Her working for Wyatt was a result of that time. Yes, this was personal. Very personal.

After rolling over, she closed her eyes, unable to shut off her mind. Her story gave the why, and her grandfather assisted her in the pursuit of those who had hurt her. All she needed was the last bits of evidence and the appropriate federal group to prosecute them. Unless she had miscalculated Tom's authority, he would handle those who popped out of the woodwork. If only . . . She let the thought hang, not willing to contemplate what wasn't ever going to happen.

Chapter 8

TO BE OR NOT TO BE

Jill was up early. Unable to sleep, she dressed in her normal cargo shorts, large T-shirt and khaki vest, and her favorite tennis shoes before preparing to leave. After placing two phone calls, she had put all her ducks in a row. It was time to force a few slime balls to pop out of the swamp where they lived, worked, and played.

One thing she wanted was to observe Billings' expression when the handcuffs snapped shut on his wrists. That picture of him being made to pay for his sins had been her talisman over the years. She was the closest she had ever been to achieving her vow to see him behind bars.

Tom, Wyatt, and Sam were sitting around the dinette table talking when she entered the room. Wyatt's gaze followed her as she poured herself a cup of coffee before taking a seat on the couch, eschewing the bagels and sweet rolls. Wyatt pursed his lips before flicking a warning glare at her. He toasted a bagel then smeared it with cream cheese before placing it on a plate, and handing it to her. With a sigh, she took the plate, staring at the food she didn't want. Wyatt waited, hovering at her side, until she took a small bite, before returning to his chair. The muscles in his jaw jumped, but it was his words which angered her.

"Tom, make sure she fucking eats. If you don't, she won't eat a fucking thing until this is over."

Tom's focus ping-ponged between her and Wyatt. "I'll do my best."

"You better fucking listen to him," Wyatt warned with a glare.

Not responding to his words, she took a deep breath and held it, restraining herself from throwing the plate and bagel at him and telling him to go to hell. Nothing like getting the hired help to force her to eat.

"You coming back here tonight?" Wyatt asked, his gaze holding hers, cognizant of her thoughts and feelings, having been the brunt of the anger she kept hidden more than once. After several deep calming breaths, she let go of the irrational anger at the man who loved her enough to fight with her over her well-being.

The worried eyes of her grandfather resulted in her dropping her gaze to the partially eaten bagel. Guilt wormed its way out of the box where it hid. He hadn't been this concerned for her in years. What had Sam found to cause Wyatt to be so worried? There was no sense in asking because he wasn't going to tell her. This was one of those times where she needed to accept he had information, but wasn't sharing.

A glance at Tom gave no hint in how to answer her grandfather. After swallowing the piece of bagel in her mouth, Jill mulled over what she wanted to accomplish today. "Not sure. It depends on what we find or if we run into problems. We may need to hide out if we find something important."

Wyatt let out a noisy breath, aware of what she wasn't saying. "You keep that fucking phone on. Understand?"

"Yes, sir," she replied, her voice that of a chastised child. That was an order she couldn't ignore, unable to put him through finding her again. "Just don't come unless I signal you. I don't need to lose them now."

Wyatt provided excellent backup, even though he was seventy. Along with running the agency, he continued to work cases, enjoying being in the field with her except in cases intersecting with her past. When she had joined the agency, he had taught her everything he had learned over the years. She had informed him of her plan to make them pay, so he made it easier and safer for her to monitor those she wanted to see punished for ruining her life.

"Honey, I won't fucking interfere. All I fucking ask is for you to keep in fucking contact with me."

"I will," she promised, hoping it wouldn't complicate things along the way. After losing her once, he expected her to check in daily when they were apart. This was one of the few times he was ordering her to check in instead of assuming she would out of habit.

Tom waited, chatting with Wyatt and Sam, while she finished the bagel her grandfather insisted she eat. After disposing of the plate, she prepared to leave. When she walked past Wyatt, he reached out and pulled her into an embrace, planting a kiss on her forehead, then studying her face.

"You better fucking come back to me. I need my fairy."

With a watery grin, she told him, "I'm like a bad penny. I keep turning up." Unable to look away from him, she patted his hand, then stood on her tiptoes to plant a kiss on his cheek before hugging him.

Without saying the words, he knew how she felt. She loved the man who gave her unconditional love. The somewhat crude exterior didn't matter in the overall scheme of things where she was concerned.

She sent a saucy wink his direction before walking out the door. Tom led her to a nondescript car parked near the front of the hotel. He held the passenger door for her until she was seated. For now, riding shotgun was fine, because when push came to shove, she would be the one driving.

After settling into the driver's seat, he asked, "Have you always had a problem eating?"

She studied her clasped hands, before admitting, "No, only when I'm stressed. Wyatt knows I'll live on coffee along with a few bites of food until these guys are in cuffs."

"Not on my watch you won't. I agree with Wyatt. You need to eat."

With a glare, her muscles tensed. She grated out, "You aren't my grandfather, so don't try to force me to eat."

"No forcing, but you will eat."

Tom didn't shy away from the challenge in her eyes, which said he could try, but it wouldn't work. When an eyebrow quirked as his gaze held hers, she accepted the challenge.

After a few seconds, she turned away, her lips compressed in a straight line, not sure if she could win the food battle with him. After folding her arms, she commanded, "Warehouse." It was time to go to work.

When he turned the key, a bored-out engine purred to life. It was a sound she loved. Power. Massive power. The man had some knowledge of cars and what she had requested in one. Hopefully it had the agility to take corners and rough terrain in a chase situation.

At the warehouse, Jill scanned the complex. Several

bays were open, but no one was paying attention to them other than a quick glance in their direction, leading her to believe they were used to different cars coming and going at this bay. Tom pushed opened the side door to the warehouse, which she hadn't locked, having left in a hurry.

Once inside, she headed to the far side of the large bay while Tom started at the wall next to the door from the small office. Boxes, bins, and bags were piled along the walls, leaving an area in the middle big enough to pull in a large vehicle. There were sleeping bags on the floor near the back wall. In the corner was a refrigerator and a cheap dinette with four mismatched chairs. On an old beat-up dresser was a microwave and a few dishes.

As they finished going through items, they moved them to the center of the floor. The local authorities would repeat what they were doing. So far, everything was benign in that there was nothing but clothes, books, dishes, and other items not being used.

Upon reaching the back wall, she opened the backpack located at the top of the nearest sleeping bag. A picture found in the side pocket verified the backpack belonged to the woman she was hoping to find. Jill set aside the backpack, along with other items belonging to the girl, to give to Wyatt, ensuring the girl or her brother would receive the recovered items.

Jill moved to the next backpack. She wanted to cheer when she found a slip of paper on the floor under it. The writing on the piece of paper indicated someone had been careless. After slipping it into the side pocket on her shorts, she continued the thorough search of the personal effects of the three women, not expecting to find anything else of interest.

She ignored the dresser, leaving it for Tom to search before moving to the miniscule bathroom. Aware of the most common hiding places, she took the lid off the tank of the old commode. Inside, along the back of the tank, was a thin object sealed in plastic, which blended in with the rusted walls of the tank.

With care, she removed the package, dried it off, then peeled the plastic back to reveal an accounts book. Opening it, she flipped through pages containing items bought or sold, names, dates, and dollar amounts. Sweet. In her hand was what she needed to tie Knight to the couple and Billings and his organization. One bow done up all nice and pretty.

Apparently, the couple hadn't trusted the people for whom they were working. It would be one of the few reasons to keep accounts like this. Too bad Billings' name wasn't on the list. Of the names listed in the book, only two were unfamiliar to her. Most of those listed were men from Billings' organization, tying the couple to him. The others were from Knight's organization, tying him into the syndicate.

Tom finished the section he was searching before

joining her in the small bathroom. Without preamble, she handed him the ledger. "Any names in there you haven't identified?"

With pursed lips, Tom took his time perusing the lists of names before answering. "Only one. I've no idea who Kingman is."

"I do, but I don't know Carlton or Fishman."

"Great. Between the two of us we know the whole group."

She handed him the slip of paper in her pocket before standing on the toilet seat to check the ceiling panel above the commode. From how it sat in the metal frame, it had been moved more than once. This was another common hiding spot for the not-so-smart criminal. Then again, they may have been using this as a temporary stash, or had paid protection and weren't worried about being raided. From the number of deputies arrested, it was most likely the latter.

"Where did you find this?" Tom asked, watching her lift and move the ceiling tile.

"On the floor under a backpack. Any idea where that combination might have a lock?"

"Yeah. The country club Billings just joined."

With a "Humph," she felt around until her fingers touched a smooth plastic-covered surface with twine around it. She hooked her finger through the cord and pulled out a tightly wrapped package. After handing it to

Tom, she pulled out a second one. On tiptoe, she reached as far back as she could, but was unable to find anything else within her reach.

With a huff, she stepped down from the seat. "You'll need to check if there's any more up there. I'm too short to reach any farther than those two."

Tom stepped onto the toilet seat and pulled out two more packages. With the flashlight on his key chain, he verified they had everything from the ceiling. Now they had the group on smuggling illegals and drugs. There was no doubt in her mind as to what was in the wrapped bricks. This added up to carelessness, stupidity, or lack of fear of discovery on their part.

They finished with the bathroom and moved into the office, working side by side. A few more personal items were added to where she had placed the backpacks. When they finished with the office, Tom put the bricks into evidence bags, then gathered up the incriminating papers discovered in the office and the account book.

Jill picked up the few things she put aside for the women, placing them into a garbage bag. At the car, he opened the trunk and placed the salvaged items and evidence into it. She didn't miss the rifle placed where it was accessible from the backseat. Okay, the man was a tad smarter than he first appeared.

When he closed the trunk, she held out her hand for the keys. The objection she expected didn't happen when he dropped the keyring onto her palm before going to the passenger side. Once behind the wheel, she asked, "Where to now?"

"The country club. Let's see what's in locker number twenty."

At the stop sign, Jill noted a car with two men parked so they could observe the complex road.

"Buckle up," she warned before whipping left onto the street. With the gas pedal to the floor, the tires spun for purchase on the blacktop, leaving a streak of rubber and smoke behind them. The car had power to spare, but how it handled the turns was the next hurdle.

With a rolling stop at the next intersection, she took a quick right, then the next left. In the rearview mirror, the men chasing them made the correct turns, but were over a block behind. At the next crossroad, the car skidded as she went to the right, not slowing for the turn, then took the next left with squealing tires, the back in of the car sliding on the pavement.

In a check in the rearview mirror prior to making the last turn, the other car was nowhere in sight. When she got to Citrus Tower Boulevard, luck was with them. There was a break in the traffic, enabling her to make a quick left across all four lanes, merging into traffic before taking the next right off the boulevard. It was at this point Jill slowed before turning into the parking lot for Uncle Kenny's BBQ. After parking so they could watch for the men chasing them, Jill, with a calm voice, requested, "Directions to the country club, my dear."

Tom sucked in a big breath before saying, "Let the rest of me get caught up first. When Sam and Wyatt said you could drive, they weren't kidding."

Jill giggled, not having missed how he had braced himself in the seat with a hand on the dash. That alone verified he hadn't ever ridden with someone who knew what they were doing behind the wheel, at speeds most drivers never attempted on a traveled street. It made her wonder if he could handle a real chase where she had to use all her driving skills.

It was her turn to quirk an eyebrow and grin. "That was child's play. I kept all four wheels on the ground and didn't do one slide and still lost them in less than five miles."

The hand he had on the dash relaxed before saying, "Hm. Sure you aren't a professional getaway driver?"

"You tell me. I know you've run a check," she challenged before she gave him a quick glance, grinning.

Tom pursed his lips, studying her for a few seconds. "There's a three-year blank in your history where no one knows where you were or what you were doing. Want to explain it?"

The grin vanished, an icy fear gripping her. That wasn't the question she expected. "Nope."

"I'm surprised no one has questioned your expert

testimony without knowing what happened during that part of your life." He turned in the seat, waiting for her answer, scrutinizing her reaction.

The lump of fear grew as she stared out the windshield. "I don't give expert testimony, just the facts of the current case and my part in it. There's no reason to question the documented facts," she told him, her voice devoid of emotion.

In the ensuing silence, he studied her with an uncomfortable intensity. No one, including him, needed to know where she was during that time. Wyatt and Sam knew part of what had happened, but only Brad and her therapist knew every detail. What the others didn't know was her secret to reveal only when necessary. What transpired in those three years was the reason she became a detective, but that information was given out on a need-to-know basis. For now, he didn't need to know.

Jill started the car and followed the directions he gave to the country club west of Orlando. The silence was heavy with her refusal to answer his question. At the country club, she pulled into a parking space in the outer portion of the parking lot where the car wouldn't draw attention before shutting off the engine. Billings was rubbing noses with the cream of society, judging from the fancy building and the people entering or leaving. Most were driving pricey vehicles.

"I'll wait here," Jill stated, not wanting to go into the

building. Just knowing Billings was a member was enough to deter her from entering the club. Then there was Tom's palpable disapproval of her keeping secrets from him. Too bad. It was her choice as to whom to share the past with and when.

"No, you need to go in with me. I may need your assistance in getting out."

With reluctance, she joined him in the walk across the parking lot. His arm came around her, creating the illusion they were a couple as they made their way into the large modern building. Tom proceeded directly to the men's locker room, showing he had been here before today.

There was an alcove with padded benches near the locker room door. It had a good view of the lobby yet was partially hidden by a low wall. Jill took a seat to wait on Tom to return. She kept watch on the lobby door while flipping through a magazine from the table beside her to pass the time. Other than her tennis shoes, she could pass for a golfer at the club. Several women who passed the small hallway had on cargo shorts and T-shirts, only theirs were brand names and fit snug enough to show off their figures.

Tom was gone for two or three minutes when she froze, holding her breath as fear zinged around inside of her. Billings walked in the front door, a big smile on his lips, dressed for a game of golf. A man stopped him a few steps inside the lobby, as if he had been waiting for him. They talked, then walked off together toward the bar and restaurant. Jill let out the breath she had been holding, keeping a watchful eye on the lobby and the small walkway to the locker room. If only Tom would return before Billings decided to come to the locker room.

It took Tom less than ten minutes to reappear, but it had felt like days with the tension of knowing Billings was in the building. She joined him, her arm going around his waist. In return, his arm slipped around her shoulders. With her head lowered, she leaned into him, acting as if she was upset and wanted comfort.

"Billings is here. He went toward the bar with another man."

Tom's arm tightened around her. "I wondered what prompted the sudden affinity for closeness."

She raised her head, a pitiful look on her face, before saying, "Fuck you."

With his bottom lip caught in his teeth, Tom kept back the laughter she had felt bubbling to the surface at her two words. At that moment, Billings walked out of the bar. With nowhere to hide, she pivoted Tom so he was hiding her, arms around his waist, her head tilted up to his, and her eyes filled with fear.

A smile twitched at his lips before he bent over and brushed his lips over hers. He nipped at her lower lip before deepening the kiss. Her arms pulled him to her, as the feelings he drew from deep inside pushed Billings from her mind. When his tongue danced with hers, she lost all contact with reality, drowning in the sensations flowing through her. This wasn't a pretend kiss. It was a real kiss!

Tom gently broke the kiss and straightened up. In a daze, she stared up at him, lips parted. Her emotions swirled around inside of her, increasing her confusion at what Tom had done, preventing her from speaking. The touch of his hand rubbing her arm had her backing away from him, not sure of why he had kissed her in that way.

"Come, darling, let's get out of here," he said as if nothing had happened before turning her to walk out the door.

Once safely out the door and on their way through the parking lot, Tom took the keys from her nerveless fingers. Acting on autopilot, she got into the car and fastened her seatbelt while attempting to control the emotions resulting from his kiss.

Before he started the engine, Jill asked, "Why did you do that?"

"Do what?" The normally melodic voice was devoid of emotion.

His answer was a dash of cold water, bringing her back to reality. His reaction was nothing more than she should have expected. "Kiss me like that?"

The lack of an answer had her rotating to him. He was sitting with his hands on the wheel, head bowed. In a voice so soft she could barely hear it, he said, "I wanted to. Just forget it ever happened."

Her eyes watered, pain spiking through her as she stared at him for a few seconds before saying, "Okay. Forgotten."

Talk about a lie! That wasn't a kiss she could forget, just as she wouldn't forget those eyes or the voice which caressed her each time she heard it. Thankful he was driving, she stared out the side window, attempting to put the kiss into perspective. What she wouldn't give for him to have meant that kiss, even if it was only temporary.

It wasn't until he pulled into a nondescript bar on a side street and shut off the engine that she pulled herself back to reality.

"Lunchtime," he announced.

"I'm not hungry. You go ahead and eat. I'll wait here."

"Not happening. You need to eat something. We can share."

"I'm not hungry. You go eat," she reiterated, refusing to face him.

"Jill, don't make me call Wyatt to get you to eat. It doesn't have to be much, but you need food."

Okay. No Wyatt. The spike of anger burned bright at his negating the kiss and now threatening her with Wyatt. She slammed the door after exiting the car and stalked into the dim bar, ignoring him, then hesitated. Her stomach flip-flopped at the smell of beer and greasy food. There were several people at the bar and most of the scarred wooden tables were filled.

The gentle hand at her waist nudged her toward a booth at the back of the room. With her back to the door, she slid onto the padded seat, sitting so he had to take the seat opposite her. It was his turn to watch for the bad guys.

A barmaid came to the table with water and menus. "What can I get you to drink?" she asked.

Tom ordered a Heineken, so Jill ordered a Samuel Adams seasonal ale. If he could drink on the job, so could she!

"ID please," the woman requested. Jill already had her driver's license in her hand, aware she would be carded.

She laid the menu on the table, ignoring the man opposite her. With her head bent over the menu, she struggled to decide what to order from the list of hamburgers and sandwiches. There wasn't a damn thing she wanted on the entire menu.

When the barmaid came back with the drinks, Jill asked, "Could I get a simple grilled cheese on whole wheat?"

"Sure, honey," the barmaid stated, dismissing Jill before taking Tom's order for a hamburger and fries.

After flicking a glance at Tom, Jill stared at the mug she held in her hands, running her thumb up and down the frosted glass. She didn't want to be here with him. Being totally truthful, she didn't want to be anywhere close to him after that kiss. The problem was, she couldn't devise a way to ditch the too-attractive detective, which wouldn't put them both in jeopardy of losing the group they were after.

A gentle finger on her hand had her freezing, unsure of what he wanted. "Jill, talk to me."

"No need to talk." She took a big drink of the ale, wishing it was a shot of Jack Daniels.

For the first time in years, she wanted to get drunk. One fucking kiss from him had destroyed her hard-won distance from men. One fucking kiss. A tear escaped, leaving a silver track on her cheek before she could wipe it away. What she wanted was for him to kiss her again.

The cool fingers caressed her hand until she pulled it away, unable to bear even that much after what she perceived as rejection on his end.

"Jill, I'm sorry. I shouldn't have kissed you, but I'll admit I've wanted to since that first conversation with you."

"Why?" she asked, meeting his gaze, afraid of where this conversation was going.

It was his turn to look away and play with the mug he was holding. He sat in silence, staring at the table, gnawing on his lower lip.

"I can't explain why, because I don't understand it myself. What I do know is how I've never met anyone like you. In all my years of working in law enforcement, I've never done what I did today." He raised his head, facing her. "I let my personal feelings take over. Somehow, someway, you've gotten to me, and I don't know what to do about it."

That simple admission gave her more information than he intended. It put what he had done in perspective and why he had said to forget about it. She picked up her mug, took a drink, then held it before her, watching him. "I lied. I won't forget it."

The wry grin on his face at her admission had her holding her breath, until he said, "Neither will I." He reached out, taking her hand in his, the caress of his thumb sending chills up her arm. "Jill, when this case is finished, I want to spend some time with you so we can get to know each other better."

"Then you better make sure I stay alive," she stated, raising her gaze to his face.

With elevated brows, he stated, "I've no intention of trying to explain to Wyatt why I survived and you didn't."

From his expression, he was serious when he said he wanted to spend time with her. With a sigh, she lowered her eyelids, not kidding herself into believing this current interest in her would be long term. The words were ones she had heard before, yet she was still alone.

She removed her hand from his. They engaged in no further talk until the barmaid delivered their meal. With a sigh, Jill examined the sandwich and potato chips before picking up a half of the grilled cheese and taking a bite.

For him, she would try to eat.

Each bite was washed down with a mouthful of ale. He had eaten his burger and fries before she finished half the sandwich. She nibbled on a chip, staring at the other half on her plate. If she ate it, she would get sick, but she didn't think he would believe her.

Tom winked at her then grinned when she stared at him. "You don't have to eat the rest of it. I only promised to see that you ate. I didn't say how much."

Leaning back on the bench, she sighed in relief. "Thanks. So, what's next?"

"Find a place to hunker down and go through the papers I found in Billings's locker."

"Okay, you drive. I'm finishing this ale, and I won't drive if I've been drinking."

"But you're only having one beer," he said, surprise in his voice.

She picked up her mug and stated, "I get tipsy on one beer," before taking another big swallow of the ale.

"Nothing like a cheap date," Tom replied, chuckling.

"Right. It isn't that I can't drive. It's my choice not to do so. Also, it doesn't mean I don't know what I'm doing or saying." She wanted to be clear on what she meant.

Without comment, Tom paid the tab, then escorted her out of the bar. He held the door for her. "Thank you," she said. The small courtesy was something few had ever given her.

Before he turned the key, he asked, "You okay?"

"Yeah," she answered, but it was only a partial truth.

Not seeing the passing scenery, Jill remembered the feel of his arms and that wonderful kiss. It proved he cared about her for now, but it would change when he learned the secret of those three years. It always did. She gnawed on her bottom lip, letting the feelings she kept hidden loose. There was enough time to hold a quick pity party for herself and the past that had destroyed any hope for a normal future.

When Jill again noticed her surroundings, trees, palmettos, and the sawgrass of the Everglades lined the road. Close to an hour later, Tom exited the interstate and turned into a motel just beyond a gas station. The place needed a fresh coat of whitewash and the trim repainted. The vacancy sign was only half lit, and the name of the motel was difficult to read with the peeling paint. From the number of local cars in the lot, she could guess the type of business this motel did on a regular basis. If Tom asked for an hourly rate, he would most likely get it.

Jill let Tom go alone into the lobby to register, not wanting to be seen by the clerk. Whereas he was hard to describe, she wasn't and knew it. Her short stature, auburn curls, elfin face, and bright blue eyes stood out. At twenty-five she could still pass for a teenager, so she would be remembered by anyone who saw her.

Tom rejoined her in the car to park in front of their

room. He scanned the parking lot before saying, "Welcome to the local flop house. I requested a room with clean sheets. Hopefully it's decent."

"Doesn't matter. I usually put the towels on the bed and sleep on the top of the covers in these types of places."

It was all she could do to hold back a giggle when his head swiveled in her direction. He stared at her, frowning, before saying, "When have you been in a place like this?"

With raised brows, she quipped, "I work for Wyatt. It isn't just penthouses and rich bastards. I've seen the seamy sides of life too."

On that, he pulled the keys from the ignition and got out. She joined him at the front of the car and waited as he unlocked the door to the room, opened it, letting her enter first. It was a small room with a king-sized bed, small couch, and two wooden chairs at a small round scarred wooden table. The room had a musty smell, but from the cleanliness and quality of furnishings, it was reserved for travelers. The sheets should be clean enough to use for the night.

Tom pulled the curtains closed, then rechecked the door locks. When done, he moved to where she was standing.

"I'm going to be bad again," he warned before his arms came around her and he kissed her again. This time she fully participated in the kiss, imagining more than would ever happen, until he raised his head, green eyes saying he wanted more than the kiss. She felt the physical response to his being bad on her abdomen.

"I better stop before I get into trouble." A hand ran through his hair after backing away from her. "Never have I experienced such a passionate kiss from a woman who looks so innocent."

The words hit her as if she had been doused with ice water. "I'm a lot of things, but innocent isn't one of them." She turned away before muttering, "I wish I was."

When his hand brushed her shoulder, she flinched but controlled the response to the unexpected contact. With a gentle hand, he turned her, tilting her head up so she was facing him. "Jill, I have a past too. It's okay."

Her hands pressing on his chest kept a distance between them. "Tom, don't. I shouldn't have allowed that last kiss. You need to forget about me. We'll both end up getting hurt if you don't back off and leave it alone."

"And if I don't want to?" he queried in a soft tender voice.

Her gaze dropped to the dark brown carpeting, blinking back tears, the pain of loss knifing through her before saying, "You'll end up regretting it."

"Why?"

"Trust me. It's best to stop now."

"Jill, tell me what the problem is with going forward. I know you enjoy being around me as much as I do you."

She moved away from him, turning so he couldn't see

the gathering tears. "Please, Tom, forget that kiss ever happened and let it go."

There was extended silence before he said, "Okay. For now, I will, but like you, I don't give up."

With the heels of her hands, she rubbed the tears from her eyes, attempting to distance herself from the desirable detective. The kiss had made her want more than she could ever expect from any man. She took a calming breath before returning to professional mode.

"Let's see what Billings had in his locker."

Tom pulled an envelope from his pocket. It wasn't sealed, so he lifted the flap and pulled out the contents, and unfolded the multiple pages. He scanned the pages then handed it to her.

A quick perusal of the document put a big smile on her face. "Signed, sealed, and delivered," she pronounced.

Tom frowned. "Not yet. We need the corroborating evidence."

Jill went to the chair where she had dropped her purse. She withdrew a folded envelope and handed it to him. It was a piece of evidence she carried with her, not willing to leave it where it could be lost.

He took the envelope, studying her with lowered brows before opening it. After scanning through the contents, he sat on the edge of the bed, shuffling through the papers she had given him. He shook his head, rereading part of the long document.

"Where did you get this?" He raised his eyes from the papers to stare at her.

She stood watching him, fighting the fear which had reared its ugly head when she handed him the envelope. Unable to meet his scrutiny, she shifted, angling away from him so he couldn't see her face. "You don't need to be concerned with where I got it. The content is easy enough to verify and I know it will hold up in court. So, what are your plans now?"

He took a few long seconds to say, "Get some sleep. Billings will be at a party tonight. I need Fred and his men in place before going to arrest him and the others." He hesitated then asked, "How long have you had this?"

Jill had her back to him, and her voice hitched when she said, "You ask too many questions. It doesn't matter how long ago I got it. You now hold the corroborating evidence you needed."

The sudden warmth on her back told her he stood behind her before he commented, "No wonder they want you dead."

Her shoulders lifted in a shrug. "Hey, a girl's got to do what she's got to do where people like him are concerned."

Before he could touch her, she walked to the window, then turned and faced him, barely constraining the hatred raging through her.

"Tom, I've been after Billings and his group for many years. The only thing I want is to watch the handcuffs being clamped on his wrists and him being put in the back of a police car. I want him to see me and know I put him there."

Tom stared, forehead furrowed, studying her face. "What did he do to you to make you want him to know it's you who took him down?"

"Don't concern yourself with what happened between me and him. Just make sure I'm there when he's arrested."

Her eyes bored into his, mouth grim as she stood with crossed arms. She would refuse to help him if he didn't do this one thing for her.

"Okay. What else do you have on him?"

"Enough to make things stick to him as if they were superglued. That's only one thing I've got on him. I'll be the star witness because I can hang him and he knows it."

"Jill, what else do you know about him and his organization?" Tom repeated, crossing his arms, feet spread, becoming the alpha male he kept hidden.

"Enough to see him behind bars for the rest of his life. You need me alive to get that information, and Wyatt knows it. I'll give it when the time is right."

Tom ran a hand through his hair, pacing in a circle before stopping and facing her. "Jill, I need what you have on him and his group."

Not shying away from his growing frustration, she nodded to the papers in his hand, "You aren't getting it. That document is enough for you to arrest him with what he had in his locker."

The muscles in his jaws jumped as he glared at her before turning away and letting out a deep breath, giving up for now. "Get some sleep. It'll be a long day tomorrow."

Doing as he suggested, she removed her shoes and vest. When she went to the bathroom, she took off her bra so she could at least have some comfort. Going to the bed, she pulled back the covers. The sheets were fresh. After making herself comfortable, she informed him, "You can share the bed. Just keep to your side."

From the look on his face, he didn't miss the warning in her statement. With closed eyes, Jill tried to relax as he prepared for bed. He left the bathroom light on and pulled the door closed until there was only a sliver of light.

The weight of his body as he reclined on the bed sent fingers of fear through her. Forcing herself to take slow breaths, she knew that for now, there was no other option. There was no way she was sleeping on the small couch, and she wouldn't do that to him.

Chapter 9

FRIENDS, ENEMIES, AND SECRETS

When Tom's hand touched her upper back, Jill woke with a start. Rapidly rolling over, she glared at him, fear coursing through her. The questions in the green eyes told her what she had feared when his hand had rested on the ridges easily felt under her shirt.

"Jill, what happened to your back?"

"None of your fucking business," she snapped, moving away from him to sit on the edge of the bed.

A firm hand on her shoulder held her in place. She attempted to quell the pending tears. Their growing relationship was over before it ever began. At least she had a couple of kisses to remember and dream about.

He shifted to behind her. She stopped any possible questions by saying, "Tom, don't bother asking. I'm not telling you a fucking thing."

Instead of asking, he pulled her shirt up to view the scars crisscrossing her back. Tears spilled from her eyes as his gentle fingers touched the ridges. He was one of three men, outside of those who had cared for her, to see one form of abuse she had endured. She waited, pushing the loss and sadness back into their boxes, while his tender probing sent a river of tears flowing down her face.

The bed moved when he shifted so he could face her.

Other than the tears, her face held no emotion. He kissed her forehead then gathered her into his arms, holding her firmly yet with care, making her feel precious and fragile.

"It's all right. I won't ask again. I'll wait until you're ready to tell me."

"Tom, you don't want to get involved with me. Please. You'll only end up getting hurt," she reiterated, her voice holding a sadness she was unable to hide. Her breath hitched. She hid her face in his chest, needing the reassurance of his embrace yet unable to look at him, the pain of loss coursing through her.

"Let me worry about me." He hesitated before adding, "I can't imagine you ever doing or saying anything, which would cause someone to whip you like that."

Turning away from him, she repeated, "Tom, don't. Just forget it and keep our relationship professional."

He tugged her closer to him, his arms holding her tightly. "I can't. God knows I've tried, but I can't."

A sense of dread passed through her. Shaking it off, she pushed away from him, going to the bathroom and closing the door. Once he learned the truth, he would become like everyone else—gone. She did what she needed to do to make herself presentable, including putting on her bra and vest. She always wore a thick vest, preventing others from feeling the ridges on her back. It never entered her mind that he would put his hand on her while she was asleep. When she came back out, he had gotten coffee and donuts for breakfast.

"Eat at least one donut. It isn't that much," he commanded as he headed to the bath.

She was hungry, and the donut was her normal breakfast when working a case like this one. When he came back out, she was finishing the second donut and her coffee. Her eyes followed him as he walked to where she was sitting. He sat on the corner of the bed so he was facing her, a hand on her arm.

"Jill, I'm going to be truthful with you. I care for you. More than I should for the length of time I've known you. No matter what you tell me, I won't walk away." She steeled herself for rejection when he hesitated, expecting a *but* to be added onto his declaration of caring.

"From what you aren't saying, I know what happened wasn't something you agreed to, but I'm a big boy. I don't believe your horror story is any worse than others I've seen and heard. What I do know is that no one in your family did that to you. I can guess as to how it happened and who was responsible from some of the things you've said. I'll make sure you see him taken down."

Okay, so he knew Billings was involved somehow, but he didn't have any facts. She moved her head, looking over his shoulder before attempting to stop what was happening. "Tom, please don't care for me," she pleaded.

His finger on her chin pulled her gaze back to him. "I can't stop what I feel. I'm not going away, so get used to it."

Okay. It was his problem, not hers. She couldn't stop him. He would still leave when she revealed the full story on the stand, if she ever made it that far. It was up to him to help her stay alive long enough to testify. At the trial, he would learn the details concerning those missing years before disappearing. Until then, she would tuck away memories for when he left.

"What are we going to do today?" she questioned, stuffing the past back into the little box inside of her where it lived, popping out to remind her of why she couldn't let anyone get to close to her.

"Find a few underlings and put them in custody, then see who else pops out of the woodwork."

"Okay, let's go." When she stood, he rose and put his arms around her.

"Jill, stay close to me. I have backup, so you don't need to be a hero."

"I won't be a hero for the underlings. I want Billings and those close to him."

"You'll get him." Tom leaned over and gave her a quick kiss before they left the room.

When they got to the car, he held the passenger-side door for her. Not objecting to his driving, she got in and made herself comfortable. They headed west toward Orlando. Turning off Route 50, he headed to an industrial complex where several trucking companies were located.

He turned into a company she knew well. A smile lit

her face when they pulled into the large parking lot. Tom parked and shut off the engine before saying, "Well, I think I'll let you handle this one. I believe he's someone you know better than me."

She didn't question his statement. He was right. This company she knew well, along with several of the men who worked here, including the terminal manager who was very special to her. The man they were after was here. His truck was only three vehicles over from where they had parked.

She strolled toward the smaller building as several men watched her, their faces creasing in smiles. With several hugs and frequent teasing, they welcomed her as a friend. There were questions as to how she was doing and if she was staying for a few days. One even asked, "Jill, you going to steal Billy for a few hours so we can duck out early?"

She chuckled before saying, "Sorry, Wayne. Not today."

"Doggone it. I was hoping." He and the rest of the men laughed.

Tom hung back, letting her greet the men until one of them noticed him. "Hey, Tom, you working with Jill or is this a social call?"

She didn't miss his answer of, "We're working together for now." It appeared he was as well-known here as she was, making her question how many times their paths had crossed on various cases.

She ambled into the large room filled with desks,

making her way to the private enclosed office in the back-left corner of the big room. The office workers acknowledged her with smiles and waves as she passed.

At the doorway of the private office, she paused, her hand on the doorframe. Her lips turned up in a tender smile, observing the man she considered her best friend on the phone. He was facing away from her, discussing business in his soft Southern drawl.

Jill leaned against the doorframe, watching him do his job, not wanting to interrupt him while he was working. When he swiveled his chair to hang up the phone, his striking rugged face lit up. He left the desk, meeting her with open arms when she stepped into the office, closing the distance between them. She relaxed in the arms holding her tight, standing on her tiptoes when he dipped his head for a kiss. It was the only show of his love for her she allowed. When he raised his head, his soft brown eyes scanned her face as if he was memorizing it. She observed the love he didn't hide, causing her to catch her breath. If only . . .

"Jill! What a wonderful surprise. How's my favorite imp doing?" he questioned, loosening his arms and guiding her further into the privacy of the office.

"I'm doing okay, I guess. It's great to see you as always, Billy."

"Girl, it's been way to long since you've come to see me. How's Wyatt and Sam?"

"Fine. They're over in Clermont with me, helping with a case I'm working."

Her words hung in the air for a few seconds. The smile dimmed as he let out a sigh of resignation, now aware this wasn't a social call as he had hoped. She lowered her gaze when he asked, "Which one of my workers are you taking this time?"

Her fingers played with a button on his shirt as she stared at his chest. Bowing her head, she wiped away the tears before answering his question. "Doug. He's in big trouble." Again, she had hurt the gentle man who loved her. When would she learn to stay away from him?

"I'll hate to lose him. He's a good worker." Billy leaned back and lifted her head, studying her face. "I take it this is about where he gets the extra money to support his gambling."

She flicked a glance at him and nodded. "Yes."

"Jill?" he questioned as she moved away from him.

"He's only one of the minor players, but yes, he's involved."

Billy moved so he stood beside her. "Does he know you're here for him?"

"Not yet. I wanted to see you first."

"Honey, what am I going to do with you?"

She planted a kiss on his cheek. "Just be my friend, Billy. I don't have all that many." His arms came around her again, hugging her close to him, his chin resting on her head before leaning back to face her.

With a crooked grin, he said, "You know me. I'll do whatever you want."

"I know." She peered up at him, a wry twist to her lips. "I wish things were different."

"Me too. I'll always love you no matter what happens." With a finger, he tilted her head up and gave her a quick kiss. "You better come back and see me before you leave this time. I still owe you a fancy meal and night out on the town."

"I'll do my best. It may not be until this case is over, but I'll be back one way or another."

"Darling, you had better come back all in one piece. I'm not good at funerals."

She grinned. "Remember, I want that wake so everyone can have fun."

"Well, it had better not be any time soon."

His glance behind her had her turning to see Tom standing in the doorway watching them, face composed.

"You know him?" Billy questioned, concern in his voice.

"Yeah. He's helping me out on this one."

Billy glared at Tom before saying, "You had better make sure she stays safe. This special lady has been to hell and back, and she's real special to me."

Tom's gaze moved to her. "I gathered that. She's pretty special to me, also."

"Don't you hurt her, or you'll have to deal with me," Billy warned.

At that, Tom shook his head, a slight smile on his lips, but it was his eyes she noticed as they bore into hers. "Don't worry. The last thing I'll ever do is hurt her." He entered the office to where Billy was holding her and ran a hand over her hair. "For now, I need to make sure she stays alive. Wyatt, Sam, and I'm sure you, will make me suffer big time if anything happens to her."

Billy peered down at her. "Jill, you stick tight to him. He'll keep you as safe as possible. Since you won't have me, I can't think of a better man for you than Tom."

Billy's words had her studying him, wondering where he got the idea there was something between her and Tom. "Forget it. We're just working together. Once this is done, he'll move on to the next job. I'm just a passing interest."

As Billy glanced at Tom, then back to her, a big grin forming on his face. "Sweetheart, you couldn't be more wrong. You'll have trouble getting rid of him."

She rested her head on his shoulder, feeling safe with his arms around her. "Wrong. He'll leave in due time, just like everyone else."

She was unable to stop the tears as they overflowed and tracked toward her chin, still not recovered from what had happened earlier with Tom. Billy tightened his arms around her.

"You'll see. He'll stick around, unlike the other creeps

who didn't love you like I do. He'll understand, and like me, he'll be right there for you."

Unable to leave his arms, she kept her eyes closed, allowing the man who hadn't rejected her to comfort her. Yes, he loved her, but for her, he was only a good friend. As much as she wanted to, she didn't love him, yet he loved her enough to accept her limits on their relationship.

Billy loosened his hold on her. "You better go get Doug before he tries to run off. He should be in the repair shop."

After drying her tears, she attempted a smile. "Thanks for keeping him around so I could find him."

"Hey, you know me. I can't refuse any request from you."

"I know," she told him with a crooked grin. "I'll keep in touch."

"You better come back to see me again real soon, and I want to see that pretty smile on your face when you return."

She gave him a quick kiss. "Billy, I'll be back one way or another."

He didn't respond as she left, heading to the repair shop. His statement concerning Tom didn't change her belief in how he would walk away once he had all the facts. Billy only knew part of what had happened. Tom would learn details which only three other people knew if she made it to court.

Doug spotted her when she entered the door at the end

of the large repair shop where he was working on one of the big trucks. He threw the tool he was holding into the toolbox beside him. With a frown and shoulders drooping, he used the rag from his back pocket to clean his hands, watching her progress toward him.

Without speaking, he started removing his coveralls, recognizing why she was here. It wasn't until she was standing by the toolbox that he acknowledged her, pulling the coveralls over his boots. "Jill, can't say it's a pleasure. I take it you're here to take me in."

"Yes. You knew it was only a matter of time."

Doug's eyes drifted to Tom. "I see you brought some backup."

"Not by choice. He happens to be working the same case from a different angle."

Blowing out a deep breath, Doug grumped, "I knew I should have left when I learned you made it out alive and was working for Wyatt a few years back."

"Why didn't you?" she questioned.

He shrugged. "The fucking money to pay my debts to some nasty pricks who would've come after me and left me dead or disabled."

"Doug, I'm sorry, but it's now time to pay the piper."

"Let's get it over with." He paused and turned, pleading for a favor. "You'll let Jackie know, right?"

"I will," she promised. He loved his wife but hadn't been able to control his gambling. This was one man she wished she didn't have to arrest because he was one of the nicer bad guys.

Tom stepped forward and cuffed him. There was a squad car waiting when they walked him to the parking lot. He remained calm as they put him in the back of the car.

"Jill, I can't tell you how bad I feel about what happened to you. They'll try to make sure neither one of us survives for trial."

Tom told him, "You'll survive. Just tell the truth on the stand, and I'll see what I can do to make you disappear when it's over."

"Thanks," Doug responded before the door closed. Tom gave instructions to the officers while she went back to the car to wait on him. She hoped Doug made it to trial. The little kindnesses he had done for her had shown he didn't like what they were doing.

Tom unlocked the car and put her in the passenger seat again. He didn't talk as he pulled out and headed to the next stop. It didn't take her long to figure out where they were headed. Hopefully, the next man would be like Doug and accept his fate.

Tom pulled into the small warehouse, which held a car restoration business. She and Tom exited the car at the same time. Jill wended her way between car parts and shelves of tools into the bay, until she stood behind the thin man bent over a fender, working on an engine.

"Leroy, I'm back," she said in a sing-song voice,

taunting the man who dropped the tool he was using onto the floor. He barely avoided hitting his head on the hood of the car when he whipped around to face her.

"Fuck you, bitch," he spat, his hand going to the pocket on the right leg of his orange coverall.

Jill jumped forward and grabbed his wrist. In one swift movement she twirled him around, bending him over the fender, his arm bent up to the middle of his back. He was gasping from where her knee had hit his scrotal area hard enough to keep him from moving for a few seconds.

"Motherfucking, cocksucking bitch, I'll see yo' fucking ass dead," Leroy snarled.

"Now, Leroy, that's no way to address me and you know it," Jill informed him, her voice calm as she put more pressure on his arm, her knee pushing against his balls as he grimaced in pain. "I hope that life insurance policy is paid up, dearie, because I don't think your boss is going to appreciate you being arrested."

"Fucking bitch. I should have fucking killed you when I had the fucking chance," he grated before she put more pressure on his arm and testicles, her other hand shoving his head down.

"If you would have, sweetie, you wouldn't have survived the night and you know it. He wanted me alive."

"Fucking bastard will fucking regret it, won't he?"

"He already does. Only, his mistake was in thinking I had no family, not in keeping me alive."

Tom ambled over and fastened the handcuffs on the arm she held. He pulled the other arm back and snapped the other cuff closed. After removing the multiple weapons Leroy had concealed on him, Tom pulled him toward the door.

"I see you have help this time," Leroy sneered.

"More than you can imagine. I hope you enjoy being a bitch, honey. You'll get some idea of what the girls went through, thanks to you."

Leroy spat at her, but she had moved. The glob of saliva splattered onto the floor. "You're fucking dead, bitch," he threatened as Tom jerked him toward the door.

"So are you, bastard. Your boss won't be happy with you being in custody."

"You won't get a fucking thing from me and he fucking knows it," Leroy gloated. He jerked, attempting to pull loose from Tom to face her.

"Leroy, you don't need to say a word. Matter of fact, I'd prefer if you didn't say a thing." She let her lips turn up in a sly grin, watching his smirk fade as understanding came to him.

Two police officers came and jerked him toward the police car. They knew him well and weren't being gentle with him. She watched as they shoved him down into the backseat before releasing the breath she had been holding. Tom stood beside her, his hand at her waist. The soft voice next to her ear startled her.

"I now have a good guess about those missing years. No wonder this is personal."

"Leave it alone, Tom," she intoned, a frisson of fear zinging through her before anger reared its head.

A hand on her arm rotated her to face him. He examined her face, his mouth a grim line. "Jill, whatever happened, you didn't agree to it. I've seen what they did to the girls." His gaze sought out Leroy. "He is one of the worst of the keepers."

Not commenting, she pulled away and stalked to the car, got in, and slammed the door. Yes, Leroy was one of the worst. It was because of him she had the scars on her back. He had enjoyed giving her each mark. His laugh still rang in her dreams as Franko watched him whip her while she was tied to a pole. Yes, this was personal. Very personal.

Chapter 10

THE ENEMY IS MINE

Their next stop was another of the minor players. Like Doug, he had known she would come for him. The tears he cried hadn't fazed her because he was the one who hadn't bothered to help her as she was being beaten by Leroy. One by one, they were being arrested and jailed. Every last one of them would pay, not just for her, but for all the others, alive or dead, who had endured the hell forced upon them.

Tom didn't make any further comments on his suppositions, but she knew he wasn't going to let it drop. When he pulled into a small restaurant on the outskirts of Orlando, without arguing, she went into the restaurant, hoping he wouldn't talk about her past. Since they hadn't stopped for lunch, there was no way of getting away with saying she wasn't hungry this late in the evening.

When they sat down, a waitress inquired at to what they wanted to drink. Jill ordered a Jack Daniels on the rocks and water. An ale wouldn't cut it tonight. Not caring what Tom thought, Jill finished the drink in minutes, then ordered another when the waitress came back to see if they were ready to order. When the waitress returned with the drink, she completed the drink in two gulps and requested another along with a cup of soup. The food choice was dictated by what she could swallow without gagging.

"Jill, getting drunk won't help."

His words increased the anger coiling around inside of her. "Back off and leave me alone," she warned, in no mood for his playing substitute parent.

"Not happening. I promised Wyatt I'd take care of you, not that I wouldn't have anyway."

"I don't need a caretaker," she snapped.

"You will if you keep downing those drinks."

The glare sent in his direction was full of ice. With gritted teeth, Jill again snarled, "Leave me the fuck alone!"

"Jill, I'm not going to leave you alone," he declared as he watched her finish the third drink.

The anger flared, but she kept her mouth shut, not willing to make a scene in public. Sooner or later she would need to deal with him, but not tonight. She had enough voices in her head without adding more. Tonight, there was the past she needed to handle and was hoping the drinks would quiet the voices for a few hours.

When the soup came, she ordered a fourth drink. Tom's disapproval was palpable, yet he held his tongue. The barmaid brought the drink and left when Tom glared at her. There was no comment forthcoming, so she finished the soup and the drink. He shouldn't complain. She had eaten without arguing.

Tom paid the bill before walking in disapproving silence to the car. Even though she was still walking straight, she was drunk. Hopefully, she would sleep tonight. Inside her head, the memories and voices were loud, driving her close to the edge. The drinks should silence them for a few hours. He didn't understand because she was the only one privy to the voices and images of her past replaying over and over.

This time he checked into a chain motel as she waited in the car. The drinks were working as planned. She could barely stand, let alone walk upon exiting the car. Tom half carried her into their first-floor room. After collapsing fully clothed on the bed next to the bathroom, she passed out, the pain numbed, and the voices silenced for the moment.

Tom's "Jill, wake up" calmed the panic of not being able to stop what was happening in the dream. Fear had her heart racing as a scream bubbled toward the surface. Not completely awake, she pushed him away from her, holding the scream back, believing any sound would create more suffering than the current pain she was feeling.

Bleary eyes opened to Tom's concerned face. An awareness that no one was holding her down entered her consciousness when he moved away. The tender hand and the worry on his face had the tears spilling over as the nightmare, which had been a reality, faded. The drinks hadn't prevented the dreams.

"Jill?" Tom questioned.

"I'm all right. Nothing but a nightmare." That wasn't the truth. Her mind was reliving a part of the past she wanted to forget.

At a gentle push from Tom, she scooted over in the bed.

He reclined beside her, placing the sheet over them before tugging her next to him. She wasn't sure what he wanted. Her muscles tensed until she realized he wasn't going to do anything but hold her. With her back to him, they were spooned together. When he remained still, a soothing arm encircling her, she relaxed.

"Go back to sleep," he murmured, his head resting next to hers and the fingers of his hand entwined with hers.

Unable to resist the security of him next to her, she became the small child who needed reassurance that the nightmare wasn't real. Her eyelids closed, as she continued to feel the effects of the drinks she had downed with her meal. The tears dripped onto her pillow as she attempted to push the last vestiges of the nightmare back into the box it had escaped from after seeing Billings and Leroy.

The comfort he was providing supported the fantasy of him staying with her. It was a much better dream than the one from which he had awakened her. Too bad it was nothing but a fairy tale. Early on she had learned there were no knights in shining armor, and she would never pass for a princess. If not for the past, she could imagine spending her nights like this with him keeping her safe from the things that haunted her mind.

One night shouldn't hurt. One lovely night of being treated like a normal woman with someone who cared enough to hold her. Just one night of being held by someone who loved her.

The pleasant dream mixed with reality as she moved into the warmth beside her, drifting toward wakefulness. When the warmth moved, her eyes popped open. She realized she wasn't alone in the bed. Tom was watching her, his emotions showing on his face.

The events of yesterday came rushing back. The nightmare. His joining her and keeping the nightmare at bay. What was she to do now?

He watched her for a few seconds then said, "Jill, we do need to have that talk."

Moving away from the dream, she sat up to move off the bed. A hand on her arm froze her in place.

"Tom, don't. I was drunk last night when the nightmare woke me, but it doesn't change a thing."

"True, it doesn't, but you need to accept that I'm not like the others. I'm not going away."

A sadness filled her before she moved away from him. "I've heard it before—more than once. They all left, and you will too."

In the safety of the bathroom, she cried, not believing his confident words. No matter how much she tried not to care, she did. The problem now was how to prevent crumbling into little pieces when he walked away. Those tiny pieces had been difficult to put back together after she had been found, but with the big chunk he would take with him, it might be impossible this time.

In the past, she had believed the promises, then felt the pain when they were broken. Even though he may have guessed where she had spent those missing years, he had no idea of what had happened and the lifelong effects of what they had done. The scars on the outside were minimal compared to what was inside, destined to never be whole again. They had taken an innocent girl and made her into severely damaged goods, mentally, physically and emotionally.

When she stepped out of the shower, there were clean clothes on the counter, making her wonder where he had gotten them and when. After dressing, she combed out her short hair, brushed her teeth, then forced herself to join the man helping her round up those who had turned her life into a living hell.

Once the trial was over, she planned on taking a long vacation. One to put herself back together, or maybe not. It was easy to understand why Susan had done what she had instead of waiting to be rescued. Life was difficult at best without dealing with all the issues from what had happened to her.

Maybe she would return to that world where no one could hurt her again. That was one option. Quinn had given her three options six years ago. Right now, everything hinged on whether it meant facing life alone or with Tom at her side. From past experiences, alone would be the most likely outcome.

If she wanted to see Billings and his group behind bars, it meant keeping herself together until after the trial. Once it was finished, she could let the thin fraying thread holding her together break. Until then, she would keep repairing it, hoping it held until Billings and company couldn't hurt anyone again.

When she rejoined Tom, he pointed to a cup of coffee and two sweet rolls on a plate before he took his turn in the bathroom. By the time he rejoined her, she had finished her breakfast. To her, he was gorgeous in the sports coat and casual pants. The man cleaned up nice. She could imagine him in a suit. What she wouldn't give . . . Her eyes dropped as she stopped the thoughts of what could have been.

"You up to taking out the club and brothel today?" he questioned.

"Do you have enough backup?" she inquired, avoiding looking at him.

"Not sure. Tell me what to expect. I'm sure you know it better than any of us."

True. She had endured three years of learning it from the inside. It was time to put that knowledge to use. Steeling herself against the memories attached to the club, she drew the floor plan to the building on the pad from beside the phone. On the map, she marked the location of each door, then explained how the club setup functioned as she pointed to the specific areas.

"There are four doors into the main club from the outside. The public entrances are here and here. Each door is guarded by two bouncers. The delivery door over here is locked unless there's a delivery."

She used the pen to point to each thing she mentioned. She could still see the tawdry red and gold curtains on the stage with the poles for the girls to use. As she talked, it was like she was there, walking through the place where she had sent three years in a hell from which she had barely managed to escape.

"This door goes to a walled yard where the privileged girls go to walk around during their time off to keep them from getting too pale. The stage is here, and the tables and seating are scattered in this area. There are normally four dancers on this side of the stage. One should be dancing, and the others will be under guard in the room here. The guards for the girls working the floor are stationed here and here. There are usually two or three more hanging in the office, which is up the stairs over here and to the right. Those in the office watch the floor through the glass panels on the walls and the video monitors."

Jill had marked each position on the little map during her recitation. She ripped off the sheet and handed it to him before drawing the floor plan to what she knew as the hole.

"They keep most of the girls who work in this area in the dormitory here. There are entrances here and here.

There are twelve partitioned cubicles in this section. One for each girl who's working. Expect several johns to be there. There are four guards in there 24/7. The woman who oversees the hole has an office here. Her room is through the door located here. There's an alarm in the office. The button to set it off is located under the desk. If that happens, you won't find one girl alive in the basement or on the third floor."

After tearing off the paper, she handed it to him. There was one more piece of information he needed. Drawing in silence, she drew the third floor with the office, a room behind it, and several more in a cluster. She added the connecting doors to those rooms along with the private rooms where the girls entertained the men.

"This is where the girls for the high-end customers and bosses are kept. Entry is through the office door here. There are two men stationed in this room, and two women over here. This first room has a keypad entrance so only those who have the code can get into it. Billings keeps the one he finds *special* in that room. She'll be well taken care of, but may be drugged if she wasn't amenable to what he wanted. She'll be okay if he isn't there because only the women have the code." With reluctance, she wrote numbers on the bottom of the page. "That's the code for the door.

With a big breath, Jill faced him. "If the men can't get to the office without being targeted, all but that one girl in these rooms and the basement will die."

Tom had the good sense not to question her knowledge. Once she went over the rest of the rooms on the third floor, Jill handed Tom the map, praying her knowledge might save a few of the girls. More than once, she had listened to the contingency plans if they were raided. All scenarios ended with all the girls dying so they couldn't talk.

When finished, she turned away from him before confirming what he suspected. "I can't participate on this one as they know me on sight. If I go anywhere near there, they'll kill me and put the place on alert and lock it down while they get rid of the evidence. I'll wait here."

The gentle squeeze on her shoulder showed he understood. "Wyatt's on his way here. Go with him. I'll come and get you when it's over. We'll pick up Billings today. There's a group of marshals and agents watching him, so he won't be going anywhere without us knowing it."

"You'd better come and get me," she warned him, meeting his gaze.

"I don't break promises. You'll be there when the handcuffs go on."

There was a knock on the door. Tom let Wyatt into the room, who studied her, a crease between his brows. "Wyatt, I hope you have a safe place to stash her for now."

"I do," he informed Tom then faced her. "Jill?"

"Yeah. I'm ready. This is one time I have to stay out of it."

"Tom, call me when you're on your fucking way, and I'll meet you if you don't want to come to us."

"Got it."

Jill followed Wyatt to the car where Sam was waiting. He opened the door, and she slid in. Wyatt joined her in the backseat, not missing how she had distanced herself by moving to the door and fastening her seat belt. At this moment, she didn't want to be touched, withdrawing in an attempt to keep control of her thoughts and feelings. Three years of her life gone because of these bastards. Three fucking years!

Those three years would affect the rest of her life. The dream she had as a teenager of someone to love her, a family, and a real home was now gone. That was destroyed during those three years. The rest of her life was destined to be spent alone, working to save others from the same fate. There was nothing else left for her.

The only reason she hadn't gone after Billings before now was the lack of a case leading to him. During the past five years, she had broken one prostitution or drug ring a year while working with various law enforcement agencies. This was the one for this year, only it was the one that meant the most to her. Five long years of waiting, watching, and hoping for just one case leading to him and his cronies.

Wyatt's voice pulled her from her thoughts.

"Baby girl, you okay?"

"Yeah. I hope he gets to them before they kill them."

Wyatt was privy to part of what she went through, so he understood what she meant.

"Honey, if he fucking can't, it won't be because he didn't fucking try. He's fucking good."

The fear skittered around inside at what would happen if those raiding the club didn't get to the office before an alarm sounded. "I hope so because if he doesn't . . ."

Wyatt's "He cares for you" had her blinking back tears.

"Grandpa, it's only temporary. It'll change and you know it."

"Humph," Wyatt sounded before saying, "I don't think so. The fucking prick's in love with you. There's no way he'll fucking leave you."

With a large exhale, she pulled her bottom lip between her teeth. If only he was right—but he wasn't. "Wishful thinking on your part. You'll be saddled with me for a long time."

"Honey, I don't mind keeping you around, but he won't fucking give up on you. I saw the way he was looking at you back there. This is now fucking personal for him because of you."

The short curls bounced as she shook her head. "Like I said, it's only temporary. He'll change soon enough." With a sadness she couldn't hide, she looked over at him, attempting to keep the tears back. "Once this is over, I'll need that vacation I wanted but didn't get to take."

"I'll fucking deal with that when this is fucking over," Wyatt growled, turning his head away.

Sam pulled into a nondescript house and parked the car in the garage. She waited, knowing they needed to ensure there were no surprises inside. Upon entering the house, she headed to the living room and plopped onto the couch. After curling up, she closed her eyes, head resting on the padded arm, planning on sleeping to block the emotions roiling around inside.

It wasn't long until she was dreaming of the man who said he'd stay with her. In the dream, Tom was giving her a kiss. Half awake, she reached out to hold him. Reality intersected with the dream when her hand contacted real flesh. Her eyes popped opened to meet twinkling green eyes set in a smiling face.

"Mm. I can handle that type of reception any time. You ready to go get your man?" he questioned, continuing to smile at her, his hand cupping her cheek.

Heat rose to her face before she dropped her arm then pushed herself to a sitting position. "Yes. Just give me a minute."

Tom moved so she could stand, his face merry. Wyatt chuckled as she hurried out of the room, aware her face was red. Wyatt's deep voice carried into the bathroom in the hall. "Son, you had better not hurt my little fairy."

She couldn't understand the words of Tom's response, but it made no difference. He would hurt her and she'd need Wyatt to help pick up the pieces, just as he had when she was brought home six years ago. It was one more thing to be pushed into that box of painful things she tried to keep hidden from herself and the world.

Upon her return to the living room, Tom asked, "Want Wyatt to go with us to arrest Billings?"

Based on his cheerfulness, the raid at the club must have gone well, so she didn't ask questions. With this collar, it was up to Wyatt if he wanted to be there. He knew the history between the two of them. She gave a quick shrug after a swift glance at Wyatt, who was studying her. "That's up to him."

Wyatt pushed his bulk from the chair where he had been sitting. "In that fucking case, I'm going. I want to see those fucking handcuffs go on him."

Tom put his arm around her as they made their way to his car. He opened the front door and waited for her to arrange herself in the seat. Wyatt folded himself into the backseat. Tom drove to the Orlando downtown business district. Aware Billings had an office there, she assumed that was where they were headed. They had gone less than four blocks when she noticed the car behind him. When she looked at Tom, he patted her leg.

"It's only Fred. He needs to be there. It's his job to arrest them, not mine. This is a federal case, and there's a federal warrant for Billings, so the US Marshals are serving the warrants and taking them into custody."

Not relaxing, she kept watch for the expected attempt to stop them. There was no way the group didn't know Billings was to be picked up today after the raid on the club. The attempt to stop them wasn't long in coming. A car sped along a side street on her side of the car. The barrel of a gun poked out the right rear window. Her Glock appeared in her hand seconds before she hit the button to lower the window.

As the speeding car aimed for theirs and a possible crash, Jill fired four shots at the driver. The driver slumped over the wheel, listing to the right, sending the car into a light pole. A squad car roared from behind them, racing up on their right, lights flashing. It skidded to a stop beside the wrecked car, another squad car stopping behind the crumpled car, preventing the passengers from running.

Tom didn't slow his speed, which meant she would have to answer for those four shots later. Several squad cars moved up to surround them, lights flashing as they continued into the business section of downtown Orlando, providing protection from any further attempts to stop them. Tom pulled into a loading zone, the squad cars surrounding the two cars and blocking the street. Uniformed police poured out of the cars, preventing the pedestrians from nearing the doors of the office building. The three of them exited the car and were escorted into the building by US Deputy Marshals and federal agents dressed in suits. Jill recognized several of the men in the lobby from the LCSD arrest.

Tom stopped near one of the agents and asked, "He still in his office?"

"Yes, sir. We've got four men on the floor, and he hasn't attempted to leave. His lawyer is with him."

"Good. Let's go get him."

Tom's arm came around her before they entered the elevator with Fred and Wyatt, along with several marshals and agents from the lobby. Fred pushed a button and the doors closed. Seconds later the car stopped on the sixth floor. Jill felt her heart speed up into overdrive with the tension, making her lightheaded when the doors whooshed open. Tom put a hand at her waist, guiding her to the business office she had never seen. She could hardly wait to see Billings' face when he recognized her.

On their trip down the hall, she hid the dizzy spell. Her heart rate returned to normal before stopping at a door on their left. They entered the office and started toward a door marked private, located down a short passageway to the right of the receptionist's desk. The receptionist stood up and started around the desk.

"Stop. You can't go back there," she stated with force.

Fred stopped her. "This is a federal search and arrest warrant for the premises." He handed the warrants to her before one of the men took her arm, holding her in place.

With an audible gasp, her eyes widened when she recognized Jill on her way past the desk with Tom beside her. The woman had been with Billings at the club at least twice a month and had seen her on multiple occasions.

"Oh. My. God!" she exclaimed, watching them stride down the hall until an officer stated she was under arrest.

Jill moved into the lead and strode to the private office where Billings was in conference with his lawyer. He would be one of several in the law firm Billings used who had kept the higher-ups out of jail. She assumed Tom had a warrant for his arrest also.

Without knocking, Jill opened the door, a smile pasted on her face, gaze focused on Billings. The two men turned to the door and stared, the conversation stopping mid-word. Both froze, not moving when she paused in the doorway of the office.

"Good afternoon, gentlemen. Remember me?" she queried as they blanched in unison. A chuckle escaped her at their reaction before moving farther into the office to allow the agents, marshals, Tom, and Wyatt to enter. The lawyer was one of several who had come to the club. "Ah, I see you do. Hope you don't mind that I brought a few friends from the feds with me. Sorry for taking so long to get back to you, but then again, you didn't believe I'd ever return, now did you?"

The lawyer pulled himself together, then pronounced, "You need evidence, my dear, to get an arrest to stick."

Tom shifted to beside her and imparted, "We have the evidence. It's nice and tidy." He handed the arrest warrant to the lawyer. Like the one for the receptionist, it was federal. He then produced a second one. "Sorry, but Mr. Billings and you both will need lawyers. You have the right to remain silent. Anything you say, can and will be used against you in a court of law. You have the right to a lawyer. If you are unable to afford a lawyer, one will be appointed for you. Do you understand these rights?" he questioned.

"Fuck you," Billings snapped, watching her, a scowl on his face. "You're dead, bitch," he threatened.

Calmly, Tom stated, "Thank you, Mr. Billings. I'll be adding threatening a federal witness to the charges."

Billings made a rapid move toward the drawer in front of him. Jill's gun appeared in her hand before anyone else could move. A quick shift to her right, and she had a clear shot.

Her eyes were filled with icy hatred as she held the gun aimed at him, a finger on the trigger, and mouth in a grim line. Several of the men in the room had guns pointed at him, only Jill didn't see them because of her focused glare at the man she had vowed to see behind bars. She didn't want him dead, but she wouldn't hesitate to shoot him if he made the wrong move.

"Go for it, bastard. It'll save the government tons of money and a lot of time," Jill dared, her voice hard and the gun steady.

Billings froze, staring at her, before his shaking hands

returned to the desk, palms down, unwilling to take the chance of her pulling the trigger. Tom pulled him from the chair.

"Hands against the wall, feet spread," he commanded before performing a thorough search, finding two small pistols, one in Billings' vest and the other in an ankle holster.

Tom took the handcuffs from Fred then nodded to her, mouth grim.

"Jill, I believe you deserve the honor of putting these on him."

Without hesitation, she put her pistol back in the holster and took the handcuffs from Tom. With a firm grip, Jill pulled Billings' right arm behind him. The man who had turned her life into a living hell was going to a hell of his own making. The sound of the handcuff snapping on Billings' wrist and the click as it tightened was loud in the quiet office. Her face showed the pent-up anger and hatred for the man who had ruined her life.

"I hope you enjoy these bracelets as you called them." She snapped the other cuff on his left wrist and tightened it as Billings' jaw worked. Jill moved to where she was facing him, before stating in a calm voice, "I promised you would see this day if I lived, but you didn't believe me, did you? I'll live to testify at your trial. My only hope is they put you where you become some big ugly dude's bitch. Then maybe you'll understand how a girl feels when you rape her."

"Fucking bitch. I'll see you in hell."

She raised her brows, eyes drilling into his.

"I've been to hell and back again, thanks to you, so that threat is meaningless."

Fred handcuffed the lawyer. The marshals removed the two men from the room while four agents gathered files and paperwork to take as evidence. Everyone who was working in the office were standing as a group, all in handcuffs. The federal lockup was receiving an influx of new inmates, thanks to whoever had killed Knight. Now if only the trial wouldn't take place years down the road. She needed closure in less than the five long years it had taken her to get him.

Wyatt's arm settling on her shoulders startled her. "Girl, I don't think I could have had that much fucking control."

With a sigh, she lowered her head, scuffing the toe of her shoe on the carpet. "I want him to become that bitch to some big ugly dude. I want him to know what it feels like when you're repeatedly raped." The anger came through in her voice. The tears running over her cheeks showed the pain and hurt she held inside.

"Jill, please don't cry," Wyatt pleaded, his arms coming around her.

Tom's gentle hands pried her from Wyatt, then walked her to the end of the hall. He held her, cradling her head, while she cried in his arms, unable to stop the feelings racing around inside of her. The massive pain she had kept boxed up had surfaced when she had seen Billings. Once the trial was over, then she could try to put it behind her. That is if she didn't do a Humpty Dumpty, ending up in little pieces on the ground, unable to be put back together again.

Tom's voice brought her back to the present. "Jill, we've asked for a speedy trial. With what you gave me and what I already had, I believe we can get this over with in a timely manner."

With a sniff, she mumbled, "We're supposed to forgive our enemies, but I can't forgive him for what he did. I know it's wrong, but I can't."

Tom's arms tightened. "Darling, I don't think your anger at him, under the circumstances, would be considered wrong. Like you said, you've been to hell and back because of him. I'm just glad it was you holding the gun on him and not me. I would have found an excuse to shoot his ass and saved us the trouble of a trial."

"Tom?"

"Yes."

"I know you care for me, but please, for your sake, don't get attached to me."

"Why?"

"You'll learn why at the trial."

The arms around her tightened. "Let me make that decision when the time comes."

As she slowly raised her head to face him, her eyes reflecting the sadness of what could have been. "You'll see. I'm not one you'll want to keep."

With slumped shoulders, she left his arms, drying her tears with her hands before rejoining her grandfather. She leaned into Wyatt, who put his arm around her, attempting to distance herself from the man she loved but couldn't have. No one, especially someone in his position, wanted severely damaged goods. No one.

Back at the safe house, after a silent trip there, Tom didn't comment as she and Wyatt left the car before he drove off to complete his paperwork. She spent her evening was completing her share of the paperwork for the agency, along with a report for the police concerning the shots she had fired in a public venue. By the time she handed her reports to Wyatt, it was after midnight. It now boiled down to how long before the case was put on the docket. She had done her part. The rest was now up to the legal system.

Chapter 11

LIKE A MOUSE IN A TRAP

Wyatt insisted on going home to Broward County after finishing breakfast. The LCSD had cleared her from the murder charge so there was no reason to remain in Lake County. It all boiled down to waiting for the trial date and staying alive until then.

The Florida Turnpike was the fastest and most direct route to Fort Lauderdale, so the decision was to take it instead of US 27, which was more picturesque but isolated and slower. It was ten before they left, due to Wyatt's taking care of business with multiple calls and texts. They were north of the Canoe Creek Plaza when Wyatt insisted on stopping there for lunch.

Settling into the booth in the dining area after getting their meals, Jill noticed three men to her left who kept glancing over at them. It wasn't until the man with his back to them turned around she became concerned. It was someone she knew from a time she wanted to forget. She squelched the rising fear and ignored them. It appeared Billings and company were stepping up their efforts to get rid of her prior to the trial.

After scanning the rest of the people in the dining area, not letting on she recognized the man, Jill took a sip of her soda then smiled up at Wyatt. "The three men over there to my left, I recognize one of them. They won't try anything here, but I'm sure they have a plan for once we leave here to stop me from making it home. Let me drive. I know I can outmaneuver them. You might want to inform the state police of what's going down. We don't want to get in trouble."

Smiling as if she had said something amusing, Wyatt patted her hand. "It's gonna be fucking fun to show how fucking good a driver you are. Sam, take shotgun, and I'll stick to the back like I normally do. I'll have the rifle ready, just in case."

Okay. Wyatt was playing along. The car could do what she wanted even though it was a luxury sedan. This wasn't the first time she was using it in a chase scenario. These men would discover she wasn't a sitting duck as assumed.

This meant that once home, she needed to find a safe place to hide. None of Wyatt's places, other than his penthouse, were secure enough to use. It was something to worry about later. The immediate problem was getting home in one piece.

As soon as she finished her meal, they left the restaurant. The three men, who had been watching them, made a point of ignoring her, Sam and Wyatt as they walked past them, acting as if they didn't have a care in the world. It wasn't until they were in the lobby area the men at the table moved from where they had remained, pretending like they weren't paying attention to them.

A stop at the counter selling sunglasses allowed Sam and Wyatt to get a good look at the trio when they passed them on their way to the exit. Meanwhile, Jill looked through the wares on the table until she found a pair of wraparound sunglasses with mirrored lenses. She rotated to Wyatt, holding them up to him, her eyes pleading. With a shake of his head and a frown, he pulled out his wallet.

"As if you don't have enough fucking sunglasses," he grumped, handing the clerk the money.

"But these are different," Jill responded with a grin.

After slipping the glasses on, she grabbed Wyatt's arm, looking up at him, acting like the teenager she appeared to be. "Thanks, Grandpa. I love them."

Wyatt returned her smile. "Child, you'll be the death of me yet."

"Uh-uh," she sounded. "You know I want you around for as long as possible."

"My little fairy had better do a good job driving. I happen to like this car," he warned when she held out her hand for the keys.

Jill, staying in the role of a teenager, played with the keys while Wyatt and Sam chuckled at her antics. She unlocked the doors with the key fob while watching the three men who hurried to a Crown Victoria, having waited for them to leave the building. The mirrored sunglasses hid where she was looking while waiting for Sam to complete his phone call. There had been a reason for the mirrored lenses. Two of the men got in the car while the third one walked away down the row of cars. She was unable to see where he was headed without making it obvious she was watching them.

This was going to be fun. Not only did the trio not know what this car was capable of doing, they were unaware of her legendary driving skills. Her acting like a teenager, along with them not having chased her before, left the hired thugs at a big disadvantage.

"You notify the state police, Sam?" she questioned before starting the engine. The last thing she needed was to be arrested for what she expected to happen upon leaving the parking lot.

Sam, with brows raised, sent a glare her way, indicating he thought an amoeba was smarter than her. "Yes, while you were getting the sunglasses. Ryan answered. He said there's a car three miles to the south and another beyond that one. The orders were for you to keep going and let them catch up to you. Between here and Fort Drum Plaza, there are three cars and a fourth in the plaza."

"Yeah, well, I'm more worried about the two trucks they have waiting on us. I don't want anybody else getting hurt in this mess."

"What two trucks?" Sam questioned.

She backed out of the parking space while answering his question. "The two from Beal Transport, which were behind us when we pulled in here. The troopers might want to pull one of them over for a safety check. That way we could get past without a problem."

Wyatt chuckled. "Wasn't sure you picked up on them. I'll text Ryan. They pull out behind us?"

"Of course. My guess is they'll wait until we're nearer the trucks to make a move."

"Jill, you'd make a good criminal," Sam chuckled.

Those words had been said to her more than once. "Yeah, only I enjoy staying on the right side of the law. It's more fun with fewer risks."

Eschewing the cruise control, she kept to the speed limit and the right-hand lane. After turning on the radio, Jill relaxed, watching the trailing car in the rearview mirror. A second sedan, this one an Impala, joined the first one within two minutes of leaving the parking lot. Nothing like making things more dangerous.

She watched the two cars in her mirrors while staying with the flow of traffic. She had gone close to five miles and she was tired of the sedate speed. Not only that, the Crown Victoria was creeping up on her and was now one car back instead of two.

"There are two cars following us and the one is too close for comfort. Let's see if they're ready to play," Jill said, pulling into the left lane to pass the car in front of her. Wyatt and Sam knew this was her warning of what was to come.

Gentle pressure on the gas pedal pushed the speed to

seventy-five. She moved back into the right-hand lane when around the car, but didn't slow down. When the drivers of the chase cars saw her putting distance between them, they moved into the left lane, passing the van behind her. Before the first car could pass her, Jill shifted to the left lane. When the distance between the cars was less than two car lengths, a grin spread across her face. Yeah, they were ready to play.

Jill gradually increased her speed, keeping tabs on the cars following them in the rearview mirror. Wyatt pulled the rifle from behind the seat and placed it across his lap. Meanwhile, Sam was watching the men in the side mirror, his finger on the button controlling the rear window. All the glass in the car was bulletproof, so the window would need to be down for Wyatt to use his weapon.

While weaving around the cars and trucks, Jill kept increasing the speed, watching for the promised state trooper. There were two trucks blocking the lanes less than two miles ahead of them. These weren't the trucks sent to stop them, but were still an obstacle in an active chase.

Instead of slowing for the short line of vehicles, Jill veered off the roadway onto the right emergency lane, passing the line of cars and trucks. Wyatt chuckled when the Impala careened into the median after attempting to pass the trucks on the left where there was no emergency lane. There had been recent rain. The car slid into the collected the water and mud in the middle of the median.

The Crown Victoria had followed her around the traffic using the emergency lane but had fallen back a quarter of a mile. Jill grinned. This was fun for her.

She was doing ninety when she passed the first state trooper. Ryan had been wrong. They were now eight miles from Canoe Creek Plaza. The trooper pealed out from where he was parked on the side of the road, pulling in behind the speeding Crown Victoria.

The Beal trucks were still ahead and would pose a major problem at this speed. Jill wove in and out of traffic as the chase continued another six miles before she saw the backup from the two trucks as they ran side by side. They were running at the speed limit, which was slow since most drivers drove five to ten miles per hour over the speed limit on the turnpike. With their slow speed, the line of cars and trucks stretched for close to a mile. This wasn't going to be easy. Again, she moved to the right emergency lane, passing the long line of trucks and cars. She kept the speed between ninety and a hundred, watching for cars pulling in front of her or debris in the lane.

In less than five minutes she was approaching the trucks. The truck driver in the right lane apparently say her and moved so he was blocking half of the emergency lane. Because she had nowhere to go other than off the pavement, there was no preparation for the violent bouncing and a short skid when she hit the grass. Jill fought for control as she sped past the truck, which didn't try to block her once she left the pavement. Upon regaining the blacktop, Jill skidded into the left lane before regaining control. She pressed the gas pedal to the floor, increasing the distance between her and the trucks. The Crown Victoria made it around the trucks after waiting for the truck to return to the right lane. It put him close to half mile behind her.

A second trooper entered the highway with flashing lights from an exit a mile after passing the Beal trucks. The speed was now a hundred and five miles per hour and increasing. The car chasing them increased his speed, the troopers with lights and sirens going following close behind them. The two men in the car were showing no signs of giving up the chase.

Okay, the man was a decent driver. He had followed her, albeit at a slower speed, around the trucks, but he was now decreasing the distance between them. It was time to become that low-flying jet.

With a finger, Jill flicked the overdrive switch, keeping the gas pedal on the floor, pushing the car to its top speed. The needle was buried as she sped past the slower traffic, the car doing one hundred and fifty with the speedometer needle inching to the maximum two hundred mark.

They flew past on the right of a trooper driving in the left lane. The Crown Victoria moved to the right, but the trooper stayed ahead of him before switching lanes, slowing the chasing car. One of the chasing patrol cars pulled to the left of the Crown Victoria and started squeezing him to the right with the other patrol car almost on his bumper. Jill eased off the gas when she saw the four cars move off the road, the troopers surrounding the Crown Victoria. The men had no place to go.

Sam's glare reminded her to turn off the overdrive and slow to eighty. The three of them continued to scan for another threat while blending in with traffic. Wyatt's phone rang, breaking the silence.

"Ryan, you get the truckers and the two cars?" Wyatt asked without preamble, then listened to Ryan.

"Good. Yeah, she's a damn good driver." He listened again and laughed. "Son, you'd have to fucking ask her."

When he hung up, Wyatt said, "You have an offer to teach a course in driving to the fucking troopers. Ryan said he hasn't ever seen fucking driving like that other than in a fucking movie."

With a laugh, Jill glanced at Sam, who was grinning. "Tell him to take a stunt driving course. It'll give him all the things I did and how to do it safely."

"Now when in the fuck did you take a stunt driving course?" Wyatt asked in surprise.

"The two months I was in LA. That's the reason why I had to be there during that time."

Sam stifled a chuckle as Wyatt glared at the back of her head. Sam had known what she was doing and had promised not to tell Wyatt. Until now, it had been their secret.

"Jill, you never cease to fucking amaze me. No wonder you're so fucking good at getting away."

They had made it to the Fort Drum Plaza. A state trooper was entering the turnpike as they passed it. Jill watched as he caught up to her then pulled in behind as if clocking her speed. When his lights came on, she slowed and pulled off the busy roadway onto the grass, not willing to take a chance of getting hit. Her driver's license, PI ID, and concealed weapons card were in her hand as the trooper walked up beside the car. He had his hand on his gun, his hat shading his face and dark sunglasses hiding his eyes.

Her first reaction was to punch Ryan, her brother, when he leaned over and merrily said, "Jill, you need to keep it to a reasonable speed. Our guys were having a major problem catching up to you."

"Then teach them to drive," she snapped, sarcasm dripping from her voice, not appreciating his pulling her over.

He tapped the car door before saying, "Get out of the car, please."

"Yeah," she said with disgust, curbing the anger at his playing with her before doing as he requested.

She wouldn't put it past him to arrest her if she refused to follow his orders. He was one of the few who could stop her from getting away. At six-five, he had a long reach and a grip like a vise. Her handsome brother had been on TV multiple times and was the supervisor and spokesperson for the troopers in this area. Most who didn't know him thought he was administration and a spokesman only, but he wasn't. She knew to obey his orders like she did Wyatt. That lean frame didn't show the strength and agility he hid until needed.

Once out of the car, she moved to the passenger side, away from the traffic whizzing by them. As she fumed, Ryan checked her IDs before handing them back to her. With crossed arms, Jill leaned against the front fender and waited to see what else he planned on doing before letting her go. If he gave her a speeding ticket, it would be the last thing he did today. Wyatt and Sam had also gotten out of the car but remained near the back door.

"Sis, what am I going to do with you? Somehow, I'll have to explain what happened today in reasonable terms to keep me from getting sent to the boondocks or fired. I may be in charge of this substation, but I do have bosses to answer to at the end of the day."

Before she could respond, a car pulled in behind the squad car. Jill peered at the driver in dismay, not sure if she was correct. Ryan turned to see who it was, relaxing with a big grin when Tom exited the car before turning back to her. "Let's hope I get help from him. If not, I'm in big trouble."

Jill frowned, studying her brother. How had everyone

met Tom and not her? Just who was he and what agency did he work for to know everyone she did?

Tom sauntered toward them, shaking his head, and from his expression, he wasn't happy. "Jill, you need to warn us before you do that again."

His presence resulted in another spike of anger. First Ryan and now him! Why were they picking on her? It wasn't like she had done something wrong. She had no choice other than avoiding the creeps who wanted her dead.

Jill snipped, "Wyatt had Sam fill in Ryan as soon as I made the three guys at the rest area. Maybe you should keep in contact with the state guys so they know to expect trouble."

Pursing his lips, arms crossed, Tom planted his feet before he shook his head. "Jill, the fewer people involved, the better off we'll be." His expression let her know he thought she wasn't exactly smart before turning to Ryan. "I'll send an official thank you for the assistance so you don't get in trouble for helping a crazy lady."

With a chortle, Ryan clapped his hand on Tom's shoulder. "She's crazy like a fox. I appreciate the help though. My boss will ream me a new asshole for what just happened, especially after Vince clocked her at a hundred and twenty-five. He'll want to know why we had so little notice of a possible problem."

"Not to worry. I'll let him know you were helping us to

protect a federal witness in an unexpected event." Tom had continued to focus on her while he talked to Ryan. When he said, "Jill, you're coming with me," she straightened up, eyes flashing, ready to refuse.

He held up a hand before she could protest. "Don't say it. I'm not going to attempt to try and catch you when you get home and go into hiding as you're planning. You can come with me on your own or I can cuff you. Your choice."

"You won't cuff me without *my* cooperation, so don't even try. I don't want to go with you. I'm going home," she spat, her arms crossed and mouth set in a straight line, daring him to try and force her to obey.

Ryan leaned into Tom, grinning at her. "Pal, you might want to get Wyatt's help, otherwise she won't do a damn thing and you won't win if you try to force her. Believe me, I know how difficult she is to contain. Plus, she'll get away if you don't and will be close to impossible to find."

Tom didn't have the chance to appeal to her grandfather for help. Wyatt moved between them, blocking Jill's view of Tom and Ryan. She glared up at him, blinking back the pending tears. All she wanted was to go home, even if it was only for the night.

"You're fucking going with him," Wyatt ordered. He held up a hand when her mouth opened to protest. "Not one fucking word. Not one. You do as he fucking says. I want you alive, not fucking dead. Understood?"

Biting back what she started to say, Jill lowered her

eyes from the angry ones warning her to behave. "Yes, sir," she responded in a contrite voice. She was so screwed. There was no way she could change his mind after the way he phrased his order. She gritted her teeth, blinking rapidly as her heartbeat refused to slow. She sucked in a big breath and willed herself to be calm.

Wyatt put a gentle finger under her chin, raising her face to his. She saw he wasn't any happier than her. "Jill, I love you. There's no way I'd trust my precious fairy to anybody if I didn't think the fucking bastard could keep you alive."

Tears welled, then overflowed. "Please, Grandpa. I want to go home," she pleaded, a hand resting on his arm.

"Not right now, honey. I want you there, but I can't fucking protect you like he can."

Her breath caught. It was the first time he had ever admitted to having limits on protecting her. Also, she didn't miss the fear he tried to hide before moving into his embrace. He had to be aware how intense the search for her would be this time. If he was telling her to go with Tom, he had to have a good reason. Over the past six years he hadn't allowed her to be away from him, even in Aruba and the Bahamas, without protection.

"I'll miss you," she admitted as he held her close to him, his big hand brushing her head.

"I'll miss you, too, baby girl. I hope it'll only be for a couple of fucking weeks. Don't you dare disobey him. He knows what he's fucking doing."

"Yes, sir," she answered, aware of the consequences of disobeying his orders. With reluctance, she left his embrace, then gave her brother a crooked grin when she got to him. "You're getting better, bro."

Ryan bent over to give her a hug and a kiss on her cheek. "Sis, you stick with Tom. He'll keep you alive. I want to see my imp turn twenty-five."

"Yeah. Right. Be careful out there. You're the only one other than Brad worth a rat's ass." Ryan laughed. She turned and confronted Tom. "Okay. I'm going with you because Wyatt commanded it, but I don't have to fucking like it."

Tom reached out and tugged on one of her curls. "Jill, get over it. For now, I'm your best hope of making that trial."

"Whatever," she commented before stomping off to his car. No matter what she did to avoid being with him, everyone kept pushing them together. She hoped he was as good as they thought he was. If not, she wouldn't make it to the trial. From what had just happened, Snake wasn't the only one hired to ensure she didn't live long enough to testify.

Tom's voice drifted to her. "Thanks, Wyatt. I'll see she makes it back to you."

"You had fucking better," Wyatt warned, glancing back at her before getting into his car.

Ryan had followed her to Tom's car. "Sis, cheer up. It could be worse. You could be sitting in solitary in protective custody."

"I may still end up there if he gets on my nerves," she snapped, not happy at the turn of events.

"Jill, chill. Granddad wouldn't have ordered you to go with him without a good reason."

Her arms went around Ryan in a hug. "I know, but there's more to it than you know. For now, I'll tolerate it."

Ryan glanced a Tom. "Hey, he's a good guy. A hell of a lot better than the last guy who dated you."

"Maybe, but it'll turn out the same."

"Somehow, I don't think so, sis. He's not the normal guy."

"Right! And pigs fly! See you later."

She pulled him down and gave him a kiss on his cheek, then got into the car. She reached up and pulled the mirrored sunglasses from the top of her head, hiding her watering eyes. With crossed arms and a scowl, she stared out the windshield, watching Wyatt and Sam leave. This was all she needed. More time to let him wheedle his way further into her heart.

Tom pulled smoothly into the traffic on the turnpike. Angling her shoulders away from him, she stared out the side window, hiding her tears from him. Fear of the unknown and sadness at being away from Wyatt warred for the upper hand. The sadness won.

When the tears stopped, she laid the seat back, planning on sleeping. Anything to keep from having to talk to him. Where he was taking her wasn't important. He was now in charge of keeping her safe. Until able to go home, she would play the nice little puppet and jump when told. Hopefully, it wouldn't take months until the trial was scheduled. If so, she would be so totally screwed.

Chapter 12

AND THE DISH RAN AWAY WITH THE SPOON

It was dark when the car stopped. Jill sat up and glanced around, not recognizing where they were. Tom took the keys from the ignition before rotating to face her.

"I know you have more than one reason for not

wanting to be here with me. If there was another way, or someone else I trusted, I wouldn't have insisted you come with me."

Okay, so he had a modicum of understanding of her refusing to come without Wyatt's order. Clarifying the reasons might help him to understand her not wanting to be near him.

"Tom, I've been hanging on to sanity by a thread for the past six years. The last thing I need is to be torn apart by someone who says they care and then walks out upon learning the truth about me. I don't want to go through that again."

"How many times has this happened?" he inquired.

"The numbers don't matter. Most didn't hurt all that much. I didn't really care for them. The last one tore me apart because I had waited until I cared, hoping for a different outcome."

"What about Billy? He's in love with you."

She released the breath she had been holding, staring at her folded hands in her lap, head bowed. "Yeah, well, the problem is, I don't love him the way he does me. Billy's this wonderful guy who would give me the world if he could, but I can't shortchange him."

"Is he aware of those missing years?"

"I haven't disclosed everything to him, but yes, he knows. Meanwhile, you'll get to listen to all the gory details. The defense will try to make me into this whore who willing did what they wanted."

"I know there's no way you willingly went along with them. You're not that type of woman. My guess is they kept you drugged, and if you resisted, they used a whip to keep you in line."

"Something like that," she admitted before undoing the seat belt and getting out of the car. Time to change the subject.

Tom came around the car to guide her toward the partially hidden front door. A man stepped from the shadows and caught the keys Tom tossed to him before going to the car they had used and driving off into the dark. With the poor lighting, it was a miracle anyone could see an intruder.

Tom opened the unlocked front door and held it for her to enter. A quick scan showed the house was spacious and decorated with comfortable stylish furniture. This would be a pleasant prison. There was a man sitting in the corner of the good sized great room, eyes never leaving the multiple screens arranged in a bank so he could watch them all at once.

"Hi, Tom. Nothing to report other than quiet," the man stated.

"Keep a good watch, Jesse. I'm expecting visitors now that we're here."

"Gotcha," was Jesse's response.

Tom led the way to the left side of the living room into

a short hallway. When he opened the first door on the right, a large bedroom with an in-suite bathroom was revealed. The king-sized bed piled with pillows on a colorful comforter could have been in a furniture ad. The folded nightshirt on the bed and the valises on the dresser were from her condo. She now knew Wyatt and Tom had planned the protective custody prior to today. The only things lacking in the room were a TV or books. Without either one, it meant she had to leave the room for entertainment.

"Go to bed. There are clothes in the bag on the chair and necessities in the bathroom. I'll see you in the morning."

After the long stressful day, Jill didn't argue with the direct order. Once alone, she scanned the room for exits or entries. There was a sliding glass door opening onto a patio with a pool. It had an added keyed lock and alarm along with a rod which locked onto the doors in the track, preventing anyone from opening the door. There was a door to the hall and an entrance to a private bath, which had a small window, also locked with an alarm, leaving no viable means of escape. Because of the alarms, there was no reason to attempt opening the door or windows.

Resigned to being a prisoner, she listened to the murmuring voices of the men drifting through the door. She and Tom weren't alone, which was a plus. The negative was how there was no way out unless she could sneak past the men assigned to guard the exits. Then there were the cameras and the man watching the screens. Nothing like being in a gilded prison.

Her clothes landed on the floor at her feet. She was too tired to care about them. After pulling the nightshirt over her head, she crawled into bed. A shower and picking up the clothes could wait until morning. Jill drifted off to sleep, the exhaustion pulling her into a dream of the green-eyed man with the musical voice telling her things no man in his right mind would ever say to her and mean it.

The house was quiet when she awoke in the strange bed and room. Her breath caught in her throat as fear sent her heart racing before she remembered where she was and why. A tiredness sapped her normal energy. The comfortable bed encouraged a return to sleep instead of getting up.

Forcing herself out of the bed, Jill found a clean pair of jeans, a T-shirt, and underthings to wear in the valise. How long had Wyatt known she would need to be in protective custody? Why Tom? There were others who could provide better hiding spots.

On the way to the shower, she scooped up the dirty clothes, depositing them in the hamper before stepping into the shower. The hot water relieved the stress as it rained down in gentle drops. For the next several weeks, until able to return home or decide where best to hide, she needed to remain stress-free, which meant staying away from Tom.

The relaxing shower didn't stop what was going on inside her mind. There was at least a two- or three-week wait for the grand jury hearing, then a year or more for the trial. That is if they were lucky. There was time to have a mini meltdown before the hardest part came—the waiting then testifying. After the trial, she could fall apart and deal with the resulting emotions from dredging up the past.

There were two men in the large living room. They were dressed in what could be called office casual. The older man peered over the top of the newspaper he was reading.

"Good morning. The kitchen is through the door there. There's breakfast on the counter," he stated then returned to the paper. The other agent studied her with an intense stare, remaining quiet. Jill ignored him, stalking to the kitchen, aware of being rude but not caring. It wasn't her choice to be here.

She nuked the McDonald's breakfast sandwich. If this was their idea of breakfast, she would become a royal bitch. The coffee was lukewarm but that didn't matter as she seldom drank hot coffee. With the food in her hands, she turned to the kitchen table, choosing a clean spot to sit. A newspaper on the table was open to the story of the arrest of Billings and his lawyer on federal racketeering charges.

There was a grand jury hearing set for today at the

Broward Federal courthouse, which was strange considering Billings was arrested in Lake County. The trial should be held in Orlando, not in Fort Lauderdale. Tom had to be at the hearing, which meant they were somewhere in Broward County. He should have information on how long until the trial was placed on the docket when he returned.

Not bothering to finish the article, she flipped to the page with the funnies and advice column, then scanned the back page. Finished with the unsatisfying meal, out of habit, she cleaned up the mess in the kitchen, ticked off that the men hadn't cleaned up after themselves. This was another issue to be discussed with Tom. It wasn't that she expected someone to wait on her, but she was a prisoner, not the housekeeper.

Jill returned to the living room when finished in the kitchen and turned on the TV to pass the time. She flicked through the channels before settling on an old Western. Turning the sound low, she curled up on the couch to stare at the screen. This wait was going to be long and boring.

The depression snaked its way out of the compartment where she had kept it contained. Closing her eyes, she let the hopelessness increase the tiredness, draining what energy she had left until sleep overtook her. It was the easiest thing to do.

Bored out of her skull and forced to stay here, she knew there were few options other than sleep. She would testify, return home, then fall apart in that order. That crash and burn she had avoided for six years was inevitable this time. No matter what he guessed, Tom would leave once the trial was over, if not before then. In her case, the truth didn't set her free. It was a prison from which there was no escape other than into the world of insanity.

Jill awoke to voices. At some point, someone had placed a warm blanket over her, which she now pulled around her neck and shoulders, using it to block out the world for the moment. Her shoulder was uncomfortable, so she turned over and opened her eyes, noticing Tom watching her as he talked to the two men who had been in the room this morning. With a sigh, she closed her eyes again and prepared to go back to sleep. There was no reason to stay awake.

The caress from a gentle hand on her cheek pulled her back to wakefulness. Tom was squatted beside the couch, his serious green eyes studying her.

"Jill, you can't sleep for the next two weeks. Come on and get up." His face conveyed the concern his voice held.

"Why not?" The lethargy held her in place. She was now aware the prosecutor would request her presence to discuss her testimony within the week. If the defense didn't know her, they could call her in for a deposition, which was okay. She knew better than to answer their questions. Her standard answer was, "You will need to ask that question in court."

"Because we need to get your testimony ready."

"Don't need to. I know how to answer the questions," she stated before turning away and facing the back of the couch. "I've been on the stand multiple times so I know what not to do."

"There are a few twists to be discussed. The defense has a good lawyer, and we don't need any of the bows coming undone."

Reluctantly, she struggled into a sitting position. "Okay, this should take five minutes."

"After we eat," he told her.

"I'll eat when I'm hungry," she stated with force. "What twists do they have in store?"

"After we eat," Tom repeated.

She crossed her arms, teeth gritted in anger. "I'll eat when I'm hungry."

He stood, his right eyebrow elevated. "Jill, this is one you won't win. Time for lunch. Let's go."

"Make me," she spat, challenging him with a glare in his direction.

In a calm voice, Tom told her, "I'll not force you, but you will eat."

She pulled her legs up, sitting Indian style on the couch, and refolded her arms. No matter what he said, she wasn't moving until good and ready. There was no way he could force her to do anything, including eating. Being a prisoner had its advantages. The only requirement was to stay put. Everything else was optional, including eating. When she got hungry, she would eat and not a moment sooner.

Tom walked away, ignoring her, the men following him into the kitchen. Jill huffed. It would be a cold day in hell if they expected her to clean up after them this time. Alone again, she reclined and covered up with the blanket. She curled into a ball, facing the back of the couch and closed her eyes. The tiredness drew her deep into the darkness of a numbing sleep, away from the things she didn't want to deal with now, or ever.

A hand shook her. The jerk of her shoulder removed the hand. Whoever was bothering her needed to leave her alone. When the hand shook her again, she whipped around and grabbed the person's arm, stopping abruptly. If she had completed the move, Tom would be on the floor with a dislocated shoulder.

"Leave me the fuck alone before you get hurt. I'm a prisoner in a nice prison, nothing more. I'll decide what I want to do and when I want to do it while here."

She sat up, warning him to back off with a glare. Tom backed up a step. Jill pushed up from the couch, then shoved past him and marched to her room, slamming the door before flopping face down on the bed, red hot anger coursing through her. Just because she was in protective custody didn't mean he could tell her what to do!

The door opened and closed. A scuff on the carpet informed her Tom had entered the room. The bed sank when he sat on the edge. Without speaking, she rolled away, hoping he'd take the hint and leave.

"Jill, I'm tasked with keeping you safe, not just physically, but mentally too. You can't let whatever is happening in your head take control. If that happens, you won't be able to testify as needed. I don't want to get into a physical fight with you, but I will if that's what it takes to make you resist what is going on inside of you."

"Leave me the fuck alone," she repeated, using her thumb to dry the tears seeping onto her pillow, barely stopping herself from physically lashing out at him.

"No, I won't. We have two to four weeks to wait until learning if the trial will be added to this docket. With a bit of luck, they won't find you while we're waiting. If they do, I'll need that feisty girl beside me."

"Not my problem," she stated.

"It is your problem. You started this, now you need to finish it. Crash on your own time, not mine." His voice had turned harsh, reminding her of Wyatt when she wasn't listening to him.

With a glance over her shoulder, she retorted, "I'm on my own time while waiting. Now Leave. Me. Alone."

"No, I won't."

She rolled over, spearing him with a glare, anger rearing its ugly head. She barely maintained control at his daring to give her orders on how to live. "Get the fuck out of my room before you get hurt."

"I'll take my chances. It's time for you to get out of this bed and eat like the lady you are so we can discuss this case."

"Fuck you," she snapped, rolling over again so he didn't see the tears or her fisted hands.

She jerked away when he touched her shoulder. His fingers came around her arm, pulling her toward him. In one swift move, she rolled over, rising to her knees, fighting him for the right to do what she wanted. Everything she did, he countered. Anger and fear fueled her moves, but it was as if he knew what she was going to do before she did it. After close to fifteen minutes of fighting him, she was trapped, her arms and legs controlled with a surprisingly gentle strength. Too tired to offer further resistance, she slumped against him, giving in to the tears she hadn't wanted him to see.

He kept her arms controlled with one hand, tilting her head up with the other, so she was facing him. The brush of his lips sent a different shock through her. Without wanting to, she responded, moving into the man holding her. Her skin craved contact with him, sensitive to every place they touched. When her hands were freed, she encircled him with her arms, answering the deepening kiss, which was bombarding her system with sensations she didn't want to stop.

Her lips parted and his tongue probed her mouth. Their tongues danced in a kiss, which created a need she didn't fully understand. It was something she had only felt once before and wanted to be fulfilled.

When he broke the kiss, Tom kept her in his arms, holding her firmly against him. A hand rubbed her back, his head resting on top of hers. The falling tears changed from anger to anguish driven. This man was going to rip her apart, and she had no weapons left to prevent it after that kiss.

"Please don't keep pushing me away," Tom pleaded.

With her head buried in his shoulder, she admitted, "I'm not sure I'll survive if you walk away from me now."

"Honey, no matter what you say on that stand, I'm not going anywhere without you."

He didn't understand what he was promising. Jill moved closer to him, wanting to remain in his arms—protected and loved, only that wasn't going to happen.

"Yes, you will," she said in a voice barely above a whisper. No one outside of Wyatt and Brad, including Billy, wanted a severely damaged fairy. No one.

His arms tightened, holding her closer to him. "No, I won't. You'll see. I'll be right there beside you. There's no way I'm letting you get away from me. No matter what was done to you, inside there's this beautiful woman, who I believe cares for me, and I want her in the worst possible way."

Cutting off a sob, she disclosed the truth. "She isn't beautiful. She's used and dirty."

His hand against her head created a longing to stay here in his arms and experience the promise of a life of love.

"The used I'll agree with, but you aren't dirty. Being used wasn't your choice so it doesn't count in my book."

Jill sat up, turning away from him. The fear of being rejected again, filling her. "I ended up with an STD that won't ever go away. I lucked out and didn't get HIV, but this one is a lifetime thing, so yes, I'm dirty."

A gentle hand tugged her back down beside him. "Let me guess, genital herpes or warts."

Unable to meet his gaze she said, "The first one," hiding her shame with her lowered head.

"Honey, we can work with it. Anyone can pick it up with one encounter. That isn't uncommon, and I'm not going to go nutso over it. If that's the only problem, then it's a minor one."

The small flicker of hope grew with his words. This was only one of the problems resulting from her three-year residence in hell. There was another far worse problem, but she would deal with it later. It was an issue unacceptable to most normal men, but for now, he wasn't running away.

"You just need to be honest with me. You've had enough hurt for a lifetime, and I don't want to add to it.

Every time you cry because of something I don't understand, it tears me apart." With a sniffle, she cuddled into him, wanting more than anything for his words to be the truth. He continued, "Once this is over, we need to discuss what's next, and I don't want to be chasing you all over creation to have that talk."

"Are you sure?" She leaned back and studied his face, still not believing he wouldn't disappear.

"Positive. As I said before, I understand what you went through and it makes no difference to me. You're the one who needs to move beyond it."

She stared at his neck. "I've tried, but it keeps coming back to haunt me in various ways. Just knowing I was one of the elites and made to dance for the leering creeps, either elicits disgust or the belief I'm an easy lay."

"Not for me. Even if you swear like a sailor when pissed, you're a lady and deserve the respect of a lady."

She wanted to believe his words. For now, it was time to trust. The worst that could happen was him leaving, taking a big chunk of her with him. If that happened, it would mean a stay in some nuthouse until able to pull herself back together. This time, there would be no talking her out of becoming a hermit, unwilling to allow the reoccurrence of the pain of rejection to rip her to shreds.

"I guess I better go eat," Jill stated, letting out a deep breath, hoping he understood this was a truce, and she was willing to cooperate for now.

His hold on her loosened so she could get up. Time would tell if she was right. Because of the one secret only Brad and her doctor knew, she didn't have any hope of his sticking around after her testimony.

The two guards ignored them as they walked through the living room to the kitchen. Jesse was back at the monitors. From the pots and pans in the drainer on the sink, someone had cooked the chicken alfredo and fresh garlic rolls. The tantalizing smell had her mouthwatering.

She filled a plate and reheated it in the microwave. Tom put a salad by her plate before taking a seat at the table. He stayed with her, reading the paperwork from a folder he had retrieved while she was waiting on the microwave. With the stress gone, she was hungry and able to eat normally.

When done, she put her dishes in the dishwasher and the leftovers in the refrigerator. Ignoring the rest of the dishes, she left the kitchen. Within a few seconds, the sound of running water, then the clink of dishes being placed in the dishwasher came from the kitchen.

When Tom joined them in the living room, he stated, "Guys, she's not the maid and neither am I. You need to clean up after yourselves. That means putting your dishes in the dishwasher, cleaning the table, counters, and stove if used."

When the younger man stood, Tom told him, "I did it this time, but I won't again."

Tom sat on the couch, angled so he was facing her. He stared past her before speaking.

"Jill, the prosecutor needs to talk to you and has requested us to be there this evening. I can arrange protection and transportation. Are you willing to talk to him?"

She kept her head lowered, deciphering what he was asking. "Sure. Why not? He needs information from me."

Tom nodded in agreement. "I'm sure he'll have specific questions needing answers. They have enough on the racketeering charges with what I turned over to them, but it's the other charges he needs to discuss with you. There's one other woman who'll be testifying, but you'll be their star witness. From what he said, he's expecting to get a lot of information from you."

"Probably. They've worked with me on several other cases. We need to discuss the direction of the questioning and some of the particulars of my testimony."

Tom placed a hand on her arm, keeping her attention. "You'll have a choice once we get there. I can wait outside or be in the room with you. That decision will be yours to make. I'm not testifying in this case because those I got the information from will need to testify as to where they got what they gave us."

After rearranging herself on the couch, she snidely stated, "I get it. They don't want you outed. I'll let you know once we get there."

He tugged on a curl. She rotated her head to face him, eyes questioning.

"They won't go easy on you. It'll be a rough session."

With a frown and a slight lift of her shoulders, she stated, "Been there, done that. It's standard for when I'm testifying. As I said, they've worked with me in the past."

"So the prosecutor said. He also said you haven't ever let them down. In fact, he told me you were the one who sealed the fate of several major criminals and wanted to clone you for other cases. Something about this sweet innocent girl, who can sway a jury, unlike other witnesses can, by stating facts in such a way that even the densest person gets it."

"It'll be harder this time," she admitted.

"Why?"

She blinked rapidly, studying her entwined fingers. "I'm one of the victims. The defense will attempt to convince the jury I've manufactured things to get him. I'll be walking a very fine line. My testimony for the agency will have to be impartial and then change into that victim when they attempt to discredit what I said. On top of that, I'll have to hide my feelings, and that will be fucking hard to do."

"Sometimes letting those feelings show is better than staying impartial. He's planning on having you testify after the other woman, so that'll help. You'll be verifying what she gave in a totally different way."

Not willing to say more in front of the men, she gnawed at her bottom lip. The prosecutor only had a small portion of the information stored in her brain. When she gave Tom the maps of the club for the raid, it should have shown him her ability to remember things in detail. In her memory were names, places, clients, connections and more. It was filed away, unable to be written anywhere because the minute she did, whoever received the information was turned into a walking dead person.

Billings' threat to see her dead was very real. He and his cronies had a long reach. She couldn't tell what she knew to anyone. Not yet. Not until the lawyers asked the questions in the courtroom where only those who were guilty would get hurt. Once on the witness stand, she would impart the information to put Billings and his whole network in a federal lockup for a long, long time.

The major problem was how to stay alive until then. Once she testified, then they could do their worst. Until then, the prosecutors needed to be satisfied with her standard statement, "I'll give you the relevant information on the stand." To help reach that information, she guided them as to what questions to ask.

"What's going through that brain of yours?" Tom asked when the silence became extended.

"Just going over the questions they'll need to ask to obtain the information to convict the ones above Billings."

"Um, what?" Tom questioned.

A glance at the two men listening to them showed an intense interest in her statement.

"You heard me. I'm not repeating it."

She met his concerned gaze before letting out a noisy breath and rolling her eyes at him.

"Honestly! You didn't think Billings was the top of the heap, did you?"

His gaze went to the two agents. "Come with me," he commanded, leading her to her room and closing the door behind him.

"Jill, talk to me," he commanded, all business.

"This is one time I can't. There's a time and place for me to give the information I've gathered. If they believe I've revealed any of what I know to anyone, those people will be killed, along with me. It's bad enough you're a target simply because of being with me.

"There are two moles in the US District Attorney's office. I'll only give them the direction for the questions they need to ask to get the information. If the one is there in the office, I won't be able to guide them very much as he'll see to it that many of the questions aren't asked." She met his concerned eyes before saying, "I hope you realize we won't be able to come back here after this meeting."

He stared at her, before turning away and letting out a snort. A hand ran through his short hair while pacing the floor. Jill sat on the bed observing him. When he stopped pacing, he faced her, his face a study in concern with a grim frown on his lips.

"Jill, is Wyatt aware you have this information?"

"He knows, but not any specifics. The plant in the agency knows I don't share this type of information with him and never record everything I know. Only evidence which is easily discovered is written in my reports. It's the reason they want me dead. It's the reason the prosecutor wants to talk to me. He knows I've got information no one else has."

"What will you do if the plant is there?"

"Dance around the issues. I'll be using some code two others will understand. They'll pick up on what to cover and the prosecutor will allow them to ask those questions. It's the reason they work as a team when I'm on the case. They know how to ask questions to get the information."

"Pack a week's worth of clothes. I'll get the bags to the transportation without them seeing it. I don't want them to know we won't be back."

"Good. One of them will turn me in for the bounty when he gets the chance."

"Which one?" Tom questioned with tightly controlled anger and a hand on her arm.

"The young one. I recognized him right away. He isn't aware I've seen him before in a place he should never have been, talking to someone he shouldn't have any personal contact with, unless working undercover."

"And you remembered him from how long ago?"

"Eight years. I've an exceptional memory for faces, names, facts, dates, times, and conversations. They thought they had me drugged, but I wasn't most of the time. It's one of the reasons I weighed 90 pounds when Wyatt and Sam got me out of there."

Tom embraced her, placing his head on hers. "We'll need to move around until the trial. I can't trust anyone to keep you safe. Fred will make sure they can't track us from the meeting. You choose the one person who'll inform us when to show up for court."

"That's simple. Wyatt. He wants me back and will use secure lines to contact me. I'll set it up. I've done this before and he'll work with me."

"In that case, I'll let you arrange it. I'll need that bag as soon as possible."

"Give me ten minutes."

"I like your style." He grinned at her before leaving, after planting a quick kiss on her lips. She loved his style with the spontaneous kisses and hugs.

When the door to the room closed, she went to her purse and pulled out her communicator. She opened the connection and Wyatt answered within seconds.

"You okay, baby girl?"

"Yes. You need to keep in contact with Gil. We're going underground after the meeting this evening. Notify me when to be in court."

"Got it. Stay safe."

He broke the connection. Less than thirty seconds. There was no way anyone could trace it even if they caught the signal. Oh, yeah, she had a way to keep them from being found through communications. This wasn't her first rodeo, and she wanted to stay alive.

Chapter 13

AND THE DIE IS SET

Jill used one of the valises to pack enough things for a week from what was in the room. Wyatt had included two dresses for her. She chose the simple slip-on dark blue dress along with matching ballet slippers, leaving the other one in the closet. Hopefully it, and her other things would be returned to Wyatt. The outfit she was taking with her would make her look like a teenager, but that was okay. Leave it to Wyatt to think ahead while she was worrying about getting the bad guys.

Going back to her seat on the couch to wait for Tom, the youngest of the guards engaged her in conversation. It wasn't long until he asked about her work with Wyatt. Aware of what he was doing, she didn't react when he asked, "You been in contact with Wyatt today?"

"What for?" she questioned, an innocent wide-eyed expression on her face.

"Well, don't you have to report in to him?"

"Not unless I'm working a case. The case I was working is finished, and he has the paperwork for it," she told him with a shrug.

The man, being persistent, questioned, "Then who are you working for now?"

Her right brow rose as she informed him, "If you don't know, then it's above your pay grade, sweetie."

He stared at her. The older agent chuckled before saying, "I guess she told you, Whitey. You ask too many questions. My best guess is her clearance is way up there in the stratosphere from the past work she's done for us and other agencies."

Jill gave no indication as to whether he was correct or not, observing Whitey as he studied her.

"Drop it, Whitey. You aren't going to get any fucking information from me just like Tom isn't, and I do believe he has a much higher clearance than you do," Jill informed him in a tone geared to let him know he had tipped his hand.

She turned to the other man. "If I were you, I'd watch my back."

Getting up from the couch, she went to the kitchen to fix something to eat. Tom was there. He winked at her before slipping out the back door with their valises. She hadn't noticed him moving through the room where she and the agents had been sitting. His wink informed her he had overheard the conversation and Whitey would be neutralized.

She heard the older man talking to Whitey. If he had half a brain, he would be questioning Whitey as to why he was trying to obtain information from her. Her statement as to clearance should have set off alarms.

Tom returned to the kitchen as silently as he had left, motioning for her to follow him. She took the sandwiches she had fixed and grabbed two small bags of chips and two bottles of water before joining him. Like him, she made no noise as she left the house, leaving the two agents talking in the living room. They wouldn't discover she was missing until she didn't return from the kitchen in a timely manner.

Jill followed Tom to the dock behind the house where a fishing boat was moored with their bags on board. She stepped onto the boat and took a seat while Tom untied the lines before joining her. Using the trolling motor, he waited until they were around the bend away from the house before he started the engine. Handing him one of the sandwiches she had made, she sat beside him and started to eat.

Her trust in him to keep her alive went up with the way he had gotten her out of the house. It would be another five to fifteen minutes before the two men realized she was gone. Heaven only knew when they would discover Tom was also missing.

Smiling down at her, he stated, "Thanks for the sandwich. I wasn't expecting to eat again until late this evening."

"You're quite welcome. Now that the stress is off, I can eat without choking. I take it you informed Jesse we were leaving so he didn't notify the other two."

He glanced at her, brows drawn together. "Of course. Why isn't the running and hiding more stressful?"

Chuckling, she shook her head. "Because I'm good at hide-and-seek. Getting all the crap lined up to make a collar is a lot more stressful. During this trial, I'll be stressed to the max until the defense starts questioning me. Then I'll relax.

"This is my normal life when I'm involved in a big case going to trial where I know they'll be trying to stop me from testifying. I hop around and stay out of sight unless I want to be found. Right now, I'm letting you do the hiding part until I see it isn't working."

"Then what?"

"I show you my way of hiding. FYI, Wyatt knows to

play tag with me. He'll let me know the when and where."

"When did you talk to him?" Tom inquired as he increased the speed on the boat.

"Not telling the when or how. It's secure and will drive them nuts if they try to intercept."

"How long were you in contact?"

"Not long enough to get more than a general part of the country. If they got a state or city, it would be a miracle."

"Even if they knew it was Wyatt you were contacting?" he asked.

"If it was caught, which is very unlikely, they would need to figure out who I was contacting. There are hundreds of bands to be monitored, including shortwave, radio, TV, satellite, and the off-the-grid ones. This communicator is set so it accesses a different frequency every time it's used. Even if they picked up the frequency, it won't be the same the next time. Also, it can change in the middle of a ten-second conversation and the changes are never on a pattern, they're random."

He glanced over at her with a frown before asking, "Who set this up for you?"

She raised her brows and relaxed on the seat beside him. "Not telling. Just know it was for my protection when I was found so Wyatt could check on me while I was getting myself together. We kept it so he could keep up with me if I missed a call."

"So, it doesn't monitor you. It's strictly communication

based."

"Correct. If I don't physically answer, he's coming after me."

"Would anyone around you know it was summoning you?"

"No."

"Hmm. It appears I need to have a talk with Wyatt when this is finished."

She chuckled, well aware Wyatt wouldn't tell him where they got the devices. The technology was new and was taken from the bad guys. Sometimes it paid to have friends in low places.

This friend was one she had helped to keep out of jail. It had been how he had paid her back. Like Wyatt, he didn't want her dead. Her association with him was keeping him alive and free.

It was an hour later before Tom pulled into a large marina, docking the boat in a slip which sported a government insignia. Two men in suits took the lines he threw to them. Once the boat was secured, Tom stepped off with the valises while one of the men assisted her onto the dock. Other than a nod, there was no communication with the two men before Tom guided her to a car in the lot above the dock. The man standing by the car tossed him the keys and winked at her. He was an agent she had worked with on another case.

"You take good care of our girl," the man warned as

Tom opened the passenger door for her before putting the valises in the backseat.

"Have my instructions been carried out?" Tom questioned.

"Yes, sir. Red level is in effect."

"Let Alpha know to contact Wyatt with any changes in the schedule."

"Got it. Droplet was trying to get info. Want us to neutralize?"

"Not yet. Need to know his contact. Let it drop we're going under and see where it goes."

"You got it. Don't use seven or ten. They're not secure and four is questionable right now."

"I believe we may drop off the radar. Let Alpha know so he doesn't panic."

The man peered at her and grinned, "Sure you don't need help on this one?"

Tom laughed, "Not happening, Sal."

"Can't blame a guy for trying."

"No, I can't."

"Tom, you take real good care of her. She's one special lady."

"In what way?" Tom questioned as he studied Sal.

Sal chuckled, watching her with a big grin. "I've worked with her before. Believe me, you'll want her on that stand. She'll tie it up so more than those who have been charged go to jail. There's a damn good reason why they want her dead."

"Yeah. I sort of got informed of that earlier. Make sure I have a day to get her to the courthouse or they'll need to ask for a twenty-four-hour recess to produce her."

Sal chuckled before saying, "One other thing. She's good at disappearing, so don't be afraid to let her do the hiding."

"We'll see what happens in this meet, then decide what to do afterward."

"Dung bug won't be there. He's having a problem and sent his regrets."

Once behind the wheel, Tom stated, "It looks as if your problem guy won't make the question-and-answer session today."

"You sure you have the right one?" she asked, her head tilted.

"You tell me once we get there."

They switched cars twice before pulling into the parking garage at the courthouse. Going to a secured elevator, he placed his hand on the pad and the doors opened. They had to be meeting in one of the rooms with special security. She had been there once before, but from a different entry point.

Tom examined the hall before allowing her to exit. He exchanged a nod with the man carrying an assault rifle in the hall near the exit. There was another man at the other end of the hall guarding that stairwell. Fear spiked through her. This was far above the normal security she had gotten in the past.

They entered the open door of one of the multitude of rooms. She scanned the faces of the men gathered there. There was one she didn't know. He was studying her, a slight upturn to his lips, giving her the impression he knew her, yet she had never seen him before now. He was a big man with blonde hair and green eyes. Her eyes went to the lead prosecutor then back to the new guy.

"I'll have to ask you to leave. I need sensitive information from her and she doesn't know you," the prosecutor stated in response to her non-verbal communication.

The expression on the man's face didn't change as he continued to watch her, unfazed by the prosecutor's request for him to leave. "Not a problem. Let me give you what I have before I go."

He gave them valuable information in a very concise organized manner. Then he added a detail she already knew. With a glance at her, the lawyer stated, "We will need to ensure we get the information on those above Billings to completely break this ring."

Jill stared at him. Where could he have gotten that information?

Before he could gather his paperwork, she stopped him. "I need to ask where you got the information on Billings not being the top guy."

"From an agent in one of the federal agencies. He said he got it from an operative with a code name of Ice."

"Name the agent," she demanded.

His eyes went to Williams, the lead prosecutor, who bobbed his head, indicating he could tell her.

The man faced her before saying, "Agent Thomas Wellington." His gaze went to Tom.

"Okay, you can stay. Sorry, but I'm not in a real trusting mood right now." She turned to Williams. "I'll warn you, if one piece of information I give during this meeting gets leaked to the opposition, it'll be the last group meeting you'll get me to participate in. The last time it almost got me killed, and I refuse to go through that again."

She took a seat and didn't ask Tom to leave. He stood behind her as the team began asking her questions. Most of it dealt with the paperwork and other evidence she had given to Wyatt, who in turn passed it on to them. Williams, the lead prosecutor, finally asked, "Jill, how did you come by that paperwork?"

"It was left on a desk in plain sight. I put it in my pocket."

"When was that?"

She took a deep breath before answering his question. "It was while I was being held captive during the second year. I don't have an exact date for you. We weren't given access to calendars or clocks. I do know it was during the winter because the people who were coming in were wearing heavy coats."

"What other information do you have from that time?" he asked in a gentle voice.

"That will need to come on the stand. You might want to ask for specifics on Billings and his dealings through the club. Follow up on every bit I give you with more questions. You might want to question me about the women who worked there. A few on the drugs being sold in the club might get you more information than you would expect." She stopped before saying, "You'll want to know about the clientele who came to use me and what they talked about, thinking I was too drugged to remember anything."

It had been hard to say, but he needed to know. There was a lot she had to give them.

"Anything else, Jill?" Williams asked, keeping his voice neutral and his eyes on her.

"Billings has many connections. You'll need what I have on those. I have names, dates, conversations, and the names of the ringleaders. It wasn't Billings. He was upper level but not the top."

"Who's on top?" Williams inquired, leaning forward and placing his arm on the table, focusing on her.

"That you'll get if I live until the trial. If I don't, you have enough to put those you have away."

"Why won't you tell us now?"

She met his gaze. "I'll not get you or the others here killed by telling you now. If you don't know, they'll leave you alone."

"How will they know you didn't tell us?"

"Trust me, they'll be informed I haven't told you much of anything, only directing you in what questions to ask. If you aren't there, I know a couple in this room who'll ask those questions."

Williams sat back and scanned the others in the room. He now knew there was a mole in the room, and it wasn't the new guy. They had neutralized only one of the prosecutors. She gave no indication which one it was of the six other lawyers in the room. She wanted Williams there because he was superb at asking the right questions.

"Anything else I need to know?"

"Just give Wyatt twenty-four hours to produce me."

"I don't like that you aren't giving me the information I need," Williams stated with a frown.

He hadn't gotten as much as he normally did. She knew what she was doing, and hoped Tom had picked up on what needed to happen once they left here.

"I'm sure you aren't happy with the lack of details. Your team needs to pay attention to every word I say and follow up with more questions on the little things. You'll appreciate the answers you'll get. I spent three years gathering information, hoping I would live long enough to use it. If I make it to the trial, don't hesitate to be rough in the questions and extract everything I know. Whatever you do, don't back off. I'm a witness. You need to ask those hard questions and make me answer them."

"Jill, are you sure? I know you had a hard time after they found you."

"I'm sure. Afterward I may crash, but I'll recover. Trust me, you'll want every bit of the information I gathered while there. If you back off, the big guys will walk. Treat me as you would any hostile witness, because I may get hostile on the stand this time."

She stood, indicating she was finished. They had what they needed to build the case.

"It's been a pleasure, gentlemen. The one who's passing information had better watch his back. He'll find out he isn't getting paid enough for what he's doing. Also, I hope he likes cages, because that's where he and his partner will end up."

She turned and left. Oh yeah. He would go to jail. One simple question would put him there, and she had just given them what to ask her. She knew her code was caught. The two who were her friends wouldn't back off when questioning her even though it involved colleagues.

Tom took her back to the secure elevator and hit the button for the garage. He hadn't spoken since they had entered the building. When the door whooshed open, he checked the garage before guiding her to a different car than the one they had arrived in earlier. He opened the back door and used his hand to show he wanted her to hide. She knelt on the floor and pulled the blanket on the seat over her. She noticed the hat he put on before starting the car.

He drove to the upper deck and parked, then guided her to a different car. When he slid in behind the wheel, he changed hats and pasted on a mustache. She took the bag he handed her. It contained a sweater which she pulled on over her shirt before putting on a black wig. At the bottom of the bag was some makeup. Using the visor mirror, she expertly applied the makeup, turning her into an unhappy teenager in partial Goth makeup.

Tom glanced at her and shook his head before starting the car. She grinned at him, aware it was her type of car from the sound of the engine. Hoping he was a good driver, she put her barefoot on the dash. He glared at her. She returned his glare, playing to the multiple cameras as they pulled out of the garage.

He began to chide her on what she had done in the meeting. "Jill, you could have been more cooperative in there."

"No, I couldn't. I want Williams to do the questioning. I don't know the new guy and if he isn't one to pick up on the nuances, he'll stop before he gets all the information."

"He won't stop, trust me on that one. Plus, he caught onto what you were saying within the first few minutes. Even though he didn't take notes, he can repeat exactly what you said. He'll analyze it and go to the right people with what you gave him. I wouldn't be surprised if he didn't break your code and now knows who, what, when, and where."

"As long as he knows who the right ones are. You don't know who the mole is and I do. If they ask the right question, they'll get both names, connections, and even payoffs. I would bet that Williams has a good idea who the two men are based on what I said before I left."

"Let's see if I have them. Nelson and McElroy."

"Bingo," was all she said.

"I take it you have the proof that ties them into this."

"Yes."

"Jill, you're playing with the big guns. You better have airtight proof."

"I do. They'll dismiss my threat because neither one of them understands what I do or how I operate. Only two people there know. One is Williams."

"The other is Helms." Tom stated as he turned onto a side street.

"You sure about that?" she asked.

"Positive. Other than the new guy, he's the only one who knows some of my part in this other than Williams."

She pursed her lips as she stared at her foot.

"Tom, don't trust Helms."

Meeting his direct stare, she kept her face neutral as real fear whizzed through her. "Does he know the planned spots for you to hide me?"

"No."

"Will you stake your life on that?"

Tom didn't answer. He turned back to the road. "Talk to me, Jill. I can't keep you safe if I don't know what you're trying to tell me."

"Don't trust Helms. How much clearer can I be?"

"Shit!" he commented as he hit the steering wheel with his hand, face pulled into a worried scowl. He shook his head, having a hard time with her revelation. His voice held anger when he said, "Good thing I don't give but bits and pieces to them. No wonder he was asking for more than I gave him."

"Like Whitey. The minute he started asking questions, I clammed up. Notice Williams didn't push. He accepted I wouldn't give him any more than I had given him and he knew why. If you were watching Helms, he was taking copious notes. Those notes will end up with the defense I'm sure."

"So," he drawled, "How many are there in the office you can trust?"

"Good question. Williams is one. He's a total good guy."

"Who else?"

Hesitating, she figured he needed to know, so he didn't get them killed. "Phillips, Levine, and Kolinsky."

"That's it?" he asked in surprise.

"That's it. Like I said, I don't know the new guy, so it remains to be seen which side he's on."

"How did you find out who not to trust?"

"Easy. You give them one piece of information only they know. If it ends up in the wrong hands, you can't trust them. What do you know about the new guy?"

"I know I can trust him with my life."

"How?"

"He's my brother."

She stared at him, finding it unbelievable they were brothers, before stating, "Hopefully you're on good terms with him."

Tom chuckled. "The best. We have different last names as he uses our mother's maiden name to keep us from being connected. Williams knows that little tidbit, but he's the only one other than Shaun."

"Kolinsky picked up on what I gave him. He'll pass information to one of the creeps and we'll see where it goes."

"What did you give him?" Tom questioned, giving her a confused look.

"A specific hideout, but we won't be there. The agents who'll be there, will get them to sing after they fall into the trap. It'll lead right back to the one. Now you know why I give nothing to anyone, including those I trust."

"Who do you trust outside of the feds?"

"Wyatt, Sam, Brad, and Ryan. You're still on

probation."

"That's a mighty small list."

"When your life is on the line, you better have full confidence in those who hold your life in their hands. Yes, it's a small list. There are a couple of others I can call on for help, but only for a very short time. They would give me up if the price was right and I know it."

"What about Billy?" he probed.

She shook her head. "I wouldn't ever put him in that position. He's a good friend, but I'd never put his life on the line."

"Jill, that one statement gave me the one thing I wasn't sure about. Few operatives have that much integrity. Many will put their friends in jeopardy and think nothing about it. Like you, I only use those who know what I do and know they may get heat for helping me. After tonight, you choose where to go next and how to get there."

"Got it. I like this getup. It'll work for tomorrow. I have the perfect person, and he'll love that I'm using him."

"And why would he love it?"

"He's into intrigue and espionage. It's a game, a dangerous one, but one he loves to play, and he does a good job at it."

"Have you used him before?"

"Not for something like this, but yes, I've used him. He hid me for a week from Wyatt, and you know how good he is at finding someone."

"Yeah, I know. He found me in forty-eight hours when no one else could."

"You'll like him."

"You sure about that?"

"Yes. He's not a boyfriend, so chill."

"Just another friend?"

"No," she said with a laugh.

"Okay, if he isn't a boyfriend or just a friend, then family?"

"You tell me when you meet him."

"I swear, girl, you're giving me gray hairs by the minute."

Merrily laughing, she didn't give him any more information. It was going to be fun to see how Brad, her brother, would hide her this time.

Chapter 14

FRIENDS AND FAMILY

Tom drove to an old section of Pompano Beach. He turned into the driveway of an old house and pulled into the open two-car garage. The garage door closed once the car was parked and the engine shut off. Jill exited the car, scanning the cluttered garage to locate the person who had closed the door. A tall thin woman with a glossy cap of dark brown hair was standing in the doorway to the house, a gun aimed at her. She didn't lower it until Tom turned and faced her.

"It's about time you got here. I was beginning to think you'd gone somewhere else without calling," she drawled, leaning against the doorframe.

"You know I would have called if my plans had changed, Sarah."

With an exaggerated sigh, the woman frowned. "It's a hell of a way to get a visit from you."

"Sorry, sis, my schedule has been hectic for the past six months."

"Right. Come on in."

Sarah turned and entered the house, leaving them to follow. Tom retrieved the valises from the backseat and nodded for her to take the lead. When she stepped into the kitchen, her eyes widened, recognizing the big man seated at the kitchen table. A grin lit his face upon seeing her. He stood and Jill ran and leaped into his open arms to give him a hug. The man held her as if she was a small child, planting a kiss on the offered cheek. Grinning up at the big man, who was a good friend and a great working partner, Jill clung to one of the few people she trusted outside of Wyatt and Sam at the agency.

"Cricket! What a surprise. How're you doing? And just how did you end up in Tom's care?" the man rattled off, continuing to hold her with a big grin.

Jill patted his cheek while returning the grin, then gave the big man, who made her feel like a tiny child, another hug.

"I'm hanging in there. Tom's providing protection for now. You know how it is with me and getting into these messes."

"Sure do. It's been what, six months?"

"Yep. I never got to thank you for getting me out of that scrape. They're serving three to five years on drug charges."

Sarah interrupted the greeting, standing with crossed arms watching without a smile yet not frowning. "Okay, Cletus, I take it this is Cricket. Now how did you end up working with her?"

"Well, I met this little lady on a case I was working for Wyatt. She got into a jam with a local gang when she walked smack dab into a drug deal I was observing while looking for a piece of slime who kept slipping away from me. I pretended to be her bodyguard when I recognized her from the office. She politely asked several questions, then told the leader to hide the baggie of smack if he wanted to stay out of jail before walking away. I swear the dealer and buyer stood there with their mouths hanging open for a good minute before moving."

Jill chuckled then imparted, "What Cletus left out was how we were looking for the same person and ended up finding him later that night by working together. We ran into each other on several other cases and at the office."

Smiling up at the big man, Jill added, "Cletus reminds me of Brad, a big teddy bear who treats me like his kid sister. He and Sam are always teasing the hell out of me." She turned to Sarah with a smile. "I take it you're the wife he keeps talking about who's this awesome lady he would go to the ends of the earth for."

Tom stifled a laugh while Cletus blushed, lowering her to her feet. Sarah shook her head, her lips turning up in a grin while gazing at her spouse. "You have the damnedest friends, Cletus," she declared before turning back to the food cooking on the stove.

"Hey, Wyatt made me promise to keep an eye on her after finding out about me playing backup for her. He didn't explain why, but she's Wyatt's brat, not mine."

"I'm not a brat," Jill snapped.

"Yes, you are, and you know it," Cletus stated with a grin.

Tom intoned, "Sarah, meet Jill, and yes, she's Wyatt's brat once removed."

Cletus's eyes widened, staring down at her once it

registered what Tom had said. "You're Wyatt's granddaughter?"

Jill sent an icy glare at Tom before saying, "If you tell anyone else, I swear you'll live to regret it."

"That explains everything. No wonder he's so concerned with you out in the field. It also explains why he left in such a hurry the other day after talking to you on the phone, then returned swearing up a storm yesterday."

"Wyatt does tend to be protective of her," Tom stated, grinning at the understatement.

Cletus glanced at Sarah before saying, "I understand. I can see her taking over someday with the way she handles the business end of the agency."

She bit her lip before saying, "Not for a long time. Wyatt still has more to teach me."

Sarah laughed. "Girl, you could run the agency and not one person would notice the difference, other than the lack of swearing when reporting in by phone. From what I've heard, there can't be much more for Wyatt to teach you."

Jill turned to study Sarah. "I don't remember meeting you, but I remember your reports. Sarah V. Rhoades. You do good work."

"I seldom go to the office, but I'm surprised at not meeting you in the ten years I've worked for Wyatt. Over the years, I've seen your name on various reports and notices. I remember you running the agency when Wyatt was sick with the flu. You did such a good job, he was a bear for a week after returning with practically nothing to do."

With a nonchalant shrug, Jill stated, "Hey, someone had to step in and run the place. Sam didn't want to make any decisions. If I hadn't stepped up, when Wyatt came back it would have been a two-week mess to clean up."

Sarah grinned before turning to Tom. "Show Jill where she'll be sleeping. Supper will be ready in a few minutes."

Following Tom, she wondered what he was thinking concerning her and Cletus, who was her backup on several cases. The large man was that big brother you love to have around. With his sense of humor, he was fun to work with, plus was an excellent PI. What she wasn't willing to share with Sarah was how the two of them spent forty-eight hours in the back of a van on stakeout, watching cameras and listening to bugs and phone taps. During that time, Cletus had teased her unmercifully and nicknamed her Cricket, saying she was always chirping the same tune, just like a cricket.

Tom put her valise on the bed. "I never associated you with Cletus's Cricket. We've had many a laugh over the stories concerning your daring feats, which always seemed to work out. He's said more than once that you're better than Wyatt, and Wyatt knows it without being aware of the relationship."

"Cletus is fun to work with. He's got this great sense of humor and is extremely capable when the shit hits the fan." She avoided commenting on her being better than Wyatt. She wasn't better, just different.

"Yeah, he is. Sarah is just as good. That's the reason we're here tonight. They know what to expect, but I won't put them in jeopardy past tonight, so your friend better be ready tomorrow."

"Speaking of that, I need to write out the message. He needs to know it's me and what I need."

"You aren't calling him?"

"Nope. Not taking any chances even though he's a PI too. We've worked together, so he'll recognize from the code I'm in trouble and what is needed. There will be a plan in place by tomorrow."

"Okay. Let's go eat. I'm starving." Tom guided her put of the room.

Upon rejoining Cletus and Sarah for the meal, from Sarah's actions, Cletus had explained their working relationship. Jill listened as the three exchanged stories from various cases while eating. Each story gave her more insight into the family dynamics, and Tom's legendary ability of catching criminals.

The fun lasted until Tom said, "Jill, you need to eat more than a few bites."

"I'm not hungry," she told him, creating a pregnant pause in the conversation.

The food was excellent, but with the worry of having missed something earlier during her meeting with the prosecutor, she was too tense to eat. While staring at the nearly full plate, she replayed the meeting in her mind from facial expressions to body movements, along with what was said by each person. She sucked in a lungful of air when what she had missed stood out like a zebra in a herd of horses. Williams had requested information, and a name based on Tom's brother's information. Since their first case, he never asked for specifics—ever!

The fork in her hand clattered on the plate before turning to Tom, fear on her face.

"Tom, other than Williams knowing the part you played in ferreting out the corrupt deputies, have you had any other contact with him on this case?"

"Minimal, why?"

"I now know who the top mole is."

Tom froze, studying her, then relaxed before stating, "About time."

Jill's mouth formed a straight line. In an attempt to keep calm, she sucked in a deep breath, then slowly let it out. Anger and fear whipped around inside while reviewing the mishaps which had occurred over the past few years when a case touched on this group. Every last one of those hiccups pointed to him being the one pulling the strings.

She met Tom's gaze. "It all fits. Fuck!" Her teeth gritted as she blew out another big breath. "Cletus, make sure you go to the office tomorrow and warn Wyatt. Williams will try to get me out of hiding before the trial.

Tell him to contact Shaun or Kolinsky. I can't call my contact as they'll have someone watching him and possibly have his phone tapped to pick up incoming numbers. My cellphone number would be tagged. Let me write the message for one of you to make the call."

"Why?" Tom asked.

"To decrease the risk of being discovered, that's why. I need a paper and pen."

Sarah slid a pad and pencil across the table, her face grim, aware how their part in hiding her just became more dangerous.

Jill wrote: *Brad, how are you doing? It's Wilson. (wait for response) Rasta told me to call you. I ran into him two days ago. He has four or five items he wanted to discuss with you, but couldn't wait around because he had a date. He wants to meet you tomorrow but needs a where and when. (wait for response and remember what he says word for word) Great. I'll let him know. We need to stay in touch more often. (Remember exactly what he says.) Will do. Talk at you later. (hang up)*

When done, she handed the paper to Cletus. "You'd be the best. Remember word for word what he says. If you mess up, I'll miss him."

"Tom should do this," Cletus stated, not taking the paper.

"No, you're the best actor I know. Just write what he says if you can't remember it. I need it word for word because if it isn't, I'll mess up the meet and might walk into a trap."

Cletus stared at her for a few seconds. "Okay, I need the number."

Sarah handed her the house extension. "Make sure to delete this number," Jill commanded, punching in the numbers for Brad's personal cell phone instead of the one for the agency.

With the first ring, Jill handed the phone to Cletus. When Brad answered, Cletus read what was written, sounding natural in the part of Wilson. Using the pad Sarah had given her, he wrote what Brad was saying then laughed and read the next line. Again, he wrote what Brad said. After reading the last lines of the message, he hung up.

She took the paper to read what he had written. "Okay, we'll be meeting him at noon. We'll take the bus to the rendezvous."

Cletus lifted his eyebrows before saying, "Tell Brad hi for me. He better not have lost a damn thing in keeping you hidden. I remember Wyatt cursing us out for not finding you when he hid you during those hide-and-seek exercises."

"He'll keep me undercover until Wyatt contacts me." At least she hoped that would be the case. This scenario was what the practice hide-and-seek had been preparing them for—keeping her alive when there was nowhere else to go.

Cletus leaned against the wall before telling Tom, "Brad will work wonders. He has this devious mind and would make a better criminal than Jill. During the last exercise, she was out in plain sight and not one person saw her. I know it taught me how to effectively search for a person, yet none of us found her, including your men, and they had all these resources."

"Considering we need to disappear until the trial is under way, I hope he gets the same results this time." Tom peered at her, a crease between his eyes. "What's your plan concerning Williams?"

"Not sure. Depends on if he stays in character or goes out. If he steps out of character, I'll meet with the judge and two of the top guys I know in the FBI and US Marshal's office. If he doesn't think I'll fucking turn on him, he's fucking nuts."

"She's Wyatt's brat," Sarah stated with a chuckle.

"Sorry," Jill apologized, feeling the heat creeping up her neck. "I guess being around him has made me somewhat less lady-like. Having a few other friends on the crude side doesn't help."

"Not a problem. I still can't believe you're his granddaughter. The only things you inherited from him is your mind and that hair color." Sarah was smiling.

"I take after my grandmother. Other than my hair color, I'm a clone of her."

Cletus sobered as he stared at her, eyes widening. "My

God. He has her picture on the desk and on the wall in the penthouse. I'll bet he's had a damn good laugh over us being so unobservant."

"More than once. He's still waiting for someone to notice. Even with me standing behind him and the picture visible, three of the guys who knew Grandmother didn't notice I'm the spitting image of her. Wyatt even looked back and grinned at me during that meeting."

"I guess there's no faking it to get the bonus, is there?" Cletus questioned with a chuckle.

"No, you can't, and neither can Tom. Just don't pass it around. If someone guesses, that's okay, but he wants our relationship kept low key."

"Understood. At least when he's bitching about you, I'll know what the damn problem is now."

They sat around the table and talked for what was left of the evening. Sarah and Cletus both had a good sense of humor. Tom said little, watching her joking around with his family.

Upon noticing it was almost midnight, she said, "It's past my bedtime,"

Sarah gave her a hug when she stood up from the table where they had been sitting. "Jill, I can see why Cletus is so taken with you. Once this is over, you better set up a get-together outside of work so we can get to know each other."

"I'll do my best. It's been a long time since I've had so much fun."

"I'm glad we could help. You better come back to us, Cricket," Cletus told her before kissing her cheek.

"I will. You take care of yourself and Sarah."

"I have to, or Tom will finish me off. He's as protective of Sarah as Wyatt is you."

"She's something special so I don't blame him."

Cletus gave her a hug. There was worry in his eyes, understanding the increased risk to her regarding Williams playing both sides.

While waiting for Tom to finish his good nights to Sarah and Cletus, she deliberated on him staying with her. With the new developments, she could be in hiding for as long as a year or more. Williams would delay the trial to allow the assassins time to find her, hoping to prevent her from testifying. If that wasn't working, he had the authority to subpoena her to show up at his office.

When Tom joined her, he needed no invitation to follow her into the bedroom and close the door. She wanted to bounce a few things off him.

"Talk to me, Jill," he requested before she could speak.

"All the odd puzzle pieces fell into place. It explains the last three times I had to hide. Williams will delay this trial, hoping I can be eliminated. There's nothing I can do because I don't have the trail that leads to him."

"Don't worry, I have that trail. We intercepted a message sent to Billings five years ago, and have gotten a few more since then. I'll alert the team that we're in trouble and why. Brad better be as good at hiding you as everyone says he is."

Jill shook her head, disgust showing on her face. "Why didn't I see it when Leroy was on trial for murder with the negation of my testimony?"

"Because he didn't make a mistake back then. He did this time."

"Yeah, he did. He asked the wrong question, not once, but twice."

"Well, at least we're on the same page now. I was thinking I'd made a mistake in believing you were head and shoulders above the rest."

"Thanks a lot," she snapped.

With a chuckle, he encircled her with his arms. "Honey, you're the most intelligent PI I've ever met. That pretty head has tons of information I want spouted where it will mean the most. I'm going to generate pressure from above and see what falls out on the bottom."

"Look, I don't want to die, so don't turn up the heat unless it can be handled without putting me in further jeopardy."

Tom patted her cheek, a grin on his face. "Now I bet that's a first for you, but I have information you don't. We need to get the high-hanging fruit out of the tree to get things moving at the bottom. Trust me. My friends are up in the stratosphere of several agencies. They'll come through to keep you safe." He paused, brows furrowed and lips pursed. "Can you get a message to Wyatt?"

"Sure, but it needs to be short to stay on the safe side."

"Just tell him 'Operation Revere.' He'll know what it means, what to do, and who to notify."

"Tom, don't make Wyatt a target."

"He won't be. This was a contingency plan and with what's happening, I believe it's time to put it into action."

"Okay."

"Now, my dear," he commanded.

"As soon as you leave," she said, not willing to reveal where her communicator was hidden.

"Okay, I'll see you in the morning."

"Right," she answered, her thoughts flipping back to Williams.

Before she could turn away, Tom lifted her head, giving her a kiss, which made sure she would be thinking of him for the night. With a wink, he tapped her nose with a finger then left.

Jill prayed he wasn't lying to her. If he was, both of their lives would be forfeited. Retrieving the communicator from her purse, she opened the channel. Wyatt answered within seconds.

"Jill?"

"Operation Revere," she said and signed off. God, she hoped Tom knew what he was doing.

Chapter 15

BRAD

Jill awakened to her communicator's beep.

"Here," she answered, her voice thick with sleep.

"Revere is riding," Wyatt said before cutting the communication.

The room was dark, meaning it was still the early hours of the morning. She needed to inform Tom that whatever he had set in motion had begun.

When she tapped on Tom's bedroom door, it opened within seconds. Either he had been waiting for her knock or he was working and close to the door. The attire of jeans and nothing else she could see had her pausing. The man's muscular bare chest made her want to touch him to see if he was real. She dragged her eyes to his face to impart the message from Wyatt.

"Revere is riding," she said, hesitating to allow him time to tell her what was happening.

A nod and a hand smoothing his rumpled hair wasn't the reaction she was expecting. "Thanks. Go back to bed. It's too early to get up."

With a sigh, she pivoted to return to her room, disappointed, yet expecting the dismissal. A hand gently touching her arm held her in place. She rotated her head to him, waiting to see what he wanted.

"Rescue is on the way. Until they arrive and things are back on track, we need to stay hidden. I can't tell you anything more."

Her shoulders lifted in a quick shrug before lamenting, "I hope someone will ask those questions like Williams would have. If they don't, the top guys will walk."

"Oh, someone will. Prepare to have one tough prosecutor tear into you. He won't stop until all the questions are answered, extracting every detail contained in that brain of yours. He may be young, but he's smart and skilled enough to become the assistant to a special prosecutor. The information you shared reached those able to put it to use, and the fallout isn't pretty."

A concern popped up with his information. It meant he was communicating with someone and that alone could enable the hunters to find them.

"Your communications had better be as secure as mine. The syndicate knows you're with me."

"They are. It'll take weeks to track just one to the city."

A sinking feeling ran through her. "That's what you think. I have a guy who can pinpoint your exact location in minutes if the signal lasts thirty seconds."

Tom's brows drew together, eyes boring into her. "You sure about that?"

"Very. He's the one who set up what I'm using. Ten seconds or less is the time frame for someone to lock onto the signal. Because it isn't telephonic, the person attempting to track it must catch the signal on whichever bandwidth it started with, then figure out how to follow which band it hops too after ten seconds."

With a frown, Tom stated, "Let me guess. Lester set this up."

"Nope. Lester's good, but this guy is way better."

"I'll strangle Walter if he gave you what I think he did."

Jill faced him, arms crossed, and eyes narrowed. "You leave Walter alone. He still owes me."

Tom reached out and patted her cheek with a gentle smile. "Not to worry, beautiful. Just keep what he gave you to use well hidden. No one else needs access to what you're using."

"I'm not worried. No one will find it."

"Bet you I can," he challenged with a grin.

She chuckled. Without a clue, he wouldn't find it. "Bet you can't."

"I'll show you in the morning," he stated with confidence.

She returned to her room and placed the communicator in her purse. This would be fun. Tom had watched more than once as she used it, not aware it was a dual-purpose item.

Jill was up and dressed early. Tom joined her on the landing, a grin in place before following her downstairs to eat. The grin expressed confidence in finding the communicator. They placed their valises on the living room sofa before moving to the kitchen. Jill emptied her purse on the table. Cletus and Sarah watched Tom sift through the things most women carry in a purse.

Cletus remained quiet for a minute before asking, "What're you looking for?"

"An object which isn't what it appears to be."

"Such as?" Cletus questioned, studying the contents spread across the table.

Jill watched as the men searched for the communication device among the items. There was a checkbook, a wallet, a brush, lip balm, and an umbrella in one pile. The second pile contained two pens, a pad of paper, a package of bandages, an open pack of gum and Mentos, two pairs of sunglasses, a dollar twenty-three in coins, her keys, and a gun. Tom lifted the item he was searching for several times, not recognizing what it was.

With the challenge from last night, Jill wasn't going to give them a clue to the device's location. The communicator was so well hidden it had to be found first. Then the person needed to figure out how to open it. If someone got that far, the next problem was getting it to function.

"When you tire of trying to find it, just dump the stuff into my purse," she said before pouring a cup of coffee.

Sarah asked, "What is he looking for?"

"My communications device."

Sarah joined the men, and like them, she lifted the communicator before putting it back on the table. All three gravitated to the pens, but they were wrong. If it was a pen, it would have been lost a long time ago. They gave up after another five minutes and returned everything to her purse.

Jill held back a giggle before telling Tom, "I told you last night you couldn't find it. I promise you, it's in there."

"Where?" he asked, right eyebrow raised.

"That's my secret. If you can't find it, nobody else will."

"I need to have a talk with Walter," Tom groused, admitting defeat.

Sitting opposite him, Jill imparted, "You wouldn't find the one Wyatt has either. It can go off and you still won't find it, just like mine."

"So, what would upset you the most if I took it and kept it?" Tom inquired with a grin.

It wouldn't hurt to go along with the probing questions. Her answers wouldn't help him find it.

"Well, let's see. My wallet because of the two credit cards and debit card in it. The checkbook I could live without. I need my sunglasses because my eyes are sensitive to the sun. My brush since my hair is always a mess. Both pens, which I use a lot, and the umbrella because I hate getting wet. I can live without the rest of the stuff, including the gun."

Tom shook his head. "I still can't figure out which one of those items holds a communicator."

He turned to Sarah. "You're a female. Which one do you think it is?"

Jill waited for her answer. Sarah laughed. "Men! I'm not answering. Even if I'm right, you won't get it. We women deserve our secrets."

Sarah winked at her. Jill rearranged the purse so the gun could be easily accessed. Sarah was right. The men wouldn't get it. The one item most women carried in their purse was one item most men would overlook and allow a woman to keep.

As they ate breakfast, Tom stayed silent while the rest of them talked. She knew he was still attempting to decipher which item held the communicator. Cletus hadn't given up either, attempting to extract a clue with various questions.

"Jill, if I kept the umbrella, how upset would you be?"

"Totally pissed if it rained."

"What about the brush?"

"What do you think?" she retorted.

"Yeah. You women and your hair things."

"Bingo!" Tom crowed, daring her to disagree.

"What?" Cletus questioned, brows drawn together.

Tom sat back with a grin, before asking, "What do all women carry that wouldn't raise any suspicions, and no man would normally take from them?"

"A brush or comb," Cletus stated before adding, "Damn it, Cricket. That's not fair."

"If it's in there, how do you get it through security?" Tom asked.

"If it's in there, it would appear to be part of the brush. It's been through security multiple times and hasn't been found yet."

Tom grinned and let the subject drop. "Okay, you mentioned taking a bus. How are we getting to the meeting point without getting caught?"

"By making everyone see us," she stated with a big grin. The confused looks from the others had her giggling.

"Explain that, please," Tom requested, his fingers drumming on the table.

"We're going as a Goth couple. They'll see us but won't recognize what they're seeing."

Tom quickly stated, "There's no way anyone will believe I'm a Goth."

Sarah patted him on the head. "You will become a really nice Goth guy. Let's go. You'll need at least an hour to get ready. This is going to be fun. My prim-and-proper brother a Goth."

As Sarah was helping her brother get ready, Jill painted her nails a dark purple from the array of polishes Sarah had in her wardrobe room. When her nails were dry, she applied a pale foundation, then rimmed her eyes in black with designs at the outer corners.

Sarah had a walk-in closet of costumes. Among the items was a short black corset, which fit even though she was at least four sizes smaller than Sarah. She located a skirt with a drawstring at the waist. It was long and would hide her tennis shoes. Because her feet were smaller than Sarah's, she couldn't wear any of the shoes or boots in the closet.

From the wigs, Jill chose a short black blunt cut. The last things needed were the black lipstick, changing the shape of her lips, and a fake nose ring. No one would recognize her, including Wyatt and Sam. Brad would see through the disguise because he was expecting a couple in unusual attire.

Brad was a master at how to hide in plain sight. The trick was to be seen but not recognized. Everyone would notice the Goth couple, but wouldn't see the people underneath the makeup and clothes. The majority wouldn't pay close attention due to fear of their unusual appearance. It was how he had hidden her several times prior to this. Everyone had noticed her but didn't recognize her.

Tom was this fantastic-looking Goth when he joined

them. The black clothes, spiked hair, nailed neck choker, and wrist bands, along with the makeup, changed him from a clean-cut man into this dangerous-looking cult figure. From the fit of his shirt and pants, he had to have clothes here to use when staying with his sister. The form-fitting leather pants and knee boots made her wonder about his private life.

Cletus laughed upon seeing Tom in the doorway. "Too bad I can't take a picture of this. I wouldn't recognize you if I saw you on the street. Love the black nails, by the way. You two will get a lot of attention while scaring the locals."

"I'm just glad Brad will expect the unusual to show up," Jill stated.

"Why?" Tom asked.

"*Rasta* means disguise. *Wilson* is me. *Had to leave for a date* means I need to hide until court with no date set. The *stay in touch* means I'm in trouble. When I added *more often*, it means multiple hunters."

"That code is great. I was wondering what you were communicating. So where are we meeting?"

"The arts district. We'll fit right in at the café. It's a hangout for the weirdoes of the area."

"I hope you know which buses to take," Tom stated, revealing he didn't use the buses in the county.

"I do. We'll need cash for the fare and transfer."

"Not a problem. Do you have a credit card that isn't traceable just in case?"

"Does Carter have pills?" she quipped.

Tom grinned. "Okay, let's get this show on the road."

Jill turned to Sarah and Cletus. "We need a way of getting to Atlantic Avenue without creating too much of a scene."

Tom chuckled. "That I can do." He headed in the direction of the back door.

Cletus pulled her into a hug before she could follow Tom. "Cricket, be careful and take care of Tom."

With a giggle, she said, "He's supposed to be taking care of me."

"Somehow, I think the opposite is true."

Cletus was right. The roles had changed. She was now in the leader role.

She followed Tom down a narrow alley to a deserted residential street. Keeping to side streets, they arrived at the main thoroughfare without meeting anyone along the way.

At the bus stop on the corner, Jill looked at the route numbers on the sign, locating the bus they needed to take to connect with the bus to the arts district. Tom took his cue from her in appearing disinterested in the people who stared at them while they sat on the bench, waiting for the bus.

When the bus arrived, the other passengers, who had drifted to the bus stop, let them on first. On the way to the back of the bus, they passed one of Wyatt's men, who didn't recognize her. Tom hadn't said a word since leaving the house. He sat beside her, ignoring the stares of the other passengers, imitating her actions.

A group of noisy young men got on two stops later and took the seats in front of them. They made derogatory comments and veiled threats until Jill faced the leader with a glare. The men quieted at her direct gaze. She returned to staring out the window, not wanting to miss their stop.

A few blocks later, she pulled the cord for the next stop. Two of the group of men stood, attempting to prevent her and Tom from leaving the bus. Not speaking, Jill again gave the leader a direct stare, daring him with the look and crossed arms to continue bothering her. The men moved, allowing her and Tom to exit.

They crossed the street to the bus stop there to catch to bus to the arts district. No one was at this stop. They sat partially hidden in the small shelter.

Tom questioned, "What did you do to make them back off?"

"You should know what I did. It's basic self-defense. When I faced the leaders, they knew I would recognize them. My lack of fear meant I would be more of a problem than it was worth. If I was in my regular clothes, they would have sat in the front of the bus and not bothered us."

"Now why would they do that?"

"The leader and I had an altercation, and he doesn't

want to repeat that mistake."

"I see. You do have acquaintances in low places."

With a chuckle, she stated, "Those aren't lowlifes. They're just stupid kids. I'm acquainted with some real unsavory characters in places no lady ever goes."

The bus arrived before Tom could ask any further questions. It was over an hour before they arrived at the north end of the arts district. No one paid any attention to them ambling down the sidewalk, being only two of many dressed in unusual costumes. Jill stopped to examine various pieces of art. She remained impassive while examining the pieces which had drawn her attention.

Tom followed her, not speaking, as they slowly advanced along the street. There were various shops and warehouses holding galleries of sculptures, paintings, metalwork, quilts, jewelry, weaving, macramé, pottery, and other types of artistic works. It was an eclectic collection of artists and their works. A smattering of shoppers wove their way through the wares for sale.

At 11:45, they crossed the street to an art déco building painted in various tones of a mauve and pink. The sign proclaimed the premises contained "The Artist's Room." Upon entering the café, Jill led Tom to a small empty table on the right of the good-sized room.

There were groups of people talking at the larger tables. Brad was holding court at a table for six. Upon scanning the room, she noticed there were men who didn't belong here, and of those, there were two she recognized. Maybe she had made a mistake in involving Brad in her mess.

A waitress, dressed in tight jeans with multiple tears and cut to barely cover her lower torso came to the table to take their order. She wore a skimpy see through shirt and was sporting multiple piercings and tattoos, her head topped by multi-colored spiked hair. Jill ordered a drink for the two of them. Tom remained in character as the passive male, allowing her to control the situation.

When the waitress left, he studied Brad while drumming his fingers on the tabletop. "You neglected to say Brad was a young clone of Wyatt."

Jill was surprised he hadn't commented on the waitress. "I sort of guessed you'd be able to pick him out in a crowd. What's funny is how he's a well-known artist and lives in this area. It's a great cover for what he does for the agency."

They kept the conversation low so the patrons closest to them wouldn't overhear. Three people, and possibly more, sitting in the café would love to see her disappear without a trace. Then there were two from the agency, which meant Wyatt was providing coverage for Brad.

She slid a glance over to the large table where her oldest brother was talking to a couple. From the animation he was using in the conversation, he was talking art. Not only was he a well-known artist, but he was also an excellent salesman with the ability to read people like he would a book.

Their drinks came, garnering a raised eyebrow from Tom. She knew what he was thinking about the blood red fluid and was aware from the reaction he had little to no experience with the Goth culture. This was a normal drink for someone dressed in the vampire style of Goth as they were today. It resembled blood, but contained healthy vegetables and fruit. She took a sip of the drink and waited on Tom to try his. With his first sip, he winked at her instead of smiling or commenting.

They engaged in a discussion of various art forms while waiting. Tom was knowledgeable in many forms of art, but the discussion became interesting when it turned to favorite literary authors. Their tastes in literature were almost polar opposites.

Their drinks were close to being finished before Brad sent the couple he had been meeting with on their way. Yes, he resembled Wyatt. Both were big Scotsmen with reddish brown hair and a personality that attracted attention. While Wyatt had light brown eyes, Brad had the grass green eyes of their mother. The main difference was in their actions. Whereas Wyatt was crude and brusque, Brad was refined and quiet.

Regardless of his size, Brad could disappear in seconds and Jill had seen him do so on multiple occasions. It always amazed her how he would be one place one minute, then you couldn't find him the next. She had learned many of his tricks, but he was still the best, and was her only hope in making the trial. Without his ability to hide her, they would be located within days, if not hours.

Brad ignored them while socializing with several other men who had moved to his table as soon as the couple left. Brad, speaking in a normal voice, told the others he had an appointment and didn't want to be late. One man glanced over at them before saying something she couldn't hear. Brad laughed and replied to the man, a grin on his face after a quick look in their direction. Jill could only imagine what he had said about her and Tom when the others laughed at his comment.

With a grin, Brad stood and left the others to continue their conversation and came to where she and Tom were sitting. He pulled over a chair from the table beside them, placing it so the back was to the table, then sat, straddling the seat, his arms leaning on the back of the chair. "Wilson, I was beginning to think you weren't going to come to look at those paintings. You need to stay in touch more frequently if you expect me to have the types of works you like when you want them."

Tom roused, becoming assertive with Brad's statement. "I've been busy and needed to make sure we had the price you wanted for the one."

"Not a problem. I actually have four you might enjoy. One is a 4x3, another 2x3, and one is a nice square at 3x3. I believe you'll love the 5x4, which would be great over a divan or bed. The main theme for all of them is black and white, but one has a few splashes of red and another one has red with a few dots of other colors. I believe the last one would be something you'd enjoy. It's different and would make for a lot of discussion as to its meaning for each person."

Thinking about the information he had given her, Jill wondered which venue would give the best cover. Tom had no idea of what Brad had just communicated to her.

"I think I'd like to see the ones with some color. Depending on the overall theme, I believe they would be better than the total black and white. When is a good time to view these works?"

"Now. I'm free for the rest of the day if you have the time," Brad informed them.

She turned to Tom. "Wilson, you did say you were free until later this evening, right?"

"Yes. Spending time with the pieces would help me to decide which I could live with," Tom stated in a bored tone.

"Good, then let's go. Wilson, you forgot to tell me what a lovely lady you had found," Brad gushed while smiling at her.

Tom slid a glance in her direction. "She's the reason I haven't been around."

"I can see why. Right this way," Brad stated, his gaze

flicking over her as he ushered them out the door of the café toward his studio.

Jill noticed a man who had been in the café following them at a discreet distance. Brad kept up a running monologue, talking about the pictures he had to show them, ignoring the shadow. She or Tom commented at the appropriate places. As Brad talked, she was learning more about the four secure apartments he was proposing they use for the days he had given her.

Mulling over the information he was imparting, she tried to decide where to start. The five-day place was the best, but the sleeping arrangements were the problem. It meant sleeping in one room on a hide-a-bed. Not exactly what was needed with Tom going with her. Why was Brad was pushing it over the others?

Brad unlocked the door to the studio, which covered both floors of the large building. He lived in an apartment on the top floor, which was comprised of a living quarters with a glass atrium which provided natural light in which to paint. A big share of the bottom floor was storage for various pieces he had completed along with a showroom.

When they entered, she scanned the large warehouse-like room encompassing most of the bottom floor. It had changed little since she was last here, other than the specific works of art he had sitting around. A canvas on an easel, which he was working on based on the box of paints and cup of brushes nearby, drew her attention. The bright colors and sunlight reminded her of the garden at Wyatt's villa in Aruba.

Brad moved behind her, holding her against him. "After I got the call last night, I became inspired to paint that for you. It's how I see you. Full of light and beauty."

Jill rotated to face him, her arms going around his waist. "Brad, why didn't you come?"

He was aware the question was referring to the family vacation. "I had a fish on the line. I couldn't leave them hanging for a week."

"What's with all the rats hanging about?" she questioned, her head tilted back so she could see his face.

"They're looking for the food. My instructions are to keep them hungry."

"You had better, because this time there'll be little chance of stopping them before they eat it all."

"I know," Brad answered with a sigh. "Let me show you the two pictures I have in reserve for you upstairs."

He guided them to the circular staircase leading to the second floor. She and Tom followed him through the warren of rooms on the upper floor before entering a soundproofed music room. He opened a hidden door in the wall containing high-end sound equipment to reveal a small room.

After they entered the hidden room, he closed the door and turned on white noise before motioning for her to sit on the couch. Brad stood, looking down at her, brows drawn together. "Okay, enough with the code talk, Jill. Why the intense heat? I haven't had so many on me since your rescue." His voice was sharp and filled with worry.

After scooting back on the large couch, she drew her legs up and crossed them to sit Indian style. Brad was the one person, other than Wyatt, to whom she couldn't lie. Lowering her head, she played with her fingers, attempting to decide how much information he needed to keep her safe. First, he needed the basics.

"The search for me will become intense until the trial. If they find me, they'll kill me on sight. It started at the resort when I found Knight murdered on the shore of the lake, then another couple dead the next day. It's all tied into the case I was working on for Wyatt where the seventeen-year-old was being held for ransom. I found the girl, but it all led to Billings."

"The heat wouldn't be this intense for that, so what else aren't you telling me?"

With a side glance at Tom, she returned her gaze to her hands, blinking back tears. He would learn a few new things.

"It was a setup. There were a bunch of dirty law officers. Tom and his group stopped them, but it all led to Billings. I gave Tom the paperwork I had, and he obtained a warrant to raid the club and brothel. I got to clap the cuffs on Billings. He threatened to see me dead, only it isn't him who wants me dead. It's his bosses."

Brad squatted in front of her, holding her hands to stop the nervous fingers. She raised her head and stared into his eyes as tears flowed in rivulets down her cheeks. Her stupidity was putting her favorite brother in the line of fire, along with her grandfather and anyone else who was in contact with her.

"Sis, I know there's more. Who are you really hiding from? I don't believe it's Billings."

She stared at his big hands engulfing hers. Her grip on his fingers tightened until the whites of her knuckles showed. He didn't move, awaiting the rest of the information needed to keep her alive.

"Williams is working for them. He made a mistake during the meeting and will hold off the trial so I'll be found. He's done it before. This time, he'll delay until forced to accept a date, wanting me dead because he has to assume I caught his error."

"How did he give himself away?"

"Asked for the names of the top guys, wanting to verify if I had it correct. He also wanted the proof. I didn't give him either, but now he knows, if I have it, his days are numbered along with four others."

"The rest, Jillian," Brad demanded.

She cried with fear for her brother, because once she told him, he would be in as much danger as her and Tom. She had a choice. Not tell him, and hope and pray he could hide her and Tom while staying alive himself. Or she could tell him who the bosses were, and maybe he could use the information to save them and himself. Neither option was good.

Tom took a seat beside her, turning her head with gentle fingers so she was facing him. "Jill, we're already major targets. We need the names of those hunting us so we know who to look for if Brad is to keep you alive."

He was right. In the soft voice of a terrified little girl, she stated, "Russian mafia. The top man here is Franko with Bobkin and Billings under him. They will use the Russian assassins from the club."

Brad's sharp intake of breath had the tears falling faster in fear and shame. Tom pulled her close to him, holding her head on his shoulder with a gentle hand.

"Brad?" Tom probed with concern while her brother, who sat on the floor legs crossed Indian style, didn't loosen his grip on her hands.

"Jill, do you have what's needed to put them away?" Brad queried, instead of answering Tom's unspoken question.

"Yes. Williams knows it too. He's scared, and will encourage them to do whatever it takes to find me. I'm sorry, Brad. I shouldn't have involved you in this mess."

He squeezed her hands, letting out the breath he had been holding. "Kid, you didn't have a choice and you know it. There's no way anyone else will help you if they have even an inkling of who's after you. First, I need to make you and Tom disappear. Once that's done, I believe the 5x4 will be the best place to start."

"Brad, what about you? They'll come after you once they figure out it was Tom and me."

"Wyatt has a whole team on me. If one of them makes a move, they'll find out I'm not that easy of a target. I'm limited in where I can go. I also have to inform him in advance if I'm leaving the area. So yeah, my life sucks for the time being." Turning to Tom, he grinned. "Wyatt said to tell you the minute men will be here sometime today."

Tom relaxed with the news. "Jill, that trial will be put on the docket after the grand jury is finished. Williams won't be able to delay. They'll force him to take the first available date. He won't have a choice because it's coming from Washington. We've had surveillance on him for years. He's passed a message about you since the meeting. We caught it, but couldn't identify the person it went to, but I believe we now know the recipient."

Jill scanned the two men. They had better determine for sure who Williams was contacting. She had given them the head honcho's name.

"Tom, do you have any operatives who'll help in guarding you? They need to be excellent at blending into their surroundings," Brad asked Tom with concern.

"Yes, but I'll need to give them where to be. There were two agents in the 'Artist's Room' for the past week, keeping an eye on you. I have more like them who won't stand out no matter where we are."

Brad sat and stared at Tom, brows furrowed. Jill could almost see him sifting through the people he had met during that time frame.

A smile formed on his lips. "I wouldn't have known they were agents, they fit in so well. Okay, that makes me feel better. Like the other artists, they need to join the discussions with all the regulars, not just me, to not stand out."

"They will. You talked to one yesterday," Tom stated with a grin.

Brad laughed. "The guy was fantastic. We had a superb discussion of the masters."

Tom quirked an eyebrow, a pursed-lip grin on his face. "He should have mega information on the masters. The man's a master art forger and one of his paintings is still hanging in a museum. It was authenticated as an original, unfound painting for that artist. Don't even ask. I'm not telling you which master."

"Wow. No wonder he was so good at the techniques they used. I'm looking forward to talking to him again. There's no way I would have picked up on his being one of yours."

"There's another one you'll love having around. Keep them close. They're ones who have helped keep me from becoming fish food on several occasions. Once we decide on where we'll be, I have two agents who'll blend in with the area to back up whoever else is assigned to guard us."

"Got it. So, baby girl, we do have extra help here and they're good. Now that I'm aware of what we're up against, you have a choice. The 5x4 is the best one of the lot. It will be the easiest to defend if located and has four escape routes, one hidden. The 3x3 would be my second choice. Like the 5x4, it has a hidden escape route. You're aware of the problem with the 5x4. It's up to you if you can handle it for up to five days."

She tilted her head to look at Tom. He wasn't aware of what they were talking about. Unable to face him, she turned back to her brother.

"The one Brad is recommending has only one place to sleep. It's an efficiency with a fold-out bed. The other one is also an efficiency, but it has a bed and a couch. It's smaller and only has three exits while the first one has four. Those two have hidden exits, which would make getting out easier if we're found.

"The second one means moving in three days as it's easier to find. The first one is safe for up to five days. We'll have options where to go afterward. In the other two, all the exits are in the open, meaning fighting our way out if we're discovered."

"Brad, do you have others besides those two with hidden exits?" Tom questioned.

"Yes, but these are the most secure. I'm working on three long-term secure hideouts. I'm hoping to have one in place in the next couple of days, but I need to stash you two until then. You'll move to a long term one when I get them set up."

Tom studied Brad before inquiring, "How did you hide her from Wyatt for a week?"

Brad chuckled, winking at her. "My secret, but he and his men looked right at her and didn't recognize her. She was in plain sight. I've not let anyone in on where it was or how we did it. It was a test for this type of situation. Wyatt realized she would get to a point where she needed to disappear then reappear when it was time for her to testify. Even your guys couldn't find her, and they're damn good." Brad faced Tom, a smirk on his face.

Tom sat in thought for a few seconds before he informed them, "I remember that exercise. We used the best and never found the quarry until she walked into the courthouse with Wyatt. I didn't see her, so I didn't know it was Jill they were hunting. Other than controlling the logistics, I wasn't involved. I now understand why they told me to come to you when I needed someone to disappear."

"I need which place," Brad requested, his attention coming back to her.

She had to trust him. He was recommending the safest place. Their choices were limited at best. The other three were only backups.

"The 5x4," she stated, hoping she wasn't making a big mistake.

Brad's gaze held hers. "Tom, you had better not hurt her or I'll come after you. Jill is the light of my life, and I love her more than myself. She isn't as strong as she makes you think, and she doesn't need another man getting close, only to leave when he discovers what happened to her."

With a sigh, Tom ran a hand over her hair, head tilted, and something she didn't understand in his eyes when he met her gaze. "Brad, I won't hurt her. Unlike the others who professed to love her, I have a decent idea of what she's been through. It isn't a problem for me. I'm as protective of her as you are."

"You had better be. I make an extremely nasty adversary where she's concerned," Brad warned, sending him a quick glance, his face grim.

"So I've heard," Tom stated, meeting Brad's direct gaze.

She hoped he had the correct information on how Brad wasn't above making him pay for hurting her. He loved her like Wyatt did, unconditionally and fully. He was the one who remained with her and helped to pick up the pieces after her three years in captivity. Again, he had supported her after the last guy had left, destroying what trust she had in men. If Tom walked, he would pay big time. Brad saw through her and knew she would fall apart, hence his warning.

Jill leaned forward and put her arms around her brother's neck. He lifted her from the couch and held her in his lap, much like he had when she was a child. Unable to stop the tears, she held on to the one person who had been there for her all her life.

Tom didn't understand how Brad was more of a father than a brother. He had been there for every crisis in her life, and there had been many. He was the only one she truly trusted to keep her safe and sane. It was him and Sam who had seen her dancing on a pole with next to nothing on. It was him who had taken her from the three years in hell, then helped her to rebuild her life.

"It's all right, sis. We have a lot of help on this one. I understand why this is so important to you. Really, I do."

Her voice hitched when she told him, "He doesn't know it all."

"Baby girl, I don't think it'll make any difference to him. You might want to explain things while you're waiting."

She buried further into his comforting arms. "I can't."

"Jill, he'll be in court. You need to give him a heads-up about part of what you'll be saying."

"I'm scared," she admitted, staring up at him, becoming the frightened little girl he had found in the corner of the partitioned room when rescued. He had been the one who had gotten her out alive. Sam had informed him of what to expect, but he hadn't been ready for the reality of her condition.

"I know you are. I'm just one call away. If you need me,

notify Wyatt. Let Tom take care of you while in hiding. In case you missed it, he cares a lot and won't let anything happen to you."

She let her eyes stray to Tom, who was watching her with concern, before turning back to her brother. She was hanging on to sanity by a fraying thread. This wasn't the greatest way to prepare for a major trial, but it was the best she could do for now.

Brad cuddled her next to him and gave the plan for making them disappear. "Jill, do you remember where the secret gates are?"

"Yes."

"Okay, you'll be leaving here soon. Go to the left. If someone is hanging at the corner, wait until they leave. Look back when you get to the corner at the end of the block so whoever is following will stop. Use the first gate if there isn't anyone on the block. If there is, go around the block and use the first gate you can get through. After changing into different costumes, I'll take you to the place.

"Don't leave the apartment until I notify you of when and where to meet me. I'll be the one to move you, so don't believe any communications of someone other than me coming for you. I'll use the code so you can verify it's me." He paused. "Jill, this is important. If you don't hear from me in four days, notify Wyatt. He knows how to get to you and what to do."

"Why wouldn't you be coming?" she questioned, fear

raising its ugly head based on what he didn't say, her heart rate going into a fast irregular rhythm.

"I may not be able to. As you saw, I have multiple people on me and my phones are being monitored. If it's too much of a risk, I won't call, and we'll go to Plan B. Sis, this was all laid out when you began to work for the agency. We have a main plan and contingency plans. From those other cases, Wyatt realized you would need to disappear at some point, and he made sure we would be ready."

Jill peeked over at Tom. He confirmed what Brad had said. "They've kept me in the loop. I've worked with them since you were kidnapped. It's how I've gotten what information I have."

He moved to be on eye level with her. "As I stated before, you have friends in incredibly high places. They want you alive. This case will have repercussions going through more than the Lake County Sheriff's Department. It involves people in important places they've been trying to link to other questionable things happening over the past ten years. You're the key, and they want you on that stand. They want the answers to those questions.

"When I took this assignment, I wasn't expecting to become personally attached to the woman I had to guard. This is now personal for me. I want my beautiful fairy to survive so I can show her how much I care about her."

She turned to Brad, trusting him to tell her the truth.

"Hey, kid, he hasn't ever shown an interest in someone he's protected before. I've no reason to question what he's saying. I've worked with him for ten years and he's always been up front with me. Normally he drops off the person who needs to be hidden and disappears until he picks them up again. He didn't know I was your brother until today. If he's going with you, not only are you important to the higher-ups, but to him too."

She took a shaky breath. "Okay. How do I keep from falling apart?" Her eyes were wide, fear radiating from her.

Brad cuddled her closer to him. "Lean on Tom. He'll keep you together if you'll let him. He kept me from losing it when I found you."

Jill knew Tom didn't understand her trust in Brad, or the particulars of their relationship. All her life, Brad had supported her with a problem they kept secret. Without his endorsement, she couldn't trust Tom to stay with her and would insist on going alone.

"Tom, there are subs in the fridge in the kitchen. Want to go get them? She needs to eat and so do you. It'll be late when you get to the place, and knowing her, she'll just crash."

As soon as Tom had left, Brad moved her so she was facing him. His voice was low and hurried. "Jill, I only have a few seconds here so don't interrupt. Tom's the best. He also cares more for you than I expected from what

Grandpa told me. Trust him. He'll take care of you.

"Anything you tell him will be kept confidential unless you aren't there to give it. He isn't a lower echelon agent and works with some powerful people. In fact, he's one of the top guys, and as he said, he's been involved from the time of your kidnapping. Protecting you has been a top priority because you have what they need. He's remained in the background, not wanting to put the heat on you until you had the rest of the evidence."

"You sure?" she queried, wanting to believe him, terrified of what would happen if she was wrong.

"I'm trusting my life to him and his men along with you. So, yes, I'm sure."

Her eyes lowered to the hand playing with his collar before she admitted, "I'm afraid he'll walk away once he learns the full story."

"Sis, he's nuts about you and knows what happened and can guess most of the rest. If he says he'll stick around after this is over, he'll be there."

She blinked back tears and moved closer to him. Her voice was filled with resignation. "I hope you're right or you'll be seeing me in a padded room."

Brad held her tighter. She could feel him fighting tears. He was with her for the last meltdown, and it hadn't been pretty. He, along with Wyatt and her therapist, had pulled her back, but she wasn't sure if they could this time. The pain would be too much. Like Brad had said, she wasn't as strong as she appeared.

His soft "Jill, I know you love him. I warned him. He had better not hurt you," told her how much he loved her.

Tom reentered the room. He stared at her and Brad, a smile on his lips. "Brad, you should get married and have a kid of your own."

Brad rocked back and forth, cradling her in his arms. "I'm not sure it'd be worth it. I'd never be able to do as good a job as I did with her."

Tom squatted and held the subs so she had first choice. She took the vegetarian, trusting Brad to have ordered what she liked on it. Brad took the turkey, leaving Tom with the chicken.

"You need to eat at least half of that," Tom told her as she held the sub, not sure if she could eat.

Brad lifted her back to the couch as if she was a small child. "Listen to him. Eat."

It was two against one, so she unwrapped the sub, took a deep breath, then bit off a small piece. Brad handed her a bottle of water from the small fridge behind him. He handed Tom one and took a bottle for himself.

"You two have a choice of personas to assume. I've seen Jill become a young kid or teen and make it believable. She can also become an old lady with makeup and a wig. The one which I like is the schoolteacher. I walked past her the last time she used that disguise, not recognizing her."

Jill considered the ideas he had given her. There was

Tom to consider. They would have to remain in character while in hiding.

"I think the schoolteacher idea would be easiest to keep up. We could pass Tom off as my husband. He could be a teacher too," she stated, eyes on Brad.

"Tom?" Brad questioned, not looking away from her, his face serious.

"I can handle that. Simple getup. Glasses and I'm there. It won't be hard to treat her as a wife."

"You sure, Jill?" Brad probed, studying her face.

She reached over and patted his cheek. "I'm sure. I can't imagine being in that small space with a father or a son."

"Glad you see the difficulty," he intoned before relaxing his shoulders.

She gave him a tremulous smile. "I'm a big girl. He's been a perfect gentleman. I don't see him doing anything without my agreeing."

Brad turned to Tom, who stated, "Like she said, it's her call not mine."

"You better heed my warning, Tom."

With a noisy exhale, he faced Jill, before stating, "Brad, I promise I won't hurt her. I care too much for her to do so."

His admission brought her focus to him. Tom winked at her, a grin on his face. "I like him. He loves you and I understand his concern, but he needn't worry. As I've told you both, I'm going nowhere without you, including when this is all over."

Her heart took a jump. He was serious about sticking around after the trial, if she made the trial. She returned to eating. Maybe this wouldn't be so bad if he was telling the truth about how much he cared about her. Time would tell.

Chapter 16

HIDE-AND-SEEK

Once they were finished eating, Brad guided Jill and Tom to the door, promising to have the commissioned piece ready for viewing in two to three weeks. She didn't see anyone around so they turned to the left and walked along the seven-foot privacy fence while discussing Brad's artwork. Ambling along, in no hurry, Jill stopped to admire the flowers on a tree when they were halfway to the end of the block, enabling her to verify that there was a man following them.

Prior to turning the corner, they stopped and faced back in the direction they had come. The man stopped and removed a shoe, shaking it as if there something in it, allowing them to move out of view around the corner. It was less than ten steps until Jill opened the latch to a hidden, well-oiled gate in the fence. The gate closed seconds before the man following them came around the corner. They watched through the slats as the man stood, searching for them. Jill didn't move, holding the gate so it didn't open. It wasn't latched to avoid any noise which might lead the man into discovering it.

When the man moved away toward the next corner, Jill let out the breath she had been holding before latching the gate. She guided Tom along the narrow path among various statues and outside art pieces to the back door to the studio. After entering the dim windowless mudroom, Jill stopped upon hearing the murmur of two men talking before opening the door. Not sure who was with Brad, she took Tom's hand, guiding him to the bench along the wall to sit and wait.

Tom put an arm around her, holding her close. He kissed the top of her head when she leaned into his embrace. The choice of husband and wife hadn't been hard. He would make a nice husband. Too bad it was only pretend.

Close to ten minutes later, a shaft of bright light fell across them when Brad opened the door. Seeing them huddled together, he let out a sigh and shook his head before saying, "Come on, you two."

Again, they passed through the main studio and up the stairs to the room where they had talked before. Jill skidded to a stop at the door. Wyatt was sitting on the couch with Sam. Turning to Brad, she stared at him, unable to speak as dread washed over her.

Brad closed the door then explained, "Hey, they showed up without calling, knowing you were to meet me today. Granddad wanted to talk to you before you disappeared."

Wyatt stood and waited for her to enter his embrace, planting a kiss on the offered cheek. "Jill, we aren't sure when the trial will be added to the docket. There's pressure from Washington to move a few cases and get this one going due to the danger to you. If it doesn't get scheduled for this session, it'll be another two months. If that happens, we'll need to move you out of South Florida."

She tilted her head back to study Wyatt's face. The lack of using his favorite word made her aware of how worried he was about her. His big hand gently held her head. He glanced at Brad then back to her, blinking back the tears she saw forming in the corners of his eyes. He seldom showed emotion, making this extremely unusual.

"Honey, this is out of my hands. There are multiple

agencies involved. You have information they want, but you don't need to testify. You have the option to disappear. Those in custody will go to jail, but you don't have to give them the rest."

Unable to turn away from the eyes pleading with her to take the option to disappear, she told him, "You know I have to finish this. I've held on to this information for years, hoping to put them out of business. If I quit now, they'll continue business as usual."

"Jill, honey, you could just give them what you have," Wyatt suggested, hoping to avoid her testifying in this case.

"Grandpa, I can't. I need to tell how I got the information or it won't hold up in court. Yes, it'll dredge up those things I've tried to put behind me, but I need to do this. They took three years of my life, destroyed my innocence and self-respect. If I don't do this, Susan and the others like her will never receive justice."

With a heavy sigh, Wyatt pulled her closer. "I fucking get it, but I don't have to fucking like it." With a glare at Tom, he warned, "You had better take fucking good care of my fairy."

The big man's threat didn't intimidate Tom. Instead, he reached over and ran a finger along her jaw, a gentle smile on his face. "Wyatt, as I told Brad, this one is personal. Very personal. She's important to me. It's the reason I'm staying with her."

"Baby?" Wyatt questioned, studying her face, brows

drawn together in a frown.

Jill lowered her gaze to his chest. "It's okay. Brad warned him."

Wyatt questioned, "You care for him, don't you?"

Her head bobbed, tears welling again. His arms tugged her closer to him. "Tom, be careful with her. She won't handle it well if you disappear."

With a shake of his head, Tom repeated, "I'm not going anywhere without her, now or later."

With the way he kept repeating the same thing, she hoped he meant it. It would take all of them to keep her with them when the trial finished without having to deal with him taking off and not returning.

Brad put a hand on Wyatt's shoulder. "Granddad, he'll do as he says. She'll be okay. I need to get her to the 5x4 before it gets too late. She'll contact you if there's a problem. You'll be the one to inform her of the court date and time. If it's longer than three weeks, touch base with me so I can arrange to get her out of town."

"Got it. Sam," Wyatt said, holding out his hand to his right-hand man.

Sam put a small item on Wyatt's palm. Jill danced in place with excitement at what Wyatt handed to her. Walter had given her a new toy.

"You can talk to me or Brad on this." He took the pendant from her. In his big hand, it looked so tiny. "Push this wing for me and that one for Brad. To answer, just touch the stone. It will allow for longer communications than the other one. Plus, it's unable to be traced or located. Tom will have one as well. There's no way you can be out of contact for that long without me going crazy with worry."

He handed the pendant to her. It was a fairy made in a silvery colored metal which appeared to have no value, including the stone in the middle. The fairy was the communicator. Wyatt fastened the necklace around her neck.

"My fairy had better come flying back to me as soon as possible," Wyatt murmured in her ear, his arms going around her.

"As soon as I can," Jill mumbled.

An overwhelming sense of loss swept through her. He was more than a grandfather. He was her rock, keeping her grounded in a world which threw her off kilter. Like Brad, he was one of the few people who hadn't abandoned her.

Wyatt turned to Brad. "What can I do to make this easier?"

"You just did it. I'm having them leave with you. There was a ten-minute interval where the door wasn't being watched. Just talk as if they're clients of mine like last week when you met that guy here."

Brad handed Tom the keys to a car. "It's a light blue Camry, four-door sedan, parked in the second row. Go to the parking garage downtown on fifth and park on the top level. Get off on the third level and there will be a silver Honda hatchback parked along the wall to the right near the far corner. The keys are under the front-wheel well, driver's side. From there, go to Sawgrass Mills. Park by the Brands Mart entrance. I'll meet you inside of the store. You have an hour after leaving here to arrive for us to get to the apartment in a timely manner."

"Understood. I need to get out of this creepy outfit into something less noticeable," Tom stated.

Jill giggled. "I kind of like it. You make a real nice Goth guy."

He tapped her nose with a finger. "Be that as it may, I prefer being less outstanding in looks."

Jill quirked an eyebrow with a glance at the leather pants and tall boots. His mouth tilted up in a sly grin before he turned away, leaving her to wonder why he had the outfit at his sister's place.

Brad showed Tom where to change, handing him a small container of acetone to remove the black nail polish. Wyatt hadn't turned her loose since he had put his arms around her.

When Tom left the room, Wyatt said, "Honey, he cares for you and will be there for you, just as Brad, me, and Sam are."

"I hope so." She hesitated before saying, "Wyatt?"

"What, baby girl?"

"I know this sounds silly, but did a package for me

from a jeweler in Taveres arrive?"

"Yes. Why?"

"It was something I found and fell in love with. I probably shouldn't have gotten it, but I couldn't pass it up." She gazed up at him, unwilling to say the rest.

"Don't worry. You'll be back to wear it." He couldn't say it either but understood what she was saying.

"I hope so. You'll love it. It matches the ring you gave me."

In fifteen minutes, Tom returned, looking like a teacher. After disentangling herself from her grandfather's embrace, she made her way to the bath to clean up and remake herself into a teacher. The clothes and shoes Brad had placed on the counter had come from the costume closet they had filled over the years. It enabled her to assume almost any persona without having to buy an outfit. A smile formed at the thought of what Tom would think of several of the outfits she had stashed in that closet which she had used on various cases.

It didn't take long to scrub away the Goth makeup and remove the nail polish. A change of clothes, her hair pulled back in a bun, and a pair of horn-rimmed glasses changed her into a different person. Loosening the dress gave a more mature look to her body before rejoining the men. Wyatt took a double take when she entered the room, peering at her in confusion.

"Girl, I fucking know you and didn't fucking recognize

you in that fucking getup. No wonder you can go places and no one fucking sees you."

"Sir, I'm quite certain I've never seen you before in my life." Jill turned to Brad. "If you'll excuse us, Mr. Potter, I believe you should have our painting ready. We need to leave since we have more errands to do before going home."

Brad, keeping to the role he was required to play, stated, "Yes, Mrs. Wilson, I have it right here. I hope you'll enjoy it in your new home. You'll love it opposite the sofa on that blank wall. It will brighten that space."

"Darling, would you carry it, please?" she requested of Tom.

"Of course, dear," he replied, taking the painting from Brad.

Wyatt shook his head, smiling at her before entering the charade. "If you don't mind, I'll walk out with you. I believe we're parked in the same lot."

"Thank you," she responded with extreme politeness.

As they left, they conversed on the merits of one of the pictures Brad had for sale.

Jill lamented, "I actually wanted one of the larger paintings, but it just isn't in our budget. I do adore Brad's work."

Wyatt asked, "What did you like about this painting which prompted you to buy it?"

After glancing at Tom, she said, "Well, it was so bright

and full of sun. The colors make you think of a tropical paradise. Not only that, it was smaller and the price was one we could afford."

Tom added, "I preferred the smaller size. That way, we can make it the focus for an arrangement on the large wall opposite the sofa. It also gives us time to save enough to commission the larger picture we want to complement the smaller one. We need to watch our money with wanting to start a family."

Wyatt asked, his gaze on her, "And when do you plan on starting this family?"

Tom smiled at her. "That will be my wife's decision. She needs to finish the last classes for her doctorate. Maybe in a year or two."

"Smart move. Most young couples won't wait and end up with children before they're ready for them."

She put her hand through Tom's bent arm. If she read him right, he was willing to wait, but questioned what a week in close quarters could do to that resolve. He may have bitten off more than he could chew.

They said goodbye to Wyatt, leaving him and Sam at his car to proceed to the vehicle Brad had arranged for them to use. Tom put the painting in the trunk before opening the car door for her. His glance before he started the engine made her wonder what he was thinking. He backed out of the parking space, using proper driving technique before pulling out of the parking lot on to the street, and headed toward the downtown parking garage.

Using the side mirror, Jill watched for anyone tailing them. There was one car, two vehicles back, which was concerning. A car between them turned off as Tom kept to the speed limit in the right-hand lane.

As they made several turns, Jill said, "There's a car sticking to us. He's made every turn we did since the other car turned off."

Tom pressed a button on his watch. "Ed, tail."

Ed came back, "Right signal."

The car's right signal blinked. "Okay, it's him."

"Got you. Keep your eyes open for a changing guard between us."

"None so far. You're driving like my grandma."

Jill giggled. Tom was driving like an old person, but it fit the teacher persona. After parking on the top floor of the garage as instructed, he took the picture from the trunk, checked their surroundings for other people before going to the elevator. When the doors opened, they entered and he punched one then three on the number pad.

After exiting the elevator on the third floor, they turned to the right while the elevator car continued to the first floor. The new vehicle was another which didn't stand out in traffic. Again, Tom put the picture in the trunk then pulled out of the garage, keeping in the teacher mode. He was a good actor, easily keeping in character.

They headed west on I-595 and exited on Flamingo

Road, going north toward the mall. In less than the hour Brad had given them, they arrived and parked where Brad had instructed. Jill insisted on going in through the mall entrance instead of the one for Brands Mart, refusing to leave the painting behind.

Brad found them checking out the SLR camera she had wanted. He greeted them as if he was a friend before going over the attributes of the various models on display.

She sighed before saying, "I guess I have much to consider before buying a high-end model. Honey, thanks for tolerating me and Brad."

Tom gave her a tolerant smile. "You might want to check the models online and compare their specs before buying something that expensive," Tom stated, as any good money-conscious husband might.

She glanced one last time at the cameras before saying, "I'm sure you're right. Let's go."

Brad and Tom began a conversation on art in history. She added an occasional comment, showing understanding of the discussion as they ambled along the concourse. They stopped in an art gallery to examine a picture, which caught her attention. After a discussion of the various merits of the picture, she nixed buying it, saying she needed time to decide if she liked it enough to pay the asking price.

They left the gallery and strolled toward the exit at the middle of the mall. The time it took them to reach the exit had allowed the sun to set, making them harder to identify and follow. Tom held the door for her to get into the backseat, then put the picture in beside her before closing the door and getting into the front passenger seat.

Brad pulled out on Flamingo Road. Ed notified Tom he was three cars behind them. After a roundabout route, they entered a development where the SUV fit in with the other cars parked before the single-story apartment houses. He pulled into a parking space at a building with four apartments.

Before they exited the car, Brad stated, "It's not fancy, but it's comfortable. If you stay inside, you'll be okay here for five days."

They followed him and waited while he unlocked the door. The efficiency apartment was larger than she expected. There was plenty of food in the refrigerator and cabinets. He showed them the exit routes and the hidden one for the just-in-case scenario.

When he opened the closet, it contained clothes for the two of them. The place had been set up, expecting her to agree to this one in the teacher persona. There was a stacked washer and dryer if they needed it. Brad, after giving her a quick hug and kiss, left them to settle into the apartment.

Jill plopped onto the couch and wondered what to do for the next five days. There was no TV, and she had already read the couple of books in the closet. Nothing like being trapped with a handsome man for five days with nothing to keep you occupied.

Tom unwrapped the painting Brad had given him. He studied the picture before turning it to her. The painting was of a teenage girl with a mass of colorful flowers in her arms. Jill feathered her fingers across the picture, staring at it as tears welled in her eyes before spilling down her cheeks. She had the history of when, where, and why Brad had painted this picture.

Tom sat beside her before saying, "Tell me why this picture is causing you to cry."

She took a few seconds before saying, "Brad painted it two weeks before I was taken. We were in Aruba on vacation with Wyatt. I was in the garden picking flowers to decorate the house. He noticed me and had me pose for him. As he painted, he told me I was this beautiful fairy who needed a crown of flowers in her hair so she could dance in the moonlight with her prince. I told him I needed to find the prince first. He promised I would. I just needed to be patient."

"So, why are you crying?" he asked, wiping away the tears.

Unable to face him, her voice full of defeat and sadness, she told him, "No prince wants a used and damaged fairy."

He took the painting and put it on the floor, leaning it against the sofa before turning her head so she was facing him. "Jill, I'm not a prince, but I want the fairy, regardless of her being used or damaged."

"You won't want her. Not after what I'll reveal in court."

"What will you tell them that I don't already know?"

"The details of how used and damaged I am."

His arms came around her, holding her head on his shoulder. "Honey, I've been privy to the horror stories of what happens to girls in places where they are forced into the sex trade, including details of things done to them. I'm very aware of what you experienced, including being made to dance, entertain men in ways no woman should without their consent, along with what happens when you refuse to do as requested.

"I know you were never a willing partner and didn't give consent. That's what's important. If you were working the streets by choice, it might be a different story, but you weren't.

"I'll not leave you for what happened in the past. The only reason I'll leave is if you tell me to my face, looking me in the eye, that you don't want me and to leave you alone. Even then, I'm not sure I could walk away without trying again."

"Why?" she asked, keeping her head on his shoulder, not believing what he was saying.

The arms around her tightened. "I see this lovely fairy who needs to fly again. She's so unique, and I've fallen in love with her. No matter what her past has been, I can't walk away from her, and God knows I've tried. I'm holding out for that dance in the moonlight with flowers in her hair, in a magical place she has always wanted to see with her prince. I may be a poor substitute, but I'm willing to be a permanent stand-in for that prince or knight in shining armor."

Her lips tilted up at his description of himself as a stand-in rather than the real prince or knight. "Okay. I don't mind a normal guy if he doesn't walk away when the going gets tough."

"I'll be right here beside you. You're the girl in that picture. We just need to get past this mess to get her to come back to us."

"Tom?"

"Yes?"

"I love you, too."

He chuckled, arms tightening around her. "I sort of guessed that. It's one reason I'm involved in this on a personal level. I can't lose you, now that I've found you. I've waited way too long for my fairy to show up."

"You'll need to help her with her broken wings," she stated, peering up with him, hoping she was making the right decision.

"No problem, as long as she wants to fly again with me beside her."

Jill stayed in his embrace. When she got herself together, she scanned the apartment. There was no choice in the sleeping arrangements.

She noticed Tom also scanned the large room. "Forget it," she pronounced. "It's called restraint, and I didn't promise this would be easy."

Tom kissed her cheek before saying, "I can handle it if you don't mind me holding you. I can't be that close without my arms around you."

With a quick shrug, she stated, "I might keep you awake or push you on to the floor." Jill knew she was a restless sleeper, frequently waking up wrapped in her sheet and blankets. Or worse yet, awakening with a scream from the nightmares she still fought.

"I'll take my chances. Let's get some sleep and see what we can find to do in the morning besides eating ourselves into oblivion."

"Okay. Dibs on the bathroom," she said before retrieving pajamas from the valise Brad had left for her. Wyatt must have given it to him before they returned to the studio.

Tom had made up the sofa bed for the night by the time she returned. It was a pullout and should be reasonably comfortable. She was crawling into the bed when her fairy vibrated.

"Hi," she answered, not sure if it was Brad or Wyatt.

"Sis, did you open the picture?"

"Yes. It was a shock to see it again."

"Hey, Tom said he wanted that one if I ever parted with it."

"He said he loved me."

"Good. He's a prince, so hold on tight to him. I'll contact you in a couple of days. There are games in the cabinet, and your Kindle is in your valise."

"Thanks, Brad."

"Love you, kid. Bye."

Okay. So, she had a prince. Now, to get rid of the crap before she could discover if he truly wanted the damaged fairy.

Tom came back from the bath dressed in pajamas. He bent over and gave her a kiss before pointing to the far side of the bed. She moved to where she was to sleep, fluffing the pillows to get comfortable. After turning off the lights, Tom joined her and pulled her next to him. Curling into him, she closed her eyes and sighed, feeling safe in his arms. Listening to the steady rhythm of his heart and breathing, she drifted to sleep, dreaming of the green-eyed man who said he loved her.

Chapter 17

ALL FOR NAUGHT

Tom woke her with a kiss. When she turned to him, he smiled before tapping the end of her nose with a finger.

"It's time for us to get up and get moving," he informed her.

"If you say so," she responded, moving away, enabling him to get up.

This was one of the rare nights since being found she had slept without dreams or awaking in fear with a scream. There was no reason to move yet when the sounds of the shower reached her. Thinking over last night, she wasn't sure if Tom would remain long term, but while together, she was willing to believe he loved her. It was better than nothing.

When the shower stopped running, she crawled out of the bed and gathered her clothes for the day before straightening the bed and refolding it into a couch. A quick hunt through the cabinets produced the filters and coffee for the pot on the narrow counter. The coffee was dripping when Tom's arms came around her, pulling her against him before running kisses from her ear down her neck. It sent chills throughout a body which came alive in an unexpected way.

"I could get used to this way too quick," he expressed, returning to planting kisses on her ear and neck.

"So could I," Jill responded, turning in his arms to face him. He had dressed as a teacher in chinos and a plaid shirt. Today, it didn't matter what persona he played, because he was hers for now.

"Jill, you're so beautiful. I still can't believe I had the honor of holding you for a night."

"Meanwhile, your holding me enabled me to sleep all night, which is rare for me. Pretty mundane, isn't it?"

"No, not really. It means a lot to me if my holding you made you feel safe enough to sleep."

Jill didn't say how she wanted him to hold her every night. Instead, she said, "I guess I had better get dressed."

He moved away so she could go and ready herself for the day. After showering, Jill pulled her wet hair back from her face and twisted it into a tight knot on top of her head, holding it in place with a big clip. Her clothes were casual pants and a big shirt for the day. The last thing she put on was the glasses chosen as part of her disguise before rejoining Tom. Breakfast was on the table, waiting for her.

Jill wanted to resolve one problem while they ate. "Okay, our last name is Wilson, but we need first names we'll answer to."

"Well, you answer to sis, so let's go with Sissy for you."

"It works. What about you?"

He leaned against the counter and studied the floor, lips scrunched together as if he had eaten something sour, before saying, "Seth. It's actually my first name. Thomas is my middle name."

"Does anyone else know that?" she questioned.

"Only HR, my boss, and family."

"Okay, it'll work. Now I know what to call you when I'm pissed at you," she told him with a smirk.

He looked up with a sheepish grin on his face. "I guess I better not piss you off. I was named after my grandfather, but I've always gone by Tom because he answered when they called me Seth. It was easy for everyone and didn't change when he died. Wyatt puts me in mind of my grandfather right down to his speech. He used to say I'd never be big enough to count when I was a teenager."

She could see his point if the rest of his family favored Shaun, who was like her family.

"Meanwhile, I'm a throwback to my grandmother. She was my size, and other than my hair color, I could be her clone. I was named after her. Her middle name was Jillian."

"Wyatt must be partial to fairies."

"Maybe. She died of a heart condition when I was two, so I don't remember her. She was the one who insisted on Wyatt taking me from my parents when I was diagnosed with failure to thrive as a baby. Brad told me he came to help care for me while Wyatt was working."

"And it was by chance that you looked like his wife."

"Yes. My sister is six feet tall and big. Not fat, just big. You met Ryan and couldn't miss how he's as tall as Wyatt and Brad, just not as bulky. Then there's Rick, who's also their size. He and Belinda resented it when Wyatt took Brad and me. They believed he gave us all this stuff without realizing we had to work for everything. Wyatt's a typical Scotsman and doesn't give money away."

"Yeah, but he pays well. If you're good, you get good wages."

"You may, but I get a pittance," she admitted with a wry grin.

"Why? He says you're one of his best operatives."

She moved the eggs around on the plate before answering. "He insisted I live in a condo he owns on the beach. I don't pay rent, plus he provides me with a car, cellphone, and an expense account. My paycheck reflects that."

Tom added with a big grin, "Plus, he gives you use of his places for vacations, and if I'm not mistaken, provides food and a maid for the condo."

"Correct. I'm not complaining because I earn enough to get what I want."

"Like the jewelry set you bought in Taveres."

"Yes." She glanced up and shrugged. "I seldom buy useless things, but that set, it was so well done."

He picked up her hand. "And it matches the ring he gave you."

She had forgotten the ring on her right hand. It could identify her, but she was reluctant to remove it. It symbolized the connection between her and Wyatt.

"Yes," she stated, not elaborating on the one word.

"Sissy, there's no harm in loving him like you do. The man would give his life for you. He loves you that much. It was the reason for the warnings they gave me. Brad will follow through on his threat if you were to say I hurt you in any way."

She peeked at his face before returning her gaze to her plate. "I know. He's done it before."

"When?"

"My first boyfriend slapped me. We were arguing, and I said something he didn't like. I thought Brad would kill him before I could get him to stop."

"I imagine that decreased the number of boyfriends."

"Only the creeps. There were plenty of guys who asked me out. I saw them as friends, and they understood I wanted to have fun without the sex or major ties."

He took a bite of toast, chewing and swallowing before asking, "What about the recent guys?"

"There've been two over the past five years who meant something to me. The first one was this respectable guy. I wanted him to know about my past before we got too close. He never contacted me after that night, disappearing from my life like he was never there.

"The second one, well, he was a piece of work. When I told him, he changed, treating me like a whore. He got mad when I refused to have sex with him. Then he tried to rape me. I was able to fight him off, then ordered him to leave and never come back."

Tom picked up her hand and squeezed it. She peeked up, afraid of what his face might reveal.

"Honey, I'm neither one of them. The girl in the picture is who you are, innocent and so exquisite."

"But I'm not innocent."

"Yes, you are. It shows in your reaction to some of the things I do. I want to show you how a fairy is supposed to be treated and loved."

Being honest, she told him, "I'm not sure if what happened won't interfere."

"You'll show me what you need or want. Like last night, you were okay with me holding you. For now, that's what you need. It's enough until we're ready for a more permanent relationship."

He said all the right things, but she had to ask, "You could have almost any woman you want, so why do you want someone who's damaged?"

Tom let out an audible breath. "You're not damaged. Everyone has a past. Most of the women your age have had multiple partners. The only difference is how yours wasn't by choice, so stop thinking that way. If anything, you have less knowledge than most women concerning sex and love."

Pulling her hand from his, she admitted, "Maybe. I went to this place inside, so I didn't cry or fight. Unless they hurt me, I remember little of what they were doing."

He studied her before saying, "Sissy, if you love someone, you'll want what they're doing. You won't hide from it. You'll enjoy what's happening and want to give back. It's very different from what you experienced."

"What about you? Anyone in your past?"

"One who was important to me. She didn't like how my job kept me away from home on a frequent basis. She ended up marrying one of my friends. It hurt for a short time, but it's part of life. I'm the godfather to their son, so that should tell you what our relationship is now."

Jill stared at her plate and shrugged before saying, "I guess I'm good at picking out the creeps. Brad told me I needed to find a better class of guy to date."

Tom chuckled. "Not bad advice. There's a lot of creeps out there who see women as things to use, believing they own them."

"I'm not a thing, and no one will own or use me again!" she vowed, anger and tenseness radiating off her.

Tom defused her by saying, "To me, you're this precious fairy who needs to fly and be what she wants to be. Only, I want her to fly back to me."

They finished their meal and washed the dishes. Jill found the games Brad had mentioned. They agreed upon Monopoly. They were still playing at lunchtime, so she fixed sandwiches and they ate while continuing the game. It was late evening when they quit, calling the game a draw.

His laughter as they played turned the day into one to

be remembered. After going to bed, she snuggled into his arms, wanting him to stay long term. If he did, there was hope for her future.

Awakening with a start, Jill listened, her heart pounding with fear. Tom, without a sound, moved from the bed, a pistol in his hand. He silently moved to the window where the bushes had scraped against the glass, gun ready as he waited and listened. The scraping sound came again, then a cat yowled. He lifted the curtain far enough to peer into the dim light for a few seconds before leaving the window.

"Fucking cat. Scared the living daylights out of me."

"Me too."

"You okay?" he asked with concern.

"Will be as soon as my heart rate returns to normal." On that, she wasn't lying. Her heart was racing at a speed which scared her. The frequency of the changes in her heartrate was only one more thing to worry about.

"Join the crowd. Hopefully, this won't be a nightly occurrence."

She didn't respond as he returned to bed, pulling her to him. His muscles were tense, but the surrounding arms were gentle. If his reaction to the unknown noise was any indication, he wasn't going to let anything happen to her.

It seemed as if she had just fallen back to sleep when

Tom's communicator beeped, awakening her. She became alert when she heard Brad's voice.

"Tom, we have a major complication."

"What's up?"

"There's a federal subpoena for Jill to turn herself in to the special prosecutor at the Broward federal courthouse."

"Which judge?" Tom asked, sitting up, sliding his gaze to her.

"Llewellyn."

"What time does she need to be there?"

"Between nine and five today."

"I was wondering how long it would be before she was summoned. I'll notify you where we'll meet you or Wyatt. No one else had better be there or we'll keep going."

"Tom, Fred is standing right here. He's saying he's not going to let you or her go in without protection. He has a handpicked group of men he trusts to protect you."

"Okay. I'll inform you of the meeting point. You'll have ten minutes to get to us or she's going so deep they won't find her until it's time for her to testify. I'm not taking any chances on this. If I see one person I don't trust, Fred can forget finding us."

"He's nodding that he understands. I'll wait for your call. Wyatt is here with me. They came to him first."

"Got it."

After breaking the communication, Tom remained still, jaw muscles working, eyes staring. To her, fate was trying to make sure she wouldn't survive. Her birthday was in two weeks, and she wanted to see twenty-five. Remaining calm, she got up to prepare to leave, aware she couldn't ignore the subpoena. Someone was trying very hard to make sure she didn't make it to trial. It was time to leave Tom so he could survive this even if she didn't.

Tom had fixed coffee and was standing at the counter with a cup in his hand when she reentered the room. Without thinking, doing what she normally did when staying in some place, she unmade the bed and put the dirty linens in the hamper, then made sure things were neat. There was no reason for someone else to clean up after them.

What she really wanted to do was scream, cry, and throw things. No matter what they did, she wasn't going to make it much beyond the pickup point. There was no way she could ignore the subpoena. If she did, the federal marshals and FBI would hunt for them, leading the assassins to them. The new judge had signed her death warrant without knowing it.

"Jill?" Tom questioned, stopping her as she passed him, finishing her cleaning routine.

"It was nice while it lasted. Tell them where to meet me. You don't need to go," she stated, resigned to her fate.

"I'm not leaving you. We'll do this together."

Unable to look at him, she studied a cracked tile on the floor. "Tom, forget it. No matter what you or the Feds do, I'm dead. I'm not familiar with this new judge, but that subpoena was issued so they could assassinate me, and I'm sure Williams was behind it. They need me in the open, and what better way to get me there. I don't want anyone dying with me."

"What are you planning?"

"You meet the others. I'll be at the courthouse. No protection. No one around. If it's a trap, then no one else gets killed but me. If it isn't, once I'm inside, I'll have one or two hours to go. Once this judge is finished with me, my life span will be less than a day. You tried but fate has a wonderful sense of humor, and it's actually funny in a way."

"Not happening. You're going in with me and you'll be leaving with me. It will mean spending time at the fortress, but you'll be safe there."

She turned her back to him. "Wrong. There are plants in your organization, and I won't be safe there. I was dead the day they took me. By a quirk of fate, I managed to live another nine years. I don't want you or anyone else to get in the line of fire when they find me."

A gentle hand turned her to face him before kissing her forehead. "Not happening, sweetheart. This is a major bump, but I won't lie down and give you to them without a fight. We do need to obey that subpoena. Besides, if the syndicate knows that the subpoena was issued, they'll be waiting for you at the courthouse, so going in alone won't work. Once we're with Fred, we can arrange security to get you in. It's getting you out which concerns me."

She moved away from him, holding back the impending tears while she cleaned everything but the coffeepot and their cups, leaving minimal traces of them behind. Tom had dressed and packed his valise. What she should have done was to leave while he was dressing, not that it would have done any good. The buses didn't run for another half hour.

There was nothing more to clean. She didn't know what else to do to keep herself together. If you're a mouse hunted by multiple cats, it wasn't a good thing if there was nowhere to run and hide. They had backed her into a corner, and the dog who protected her was chained and couldn't help now. There was no escape route, and there were too many cats. If one didn't get her, another one would, even if they began to fight among themselves.

Jill stood at the sink, not moving as the tears she had held back ran unchecked over her cheeks. Tom's arms came around her, causing her to jump, then to cry harder.

"Jill, work with me. I can't protect you if you don't."

"There's nothing you or anyone else can do. You don't need to get yourself killed because of me."

He turned her to him. She put her arms around his waist, resting her head on his chest, needing to be close. She didn't want him to die because of her.

"I'm not giving up. I'm well acquainted with Llewellyn. He'd have to have a good reason not to reverse the subpoena, so it wasn't only Williams's doing. There's something happening and we need to find out what. He'll work with us to keep you safe."

"He can't. There are too many and in places you wouldn't expect. In those three years, I discovered how deep this goes. They're scared because I have the evidence against those I encountered and have the links to the people who've been protecting them."

"We need names, Jill. Until we know who, we can't stop them. That's been the major problem right along. We can't ferret out the connections to those pulling the strings, and until we do, many of us have our lives on the line."

"I don't know all the names, but I can recognize the faces," Jill admitted. "You and Fred have two in your group. I noticed them when the men surrounded us at the station in Clermont. They aren't aware I saw them, let alone recognized them.

"Brad was the only one who could hide me well enough to keep me alive. He's now out of the picture due to the subpoena. I won't make it to testify, and you won't be able to stop them. Whatever you do will only delay the inevitable."

Tom held her as she cried, defeated in putting those who had tortured her behind bars. There was no place to run where they couldn't find her. No more delays. No more hiding. No more life.

"You ready to go?" he asked when her tears had dried.

"Sure. Let me clean this last bit up."

"Leave it." He reached over and turned off the coffeepot. "I want to be in a specific spot before I notify Brad where to meet us."

She retrieved her bag. The picture on the chair drew her attention. They couldn't take it with them. Hopefully Brad would be able to retrieve it and keep it safe for Tom.

Following Tom out of the apartment, Jill closed and locked the door on the two days of believing she had a future. She stayed away from him as they made their way along the deserted sidewalk, hoping if they were seen and recognized, they would miss him.

The first bus was pulling up as they arrived at the bus stop. After paying the fare, he headed to the back section of the double bus with her following. Jill watched the buildings pass, not wanting to see if an assassin found them.

Her life span was now counted in minutes. The likelihood of her honoring the subpoena was slim. If she was lucky, she might make it to the federal courthouse. That meant an extra hour. If she made the meeting with the judge, depending on what information he wanted, it meant another two hours at the most. One of the men in Fred's group was willing to die to make sure she didn't make the meeting. She wasn't sure if he was one of the trusted men, not knowing his name, just his face.

Tom had them switch buses. She did as he directed, her

time running out, positive he was merely delaying the end.

They got off at the stop at the main library downtown to empty sidewalks. Tom called Brad using the communicator Wyatt had given him.

"You have ten minutes to meet me at the main library coffee shop. You, Wyatt, Sam, Fred, Lance, Tip, Jim, and Aaron are the only ones allowed to come with you. Bring the armored SUV. If I see one other person hanging around, we'll disappear."

He broke the connection. They were at the library, but they disappeared into the shadows near the café to wait on their ride. No one noticed them as they sat on the bench sipping coffee under the overhanging palms.

The SUV came around the corner, but there was a car following it. Tom didn't move, eyes following the unknown sedan. When the SUV slowed, the car changed lanes and sped off, turning into the garage. The SUV stopped at the curb and the four-way flashers blinked on.

Fred exited from the front passenger side and strode toward the coffee shop. He was alone. He stood near the outside tables, not seeing them before starting back to the SUV.

They waited until he was at the steps to the sidewalk before appearing at his side. Fred escorted them to the vehicle and held the rear door while scanning the surrounding area as they got in. She would make it to the courthouse. That meant another hour, two at the most, to live.

She sucked in a big breath, willing her heart rate to return to normal. The stress of the morning had sent her heartrate into the stratosphere. It was now a matter of discovering why this new judge had kept the subpoena active.

Chapter 18

ONE RAT, TWO RATS, THREE RATS GONE

Sam was driving the armored SUV with Wyatt waiting in the backseat. As soon as Jill entered the vehicle, Wyatt pulled her to him. From the glower on his face, he was furious at the turn of events.

"I don't know what the fuck these cocksucking bastards are pulling, but I don't fucking like it," Wyatt growled, glaring at Tom and Fred.

With disgust, Fred stated, "This wasn't Llewellyn's idea of a good time either. Someone at the top signed the subpoena, but put Llewellyn's name as the issuing judge. We're following the trail from Williams to discover who was contacted to get the subpoena issued at that level."

"You better find that fucking trail or my little girl won't survive to testify," Wyatt grated. He knew the problem of taking her out of hiding to answer a subpoena.

Tom turned to Wyatt. "We're doing our best. Jill has what we need, but we have to keep her alive." The green eyes focused on her, his face serious. "This isn't the time to keep secrets. Everyone implicated during the conference will be arrested and charged with racketeering, then he'll get the rest of the information you have on them during the trial. The insiders need to be neutralized to keep you alive."

Tom apparently had better access to what was happening than the rest of them, making her question his position. Whatever that position was, in whatever agency, it had to be upper level to acquire the information he just imparted to them.

Jill glanced at Wyatt before facing Tom. He blanched when she stated, "Then keep Payne and Harrison away from me."

"What?" he questioned, brows furrowing, leaning toward her.

"You heard me. There's one more, but I don't know his

name. The short dark-haired guy with blue eyes, who has a half-inch scar just under his right eye and looks as if he had his nose broken more than once, is the other one."

Fred's eyes bounced between Tom and her. "All three of them are at the courthouse with the entry guards."

Tom took out his cell phone and turned it on. Sam turned to the left, heading to the beach to give them time to neutralize the three men. When the phone had booted up, Tom punched in a number.

Without a greeting, he snapped, "Pick up Payne, Harrison, and Rhodes. Take their weapons, IDs, and all communication devices. Search them and remove everything you find. Don't allow them to talk to anyone once they are contained. Make sure it's done on the QT. Put them in a secure room where they can't escape." He listened for a few seconds before he ordered, "Add them to the list." He glared at her, brows drawn together as if it was her fault.

Jill moved closer to Wyatt. Yeah, the Feds were clueless with the number of infiltrators or traitors they had in their employment. There were four more, but Jill knew they wouldn't be at the courthouse today. She would worry about them later. It was the reason she had told Tom that she wouldn't be safe at the fortress.

Tom hung up and scowled, his hand gripping the phone. A few seconds after letting out a deep breath, he turned to her. "Jill, thank you. If you give Llewellyn the names of those involved, we can neutralize as many as possible and increase the chances of keeping you alive."

"When's the trial supposed to start?" she questioned. The answer from Tom would determine how much help she could give. Those arrested could only be held for a finite time without a hearing and setting bail unless charged with an offense with no bail.

"We'll learn that while there. From what's going on, I'm expecting within the next two weeks. The grand jury indicted all those whose names were associated with the club, so that is out of the way."

"Can they hold them without charges for over three days?"

"There will be charges, but again, we need your help to get them on racketeering, money laundering, kidnapping, running a place of prostitution, smuggling, and dealing drugs."

She glanced at Wyatt, who was closely watching her, before saying, "For now, I just want to make it to the courthouse. With what he says and does during the meeting, I'll be able to determine how much to give him. What I'm sure of is, if I don't make the trial, they'll all walk."

Wyatt spouted a string of obscenities indicating his thoughts on what was happening. Tom chuckled at the old man's verbiage.

Jill giggled before saying, "Grandpa, I totally agree."

Wyatt glanced at her, a wry grin on his face. "Sorry. Bad habit from the docks."

She leaned into his embrace, putting her head on his chest. "If you didn't swear, I'd think you were losing it."

Brad chuckled, leaning around Wyatt so he could see her. "Yeah. I've heard you put a few together, too. It's hard to see you and listen to you swear and not laugh. That innocent look just doesn't fit with those types of words."

"It does make one wonder when she talks like a street urchin," Tom imparted with a chuckle.

The men's laughter had her burrowing deeper into Wyatt's side as the heat rose from her neck to her face. True, she didn't look to be the type to swear, but she had heard it most of her life. It was a part of her grandfather's personality, and she didn't mind. She and Brad seldom swore, but when they did, it was with the words Wyatt used frequently, with a few others thrown in for good measure.

It was another fifteen minutes before Sam pulled into the garage at the courthouse. He followed the directions of a guard to park next to an elevator in an empty slot blocked off with cones. The sign on the chicken wire enclosure around the elevator read "Prisoner Entrance, No Unauthorized Personnel." Two guards in fatigues, assault rifles in their hands, were posted there, awaiting their arrival.

There were no choices left. If she made it through the meeting, it depended on this new judge how long her life lasted. She had to trust Tom and Fred to ensure she lived to see another day.

Fred exited the vehicle and held the door for her, with the rest following them. One guard opened the fence while another held the elevator door for them to enter. He punched the button for the second floor. When the elevator opened, the men Tom had requested to protect them were waiting in the hall, guarding the elevator. These new men were in fatigues, also armed with assault rifles.

The corridors were empty as the contingent of guards escorted the group to another elevator, secured by two armed guards. One nodded to Fred, then motioned for them to enter before two more men joined them in the car. One of the men in fatigues put a key into a slot before pushing a button for the fourth floor.

When the elevator stopped, the armed men exited and checked the corridor before allowing her to step into the hall. Two agents led the way. Tom and Wyatt flanked her, with Brad and Sam behind, forming a protective ring. They turned to the left, moving along a hall with multiple doors.

The guards stopped halfway down the hall before knocking on a door in an odd pattern. A man in black pants and T-shirt, a pistol in his hand, opened the door. He holstered the gun before motioning them to enter.

This was a secure conference room with drab brown carpeting, one narrow window covered by partially open vertical blinds, a table with eight chairs, and two pictures of landscapes on the facing plain drab yellow-brown walls. An elderly man, who was standing behind the table, studied her as she entered the room. He wasn't tall, yet had an imposing air even though he wore casual slacks and a collared light blue pullover knit shirt with short sleeves. The white hair and a face filled with creases gave him a distinguished appearance. Deep-set alert eyes of gentian blue monitored her progress into the room. The face had deep crevasses going from his nose to a mouth set in a grim line, making her think of a bulldog in human form. He waited until the door closed, to speak.

"The fewer people privy to what Ms. Potter has to say would be best. I want everyone but Tom to leave until we are finished. Fred, please remain close by. Notify Elam that I want him here and ready when this conference is completed. I'm taking no chances on this case.

"Wyatt, Brad, I'm sorry, but for now, it's best if you have no more information than you already have. It's well-known that she hasn't talked to anyone, and I want it very clear you have no vital information. We need as few targets as possible for this group. The guards will show you to a room where you can wait with Fred until we're finished. I'll inform you of what we'll need as soon as this meeting concludes."

His voice was pleasant but held a thread of steel. This man was used to being in command, along with having orders obeyed without question. Also, he wasn't making more targets. That was a plus.

Wyatt gave her a hug and kiss before leaving with Brad in tow. The rest of the men followed them out, with Fred being the last one to leave. The elderly man closed the door, locking it before returning to the conference table. From the way he was handling this, he knew there was an informer in the courthouse who would pass on the names of those behind the locked door to the syndicate.

Before the man regained his seat, Jill stated, "You'll now be a primary target due to meeting with me. Because they won't be sure of what I've told you, they'll try to kill you too."

He chuckled, "Ms. Potter, I've been a target for years. I'm organized crime's most hated person. It's the reason I'm here. Tom and I have worked together for ten years. When he called for help, it told me this was the break we needed. You've rattled the rats' cages, scaring them. Have a seat and let's see if we can decrease the number of rats and increase the odds of you living to testify."

She took a seat to his left and studied him. He remained calm, and she could see no fear in what he was doing. Tom put a hand on her arm, drawing her attention to him.

There was concern in the green eyes, mixed with worry in the furrowed brow and grim mouth. "Jill, he knows what he's doing. You need to trust him."

The intense gaze telegraphed his concern. Yes, she was

out of options. They needed help, and she was the one who had the information they needed. Lowering her gaze to her clasped hands, she weighed what the two had said.

If she didn't give the information they wanted, they'd become targets with no place to hide. If she gave it to them, she might make it to the trial. There was nowhere else to turn. This subpoena put her into a spot she'd been trying to avoid.

"Why did you insist on making me come in?" Jill asked, not raising her gaze from her hands.

"I need to get as many of this group as possible in custody today to create a clearer playing field. From what Thomas didn't say and my conclusions from his communications, you have information and links to those involved in the higher echelon of the justice department. There are four who I suspect may be involved, but I need the trail to them. We've been working this case for ten years, and this is the closest we've ever been to breaking this ring. You're our key, and we need what you have."

She released a breath of resignation before asking, "What do you need?"

"Names for right now."

Keeping her eyes lowered, she admitted, "I have some names, but not all of them. When I see them or hear them speak, I know who they are and where they fit into the syndicate structure."

"Good, I like that better." He bent over and produced

a long narrow box and placed it on the table. "Go through these and pull out the ones you know are part of the syndicate or consorting with them. Take your time. We aren't in any hurry."

He opened the box, placing the lid beside it. The box was full of photographs. Some were portraits, some mug shots, and the rest were snapshots. She pulled the box closer to her and pulled out a handful of the pictures. After examining each photo, she placed them into the lid or onto stacks on the table. It took close to three hours before Jill finished sorting the pictures. The two men had sat in silence as she sifted through the photos, texting or just watching her. The only sounds had been the dings of messages and the release of deep breaths.

With a noisy sigh, she reached for the smallest pile in front of her, which contained four pictures. Jill fanned them out on the table before pushing two of them above the other two. Her finger tapped the top two before she spoke.

"Those two are assassins. I'm aware of at least four people outside of the club they received orders to kill. They are the enforcers and killed several of the girls, one of which I observed. The four of them are extremely dangerous and will kill to keep from getting caught." She pointed to the picture on the top right. "This man is Demetri Ivanov. He bragged about killing two cops, and this one," she pointed to the other photo in the top row, "killed a judge and made it look like natural causes."

With a glance at the elderly man, she could see his eyes harden as he took the photos and studied them. She fanned the next pile over the table before pushing several of the photos above the others.

"This group is in the inner circle. They're part of the ring of procurement, distribution, and protection at the club. Each of them participated in what was happening."

She moved one photo above the others and tapped it before saying, "This is the one who took me. He said his name was Dave. He and these three got the girls for the club." She pushed the photos next to Dave's.

Her finger moved another one out. "This is Sam Lopez. He oversaw the drug portion of the enterprise. He controlled the labs making the designer drugs sold in big quantities to various dealers. The various police officers on the take ensured that they received protection for the brothel and labs. He was the one who provided the drugs they used to keep us from creating problems."

Her hand went to the next stack. She shuffled through them, taking out several photos, staring at them, before spreading them out on the table. The two men came to attention, staring at the photos. Jill leaned back in the chair, arms crossed, waiting for the questions.

Tom's "Jill, are you sure?" wasn't unexpected.

Her gaze remained on the photos. She let out a noisy breath before with sadness in her voice she stated, "Positive. If you go through the rest of those in this pile, you'll see a bunch of well-known faces. Those there were frequent fliers. I have information concerning what they were doing, what they were getting paid, and how they ensured that certain men never went to jail for the crimes they committed. I also have how they protected the syndicate on various levels. There's one big one missing though. I didn't see his photo among these."

The last set of pictures were those in the state judiciary connected to the syndicate. Yes, there was justification for the concerns for her safety. This went deep. Very deep. These were the locals who were taking bribes or being blackmailed. What they didn't have were the federal judges and agents working with the ring.

Without comment, the elderly man produced another smaller box from under the table. There was a slight hesitation before he opened it and scooted it over to her. Sitting up to the table, she sorted through the photographs from the new box. As she had before, Jill sorted the pictures into piles. With this box, the greater share of the photos ended up in the lid rather than on the piles. Toward the end of the box, she pulled one picture out and stared at it before putting it in a pile with a sigh. There were two more added to that pile prior to finishing the box.

Her hand lifted the smaller of the two piles before saying, "Those in this group were well-known at the club. They had multiple conferences with Billings and Franko."

The man she assumed was the judge took the photos

and shuffled through them, disgust on his face as he shook his head. She moved to the larger pile. "All of these are real dirty." She pulled out the photo she had stared at, then laid it on the table. "This person is one of your key men. He was the one who recruited the protection by getting the dirt on the rest. That information was then used to force them to give minimal sentences, or stifle the prosecution with discretionary rulings based on obscure law. On numerous occasions, he bragged about what he was doing and his successes, which are the others in that pile."

The elderly man took the pile and shuffled through it. He stopped at one, shook his head after studying it, but continued without speaking. Pulling a photo out, he put it on the table in front of her.

"Tell me about this man," he requested, his eyes meeting hers, mouth pursed.

After picking up the photo, she stared at it. What she wanted to do was to rip it to shreds, then rip the man apart as she had the photo. Multiple times she had testified in his courtroom, and each time had been a chore when he blocked the prosecution testimony and cross-examination. Then again, Williams hadn't pushed the issues. It was crystal clear now why he hadn't fought the judge. Looking back, after her second trial with him prosecuting, he had changed from a zealot to letting things slide. She now knew that was when Williams had changed sides.

Her voice was venomous as she imparted the

information concerning the man in the photo. "He was on the bench for many of the lower-level creeps in the syndicate being held on federal charges. He suppressed evidence if it benefited the defense. On one case, he negated my whole testimony as being hearsay, even though I had been a part of the conversation, and had observed the drug deal and resulting murder.

"A murderer walked out of court a free man to kill again, which he did. Twice more that I'm aware of, but they couldn't successfully prosecute him because the evidence in each subsequent case was contaminated. That murderer is one of the four from the first box.

"This judge also threatened to have me banned from testifying in future cases after the last time I was in his court. I argued with him when Williams didn't object to my testimony being thrown out. Wyatt paid a $50,000 fine to keep me out of jail when he charged me with contempt of court." Jill hesitated before saying, "I believe he saw me at the club when he was there the last time. I can't be sure, but he did everything he could to negate my testimony when he was on the bench."

"Tom?" the man questioned, brows raised.

"Bingo."

"Jill, you gave us the means to shut them down. Franko and Bobkin are in custody with Franko and his lawyer objecting to being held on federal charges without bail. Before today is finished, I can expect to be hearing from a slew of lawyers, with more chiming in tomorrow."

Tom asked, "Okay, what's next, Malcolm? We now have the players, but there are two active contracts on Jill. How long to pull these in?"

She peered at the man Tom knew well enough to call by his first name, waiting for his response.

"It'll take the better part of today and tomorrow. Those pulled in will have enough charges against them to keep them in jail until the trial, but that won't stop the assassins hired to kill her. I'll request those arrested be denied bail until after the grand jury is completed due to the risk of flight. I'm sure Llewellyn will follow what I recommend. Our problem will be how to keep her under wraps until the trial."

She stared at the man before turning to Tom, her heart racing as a sense of doom slammed into her. This wasn't the judge! Fear gripped her, not knowing who this man was or his role in the case.

Tom quirked a brow before stating, "Malcolm, we neglected to say who you were."

Jill's eyes returned to the elderly man, awaiting his response. His gaze shifted to Tom, then back to her, lips turned up in a tight sly smile as his fingers moved the photos on the table. "If I had, there was a good chance she wouldn't have cooperated."

Malcolm faced her, his eyes twinkling with merriment. "Let me introduce myself. I'm Malcolm Phillips. I'll be prosecuting this case. It was because of me you're here, and will be on the stand testifying, ensuring these men get their just rewards. I'm a special federal prosecutor, and when Tom put Operation Revere into play, it brought me here to put this case together for trial.

"One reason I didn't negate the subpoena is because several of those you have given us tried to leave the country when I showed up. They're being held, pending what you gave me. A lot of little players are still out there, but we can pull them in as the case progresses. You gave me the ones I wanted." He shuffled through the last set of photos and shook his head. "Some of these men had illustrious careers. What a way to end them—in disgrace."

Her lips turned up before she stated, "I'm glad you're here. If Wyatt had known you were the one who didn't negate the subpoena, he wouldn't have been so upset."

Malcolm chuckled. "I guess my fame has preceded me."

"It has. I thought the subpoena was Williams's doing to get me into the open."

She had learned who Malcolm was from the years she had worked with Wyatt. The agency subcontracted with federal agencies to assist them and provide information on organized crime. Malcolm's name came up frequently when she sent reports. Jill had obtained more information on him from several sources in the agency, making her comfortable giving the information he had gotten from her. She grinned, glancing at Tom before turning back to

Malcolm, happy to meet the man who was determined to shut down as many of the syndicates as he could.

He sat back in the chair and steepled his fingers. "It wasn't me who got the subpoena, but I wasn't going to negate it once I arrived. I needed to find out who you could give us for the case to progress. Now, we have to figure out where to stash you until it's time for you to testify."

Tom shifted in his seat, facing the prosecutor. "We had her well hidden, but we can't go back to the person we used to hide her again. When do you expect to go to trial?"

"As soon as we have those she identified rounded up and behind bars. For your information, I arranged for the transcripts of her testimony from this trial to be used in the others due to the danger to her, along with the nature and difficulty of testimony she'll be giving. Most of those arrested will be under the same charges, and her testimony in this case will incriminate them. This way, she'll only need to testify once. I'll reinforce the arrangement with the defense and judges before I leave. The only time she'll be called to testify again is for issues not covered in this trial, but I don't believe there will be many of those. If I'm correct, her testimony will put the biggest share of this ring away in one trial."

He pursed his lips and sat staring at the picture on his right, tapping his pen on the table. He had taken her out of hiding. It was now up to him to keep his star witness safe.

Malcolm sighed. "You'll be sharing my digs. They have

no more rooms available here because our team needed to be in a secure place. It'll be close quarters, but I see no other options. There isn't another safe place to hold her that I can come up with at the moment. Llewellyn is here with his assistants also, so we have the last available rooms filled with our people. Because we bring our own guards with us, that adds more than they are used to having stay here. Like her, I have two working contracts on me related to this case."

From the merry expression on his face, he thought it funny how they had declared him a target. Gathering up the photos, he strode to the door and unlocked it.

"Fred, front and center," he bellowed upon opening the door.

Within seconds, Fred entered the room. Malcolm handed him the photos from the last box.

"You'll be getting federal warrants for these men within the hour. I want them picked up today." He handed him the second set. "These, bring in as many as you can find between now and tomorrow at fourteen hundred. Arrest them with charges pending until they get here." He handed him the last four photos. "These four here, find them and lock them in a cell together. Hopefully, they'll kill each other before I get to them. Use the minutemen and any other local resources you need.

"Wyatt will be a big help in finding many of them. Use him and give him and his PI's power to serve and arrest.

By 2 PM tomorrow, I expect to be informed of who's still among the missing."

Fred shuffled through the stack and grinned. "You got it. We have most of them under surveillance, hoping we could sweep them off the streets. This is going to be as much fun as Philly."

"More fun because we have the proof to hold them this time. I can hardly wait to see their faces when our little fairy starts talking."

Fred winked at her. "She'll bury them. Let me get the troops moving." He took out his phone and sent a text. "There should be twenty, give or take two or three, arriving within the next two hours. I hope you reserved accommodations for them."

"Done. We have space for a hundred, so bring them home to papa."

Fred left with a grin as he was dialing another number. Wyatt entered the room to find her sitting with Tom's arm around her, watching the prosecutor.

"Malcolm. Always nice to see you. I guess you got what you needed."

"More than I expected. She's fantastic. Your men ready to bring in the group they've been monitoring?"

"Waiting on authorization. She's a smart kid, keeping me abreast of who to keep tabs on over the years. To think that this all started as a case of a missing seventeen-year-old she was working for me. Jill's been waiting on this break for six long years."

"Meanwhile, I've been waiting for ten, so we both will get what we want this time. She and Tom will stay with me. I can't trust her to anyone else right now."

"Malcolm, Jill's my granddaughter and very special to me, so you had better take damn good care of her."

"I've a feeling you aren't the only one beyond me who wants her well taken care of," he imparted with a chuckle, letting his gaze go to Tom.

"Hey, I do have an interest in keeping her alive and kicking," Tom said with a grin.

With a serious voice, Malcolm ordered, "Wyatt, get to work. You have until tomorrow at two to inform me of who you rounded up. Bring them to the county jail. We have reservations for them."

Like Fred, Wyatt sent a text. From what she observed, they had everything arranged for this scenario. A short rotund man appeared at the door, a big grin on his face, brown eyes examining her.

"Elam, I want those brought in processed in a timely manner. You know the drill."

"Yes, sir," the short man answered, the grin widening. "Any restrictions on accommodations other than the four you mentioned earlier?"

"No. None," he stated as he strode to the table. A smile formed before he turned back to Elam. "Although, on second thought, it might be fun to see how our big guys enjoy being in with the lower classes. It might make them more amenable to answering questions."

Elam dipped his head before leaving with a bounce in his step. From his actions, the man was enjoying the prospect of processing the throng of soon-to-be federal prisoners.

Malcolm sent a text. A few seconds later six men entered the room. They were dressed in black jeans and T-shirts and armed with machine guns. Jill assumed they were the guards Malcolm had mentioned earlier.

"We're ready to leave. Treat these two as if it was me you're guarding. If anything happens to either one of them, heads will roll. Understood?"

"Yes, sir," one man responded as he studied her, then grinned at Tom as if they were friends.

Malcolm packaged up the leftover photos, placing them in the rolling bag he had under the table before starting toward the door. He stopped, grinning at the tall, thin, dark-haired man whose age was in the late forty to fifty-year-old range, leaning against the doorframe.

"You ready for action the day after tomorrow?" the man questioned, studying her before shifting to Malcolm.

"Yes, sir," Malcolm answered.

The man's merry brown eyes moved back to her. She had seen him before but couldn't remember where. He chuckled at her scrutiny before saying, "Yes, you've seen me before. I'm one of the good guys." With a raised brow, the man turned to Malcolm. "Bet you fifty she'll remember where, when, and will be able to quote word for word our conversation during that meeting."

"No bet."

"Smart man. If you need anything else, contact me. I delivered the items you requested. You'll only need to add the names."

"Will do," Malcolm answered as the man winked at her before he left with several guards surrounding him.

She turned to Tom, but he wasn't giving anything away. The man had her puzzled after his statement of them having met before today. It was the voice she recognized more than him. Not paying attention to where they were going, she sifted through her memory for that distinctive voice. It was low, with a vibrant timbre which held your attention.

When they stopped, she came back to the present. They were in a section of the courthouse she hadn't ever seen. Malcolm unlocked the door and opened it for her to enter. It was a suite, roomy enough to enable them to coexist without stumbling over each other. After she and Tom had entered the living room, Malcolm followed, closing and locking the door.

"It isn't fancy, but it's safer than trying to get you in and out of here. I'll admit to not being willing to give up my bed, but the sofa pulls out into a bed. I'm sure you two will be able to decide on how you want to sleep. There's a half bath through that door. We'll share the shower. I requested take-out for supper and it should be here soon, so make yourselves at home." He started to the bedroom before turning back. "Oh, before I forget, don't attempt to leave the suite. The orders are for you to remain here unless with me, so the guards won't let you leave."

Jill took a seat on the sofa and continued sifting through her memory, ignoring the others until she smiled at a picture from her past. Yes, he was there. It was right after she started to work for Wyatt as a PI. She had stumbled into a federal case through the case she was working on for Wyatt. She hadn't known how big her case was until she found a cell of smugglers. It wasn't until after she had the information needed to arrest the group she discovered she had become involved in a case the FBI and US Marshals had been working for over six years.

It had surprised her when Llewellyn was introduced as a federal judge. He appeared to be too young for such an elevated position. He wasn't on the bench for the case being tried, so he sat with Wyatt as she gave her testimony, which produced a guilty verdict. Afterward, he complimented her on the testimony and told her he would see her again when she testified in his court.

Tom noted her smile. "I take it you placed him."

"That was Judge Llewellyn and he'll be sitting on the bench as I testify this time. I met him five years ago, in another federal case I had stumbled into during the one I was working. It was his voice I recognized."

Malcolm intoned, with raised brows, "Glad I didn't take that bet. When he said what he did, there was no question of you having met him prior to today. I remember him telling me, after a visit here to talk to Wyatt, how he had heard this cute little imp testify. He said you were the best witness he had ever seen on the stand. You led the prosecutor into getting every bit of information you had, and it was concise, complete, and given in a manner that included all the relevant details. The cross-examination couldn't shake you, no matter what they tried. I hope that'll hold true for this trial, because they'll try to confuse you and trip you up on the details."

She shrugged. "You can't change the truth. I don't embellish and don't give questionable things without indicating the information isn't supported. What you'll get will be facts, and they don't change no matter what they try."

Malcolm took a seat in the chair opposite the sofa. "I hope not. We have a lot riding on your testimony. You'll be grilled by both sides. You'll probably be on the stand for several days. Are you sure you'll be able to hold up for that long?"

"I'll hold up. I can have a meltdown later when it's over. If I start to cry, don't stop unless I can't talk. Some of what needs to be covered will be painful for me, but you want that information." Jill knew he understood what she was telling him. On the other hand, she hoped she could make it through the trial without collapsing. To do that, she would need to stay extremely calm.

"I'll give you time to recover, but I won't stop unless you're sobbing to the point where you can't talk. I'll stop the defense if they get too rough and request a recess. Wyatt and Tom have informed me of what you went through. Brad will literally murder me if I don't protect you on the stand. As I said, we need every piece of the information you have, but not if it puts you at risk."

"You'll get it. Just follow where I lead you until I can't give any more information along that line, then go back and start on the next area. There are five major lines of questioning for you to follow. My best guess is I'll be testifying for upward of four or five days to cover each section."

"You can give me what questions to ask. You aren't going anywhere but from here to court. I've never worked with you before, and Williams won't be there, so I'll need all the help I can get."

Tom jumped in with, "Shaun has what she gave the other day at the meeting. I'm sure he'll fill you in on what lines of questioning she gave them to use. She never reveals details until under oath for good reason. The one time she did, the information ended up with the defense who used it to negate her testimony and a guilty guy walked."

"I get it." There was a knock on the door. "That should

be supper," he pronounced, pushing himself from the chair to answer the door. Tom's brother, Shaun, walked in with two pizzas.

"Well, I see you managed to get here alive," Shaun stated, setting the pizzas on the coffee table with a glance at his brother.

"I don't ignore a federal subpoena. Especially one from a top federal judge," Tom retorted.

Shaun smiled at her before stating, "Jill, it's good to see you in one piece. I was wondering after that session if they would find you."

She stated with a quirked eyebrow, "I'm pretty good at playing hide-and-seek."

"So I see. Malcolm, I have the stuff from that session with Williams. I'll give you the lines of questioning she gave to us to follow plus a few side trails to follow."

Malcolm opened both pizza boxes before taking a piece of the pepperoni pizza. "Good. Keep a copy for yourself as you'll be doing most of the questioning, seeing as how you were there when Williams screwed up."

Shaun stared at him. "Are you sure? I haven't been the lead on a case this big, and this one is very important to you and her both."

Malcolm swallowed the bite of pizza he had taken. "Son, you're as good, if not better than me at catching the nuances. She'll give you unexpected lines of questioning if you pay attention. Miss nothing, because she has vital information in that pretty head of hers, which we need to shut this cell down for good."

Shaun turned to her, his eyes boring into hers. The grim face sent a shiver up her spine, sending her heart rate into overdrive. "Jill, I'm not very nice in the courtroom. Please don't hold it against me."

"I don't expect you to be nice on the job. I'm not either. As I told Malcolm, if I cry, ignore it unless I can't talk. I'll answer if I'm able."

Shaun came over and squatted in front of her. He put his hands on her shoulders, his gaze holding hers. "I know Tom thinks the world of you. In that courtroom, I'll tear you apart, then try to put you back together again. I won't let up until I get everything you have, and probably some things you weren't aware you had, in that brain of yours. Tom's seen me in the courtroom, so he knows it's nothing personal. It's all about making the case and putting the bad guys away."

She gave him a wry grin. "I understand. Part of my testimony will be difficult at best. That's my problem, not yours. Just ask the questions no matter how embarrassing or nasty they may be. The jury will need to understand how I was also a victim, and that's how I got most of the information."

Shaun stood and moved behind Malcolm while she continued giving what to ask.

"One of the things to be very specific about in each

section is my state of mind. Make sure you cover how I was given drugs at various points in time. It'll be important to establish if I was lucid or not, because if you can't establish that, several will walk."

Shaun stared at her, eyes wide. "Girl, I can see why the prosecution liked you. You tell the truth and don't play games. That aspect was one concern, but I have my line of questioning from that statement. I believe we can show you were lucid by eliciting details a drugged person wouldn't normally notice or remember. Were there times when you didn't remember much due to being drugged?"

"Yes. You'll get that when you get into details concerning Billings. I'll be up front if I was drugged and unable to remember things clearly, such as the first week or so I was there. I can give you impressions, but little that is concrete."

Shaun turned and paced as he assimilated what she had just told him. Facing away from her, he asked, "Tell me, how many men did they bring you each day?"

She guessed at the reason for the question. "It depends on what period of time you're referring to."

"When you first got there," he requested.

"Billings kept me for himself for three months, give or take a week or so. The first man after him was Franko. Then the second was Bobkin."

"You're sure of the order?" he asked.

"Positive. I metabolized the drugs quickly, but they

weren't aware of it. I was never so drugged that I didn't remember someone being there."

"Are you positive Billings was the first?" he asked, turning to stare at her.

Jill stared at the rug, returning to the white room where she had been kept. There was no question he was the first. He had made sure she hadn't been able to fight him as he raped her. She would never forget his words: *"Who would've thought you were a virgin? No wonder you fought me so hard. We don't get many like you here, and I think I'll keep you for myself for a while before sharing."*

"Jill, please answer my question."

His words brought her back to the present. Her voice was flat as she stated, "He was the first. The very first. He kept me for himself for just over three months. He didn't drug me after the first time because he wanted me awake and aware of what he was doing." She glanced up at him with pain in her eyes.

"Why?" Shaun requested, his gaze direct, demanding an answer.

"Because I hadn't ever had sex before," she told him, taking a shaky breath. "I was a sixteen-year-old virgin, and he was making the most of it." She turned away from him, tears welling as she blinked rapidly to hold them back, pain and anger roiling through her.

"Shaun, explain what you're doing," Tom said, his arm coming around her as if to protect her from his brother's questions.

Shaun took a position behind Malcolm. "I'm verifying some information I was given. I have one more question, Jill, and I need the answer. Who did the abortion when he found out you were pregnant?"

Jill twisted her fingers in her lap, the tears dripping onto her clothes as she remembered what they had done to her. She took a few seconds to answer him, stuffing the sharp loss back into the box from which it had escaped.

Her voice was close to a whisper, riddled with pain, as she stated, "A Dr. Torres. He brought in this machine and did it while four men held my arms and legs. Billings told me he was sorry before Dr. Torres started. He hadn't meant for me to get pregnant. He forgot to have them put me on the pill. They gave me one every day after that. It was after that when Franko and Bobkin had access to me."

Shaun turned to Malcolm. "Torres is in custody. He was the one who told me about her. To save his skin, he gave information concerning her and several of the others. The description of her was accurate, and he remembered her name because she didn't scream. He said the men who were holding her had major bruises and fingernail marks from where she held on to them."

Malcolm sat in thought before saying, "You'll need to make sure you start there for Billings to get him on rape and sexual assault of a minor. I was wondering where you were going with those questions."

"I needed to verify if Torres was telling the truth. I didn't want to start that line of questioning to only find out I was working with lies." Shaun turned back to her, his face showing the pain he was feeling for her. "I'm so sorry, Jill, but I needed to verify he had told me the truth about what Billings had done. I see it as a starting point to what he did to the women there."

She kept her gaze on the carpet. "It's okay, Shaun. That's the nice part. It gets a whole lot worse." Tom's hand on her arm pulled her gaze to him. Blinking rapidly, she tried to stop the falling tears. Without speaking, Tom embraced her and let her cry.

"It's all right, honey," he murmured as she cried for the baby they had taken from her in such a cruel manner. He had needed to hear the truth.

She kept her head on his shoulder, muffling her voice. "While there, they did major damage as punishment before I was rescued. I might never be able to have children of my own. I wasn't lying when I said I was damaged."

"We'll cross that bridge when we get to it. It doesn't change one thing for me." He raised her head, admitting, "Sweetheart, I already knew, but I needed you to tell me when you were ready. You see, Brad and I are good friends. He told me when I found him crying over what had happened to you. He never mentioned your name, but was hurting for his beautiful little sister. She hadn't known of the permanent damage caused by the abuse from her kidnappers until she had problems and needed to see a doctor.

"Until I discovered Brad was your brother at the café, I didn't connect what he told me to you. I should have made the connection when you said you were Wyatt's granddaughter, but didn't, not aware you were from Brad's family."

"And you still love me?"

"Yes. I do. Very much. As I said, we'll worry about that when the time comes."

She gave him a watery smile. He kissed her forehead, then held her close, her head on his shoulder. It didn't matter what the others thought. He wasn't going to leave her. As long as he was there with her, she could tell them whatever they wanted to know from her past.

"Shaun," Tom uttered.

"Yes."

"You better do as good a job in court. There's more there, and I'm sure that was just the tip to the iceberg."

Shaun ran a hand through his hair, pulling himself from lawyer mode. "Yeah, it is. I can see her testimony will be excellent with the way she answered those questions." He faced his brother. "Tom, you had better do right by her. She's been to hell and back and doesn't need you to get close to her, only to walk away later."

Jill giggled through her tears. She gave Tom a watery grin.

He tilted his head, a smile on his lips, then kissed her before she buried her face in his shoulder again. "You're only the fifth person to tell me that. Brad will beat me to a pulp, after Wyatt and Sam get through with me, and Billy will get his guys to punish me if I don't stick with her."

Shaun and Malcolm laughed at his admission of threats of bodily harm.

"Nothing like having tons of pressure applied, is there?" Malcolm merrily asked.

Tom's arms tightened around her, chuckling. She raised her head and grinned at him before he stated while gazing at her, "Hey, I understand. She's this real special lady, and they want to make sure I won't walk out on her. As I've said before, where she goes, I go, and that won't stop when this is over."

Shaun shook his head and chuckled. "Big brother, when you fall, you do it up right. I can see Pop when you bring her home. You'll have trouble keeping him from spoiling her to death."

"I know. He always wanted a girl, and she'll look like a child next to him."

"You're telling me. I'm four inches taller than you, and he makes me look small."

Jill turned her head to Shaun, eyes wide. He was around six four, but not huge, just tall.

"So, your father is bigger than Brad and Wyatt?" she questioned, needing verification of what he had just said.

"You tell her. I can't," Shaun requested, laughing.

With a chuckle, Tom told her, "A bit. He's six seven and runs around two fifty and is all muscle like Wyatt and Brad. I'm the runt of the family, as I'm only six one."

Her brothers and grandfather were between six four and six-six and weighed from two thirty for Ryan to two fifty or more for Wyatt and Brad, with most of their weight being muscle. Wyatt had more weight on him than Brad, but he was still in great shape. Yeah, their father would be imposing, but then again, so were Wyatt and her father, who was six-five and somewhere around two forty, and like Wyatt, muscled from hard work.

Jill beamed up at Tom and patted his cheek. "It's okay, Tom. I'm the runt in my family. I don't look as if I belong because I'm so tiny."

Tom glanced at his brother before asking, "You did say your sister was somewhere around six foot and solid, right?"

Jill giggled, "Yes."

Shaun stared at her and Tom. "Have you seen her?" he asked.

"Yes. Nice-looking girl, but I'd guess somewhat on the feisty side. You'd have your hands full with her in more ways than one."

Malcolm laughed at Tom's description.

Jill offered, "I can arrange an introduction. She's always complaining how she can't find a man who wants to take her out who isn't looking at her boobs when she stands up."

The men roared with laughter at her description of her sister's boyfriends. When Shaun sobered, he stated, "I may take you up on that. I'm tired of patting women on the head." Jill giggled again. She could picture him doing just that to her.

Shaun ended up staying late as they talked and joked around. He was very likeable, but from his questions earlier, he wouldn't back away from the harder questions when in lawyer mode. When he left, she stopped Malcolm before he could leave the room.

Her eyes were direct as she inquired, "Why are you having Shaun question me instead of you?"

Malcolm turned and leaned against the doorframe to his room, meeting her gaze.

"Because he's much better than me in questioning. Yes, I'm the lead and will direct things. He'll come to me when he needs suggestions, but he'll cover every detail. He's been with me for six years, and I've been training him for this particular trial.

"I'm getting to the point where I'll need someone to take over my position, and he's the best trial lawyer I've run across. He has a memory like a steel trap and can quote case law the judges are forced to look up and verify. He does his homework and is prepared for every case no matter how small or big it is. If he does as well with this case as I expect he will, he'll become my partner until I retire. At that time, he'll take over the position as special prosecutor for this division."

She drew her brows together, staring at him with concern. "So, you won't be asking me any questions?"

"I didn't say that. There's a section where you'll have to deal with me. By the time I'm done, you'll hate me, but that's okay. I'll have elicited the information we need to put them away. Shaun will learn in that session what he needs on how to get information from a hostile state witness, because you'll be hostile by the time I'm finished."

A wry grin passed over her features. "Just remember, it won't be personal. I can guess which portion you'll be taking over."

Malcolm gave a quick bob of his head. "I'm sure you can. Good night." He entered his room and the door clicked closed.

Tom stared at her. "Okay. What was that all about?"

She walked over to the sofa where he was sitting and sat beside him. Tom didn't understand how certain questions could anger her, making her hostile with further questioning.

She glanced at him then focused on the floor before answering his question. "Most of the time, the lead guy does the most important questions, then gets the others to do the not-so-sensitive questions. Not this time. I know what he wants, and he'll have to ask the right questions in the right way to get that information. Shaun needs to see how to handle a hostile state witness when they are a victim of those they are prosecuting."

"Why would you become hostile?"

"You'll see. It won't be pretty, but he'll get what he needs."

"I feel like I'm missing something here."

"You are. But then again, you don't have the information; he does. He figured it out when I was going through those pictures."

She pawed through her valise, found her pajamas before going to the half bath to change. She hoped he didn't change his mind after Malcolm was finished with extracting all the information the prosecution needed. He would learn how she was damaged. It was something she had only told Brad when she had problems several years later. The other person who knew was her therapist, Quinn, who had helped her to put her life back together.

Chapter 19

REASONS WHY

Tom and Jill had shared the pullout bed for the night. Like in the efficiency, he held her, keeping the nightmares at bay. He had just awakened her with a kiss when Malcolm joined them, dressed in casual clothes for the day. Her face heated as he stood peering at them. A chuckle escaped him and Tom when she hid her face on Tom's shoulder.

"You two had better get up. Shaun will be here soon with breakfast." With a shake of his head, Malcolm watched them, his hand resting on the back of the couch. "Tom, you're one lucky man. There aren't many women like her running around free."

The arms around her tightened. "You aren't telling me something I don't already know."

Malcolm turned a direct gaze to her. After a quick glance at Tom, he spoke to her as if Tom wasn't there.

"Jill, while everyone keeps warning him to do right by you, unlike them, I'm warning you. You had better not hurt Thomas. He hasn't allowed someone to get to that heart of his before now. Treat it with care. If you don't, it'll shatter and I'm not sure he'll be able to put it back together again."

Turning to Tom, she noticed the glare he gave Malcolm, whose words had disclosed more than he had wanted her to know. She reached up and ran a hand over his cheek, staring into the serious green eyes watching her.

"Don't worry, Malcolm. He still needs to fulfill his promise to take me dancing in the moonlight in a magical place. Plus, I'm not letting him renege on his promise to go where I go. I hope it'll take a few years before he tires of me. I'll stick around until then."

"You had better," Malcolm warned and moved away.

Tom raised a brow. "You do realize that it'll take a lifetime for me to tire of you."

"I hope so," Jill admitted, snuggling into him. Her intense fear of his leaving was mitigated by his reaction to her answers to Shaun's questions. His total acceptance of her after her revelation wasn't expected. Most men wanted children of their own.

"Darling, you might want to get dressed before Shaun gets here, or be ready for him to tease the hell out of both of us," Tom warned with a laugh.

Unwilling to be embarrassed, Jill moved out of his embrace. Taking her valise, she went to the bath in Malcolm's room to shower. Dressed in jeans and a snug T-shirt, she returned to the living room. Malcolm studied her, frowning, causing her to wonder what the problem was.

Malcolm asked, "When they took you, what were you wearing?"

"Jeans and a tank top."

"Was the tank top snug?"

Okay, she understood where he was going with his questions. Her manner of dress could have caused them to target her rather than her friends.

"Look, I was a teenager and dressed like most of the girls in snug jeans and a tank, which showed my figure. I'm sure it was part of what made me a target. The other part was that I had come in alone and didn't partner with anyone while there. What they saw was this childlike female who looked good and didn't have a protector. Their mistake was in not knowing who I was."

Malcolm studied her, his face showing concern. "Jill, you're still that childlike girl who projects an innocence to those around you. That's what they were wanting, and we'll use that innocence to hang them. Be yourself on that stand. Don't be professional. Let those emotions show."

She scuffed her foot on the carpet, focused on her feet, chewing on her sucked-in cheeks. It took a few seconds for her to respond. "I know you've never seen me on the stand. Llewellyn has. What you'll see is the real me. I can't pretend to be something I'm not because it would fall apart in no time.

"It'll only take a few questions to elicit the emotions behind the words. I won't be able to hide the pain you'll cause me with those questions. That's part of why the defense hates me on the stand. I can't hide what I'm feeling. You'll get what you want, and it'll be real. I know I'll fight the tears and try to hold in the anger, but it'll come out no matter what I do."

Malcolm moved to where she stood and lifted her head with his fingers under her chin. "Just remember, it'll hurt Shaun and me to ask those difficult questions. I know you'll be reliving a very painful time. In truth, I'm not sure who's going to have the more difficult job, me or you."

She gave him a crooked grin. "You, because you have to hide how you're feeling and I don't."

He let out a big breath, his face controlled. "Glad you understand. I wanted to be sure you didn't pretend to be unaffected by the questions and your answers. While I rely on years of experience, it's still hard to be the bad guy. This time, it will be extremely hard for me to stay in lawyer mode."

"Why?" she questioned, brows drawn together.

He lowered his hands and turned away from her. She heard the strain in his voice.

"Because you remind me of my daughter. She was kidnapped by them at age fifteen, but she didn't make it out. Unable to take what they were doing to her, she committed suicide. This is personal for me, because of what happened to her. As I'm questioning you, it will be as if I'm having my daughter reveal what they did to her. Like you, I don't want them to walk."

"When did she die?" Jill asked. She was almost certain she had known his daughter by what he had said.

Malcolm turned back to her, eyes filled with pain, a

deep abiding grief on his face. "Around eighteen months after they took you. Her name was Susan."

Jill sucked in a deep breath, again feeling the pain of losing her one true friend while in captivity. She had been right, but it wasn't any consolation when the understanding of Susan's last words rose up from where she had buried them. Susan had committed suicide to protect her father, allowing him to continue his work. Only, she hadn't known what Susan's father's work was at the time. It all came together with Malcolm's revelation.

"I knew her well. We were together most of the time when I became a dancer. I tried to talk her out of killing herself, but she said that even if she got out, she couldn't live with what they had done to her."

Jill didn't try to stop the tears running in silvery streaks over her cheeks as she imparted what happened to his daughter.

"She and I attacked the matron when she tried to get us to do a lesbian-type show because we looked so much alike. Susan hung herself that night after telling me I needed to remain strong."

His arms came around her, allowing her to cry for the girl who had made her promise to help the others if she ever got out. Susan was the one who had made her want to live to see Billings and his cronies punished.

"Jill, I'll be asking you about her. I know you befriended her. Be honest and don't hold back."

The death of his daughter explained why he had been a zealot in prosecuting the racketeering cases involving kidnapping and the sex trade he was assigned over the years. He had a personal interest in seeing them shut down. Like her, he hadn't quit when he could have, wanting justice for his daughter.

"Malcolm," she intoned, not wanting to tell him the rest but knew he needed to hear it now, not during the trial.

"Hmm?"

"She knew you were close to getting her out. It was one of the reasons she did what she did. She told me she didn't want what happened to her to affect what you were doing. Also, she couldn't stand the thought of what her life would be like, and the pain it would cause you. She also let me know there was an inside guy working on getting me out. You might want to explore that avenue. It'll explain many things."

Malcolm didn't turn her loose, needing to comfort her as much as himself. The tears dropping on her head showed he was still grieving for the daughter he had loved and lost. "Thank you for being her friend. Our man informed me about you and the friendship you two had. He did his best to protect you without giving himself away."

Jill admitted, "He was the one who told me to dance to stay out of the hole and have access to a better class of men. Because of him, most of the johns sent to me were decent. It helped."

At the knock on the door, Malcolm gave her a kiss on the cheek before answering the summons. It was Shaun with their breakfast. Tom took Malcolm's place. His gentle hand drying her tears had her peering up at him.

"I can see how difficult this trial will be. Just let me know what you need from me," Tom murmured, drawing her closer to him.

"Mostly I'll need reassurance that I'm not this horrible, ugly, used whore. But I'm not the only one who'll have a difficult time this go-around."

"You're correct, Jill," Shaun stated, having overheard her last statement. "I'll be tearing my brother's girl apart, and it won't be easy for me either."

"And it isn't going to be easy for Llewellyn. He has to remain impartial while his friends are being emotionally torn apart," Tom stated. Her quizzical look had him adding, "Honey, he's friends with Wyatt and has been for years. When he was in the courtroom listening to you testify, he needed to know what to expect. This will be one of the most difficult trials he'll ever preside over. He'll have to remain impartial and rule by the book while watching you being torn to shreds."

Tom sent a quick glance to Malcolm then said, "He attempted to recuse himself from this case because of you. His bosses refused to allow it, even after revealing his friendship with Wyatt and your relationship to him. He was instructed to let the lawyers provide the evidence and do what he's always done: be fair and impartial in the courtroom and in his sentencing."

Sighing, she stated, "I hope the defense doesn't use his relationship with Wyatt to get a retrial. I don't think I can go through this twice."

Malcolm patted her on the shoulder. "You won't. They won't have a leg to stand on as it's me doing the questioning, and he'll be so fair they won't have a thing to use. It'll be up to the jury to determine guilt, not him. He'll just give the sentences. Those are based on the charges, their history, and the recommendations of the attorneys and any other interested parties."

They dropped the subject of the trial while eating breakfast, waiting for the calls notifying Malcolm of those who were in custody. The trio spent the day talking about mutual acquaintances and family, along with playing cards. Shaun was the one who made the food runs. For some reason, he wasn't a target. She expected that to change when the syndicate found out he would be doing most of the questioning.

At 2 PM, the calls came in one after the other. Out of the outstanding criminals with arrest warrants, only ten were still on the loose. They were expecting them to be in jail before the trial started.

Jury selection was scheduled to start in the morning, with the trial expected to begin the day after the jury was approved. The defense had requested a delay, objecting to the lack of time to prepare for the trial. Llewellyn denied the request, stating they had been given over six years to prepare, and due to threats to several witnesses, there would be no delays for further preparations.

Malcolm explained this meant that she was to be confined to the courthouse and his apartment for the duration of the trial. Even then, she may need to stay in hiding until the contracts on her expired or were called off. He expected her to be on the stand for four to five days for the prosecution, then another two to three for the defense.

With the talk of the contracts on her, Tom remembered Snake and how he had refused to kill her.

"Jill, I know Snake negated his contract on you. Why?"

That was a question she had avoided answering. There was total silence while everyone waited for her response.

She flicked a glance over the men before saying, "It was during an extraction of an undercover agent from a drug syndicate for the DEA. Snake was working a contract to assassinate the leader of the group. He got caught, along with the agent, when the leader discovered a plant among his men. The plant ratted on the agent and Snake, hoping to save his life by making the leader believe he was working for him. I freed Snake along with the agent, leaving the rat to his fate, not trusting him after he rolled on his own gang.

"Because I let him go for helping us to get away, even after finding out who he was, he said he owed me. Figuring he might take a contract on me in the future, we agreed that if he missed me on the first shot, he had to let me go on that contract. That's what happened at the warehouse. In the text he sent me, he said he still owes me, as that wasn't enough to fulfill his debt. He's honorable and pays his debts of honor."

"Uh-huh. So, describe him for me," Tom requested, aware she wasn't about to help him capture the assassin who charged a million per hit.

Jill laughed. "I'm not telling. It was part of our agreement. Nice try though."

Malcolm chuckled, "Tom, forget it. She has her friends, and Snake is one. Her life would be forfeit if she told you what he looked like."

With a sigh and shake of his head, Tom didn't push the issue. It was a good thing, because she didn't break her word to any of the friends who protected her like she did them. Not only that, Snake only took contracts for non-government targets.

The next morning, Jill stayed in the suite during the jury selection. It didn't matter who was on the jury for her. Tom had gone with Malcolm and Shaun, leaving her alone. Her day was spent reading a sci-fi novel, not wanting to remain in this world for the day. It was a way of staying stress-free. Her heart rate had gone from normal to out of control with each stressor over the last two days.

A guard brought lunch to her. He stayed and talked while she ate. She had enjoyed the company because the man had a great sense of humor and had kept her laughing as she ate. The laughter was something she had needed.

It was late afternoon when she fell asleep on the couch while reading. A gentle hand on her cheek awakened her. Her eyes opened to Wyatt's smiling face.

"How's my little fairy doing all cooped up?"

"Not too bad. It's just somewhat boring."

His face showed concern when he told her, "They should have the jury picked by tomorrow, but it'll be another day or two before they get to you. They need to lay the groundwork first."

"It's okay. I have my Kindle and can keep myself from thinking about it." She couldn't face him before saying, "You and Brad don't need to sit through my testimony if you don't want to."

"Would you prefer us to not be there?" he questioned.

She held on to his hand. "I honestly don't know. I will reveal things I never told you."

"Child, nothing will change my love for you. You'll always be my little fairy. If you want us there for support, we'll be there, but if there are things you don't want us to know, then we'll respect your privacy. Right now, it depends on your comfort level, not ours."

She peered up at him, blinking back tears, and admitted, "I wish you could hold my hand through it all, but I know they won't let you. If things get to be too much, I'll understand if you leave."

Wyatt pulled her onto his lap, cradling her next to him. "Brad and I will be there for you. Just let us know what you need."

Her arms went around him, fighting the fear of what was to come. "For you to continue to love me, and maybe help me to put the pieces back together again when it's over."

"You got it, baby girl. Thomas will be here for you. This is the last time I'll be able to see you until the trial is over. Because I'm a witness, along with Brad, they don't want us discussing the case. If you need anything, let me know now and I'll see that you get it."

"I need my court clothes. The blue dress you packed is the only one I have to wear. I'll need underthings and shoes to go with them."

"Anything else?" he questioned as he held her, rocking slightly.

"The new jewelry. I want to wear it."

Wyatt understood why. She needed something to make her feel pretty, because what she was going to say would make her feel dirty and used. He and Brad had gifted her with nice things during her recovery. The clothes and jewelry were their way of telling her she was still beautiful. It was what she needed then and now.

"I'll make sure it's packed. Shaun will bring it to you.

My time is up. Malcolm is motioning for me to leave. I love you, baby girl. No matter what you say, that won't change."

He gave her a kiss and a hug before setting her back on the couch.

"Thank you, Malcolm. You have witnesses we didn't discuss the case. Take good care of her for me, please."

"I will. She'll be fine. It's the aftermath that concerns me, so make sure you're available then."

"I've a fucking feeling she won't fucking need me as much with Thomas around, but I'll be here just in case."

Wyatt left with the guards who had stayed in the room. It would be a long few weeks or more for her and him both. She knew he was worried about her when he didn't swear like he normally did. Since her rescue, he had been there when she needed him. Now, Tom and Malcolm were going to attempt to take his place. She hoped it would be enough.

Chapter 20

SEX AND LOVE

Wyatt sent the clothes that he knew she needed along with all the accessories two days later. When she opened the suitcase, her grandfather had placed a note on top of the things he had packed. Her face turned red as she read what he had written. This was the last thing she expected from her grandfather.

Tom, noticing her red face, asked, "What did Wyatt do to cause you to blush like that?" She handed him the note.

He read the note, which said, *Jill, you be good to that boy. He loves you. I have no objection to you getting as close as you want to him before the wedding.*

"You know, I never expected that from Wyatt," Tom told her with a chuckle.

"It's a first for me, too. He likes you and knows how much I love you."

Tom tugged on a curl and admitted, "Again, this isn't something I ever expected him to condone for his precious fairy."

"I wasn't expecting it because he's so old-fashioned most of the time."

Tom met her gaze. "Honey, it's up to you to decide when the time is right. I'm content to wait. I won't say it's always easy, but I'm not in any big hurry."

She studied the note, thinking over what she really wanted. "I guess I'm one of the weird ones who prefer to wait for a more permanent commitment."

"Then, that's what will happen. Like I said, I'm willing

to wait." He sat beside her on the floor and took her hands. "Jill, I'm in this for the long haul. You'll get that permanent commitment, but I want to wait until this is over and you're back together. Once we're no longer under major stress, we'll have the time to make sure I'm what you want in a man."

From his statement, he was insecure in her wanting him long term. She understood because she was unable to squelch the fear of him walking away after the trial. Once he learned what they had done to her, he would need to accept her, garbage and all.

The trial had started that afternoon. She would have another day or two to wait. It was on Friday, two days later when Malcolm said, "Jill, you'll begin testifying Monday morning."

His pronouncement put her heart into overdrive for a few minutes. It subsided with a few deep breaths. It flitted through her mind to call Wyatt, but quickly dismissed the thought. She would have to inform Malcolm of why she needed to talk to her grandfather, and for now, it was information she wanted to keep to herself. She had faith it would all work out.

Malcolm woke them early Monday morning after an uneventful weekend. Tom held her as he had every night since their time in the efficiency. She left the comfort of his arms and went to prepare for the day, having slept without dreams. It was the longest she had been without the nightmares since her return home.

The outfit she chose for the first day was a conservative suit. Opening the box containing the jewelry set she had bought, she put on the earrings and bracelet. Tom took the necklace and fastened it around her neck, kissing where his hands had touched her neck before she turned to face him.

"I'm not sure what sort of shape I'll be in tonight," she informed him.

"I'm ready for the worst and hoping for the best." He pushed a curl into place. "Jill, I wish you didn't have to do this, but I do understand why. No matter what, remember I love you."

She spent a few seconds in his arms then reluctantly joined Malcolm for the walk to the courtroom. He kept his hand at her waist. She knew he was steeling himself for what he needed to do, just as she was. It would be a very long day for both of them.

Shaun met them at the courtroom door. He waited with her outside, surrounded by guards, until the bailiff motioned for them to enter. A fast perusal of the room showed a group of men and women she recognized guarded by deputy marshals. Jill surmised they were all defendants who were here to testify, identify, or being charged with the three at the defense table.

She lowered her gaze to the floor, following the bailiff

to the witness stand. He had her repeat the oath to tell the truth, then requested her to state her full name and occupation. She sat in the witness chair and waited for the questions to begin, keeping her head down, not wanting to show the anger and fear coursing through her with those from her nightmares so close.

Shaun, not Malcolm, started the questioning. He began with how she became connected to the federal case through the one she was working investigating Charles Knight. He followed her answers in to how it led to Billings, covering the details of what she and Tom discovered in breaking the case. Malcolm was right. He was very good and tenacious in following up on the nuances in her testimony, covering all the side areas while working his way to her abduction and the time she had spent in the brothel. It took him all day to get to this point. She had to admire his thoroughness.

The next morning, Shaun picked up where he had left off. He picked on a couple of areas where he wanted to get more information into the record. He went back the Knight and his ties to the syndicate. She knew this was a background work leading to the real issues.

Jill tensed when he started a new line of questioning leading up to her missing years. Shaun returned to the prosecution table after having her state how she was held in captivity for three years. He nodded to Malcolm, who hesitated, reading what he had written on a legal pad before walking toward her. He stopped before the rail, peering at her and asked, "Ms. Potter, I will be asking you a lot of questions. How would you like me to address you?"

"Please, call me Jill."

"Jill, from what we have learned, you were kidnapped and held for three years give or take a few months. Is that correct?"

"That's correct."

"Where were you held?" he questioned.

"At a place called The Underground Playground."

"Please tell the court about how you were kidnapped."

"I went to a party given by one of my friends. I drove there because I didn't normally stay late at parties. During the evening, I met this older man who started to talk to me. When I was ready to leave, he offered to walk out with me, saying he was leaving too. When we got to my car, he grabbed my arm and said I was coming with him. Before I could do anything, someone came up behind me and put a cloth over my face with this funny sweet smell. The next thing I remember is waking up in this strange white room."

Malcolm's next question wasn't unexpected. "What were you wearing that night?"

Jill let her gaze go between Malcolm and the man who had taken her. "A fitted tank top and snug jeans with sandals."

His next question was for the jury, so they had a decent idea of what she looked like when kidnapped. "How old would you say you appeared to be at the time?"

Aware she appeared much younger than twenty-five, she shrugged before saying, "Around fourteen or maybe younger. I still get carded when I order a drink where I'm not known. They don't think I'm twenty-one yet."

"If you were to see the man who kidnapped you today, would you recognize him?" Malcolm questioned.

"Yes. He was frequently at the club."

"Is he here in the courtroom?"

"Yes," she stated, focusing on the man who had kidnapped her. He was seated with the prisoners behind the defense team.

Malcolm turned to the people in the courtroom. "Will you please point him out to the court?"

She made eye contact with the man who had kidnapped her. "He's the man on the far left of the first row as I'm facing."

"Do you know his name?"

"I know him as Dave. That's the name he gave me at the party."

"Did you talk to him after that night?"

"No. He never came near enough for me to talk to him."

"Jill, how old were you at the time you were taken?"

"I was just two weeks shy of my sixteenth birthday." It was nine years ago when she had been thrust into the nightmare.

"How old are you now?"

"I'll be twenty-five in nine days."

"And you're positive this is the man who took you nine years ago?" he questioned, verifying her statement.

"Yes, I am."

"How can you be so sure?"

"I may not remember the name, but I seldom forget a face or a distinctive voice and what we talked about, even years later."

"Okay. What did you and this man discuss at the party?"

"My car. It was new, and I was thrilled to have something so nice. We briefly discussed the merits of the Mustang versus the Corvette and Miata convertibles. I gave him a good argument for the Mustang. He laughed and discounted my arguments since he liked the Corvette."

"Why would you remember such a conversation so many years later?"

"I don't know. Ever since I was a child, I have remembered conversations. It used to drive my parents crazy when I could repeat almost word for word their arguments months later."

Malcolm turned away and asked, "What type of job do you do today?"

"I'm a private investigator and have been since I turned twenty."

"Have you used this memory for conversations in your work?"

"Of course."

"Do you remember a case where you repeated a conversation, and you were called a liar during a trial?"

"Yes. It was *Harrison vs The State*. He tried to say he didn't tell me that he had stolen several cars and firearms. I repeated almost word for word what he had said to me."

"This was how long after the conversation with him?"

"Two years."

"What happened when the defense attempted to deny what you remembered?"

"They played the recording from the police wiretap I was wearing at the time."

"Had you ever listened to the recording?"

"No. I didn't need to because I knew what was on it."

"What happened?"

"The man was convicted. What I told the court was what he said on the recording other than a couple of words."

"So, when you say you remember the conversation with the man you know as Dave, if there was a recording, it could confirm the accuracy of your memory."

"Yes," she answered, wondering why he was asking. He had just proven she could remember conversations.

"I would like to submit the following CD as exhibit P. It contains the conversation between her and David Collins, the man she identified as her kidnapper."

He proceeded to play the CD. She hadn't known the

party was being recorded. It verified what she had told them. He had proven beyond a doubt her memory of conversations and faces. She remained impassive, listening to the conversation she had with Dave so many years ago..

When her conversation was over, Malcolm stopped the CD, and addressed the court and jury, "Jill had no idea this recording existed since it's been in police custody since her disappearance. As you heard, she remembered the man and the conversation they had over nine years ago. As we go through her testimony, she will give other instances of where she participated in conversations. For some of them, we will have recordings backing up what she is saying, but for many there will be none."

He let what he had said hang for a few seconds as he consulted the notepad on the table. She knew why he was hesitating. This was going to be difficult for him and her.

"Jill, describe the room where you woke up."

She described the soundproofed walls, the small bath, the ceiling with the slits along the wall with mirror-like glass, and the locked door. He asked her to describe the soundproofing in the room. With her head lowered, she related how the panels in the room were offset with the rough surfaces and holes.

Next, Malcolm had her give details of the furniture in the room. She could still see the bed with the bent metal pipes as head and foot boards with the white chipped paint. The frame was sturdy enough to hold up to someone pulling on it with all their strength while tied or handcuffed. It was one of the things which showed up frequently in her nightmares.

"What were you wearing when you woke up?" was his next question.

"Just my underthings. The rest of my clothes were gone."

"How long were you alone in that room?"

"I'm not sure. I remember eating, but everything was hazy and I'm not sure how long it was until the haziness went away. What I do remember is when I became fully alert, I was brought a sandwich to eat. They turned off the lights when I was done. They turned on the lights and brought me cereal and then another sandwich before anyone talked to me."

"So, they brought in this food but didn't speak to you."

"Yes."

"Who came in and talked to you?"

"Mr. Billings."

"Is he here in this courtroom?"

"Yes."

"Please point him out for the court."

She glared at Billings, her mouth grim. "He's the one on the far left at the defense table."

Malcolm again paused before asking, "What did he talk to you about?"

Swallowing, she bit her lower lip before replying in a

voice so soft it could barely be heard, even with the microphone. "He said, 'You are so young and pretty. I'm going to keep you for myself until I tire of you.'"

"What did you say?"

"I told him I was scared and wanted to go home."

"And his response?"

She stared at her hands but not seeing them as her fingers twisted together to prevent them from shaking. "He told me I was in my new home and to forget the old one." She peeked up at Malcolm. "He then told me he would teach me how to be a real woman."

"What did he do after that?"

"He started touching me. I told him to leave me alone, but he just laughed and said I could fight all I wanted, but he would win in the end."

"And did you fight him?"

"Yes. He finally overpowered me, then tied my hands and feet to the bed."

"Then what happened?" Malcolm's voice was kind, but it didn't help.

She took a deep breath and kept her head down. "He ripped off my underthings and proceeded to rape me."

"Did you give him consent at any time to touch you?"

"No!" her answer was quick and sharp with the anger she was holding in check.

Malcolm picked up a paper from the table and handed it to Llewellyn. "Your Honor, we would like to amend the charges on Mr. Billings to include charge of rape of a minor and felonious assault with intent to do bodily harm."

The defense popped up, "Objection. It's her word against his."

Llewellyn quickly replied, "Overruled. It was established in prior testimony given by Dr. Torres and Mr. Garrett that she was held against her will and didn't give consent. Continue, Counselor."

"Jill, had you ever had a sexual relationship before Mr. Billings raped you?"

"No."

"So, you were still a virgin."

"Yes."

"What did he say when he discovered that fact?"

She glared at Billings before answering the question, unable to stop the anger from coming through in her voice. "He told me he hadn't ever had a real virgin before and was going to keep me for himself."

"Jill, how many times did Mr. Billings come and force you into having sex?"

"Every day for almost three months."

"What happened at that time?"

"He asked me if I normally had my monthly cycle on a regular basis."

"What did you tell him?"

"Yes. This was the first time I had ever missed one."

"What happened then?"

"He got upset and started cursing. He blamed me for not telling him. I didn't know what he meant."

Malcolm gently questioned, "You didn't know?"

"No. I didn't know that missing my cycle meant I was pregnant. I knew about sex and the results, but no one had told me that one fact."

"So, you didn't know you were pregnant?"

"No."

"What happened next?"

She gripped her hands together until they hurt, blinking rapidly while attempting to hold back the pending tears. Her voice held the pain she was feeling. "He had Dr. Torres come and examine me. He confirmed I was pregnant. They brought in this machine. I didn't know what they were going to do. Two men held my arms and shoulders while two more held my legs. Dr. Torres used the machine to abort the pregnancy."

"Did they give you anything for sedation or pain before doing this?"

"No." Her one word was sharp as she bit it off, reliving that time.

"What did you do?"

"I gripped the arms of the men holding my hands and did what I could to keep from screaming with the pain and to not move." She rubbed her eyes with her knuckle to stop the tears before they started.

"How long did this all take?"

"It was over in about ten minutes. I was bleeding, but they didn't care. Everyone left me there, alone, lying in the blood." She raised her head and glared at him. The anger over what they had done to her showing on her face and in her eyes.

Malcolm ignored her glare. "How long were you left like that?"

"Until I was able to get up and shower. I took the sheets off and used a towel to catch what blood was still coming out. It wasn't until the next day someone came in and brought me clean sheets, towels, and food."

Malcolm leaned on the rail of the witness stand. "How long before someone, other than those bringing you food, came to see you?"

"I'm not sure. It had to be several weeks. There was no clock or calendar in the room, so I have no real idea of how long I was there."

"Did they start giving you a pill each day?"

"Yes. The woman who gave it to me told me it was so I wouldn't get pregnant again."

"So, you took it."

"Yes. I didn't want to go through that again."

Malcolm moved away before asking his next question. "Jill, did Mr. Billings come back to see you?"

"Yes. He told me he was sorry, but he couldn't allow me to have a baby. I was too valuable."

"What did he do?"

"He had sex with me again."

"Did you let him know that you didn't want him to have sex with you this time?"

"No. He would have just tied me up again if I tried to fight, so I just laid there and let him do what he wanted. It didn't really matter any longer. I couldn't stop him, and it was easier if I didn't fight."

"So, you let him do what he wanted because you knew you didn't have a choice, is that correct?"

"Yes, sir," she responded as tears ran down her cheeks. She didn't know when she had started to cry. Wiping the tears from her face with her hand, she attempted to stop them, but they just kept falling.

"Jill, what happened after he started having sex with you again?"

"He came in one day and said that he now had to share me. One of his bosses wanted me, and I needed to be nice to him."

"Is that man in this room today?"

"Yes."

"Please point him out to the court."

"The man next to Mr. Billings. His name is Mr. Franko."

Malcolm went to the table and picked up another piece of paper and handed it to the judge. "We would like to amend the charges on Mr. Franko to include statutory rape using force on a minor."

"So noted," Llewellyn stated. The defense didn't object this time.

"What did Mr. Franko do?"

Jill's glare went to Franko. She couldn't hide the hate coursing through her. It showed on her face and in her voice as she said, "He came in and undressed, then put his hand between my legs. He became angry when I started to cry and slapped me. He told me to stop acting like I didn't know what he was going to do. Then he forced me to get on my hands and knees, then did what he wanted even though I told him he was hurting me. When finished with that, he pushed me down and told me to open my mouth. When I wouldn't, he hit me with his fist and tried to force my mouth open. I bit him, and he got really mad and hit me with his fists until he finally gave up and left."

Malcolm moved so she had to look at him. "Did he leave any marks on you?"

"Yes. I had a black eye and bruises on my cheek. Multiple bruises on my abdomen, arms, and legs, and a cut lip."

"Did anyone come to help you?"

"No."

"What happened next?"

"Mr. Billings came in the next day. He told me I deserved what I had gotten. I should have done what Mr. Franko had asked. I needed to learn to be nice to the men and do what they wanted."

"Did he do anything that day?"

"No. He left and didn't come back until the bruises were gone."

Malcolm kept his eyes on her, ignoring everyone else in the courtroom. He wasn't letting up. He was going for the information she had for him in little bits and pieces. "Did either of them come back to talk to you?"

"Mr. Billings came back and told me that he was almost through with me, but his other boss wanted to have a go at me. He said and I quote, 'When Bobkin has had enough of you, you'll be going to the next level. That innocent look will get us some good money.'"

"Did this Bobkin come to see you?"

"Yes."

"Is he here in this courtroom today?"

"Yes." She didn't wait for him to ask her to point him out. "He's sitting next to Mr. Franko."

"What did Mr. Bobkin do?"

She let her gaze rest on the man she had pointed out, crying at what she had to say. "He came in and sat on the bed and started to talk to me. He asked me my name, so I told him. He asked me how old I was. I told him sixteen. There were a lot more questions like what type of cars I liked and if I liked pretty clothes. He then said that I was so young and pretty. He lay down on the bed and kept talking to me as he ran his fingers over my face, then down my neck, shoulder, and arm. He kissed me and then he started playing with my breasts and it went on from there."

"Jill, did you like what he was doing?"

"I was scared, but he made it feel so good. I couldn't stop what I was feeling even though I tried. He made me want what he was doing."

She broke down in tears as she remembered the gentle man who had made what he was doing feel good and not dirty.

"Jill, complete what you were saying."

"He did what the others had done, but it was different. When he was done, he held me and let me cry. As I was crying, he told me to remember how he treated me, because that was how a real man treats a woman. He makes sure she enjoys what is happening. He also said that if he had known I was there, he wouldn't have let them hurt me. Fairies were to be treasured, not used."

"Did he come back and see you again?"

"Yes."

"And did he treat you the same way each time?"

"Yes."

"Did you look forward to his visits?"

She was sobbing when she said, "Yes. He would talk to me and make me laugh and he never hurt me. I knew he was using me, but he was kind."

Malcolm handed her a tissue and let her gather herself together before asking his next question.

"Jill, how many times did he come to see you?"

"About ten times. The last time, he told me he wouldn't be back. I was to go to another area, and he wouldn't see me again."

"Did he do anything else?"

"He told me I was very special and gave me a necklace. It was a little locket."

Malcolm produced the locket she had kept. "Is this what he gave you?"

She took it and opened it and started to cry. "Yes. It has this poem in it. He told me to read it when things got too bad. It would make things seem better for me."

"How long did you wear this necklace?"

"Until I was rescued."

"Why?"

"It reminded me of one of the few kind people I met there. He was right. The poem did help. It let me know that not all men were pigs."

Malcolm had the locket entered as evidence, giving her time to stop crying.

Llewellyn stopped him and requested a lunch recess. It had taken four hours to get to this point. She wasn't hungry, but she needed the break. Malcolm took her back to the suite for lunch. It was just her and him. She picked at her food, thinking about Bobkin and how he was different from all the other men who had used her. Testifying about what he had done had been extremely hard for her. He was one of two she hadn't wanted to see arrested for what they were doing at the club.

"Jill, you need to eat something," Malcolm told her.

"I'm not hungry."

He sat for a few seconds before saying, "Jill, Bobkin treated you like a woman should be treated. He made sure you enjoyed what he was doing because he wanted you to have as much pleasure as he did. It's what a man is supposed to do, so don't feel bad about what he did. He showed you what making love is really about. It's a give-and-take. It isn't just sex. I can't bring myself to charge him with rape. I don't think we could prove it from your testimony anyway."

"Why do I feel so guilty about enjoying what he did to me?"

"Because you didn't agree to it. He used your physical response to allow him to do what he wanted. He cared about you, and that's evident with the locket he gave you. Accept that he was a reasonably decent man and remember what he did. It's what you should feel when you're with a man."

She couldn't look at him as she admitted, "It was hard for me to name him. If it wasn't for the other things he was doing, I don't think I would have implicated him for the kindness he showed me."

Malcolm patted her hand. "I get it. In the situation you were in, a small kindness can go a long way."

She now knew what to expect from someone who cared

about her. Tom would be like Bobkin. He would be kind and considerate and make sure she enjoyed what he was doing. No, she didn't have to feel guilty. Bobkin had known she couldn't stop the physical feelings he had created, wanting her to enjoy what he was doing while showing how much he cared for her.

Chapter 21

LET'S MAKE A DEAL

Court reconvened two hours later. Malcolm reminded the court and jury where they had left off before resuming his questioning.

"What happened after your experience with Mr. Bobkin?"

"They moved me to this other room. I was given a robe to wear, but that was it. The woman who took me there told me she'd make sure I enjoyed what was going to happen.

She gave me a liquid to drink. In a little bit, I began to feel like I was drunk."

"Had you ever been drunk before?"

"Once. When my grandfather found out that I'd had a drink at a party, he said it was time for me to learn the dangers of drinking too much. He encouraged me to drink as much as I wanted. Then one of the guys from the agency came and started trying to kiss me. I pushed him away, but I was giggling. He got more persistent, but I still thought it was funny. It wasn't until he started to unbutton my blouse I got scared and started to fight, but I was too drunk to be effective.

"My grandfather stopped him. He then told me that if it would have been anyone else in a different place, I wouldn't have been able to stop him from doing what he wanted. I learned that being drunk wasn't very much fun. It would make you do things you shouldn't."

"So, this drug made you feel like you were drunk, correct?"

"Yes, sir."

"Once you were feeling drunk, what happened?"

"This man came in and he didn't seem to care I wasn't all there. He did what he wanted and left. Another soon followed and then another one. There were seven in all before I was left alone to sleep it off."

"Are you sure about that number? You just said that you were feeling like you were drunk?"

"I'm sure. It made me feel drunk, but it didn't affect my memory. I counted them. I wanted to remember it. I thought I would be rescued soon, and I wanted to have concrete evidence. I also remember those seven men. I can still see their faces up to this day."

"When you woke up, what happened next?"

"She gave me more of the drug and there were more men who used me."

"How long did this go on?"

"Not very long. The men started complaining I wasn't participating. They moved me to the basement. They would put the drug on my tray at mealtimes, but I wouldn't take it. The men still came, but not as many, and they didn't complain of me laying there and not participating."

"How long did they keep you in the basement?"

"I don't really know. There was always a light on, and there would be long stretches of time when I wouldn't see anyone and then there would be several. They brought food, but it wasn't in any regular fashion. I was hungry most of the time."

"Hmm, they kept you in the same place for all the time you were there?"

"Yes. I didn't know that most of the others were taken to the dormitory or sleep room, and others would take their place. For some reason, I was never sent to the dormitory."

"Did it stay that way until you were rescued?"

"No. This man who brought me food told me they were going to ask me to dance because I had a good figure and looked so young. He said to go ahead and do it. It would get me out of the hole, which was what they called the basement. It would make it so I got a better clientele until I was rescued."

"And did you do as he recommended?" Malcolm asked, watching for her reaction.

Jill couldn't look at him. She still bore the shame at what she had done. Yes, it had gotten her out of the hole, but it came with a price—her self-respect. She also knew what was coming with this line of questioning.

"Yes. This woman came and got me. She said I was going to learn how to pole dance. I couldn't do it at first. She made me take the drug and was happy until I sat on the floor giggling. She slapped me and told me to get up and dance. I did as she ordered. There was this other girl there who sort of looked like me. She said her name was Susan and that we could dance together so it wouldn't be so bad. We paired up and did what the woman wanted."

"Is the woman who had you dance here in the courtroom today?"

"Yes."

"Please point her out."

"The woman in the blue dress with the mole under her left eye and the scar on her cheek."

"Do you know her name?"

"We called her Madeline."

"When did you and this other girl start dancing?"

"The next show. We ignored the leering men and danced. When we were done, we were told to go with these two men and dance privately for them."

"Did they just want dances?"

"No. They did what they wanted then left. Both of us were crying."

"What was your relationship with Susan like?"

"We helped each other and became friends. Because we were dancers, we were allowed outside, in what they called the garden, to walk around most mornings. Susan and I talked a lot. She had been there longer than me. She had learned there was an inside man who was working on getting her out. I couldn't believe it when she said she couldn't let them take her because it would destroy her father. She told me I needed to keep going and they would get me out."

Jill couldn't look at Malcolm. It was hard enough without seeing the pain she knew his eyes would show.

"So, you and Susan became friends. Were there other instances where you and she did things together?"

"Well, Madeline wanted Susan and me to do this threesome where we did this stuff together and then let the man join in. We both refused and ended up fighting her until several of the bouncers came and pulled us off from her. We were punished, but we didn't care."

Waiting for the next question, she peeked up at him. Only his eyes, which he kept on her, showed the pain she knew he was feeling. There was nothing she could do to stop it.

"So, you and Susan were together a lot?"

"Yes. We were."

"What happened to Susan?" Malcolm asked. She met his gaze, unable to stop the tears. He was tense, but he kept his voice as normal as possible and his face blank. She noticed the strain in his stance and trembling hand when he grasped the rail before him.

"She told me a few days later she was supposed to be taken out within the next week. I couldn't believe it when she said she couldn't go. She said not to not feel bad at what she was going to do, because it was better for everyone. She also told me I needed to be patient and strong because they would get me out. I promised her to get justice for her and the others, not knowing she was going to carry out her plan that night."

Jill hung her head, crying as she sadly told him, "That night, she hung herself. We had been put in the hole because we had refused to service a guy who would regularly hurt us. I found her just before the busy time. I had wanted to try and talk her out of her plans again."

"How long did they keep you in the hole?"

"They let me go back to dancing a few days later. They started putting the drugs in my food when I refused to take it on my own, because I wouldn't smile and was always crying. When I discovered what they were doing, I ate very little. I wanted to get as much information as I could on them for the others like Susan, whose lives they had ripped apart and destroyed.

"I discovered by accident that the drug in the food was different. It would wear off quickly, yet my eyes looked like I was still under the influence of it. I just didn't want to get too much of the drugs."

"Why was that important?"

"Because from my eyes, they would think I was too drugged to be able to remember things, so they talked in front of me. They also left important things lying around, not aware I was totally lucid."

"So, you made it your mission to get the information to help the others like you and Susan?"

"Yes."

He went to the table and came back with a folder.

"Do you recognize these documents?"

She studied the sheaf of papers he handed her. They were the ones she had taken and given to Tom.

"Yes. The top four were the ones that were lying on the desk in Mr. Billings's office. These two were on Madeline's desk, and the bottom two were again on Mr. Billings's desk. Each time, they thought I was under the influence of the drugs and left me alone in the offices where I would take what I could."

He held up a small ledger. "Do you recognize this?"

Opening it, she knew what it was. She had given it to Wyatt for safekeeping. He must have given it to Malcolm.

"Yes. That was left on a table in the backstage area. I took it as it had all the names, dates, and amounts the various people were being paid and for what. It's divided into sections for the club, drugs, smuggling, and for payoffs for various officials."

"Where did you keep these things after you took them?"

"The papers were in the Bible I had in my room and the ledger I had lodged under the table."

"What do these papers contain?"

"The top four are the end-of-year accountings. The two from Madeline are the club finances for the period of time on the pages. The last two are a communication from Mr. Franko and Bobkin and gives their relationship to the club and other activities. Mr. Billings was being told what to do for the next few months and which areas to increase income."

"I take it from what you just said that you understood these papers and their significance when you took them."

"Yes. I had done some work with my grandfather and I learned about financial statements, accounts, and that type of thing."

"Your grandfather, who is he and what does he do?"

"He's Wyatt Potter and owns the Wyatt Detective

Agency."

"You work for him, correct?"

"Yes."

"Did you ever do work for him before you became licensed?"

"I would go along on stakeouts when he didn't have anyone to watch me. I was used several times to help others when they needed a cover. I was a good cover. You don't think of a man with a child as being a PI. I also did things around the office and worked as a receptionist during the summers when I was a teenager. My grandfather liked it when I was nearby due to the type of work he did."

"So, you knew what you were doing when you took these things?"

"Yes."

"What did you do with the ledger when you were rescued?"

"I gave it to Wyatt, my grandfather. I told him I wanted everyone who was listed in there, including the bosses, to eventually be caught."

"Did you have a copy of this ledger?"

"No. I didn't need it. I had memorized it. I had plenty of time to learn everything in it down to the dollar amounts."

"Back to the club. You were dancing and finding out as much as you could as to what they were doing after Susan died. Did you overhear any conversations indicating who these people were working for?"

"Objection. Hearsay," the defense attorney exclaimed.

"Sustained. Overheard conversations are inadmissible as evidence."

Malcolm rephrased his question. "Did you ever participate in any conversation where you learned who was controlling these enterprises?"

"Yes."

"Please elaborate."

"I was in the main office of the club. They thought I was still drugged since I acted drunk. Billings and Franko were talking, and I giggled and commented, 'Sounds like the Mafioso has been having a field day.' Mr. Franko laughed and said, 'Sweetie, wrong part of the world. We Russians are putting them out of business. We just need to keep the chinks from cutting into our territory.' I giggled again and said that the chinks needed to learn more about the real men. They laughed, then ignored me as they continued to talk business."

"Was there any other conversation where you participated where they mentioned being part of the Russian mafia?"

"Yes. Franko came to me one day and told me I was a real prize because the men spent more when I was dancing. He said he should send me to his boss in Russia because he would love having a little elf to play with. I told him I would be a big disappointment as no guy wants well-used goods. He laughed and said that I was very wrong. His boss would be glad to get me. He said to get ready for the cold because as soon as he sent the picture of me dancing, I would be on my way there."

"Are you sure he wasn't teasing you?"

"No. He wasn't teasing. He meant it. He showed me later what his boss had written. He was serious about sending me there. He just needed to get a passport for me. It would take a month to get it after he got all my other papers in order."

"What happened?"

"I was dancing one night, and I noticed this big man at the back of the room. It was my brother, Brad. I wanted to die as he watched what I was doing. Later that night, Sam, one of the men who works for the detective agency, came to me and told me to be ready to leave in two days. He would come back to me, and we would be leaving at that time."

"Did he come back?"

"Yes. They spirited me out of the club."

"And you brought these things with you when they took you out?"

"Yes. It was the proof of what they were doing, but it wasn't enough to convict them, and I knew it."

"What did you do once you were rescued?"

"I had a meltdown and it took me almost six months to be able to function normally."

"Explain that, please."

"I fell apart. I didn't want my family around me. I believed I was contaminated. I went into a depression and tried to commit suicide over what they had done to me. My grandfather took me to one of his houses. He and my brother stayed with me until I got better."

"Why did you become a private investigator?"

"I needed to work, plus it would allow me to keep tabs on those who had destroyed my life. I've had several cases involving them, but none had implicated them to the point where they could be brought up on charges."

Llewellyn cut in, "Counselor, if you are moving into a different area, I believe this would be a good time to recess until tomorrow."

Malcolm glanced at her before stating, "I agree this would be a good place to stop for the day."

"Ms. Potter, you are to discuss this case with no one other than Mr. Phillips and his team. You will still be under oath when we reconvene. Court adjourned until 9 AM."

She stepped down from the witness stand. Malcolm put an arm around her when she started to cry. He motioned to someone. Tom came and took her from Malcom, pulling her close to him as he guided her toward the side exit of the courtroom. She made it to the door before collapsing. Someone picked her up and carried her to the room. She gave up the fight to stay awake and drifted into nothingness.

Tom's stressed voice reached her in the darkness. "Jill, wake up. Come on. Open your eyes."

Struggling, she opened her eyes before pulling his head down for a kiss, hoping to forestall any questions.

"Hmm. Nice move there, slick, but you need to get up and eat some supper. It's getting late and I can't let you go without eating."

"Thanks. I'm hungry. I couldn't eat much lunch." She sat up before saying, "Sorry about the fallout."

Malcolm intoned, "I'm just glad you didn't do that on the stand."

Tom moved so she could put her feet on the floor.

She kept her head down as she said, "It's just a reaction to the hours of constant stress. It may happen again, but with a bit of sleep I seem to recover. As you can tell, it's happened before. Usually Brad's the one to catch me as I go down."

Shaun shook his head. "Ya could a warned me. Tom caught you, but I carried you back here."

Tom grinned at his brother, chuckling, "He's the weightlifter and said it was like carrying a sleeping kid. I'll admit, it was all I could do to get you off the floor."

"Wyatt and Brad have scraped me up more than once. I get it. One hundred and twenty pounds isn't all that easy to carry when it's dead weight."

"Jill, you said this has happened before when you've been under undue stress. Has a doctor checked you out for medical causes?" Malcolm questioned with concern.

"Yes," she told him but didn't elaborate. There was no way she was going to tell them about what had caused her to pass out. As normal, she had forgotten her medication. She hadn't taken any since she left the villa in Clermont, but it shouldn't make that much difference. Other than a couple of times over the past week, she hadn't had the long bouts of her heart racing, so she should be okay until the trial was over.

"Well, at least we know it isn't new and you recover pretty fast," Tom stated with a grin.

"Food, please," she requested, attempting to defuse the situation.

Tom made a plate of food for both her and him. It looked like he had stayed with her until awakening her.

Shaun watched them as they ate. "You know, Tom, I'm totally jealous."

"Why?"

"You got the fairy."

Tom grinned at his brother. "I know, and you aren't getting her. She's mine."

"Looks like I'll be stuck with an Amazon of some sort."

Jill couldn't resist. "My sister would fit that description. You might like her."

Tom laughed, "She's not kidding either. You definitely couldn't misplace her."

"Okay. What does she look like?"

Tom honestly stated, "She's decent-looking with a good figure. Not sure about personality, but it couldn't hurt to meet her. I saw her when Jill went to get her things. She wasn't clumsy and had these pretty eyes. She also has hair like Mom's."

Shaun raised his brows with a crooked grin on his face. "Maybe when this is all over. It would be worth seeing what it's like to go out with someone who I can actually find."

"Hey, Amazons need men who can handle them. We fairies break pretty easy," Jill joked.

Shaun gave a peal of laughter at her statement. "From what Brad told me, you can take him down and not break a sweat."

She stared at him, not sure what to think. "And just when did you speak to him?"

"When I was preparing this case. He told me not to let your size fool me. You were one tough cookie who he had only seen crack once."

She returned her gaze to her food. "Yeah. It was a six-month crack."

Shaun shook his head. "It's okay, Jill. You did great on the stand. I know you don't know about the testimony which came before you, but it supported everything you said. You added details to what the others had said in their testimony. I can see why Williams loved it when you were the key witness. I'd love to know how your brain works for you to remember all that stuff."

"Can't help you out there. It started as a child, and I have no idea. It's always been that way. I learned to read by memorizing the words as my grandfather or Brad would read to me. I can still see the pages of Dr. Seuss when I want to escape from being an adult."

Shaun and Malcolm both stared at her. It was Malcolm who queried, "You see the pages?"

"Yes. My mind takes a photograph like a picture of the page and I can bring it up when I want to read it."

"That ledger, you have it stored in that memory of yours, right?" Malcolm questioned, changing his position from lounging to sitting upright.

"Yes. I wanted it as hard proof, but I didn't need it. I can tell you what's on every page. Just as I can tell you what is on every page of the ledger they left out in the office when I was there." She turned to Malcolm's startled face. She hadn't told anyone else about seeing the second ledger.

"You have a photographic memory, don't you?"

"Yes, but it doesn't help if you don't have the hard proof."

Malcolm leaned forward in his chair, smiling. "Wrong. I just need to prove you have that ability. Shaun, this case just got a whole lot easier. Watch as I set it up. The defense will need to shake her memory, but I don't think they can. Let me show you."

He went to his briefcase and handed her a sheet of

paper. She looked at it and handed it back to him. It was a legal brief. Malcolm handed the page to Shaun.

"Ask her about this page," he commanded.

Shaun asked her about paragraph three and what it said. She gave the exact words on the page as if she had been reading it, then explained what it meant. She waited for him to ask her something else about the page, instead he handed it to Malcolm, watching her, but not commenting on her freakish ability.

"Forget you ever read that page," Malcolm requested.

Shrugging, she stated, "Not happening. It'll remain there. I can get it in, but can't seem to get it out. It'll just go to the miscellaneous storage area unless I need it again."

"Jill, does anyone else know about this ability?" Tom inquired.

"Other than Brad, I don't think so. I've more information, but I knew better than saying so because I don't have the hard copy."

"Why are you telling us now?" Shaun queried, leaning forward in his chair and studying her.

She stared at her hands. It was the time to be honest. "I made sure I got as much information as possible. I have letters with dates, e-mails, phone numbers, and other data stored. It all points to what Franko told me. They were being controlled by a group in Russia. They sent part of the profits there through an offshore company. I can give you that trail, but you need to establish I'm able to do so. I really want that trail to be revealed, so you just need to verify I'm able to memorize the information in seconds, and have it correct."

Malcolm grinned. "That's the easy part. Getting the questions right will be a lot more difficult."

"Not really. Just start with the open ledger on the desk and the twenty minutes they left me alone with it. You'll know what to ask when I give you what it contained."

"Honey, I would love to clone you. You'll make our case on racketeering in one day. All that will be left is the smuggling and murders."

"Ask the right questions, Malcolm, and you may not need more than tomorrow to prove your total case."

They all stared at her. Tom put his arm across her shoulder. "Now I know why they have four contracts out on you, not just two."

"Yeah, well, one of those men was in the courtroom yesterday. I just hope they frisk the spectators before the trial starts tomorrow. I have a feeling he may try something if I say the wrong thing. I'm sure one of their people working in the courthouse has planted a gun or two for him."

"Who?" Tom's sharp voice asked.

"He was sitting in the second row, third person in, dressed in a dark gray suit, light blue tie, blond hair, blue eyes, and a scar on the right side of his mouth at the outer edge."

"Where did you see him, and do you have a name?"

"At the club. The name's Georgi Volkov, and he speaks fluent Russian, making me think he's from there. His English has a slight accent. From what I've seen, he carries two guns, and isn't afraid to use them. He killed one of the girls who tried climbing the wall to escape. When he made sure she was dead, he told the man with him to get rid of the garbage where it wouldn't be found."

"And you think he'll sacrifice himself to ensure you don't complete your testimony." Shaun hadn't taken his gaze from her.

"Yes. He knows he's a dead man, so it isn't a sacrifice to him. His job is to make sure the trail doesn't lead back to Russia. They want it to stop here with Franko and Bobkin."

Tom used his fingers to turn her head so she was facing him. "Jill, you knew this was a Russian-controlled enterprise. Why didn't you get the Feds involved when you found out it was across state lines?"

"They have been involved. Other than what I have in my brain, there was nothing they could do other than bust the little players. What they needed was a big break leading up the ladder. It just happened that I found the crack and followed it. I didn't know it was going to lead to this group until Knight's death. I had seen Knight at the club a couple of times, but didn't know who he was until later. I was aware he was connected, but I needed hard proof, not just his name in a ledger no one else had access to."

Malcolm shook his head, staring at her before he stood. "Well, you need to get to bed. It will be a long day tomorrow. It won't be as hard though because the questions will be less painful. I'll still need to go over some things I skimmed over today, but I believe the worst part is already done."

She shook her head. "No, it isn't. You need to question me about what happened before I was rescued. It'll give you four more people. They were the ones who held, punished, drugged, and killed several girls. I want those four to be tried for murder, and you had better ask those questions if you want the rest of the information."

Malcolm's narrowed eyes bored into hers. "That's blackmail, Jill."

"No, it's a trade. I get the ones who daily made our lives miserable, and you get your connection. I believe it's a fair trade for a couple of hours of questions, which will give you those four as a gift with all the bows neatly tied."

"Why is this so important to you?"

It wasn't something she wanted to remember. Her large crack was partly due to the permanent reminders of what had been done to her.

"Ask that question in a different way in court," she stated before rising and leaving the room to change into her night clothes. The men were talking, but she couldn't understand the words.

When she came back out, Malcolm's hand stopped her. He turned her so she was facing away from him before lifting up her top in the back. His and Shaun's gasps were audible as they stared at the scars on her back. Malcolm let her top drop back into place, rotated her, and put a gentle hand on her shoulder.

"You'll have your four. I'll make sure they don't get out for a long, long time, if ever."

"You'll have your connections in a very nice neat line. Just have me give you the ledger, line by line, starting on page 101. It's all there from the lowest to the highest with the names to go with the numbers."

Tom had their bed ready. She didn't care if they stayed up. The time on the stand along with her episode of passing out had tired her. She needed sleep. Shaun followed Malcolm to his room to talk. It didn't take Tom long to join her. His arms around her gave her the shield she needed to sleep without the nightmares, which normally increased when she thought of her time in captivity.

Chapter 22

FEARS

Malcolm and Tom left to talk to another witness, leaving her to be escorted to the courtroom by four guards. She stopped at the entrance to the courtroom, refusing to move. The bailiff came to her. "Ms. Potter, they're waiting on you."

Staring at the man who would kill her if he could, she told the bailiff, "There's an assassin in the courtroom, and I like living. Until he's removed, I'm not going in there."

Her guards moved so she was hidden. Fred heard her statement when he joined them to discover what was wrong, and simply asked, "Which one?"

"The blond man in the second row, third one in from the aisle in the gray suit, silver tie, with a scar at the outer right corner of his mouth."

Fred motioned to several men who were heavily armed. They moved to the front of the courtroom. Two of the men had the outer two people move, then motioned to the man she had pointed out to stand and move to the aisle.

Llewellyn calmly said, "I hope there's a good reason for

this display of force in the courtroom."

Fred answered without looking at him, "There is. The man who's being removed is under contract to assassinate Ms. Potter."

"And what makes you think he'll try to fulfill an alleged contract in a federal courtroom?"

Two of Fred's men frisked the man and removed a loaded gun from under his jacket as he glared to where she was standing. She scanned the rest of the crowd and whispered to Fred. "He has a backup. The man in the back row on the left in the black suit with the striped tie. I've seen him before with Ivanov, but I don't know his name."

Fred motioned several more men from behind her. He informed them of what she had told them. Before they could move, the man she had pointed out stood and aimed a pistol at her. One of the guards who were hiding her from the courtroom quickly flashed a laser beam across the man's eyes, temporarily blinding him. The men Fred had motioned to the forefront moved swiftly as a well-coordinated team when the laser flashed. They had the gun out of the man's hand and him on the floor before those in the courtroom understood what was happening.

Llewellyn's voice was hard as he commanded, "I want this courtroom cleared. No one is to enter this room without being physically checked for weapons. If anyone leaves at any point, they are to be rechecked before being allowed to reenter. Fred, your men are responsible for making certain there are no further threats in this courtroom until this trial is concluded. Please take the witness to a secure area, to be held under protective guard until you notify me the courtroom is secure."

He banged his gavel before leaving the bench. As he passed her, he winked and said, "Good catch, my dear," without pausing on his way to his chambers, his guards surrounding him. The few words showed he was aware of the possibility of their trying to stop her testimony, but had needed a reason to order the body searches. She had given him that reason.

The men guided her to a small room with four chairs and a table. Malcolm and Shaun joined her while the guards remained outside of the room.

"Well, it looks like they'll have to come up with another plan. What made you stop?" Shaun questioned, studying her intently.

"The way he was looking at me. I knew if I went into the courtroom, he would do his best to see I never left it alive. Yesterday, his eyes followed me, but today he was expecting to die, as was the other man. That makes two down and two to go."

"After today, they may just call off the other two since it would just be a waste of good talent. We'll have our case made by the time court is over today. I'll attempt to get the groundwork completed before lunch and then follow the trail in the afternoon. After that, Shaun gets to have fun tying all the knots and putting all the bows in place. The defense may untie a bow or two, but they won't be able to untie the knots," Malcolm declared confidently as they sat and waited.

She casually stated, "Just make sure that what is given me isn't going to create problems if revealed in a courtroom. I don't need to embarrass the hell out of someone with personal or confidential information."

Malcolm took a seat beside her. "Not to worry. I'll make it clear that it'll be shared with everyone."

"Don't forget to have them time how long it takes me to look at what is given me. The time factor will come into play as you extract what you need."

Malcolm's brows drew together as he questioned, "Why?"

"I memorized a ledger of 175 pages in just around twenty minutes. You do the math."

"Shaun, do you have a stopwatch with the capability of monitoring seconds?"

"Yes. I'm sure there are a few others who also have one. Last night, it took her all of five seconds to learn what you gave her."

"Okay, stage set. Let's see what happens," Malcolm gloated.

"You think Llewellyn will allow this?" Shaun questioned.

"Yes. The defense will object strongly as they see their

case going down the tubes if we can prove she has a photographic memory."

She lowered her gaze before saying, "He'll go along. He already knows."

"What?" the two men stated together.

With a shrug of her shoulders, she told them, "He's known for years. When I first met him, he dropped a paper and I picked it up, glanced at it, and handed it back to him. He could see me trying not to laugh. When Wyatt left the room, he asked what I found so funny. I repeated what I had read. It was a story about a man with a cow and how he ended up back to where he started after selling the cow to a man and then making several other hilarious trades."

Malcolm laughed as Shaun stared at him.

"It was the one I sent him. It was funny."

"I know. Your name was at the bottom of the page, your e-mail address, and other information you wouldn't want to be shared."

"The e-mail address was what?" he inquired, leaning forward, intently watching her.

"Mphillips.justice@usao.gov. . ."

"Enough," Malcolm said with a shake of his head. "I don't need to get into trouble here. That alone tells me you read the paper. You had no way of knowing my e-mail address."

He didn't say any more. Shaun's slight grin and merry eyes showed he had enjoyed her putting his boss on the hot seat. He wasn't supposed to be using government e-mail to send stories. The rest of the morning would be sort of fun. It was the afternoon she would like to skip.

She was beginning to get bored when they were called back to the courtroom. Another man was missing from the spectators. That left one to find. She was escorted into the room.

Llewellyn stated, "Ms. Potter, you are still under oath," after she was seated in the witness stand.

Malcolm stood at the prosecution table. "Your Honor, we would like to ask for the indulgence of the court as we lay the groundwork for part of the witness's testimony."

"Mr. Phillips, right now, I'm not exactly in the best of moods for games."

"Your Honor, this isn't a game. It will prove the information Jill will impart is fact and taken directly from written materials she had access to during her captivity."

Llewellyn glared at Malcolm before saying, "Continue, but be aware that I'll stop you if it's deemed irrelevant to your case." The sharpness in his voice showed his irritation at another delay.

"I would like anyone who has one or two pieces of printed or handwritten material, which they don't mind sharing with everyone, to please give it to the bailiff."

The defense counsel stood up, "Objection. Relevancy."

Llewellyn glanced at her, then back to the defense before saying, "Overruled. Mr. Phillips has already stated the relevancy of what he will be doing."

Malcolm waited until Llewellyn reached under the bench and pulled out two pieces of paper. He handed them to the bailiff without comment.

"Would you please make five copies of those papers," Malcolm instructed the bailiff.

Llewellyn indicated with a nod to do as requested.

"Now, as everyone observed, I have no idea what was given to the bailiff nor does anyone else in this room other than His Honor. I would like the defense, one person on the jury, one person for the prosecution, and any others who have access to stopwatches capable of recording seconds, to please set them up."

Jill gnawed on her bottom lip while waiting. The bailiff returned with the copies. Malcolm took a copy and gave the original back to the judge. He passed out a copy to the defense attorneys, one to a juror, and the rest out to random spectators not associated with the case.

He moved beside her, standing, so everyone, including the jury, could see her, keeping the papers in his hand so she couldn't see the printed side of them.

"I'm going to hand these papers to her. I would like everyone to time how long it takes for her to finish with them."

He allowed them to get ready, then handed her the papers. She glanced at each page and handed them back to him.

"Okay, time."

Most had recorded a time of ten seconds for the two pages. Llewellyn stated, "It took her 4.2 seconds for the first page and 4.1 for the second page for a total of 8.3 seconds for the two pages before she looked up from them."

Malcolm looked at the pages, glanced at the man on the bench, raised an eyebrow and said, "Jill, page two, paragraph two, third line."

"Let me just give you the paragraph," she told him. "It will be easier for everyone to find and follow." She repeated the paragraph, indicating the words which were italicized.

"First page, under the second bolded heading. Please give the third sentence."

Jill quoted the sentence, including the punctuation.

"The first quote under the bolded name on the second page."

She gave the quote while those with the papers read along.

Malcolm faced the courtroom before asking, "Any mistakes in her quotes?"

Those with the copies indicated she had made no mistakes.

"As you noted, it took her less than ten seconds to learn what these pages contained." He turned back to her, "Jill, I'm now going to ask an unexpected question. His Honor will verify if you are correct. Do you know what book these were taken from?"

"Yes. It's *The Secret* by a Rhonda Byrne."

Llewellyn stated, "She's correct," for the record.

Malcolm continued with his questions. "When did you read the book?"

"Five years ago, during my recovery. I would highly recommend it for the insights it contains."

"Your Honor, would you happen to have the book with you?" Malcolm requested.

He pulled it out and gave it to Malcolm.

"You have not read this book in five years, correct?"

"Yes. The one I have has a different cover. This one, I'm sure, is a different edition."

"I would like one person from the defense counsel to join me. He will choose the spot to use in the book to ensure I'm not giving her some prearranged pages."

The lead defense lawyer joined him. He glared at her. She quirked an eyebrow and dared him to find something she couldn't quote. He made his choice and stated, "Page 100."

"I'm going to hope the page numbers are the same in that edition as they were in the one I have. On page 100 of my book, it says . . .," she quoted the page word for word as the defense attorney followed what she was saying.

Malcolm turned to him. "Well?"

"Other than the first two lines and the last one, that

was word for word what was on the page."

"Then you will agree she has a photographic memory and is capable of repeating exactly what she has seen and read."

"Yes. I'll agree after one more example." He pulled out a pocket calendar and opened it to a page before handing it to her. She glanced at it and handed it back to him.

"Ms. Potter, please tell me what was on the calendar for that week." He kept it so Malcolm could see what it said.

"Please call me Jill. I'm not my mother," she stated before reciting what was on the pages he had shown her, down to the times and notes he had entered. She even gave the saying at the top of the page.

He glared at her when she had finished, "You've proven beyond a doubt that you have a photographic memory. We'll not object to the information you have obtained in that manner."

"Please note the defense has agreed to allow Jill to give testimony containing information she gathered while in captivity concerning the defendants, using her photographic memory to store the information."

Llewellyn stated, "So noted. At this time, we'll break for lunch. Court will reconvene at one." He gave one rap of the gavel. Everyone rose as he left the courtroom after retrieving his book.

She was escorted from the witness stand. The defense attorney stopped her.

"When did you discover you had this ability?" he questioned.

"As a child. I just never let anyone know. The one time I did, I was ridiculed. It's like my ability to remember conversations. I've had that for as far back as I can remember. For cases, I usually have a recording or hard copy to back up what I say, but in this case, I couldn't do that. You can ask me that in cross-examination, and I'll tell you the same thing."

"I was warned about you. Now I know why," he stated, forgetting he had cross-examined her in another case four years ago.

The guards surrounded her as they left the room and made their way along the hall and back to the suite of rooms. The food was already there when they entered, as was Tom. He gave her a hug and kiss but didn't comment on what had happened in the courtroom.

Shaun stated, "I think the kicker was when you spouted back that calendar after only glancing at it. I believe he didn't believe you could do it."

"He didn't. He expected the handwriting to make a difference. Most people don't understand that I'm reading it as it appears on the page or screen. He should have asked me a specific date. It would have been more scientific, but my guess is, he doesn't understand my abilities or how to really test them."

Malcolm warned, "He'll most likely ask you about that

conversation you two had in cross-examination."

"Not a problem. I'm sure Franko had a bit to say on his allowing me to testify to what I read while in the club. He's wondering what I have that he doesn't know about."

Shaun hesitated then said, "Jill, I have to ask this, so don't yell at me. Would you ever make up information to convict someone?"

"No. If I did, it would destroy my whole career. I like what I do and wouldn't ever do anything to jeopardize it. That ledger was in the club. You only need to find it. Did you ever get into the safe?"

"Yes," Malcolm stated but left it at that. She surmised it wasn't there. Hopefully, they would eventually locate it to verify what she was saying. If they asked her about the other things they had found in the safe and she had seen, it would solidify the things she would say without hard proof.

Again, she didn't eat much for lunch. Curling up on the end of the couch, she closed her eyes to relax. It felt like only seconds when Tom woke her with a kiss.

"Time to go, honey," he told her when she peered up at him, still half asleep.

"Give me a couple of minutes," she told them and headed to the bath.

The cold water she splashed on her face helped to take the last tendrils of sleep from her. Hesitating, she hoped she wouldn't pass out again. The funny feelings she normally got prior to passing out weren't going away this time.

They were on their way back to the courtroom when Llewellyn came up behind them and commented, "Malcolm, hopefully you aren't going to drag this out."

"No, we should be finishing in another day, two at the most. You'll get out of here in time for your anniversary."

"I hope so. She threatened to take a world tour if I'm not."

Malcolm merrily chuckled, "Not likely. It's more likely to be mine joining yours for a shopping spree, which will keep us working for a while longer."

"Right. You're retiring soon. I still have ten more years to go."

"You'll have to put up with me for another year or two. I'll be hanging around to help Shaun, not that he'll need much after this case."

"He put it together?"

"Yes," Malcolm stated as they separated. Their conversation showed they were friends outside of the courtroom.

The guards stopped her at the door until Llewellyn called the court to order. She was shown back to the witness stand and reminded she was still under oath. Malcolm continued with the questioning.

He went over several details he had neglected from her previous testimony. The questions led to when she found the ledger. She answered his questions about it, including the front page, which told what it was. His questions got very specific as she quoted what she had seen in the ledger. When he got to the page she had told him to question her about, he asked her to quote exactly what the pages said. She held Franko's gaze as she repeated what was on the pages, going in the order the entries had been written, giving each line with the company or person and the dollar amounts.

Franko was gritting his teeth as she quoted each line. She knew he would have done her bodily harm if he could have as she went through the pages. Malcolm didn't interrupt her recitation, wanting it all recorded in the official record. It took her over an hour to give the pages they needed. The courtroom remained silent as she read from her mind the innermost records of the organization.

Bobkin did his best not to grin. He knew he was going to jail, but he seemed to find it amusing. The defense lawyers weren't happy with what she was reciting. It was proving, beyond a shadow of a doubt, the racketeering charges.

She finished the accounts with the amounts sent to Russia and their bosses, giving the names of the bosses as recorded in the ledger. Bobkin said something to Franko, who gave him a nasty glare. Billings had remained impassive. His fate had been determined the first day, and he knew it. They had no real out now. The three of them would be going to jail for multiple charges from racketeering to income tax evasion, smuggling, drug dealing, prostitution, and Franko and Billings for rape.

One of the aids for the prosecution entered the court. He was carrying a box and set it on the table. Malcolm searched through the box. He produced the ledger and turned to the pages she had quoted before he smiled.

"Your Honor, I would like to enter into evidence the ledger Jill quoted from. I believe it will contain word for word what she just gave the court." He let what she had told them stand on its own merits and moved on to the next line of questions.

He started asking about her time in what was known as the hole. She scanned the multiple prisoners behind the defense attorneys. All the ones who had tortured her were there. It was time to seal their fates as she had Billings and Franko. As he asked the questions about those who had worked at the club, she mentioned each person by name if she knew it or by their job, then pointed them out for the record. Malcolm finally got to the part were the four she wanted charged were involved.

"Jill, you keep mentioning a place called the hole. Please tell us about this place and how it got its name."

"The club has two levels. The hole was on the lower floor hidden in the back behind the stage area. It was where they kept the girls who serviced the low-paying customers. The rest of us had better quarters on the upper floor and were allowed off for eight hours a day. If we created a problem, we were shunted to the hole as punishment."

"Were you ever put in the hole?"

"Yes. I was considered a problem, but they had requests for me to dance, so I seldom stayed there very long."

"Who was the person in charge of the hole?"

"Her name is Rosalyn."

"Is she here today?"

"Yes, the lady behind the defense attorney in the dark blue dress."

"What did she do?"

"She was the one who assigned clients to the girls. She was also the one who determined who got fed, drugged, beaten, or disappeared."

"What do you mean by disappeared?"

"They would take the ones who were too sick or too much of a problem and let the other workers in the hole do what they wanted with them. Those girls left in a body bag."

"You personally witnessed them carrying out bodies?"

"Yes. Rico, Paul, Leroy, and Marvin were the others who worked there regularly. On more than one occasion, they carried out a body of one of the girls."

"Do you know the names of any of the girls who disappeared in that manner?"

"Yes. Erica, who they beat to death. I was next to her

and listened to the blows as they fell for over a half hour. Jane, who they drugged and had several of us sit and watch as they whipped her until she lost consciousness. Then they raped her unconscious body. Rico strangled her when he couldn't wake her up.

"There was Lena, who Rosalyn shot for refusing a customer, and Gail, who Marvin threw into the wall then bashed her head into the floor as she lay on the ground. Paul had a wonderful way of killing the girls. He enjoyed breaking their bones then hanging them, laughing as they flopped around. Those are the ones I witnessed. I'm sure there were others."

"When were you last in the hole?"

"I spent my last five days there."

"What did you do to get sent there?"

"I refused to allow one of the customers to do something I found repulsive and painful."

"What did they do to you during your time there?"

"I was isolated, which is never a good thing. The five of them came into the room where I was. Rosalyn told me I needed to learn that I had to do whatever the customer wanted. Paul and Marvin grabbed me and tied me to the post in the middle of the room. Rico came and showed me the whip he was going to use and told me I would learn the lesson or see him again for a reminder."

Tears were rolling down her cheeks as she talked. She could still feel the terror of what he was going to do. Her eyes went to where he was sitting among the spectators. He was grinning. That grin gave her the courage to continue.

"The first blow wasn't hard. Rosalyn stopped him and came over and ripped off my shirt. Marvin and Paul cut off the rest of my clothes. The next blow wasn't soft. Leroy joined Rico, and they took turns whipping me. I refused to cry out. The last thing I remembered was them cursing my silence."

"When you woke up, where were you?"

"I was still tied to the pole. Rosalyn told them to untie me and put me on the bed in the room I was assigned. She threw a bucket of water over my back, then they left."

"When did you see anyone again?"

"When Sam came to get me. He dressed me in clean clothes. I got the things I had hidden before they took me out a side door."

"Jill, I can see the defense is doubting your story."

She had worn a loose blouse. Her eyes went to Malcolm. He stated, "Show them the proof, Jill."

She stood and turned her back to the jury. Malcolm lifted her blouse, exposing the scars on her back. The gasps were audible. Malcolm put her blouse back in place and she sat back down, eyelids lowered, unable to look at anyone as tears flowed in rivulets down her cheeks, dropping onto her hands.

"The prosecution would like to enter charges of murder in the first degree, distributing drugs to a minor, felonious assault with intent to do bodily harm against a minor, false imprisonment, sex trafficking, and forced prostitution against those she just named. We would also like to amend the charges for all those who are indicted in this case for accessory to murder before and after the fact."

Llewellyn stated, "So noted."

He had her point out the four perpetrators again. She managed to name and point to them all before the funny feelings got worse. Sucking in a deep breath, she looked up at Malcolm, who was watching her as her world suddenly went black. Her eyes flickered open in what she thought was seconds to see Llewellyn squatted beside her, watching her. He was holding her hand, concern on his face. She was on the floor beside the witness stand.

"Welcome back," he said, studying her, his mouth in a grim line. "Nothing like giving us a good scare."

"There's an ambulance on the way. We need to get you checked out," Shaun stated.

Llewellyn stopped her when she attempted to sit up. Jill had trouble focusing her eyes on him but stated anyway, "I'm okay. Really. I just fainted. It isn't anything unusual for me." She knew she wasn't okay, but didn't want them to know that. The funny feeling was still there, and she wanted to go to sleep.

"Jill, I'm totally uncomfortable with what just happened," Malcolm stated. "One minute you were fine, and the next second we're stopping you from falling. You turned as white as could be, then passed out."

"I told you what it is. It's nothing. I'm okay now," she stated, eyes widening as fear snaked through her. There was no way she wanted to go to a hospital.

Llewellyn shook his head. "No, you aren't okay. I'm used to people who faint. What happened here wasn't simple fainting. Malcolm, take my place as I adjourn court for the day."

The four she had pointed out were arrested and charged, along with Rosalyn. When he returned to the bench, a rap of the gavel adjourned court until the following Monday. Returning to her side, he held her hand. She silently cried, aware he was taking her pulse. It wasn't supposed to happen like this.

"Jill, the truth. What's wrong?" Llewellyn sternly asked.

She refused to answer. Let the doctors tell them. The guards allowed Wyatt and Brad to come to her. The tears increased as she met Wyatt's glower, aware she had scared him again.

"Jill, baby, you all right?" he questioned, worry lacing his voice.

"I didn't have my medications. I forgot them," she admitted to him.

"Jill, you know better," he chided as he laid a gentle hand, which trembled slightly on her cheek. "She'll be okay. They should release her tomorrow. Let me call her doctor and let him know what happened."

Wyatt pulled up the number for her cardiologist. When someone answered, he said who he was and only had to wait a few seconds. He quickly told the doctor what had happened and that she would be in the Broward Health Medical Center emergency room shortly via ambulance. He hung up a few seconds later.

"He'll be there when you arrive. You know better. Those pills are supposed to be in your purse and you know it."

"I'm sorry. I forgot to pick them up off the counter when I left the resort. Daddy should have them."

"I have some in the car. I'll give them to Tom. At least I know he'll make sure you take them."

Malcolm finally asked, "Wyatt, what's wrong?"

He hesitated before explaining, "She has a heart condition. It wasn't of any major concern until they gave her the drugs during her time with them. Then with what she took afterward, it created a major problem. She's on medication, which stabilizes her rhythm and blood pressure. When she doesn't take her medication and gets upset, it causes an irregular heart rate and plays havoc with her blood pressure."

Malcolm shook his head. "Jill, all you had to do was to tell us you needed the medication, and we would have made sure you had it."

"I didn't want anyone to know," she softly told him.

Tom squatted at her head, "Jill, that wasn't very smart. You need to take your medication. You aren't the only young person who has heart problems. I want a promise you won't do this again."

"Promise," she told him, ashamed for worrying him.

"You had better keep that promise," Brad told her. "If you don't, you'll have that surgery whether you want it or not. I'm not about to lose you because you don't want to let others know you have a problem."

"Yes, sir," she told him. She knew he would follow through on his threat. The reason she hadn't opted for the surgery was due to her unreasonable fear of doctors. "Please don't leave me alone," she begged.

"I should let you deal with this on your own because you did this to yourself," Brad roughly told her.

She paled, gripping his arm, terror in her eyes.

Tenderly, he reassured her, "I won't leave you alone. Relax."

She closed her eyes as her heart raced. She was scared. It wasn't changing back into a normal rhythm. This was the worst episode she had ever experienced. A paramedic showed up at her side and put a blood pressure cuff on her arm. He took her pressure once, then he took it three times before calling the base. When he gave her blood pressure as 70 over 40, she knew she was in trouble. It was worse when he gave her heart rate as 240 and irregular.

"Jill," Llewellyn softly called to her. She opened her eyes. "You're not to leave that hospital until the doctors give you a clean bill of health. If you need that surgery, do it now. You have a lot of people who'll be here for you, including me. They're going to transport you now. Who do you want to go with you?"

"Brad or Tom," she softly said.

Tom looked down at her, his composed face hiding his feelings. "Brad will go with you. I'll meet you there."

The men moved so a stretcher could be put beside her. Brad gently picked her up and placed her on the stretcher. He held her hand as they made their way to the ambulance. The EMTs attempted to stop him from going with her until he told them, "If you don't let me go with you, when you get there she'll go off the deep end and most likely go into cardiac arrest." They relented and let him into the ambulance to sit beside her. She gripped his hand, unable to hide her terror.

At the hospital, they unloaded her from the ambulance and hurried her into the emergency entrance, their eyes on the monitor they had attached to her. Brad helped to move her to the emergency room stretcher. She gripped his hand, her fear increasing by the second.

Mark Weinstein, her doctor, was waiting as he had said he would be. He set up the monitor, not waiting on the nurse, and started snapping out orders. He watched her rhythm as the nurse gave her the medication he ordered through the IV they had started in the courtroom. He had her other hand in his and held on to it as he waited for the medication to take effect. Finally, he spoke to her.

"Jill, we need to do that pacemaker right now. The medication isn't helping. There are no more options."

Brad bent over her head. "Jill, you can't say no. You will do this."

She closed her eyes. "I'm scared," she softly told him.

Her doctor tapped her arm. "Jill, you've been seeing me for a long time now. I'm not about to let anything happen to my little imp. Now, here's the deal. Brad will stay with you until we get to the surgery suites. I know the surgeon who'll be doing the pacemaker, and he's very good. You'll like him. I'll be there with you through the whole deal. Brad can't go in to the operating room, but I can."

She was unable to talk, terrified at the prospect of surgery. Her doctor inquired, "Do you want Brad to sign the papers? I know he has power of attorney for you."

A nod was her agreement as she resigned herself to what was happening. Dr. Weinstein, or Mark as he insisted she call him, lifted the phone and dialed a number. He told the other person what was occurring and what needed to be done then gave her vitals. He hung up and waited. The phone rang, making her jump before Mark picked it up. He quickly spoke and hung up, returning to her.

"Jill, we're going to have to put on external pacing pads. It'll hurt like hell, but I can't leave you in this rhythm. Brad, please remove her jewelry, including the earrings."

Doing as requested, Brad put her jewelry in the pocket of his jacket as he removed each piece. A nurse apologized as she cut off her blouse and removed her bra before she laid a gown over her. Mark placed the external pacing pads, then turned on the machine. She whimpered with the pain. He ordered medication as he stayed by her side, his eyes on the monitor. The frown and his tenseness let her know he was worried.

Brad bent over and kissed her cheek, then held her hand as she gave into the fear and pain from the external pacemaker. A man she didn't know entered the room and took one look at the monitor and calmly stated, "They're opening the room. Let's get her upstairs. Luckily, Bob was here for the case I just finished and has another set up for me."

"Thanks, Al. She's this really special lady, so I'll be going in with her."

"Now, that's a first."

"For my little imp, I'll do whatever is needed to help her."

She couldn't quell the fear as she did her best not to cry.

Al glanced at Mark before saying with a grin, "Hey, cutie. This won't take long, and you should be able to go home tomorrow. I have to do a great job since Mark will be there and will critique everything I do."

He sobered before telling her, "This is done under a local with a bit of anesthesia. I'm not going to lie. We're walking a real fine line right now, and you're going to remember most of what I'll be doing. If you feel any pain during the procedure, let me know. I'll give more local. Once we get that pacemaker working, then we can put you into twilight sleep to do the pocket for the battery. Until then, we can't give you much of anything."

Al reached over and patted her cheek. "Honey, I know you're terrified. I can see it in those beautiful eyes. The worst part will be the local injection and then having to lie still until the wires are in place. I'll accept your cursing and yelling, just don't move."

She stared at him, trying to figure out why he would think she would curse or yell. He gave her a big grin before she could say anything. "I recognize the giant behind you. You must be the Jill I've heard so much about. I know Wyatt very well."

"Okay," she told him, relaxing enough to give him a fleeting smile.

Two orderlies and an anesthesiologist came into the room. The anesthesiologist asked Brad questions as they followed the stretcher out of the room to the elevator. Mark kept her hand in his and the surgeon remained close. He didn't terrify her like most other doctors did. The elevator opened, and she was pushed to the door of the operating rooms. Brad gave her a kiss.

"Granddad and I will be right here when you come out. Now be good."

Her fear level went up as they moved away from him. Mark took her hand. "Jill, I'm right here. Nothing bad is going to happen. We'll explain everything to you before we do it. Right now, I want you to close your eyes and find the inner you who is calm and go there. You need to decrease whatever is going on inside of you."

She stared up at him. "Mark?"

"Yes."

"I'm going to be okay, right?" she whimpered, terrified at how the events were spiraling out of control.

"I certainly hope so. If not, I'm in big trouble in more ways than I want to contemplate. Now help me out here and do like I told you to decrease some of that pressure you're feeling. I want you to stay in that calm place. I'll tell you what we're doing so there'll be no surprises."

She took a deep breath, closed her eyes, and started the meditation routine he had taught her. Calmness seeped in as she blocked out her surroundings. She started to panic when his hand left hers, but she heard him talking nearby. Someone put a hat on her head and tucked her hair under it, then his hand was back in hers.

They started moving again. She knew they were entering another room from the change in sounds. The rail on her left went down followed by a gentle bump as the stretcher moved next to something else.

Mark whispered in her ear, "Stay where you are, Jill. We're going to move you to another bed. Just relax and let us do the work."

Several hands lifted her to the cool sheets covering a thin mattress on a hard surface. Someone changed the wires for the monitor, then put the tube for oxygen under her nose.

Mark's soft voice told her, "They're going to move the gown off your left side. You'll feel cold wet stuff as they clean that area. Stay where you are. Things are looking a lot better."

Doing as he requested, she ignored the wet as the nurse scrubbed her left shoulder and chest. Someone entered the room. Her surgeon started issuing orders. The first one was for some music as soon as they could get it going. Mark chuckled before requesting Bon Jovi for her. He had remembered her request when he had been doing testing. Something heavy was placed across her abdomen.

Al joked, "Good thing I don't dislike him. I was betting on Elton John."

"She likes him, too, but I think Bon Jovi will be a bit better for this."

"What did you do?" Al asked. "That strip has really improved."

"My secret," Mark stated, squeezing her hand.

They placed something over her, which covered her

head. The person at her head lifted it off her face, but she didn't open her eyes or speak.

Al told her, "Jill, I'm going to feel around the area where I'll be putting in the wires. You'll feel pressure. When I find the spot, you'll feel a stinging pain as I give the local. I need you to stay really still during this."

She moved further into her meditation as his fingers probed where her neck and shoulder met.

"Injection," he warned. It hurt, but she didn't move, concentrating on staying in her peaceful place. Mark wiped away the tears from the pain when Al completed the injection.

"I'm going to give that a few seconds to take effect while I get everything set up," Al informed her.

There was soft talking and the clanking of metal against metal. He returned to her.

"Can you feel my fingers?" he questioned.

"Just a bit. It feels funny," she softly told him.

"Okay. Let me know if you feel anything other than pressure. You should not be feeling any pain with what I'm doing now."

He was right. There was no pain. Mark continued to hold her hand as she stayed where he had told her to go. It had been the only way she had been able to get through the testing he had needed to do when she first started having major problems. He had understood her fear and had worked with her, enabling her to tolerate what he was doing.

"C-arm," Al stated. She tensed as the bed was being adjusted but didn't move.

There was more pressure. She relaxed, the music her focal point in keeping her in her calm place. The silence of the team didn't bother her. It wasn't until she started to have difficulty breathing she stirred. Mark squeezed her hand.

"Don't move, Jill. It'll pass in a few seconds. Take slow deep breaths. That's it. Good girl."

Her fingers tightened on his hand as she attempted to stuff the panic back in its box. There was no reason for it to sneak out now. Mark was with her.

"It's all good, Jill," Mark said next to her ear. "Nice, slow, deep breaths. We're almost done. Picture that sun on the water in Aruba and all those colorful flowers. Feel the soft warm breeze as you're walking through the garden. Feel the sun kissing your skin and shining on all those colors. Listen to the waves. Look at how pretty the gentle waves are. See those pretty colors you love."

It didn't take much for her to see the scene he was describing. He had walked with her in the garden and had seen the beauty he was describing as they discussed her heart problem. Like now, he had held her hand. Panic receded as she went to Aruba, the villa, and the garden in her mind.

Al stated, "Jill, we're going to give you some anesthesia

so I can make the pocket for the battery. You did great."

There was a burning in her arm. A black nothingness enveloped her.

Chapter 23

PAYING THE PRICE

An annoying beeping was disturbing her sleep. Jill's brows drew together, attempting to determine where she was and what was causing the irritating sound. When she attempted to turn, there were cords running over her. She couldn't move her left arm. It was tied down.

Panic surged to the surface. Her eyes popped open. Upon seeing the white walls, she screamed, her past mixing with the present. She attempted to free herself from the cords across her and whatever was holding her left arm. Hands held her while she fought to get away. She screamed again, her fear escalating when someone grabbed her legs and another person pushed her down on the bed.

Brad's face entered her vision, quelling part of the panic. She reached out with her right hand to make sure she wasn't imagining him, her breath coming in gasps as the terror continued to grip her. He took her hand, holding it tightly.

"Jill, it's all right. They don't want you to move your arm, so it's in a special sling. You can move everything else. You just had surgery. Remember?"

She gripped his hand, attempting to integrate Brad being here with what her brain was telling her as she wildly scanned the room for those who would hurt her, still gasping for breath. It took a few seconds before his words made sense. The fear slowly receded, replaced by shame when the nurse and orderly loosened their holds on her. She blinked back the tears, not wanting to cry. Brad ran a gentle hand over her face. The tears spilled over, her memories receding into reality.

"I'm sorry," she whimpered as multiple people surrounded them, having responded to her screams.

"It's okay, sis. At least you know help is only a scream away," he joked, a forced smile on his lips. He squeezed her hand, reassuring her with his action that everything was fine now.

Al put a hand on her shoulder and shook his head, the smile on his face not matching the concern in his eyes. "Should have known. My best patient scares the hell out of me when she wakes up."

Brad kept her hand in his as he explained her screams. "She has this thing about not being able to move. The left arm being restrained scared her, that's all."

Al leaned on the rail of the stretcher, his face serious. "Jill, I don't want you to move that arm for at least two days. Those wires need to imbed. The one was somewhat difficult to place, and I don't want to have to go back and redo it if I can avoid it. Will you be okay with the sling for that time?"

"Yes. It just scared me when I woke up." Her eyes went to Brad. He smiled, but she could see the fear and concern he was attempting to hide. She had scared him, even though he had been expecting her to wake up screaming.

Brad squeezed her hand. "It's okay. That's why I'm here. I'd better go and let the others come in and see you, especially after those screams. Wyatt will be climbing the wall about now."

Her mouth turned up in a timid smile. "Thanks, Brad."

"Goes to prove I'm worth something other than to scare off the boyfriends."

She giggled, "Yeah, like you're going to scare off Tom. His brother is your size."

Brad chuckled merrily, "Yeah and he threatened to sic his father on me if I tried to run him off. I countered with Wyatt and Dad."

She giggled as he left to find those who were still

hanging around and bring them in to see her. She was surprised when Wyatt, Llewellyn, Malcolm, and Tom all entered the room. Wyatt noticed the sling and immediately understood the screams.

"Nothing like making sure we all knew you were fucking awake," Wyatt grumped.

Her wide eyes watched him, aware he was still in fear mode. He came over and kissed her forehead, assessing her before believing she was okay.

She stared up at him, her gaze pleading for understanding. "I'm sorry. The sling scared me, and I didn't remember where I was."

"I fucking get it, but it scared the fucking hell out of me and I'm sure half the fucking hospital."

She giggled, "I don't think it was quite that loud."

"I'm not too sure about that," Malcolm stated with a grin, moving to her side to lean over and kiss her cheek. "They said you'll be able to be discharged tomorrow. We've arranged for a guard for tonight and a private suite for you. I was beginning to think your men were about to come to blows as to who was going to stay with you."

"Who won?" she questioned, a big grin on her face, finding the idea of them fighting over her weird.

Malcolm grinned. "Tom and Wyatt. It's the first time I've ever seen Tom pull rank to get his way."

Her gaze went to the man in question. He shrugged, "There are times when pulling rank is needed. Like I said,

I'm going nowhere without you. The only reason I opted for Brad to come with you was because I knew he could sign for you and I couldn't."

Her gaze went to Llewellyn. He was calmly watching her, shaking his head, eyes twinkling with merriment with his arms crossed at his waist.

"Young lady, I don't know what it is, but you have every one of us at your beck and call. Whatever magic you possess; other women would pay a small fortune for it."

"It's what fairies do. We bewitch men and put them under our spell," she joked as the men chuckled.

"I know Malcolm has neglected to give my first name. It's Jared. Tom, Malcolm, Wyatt, and I are friends and have worked together for years on some of these racketeering cases. I've avoided you and, I'll admit, it was knowing this trial would eventually take place. I simply can't avoid you any longer. Once this is over, you, Wyatt, Brad, and Tom need to come for a visit. I can introduce you to Tom's boss, who won't believe he's finally attached himself to a woman."

"Sounds like a plan. Thank you for the invite."

Llewellyn's grin broadened, his gaze held hers. "It'll be fun standing back and watching the fireworks when you show up. They're expecting someone quite different to capture his attention. I haven't let anyone know I met you before now." He glanced over at Malcolm before stating, "Malcolm and I are going to disappear, now that we know you're all right. I'll see you Monday."

He and Malcolm left as the guards split; half of them surrounded the two men while the rest stayed close to the door, guarding her.

Al pulled her attention back to him. "Jill, I explained to them that you needed at least two days to recover. Whatever you're doing will be delayed until next week at the earliest. I would prefer if they could delay it for at least four to five days."

Jill told him, "It's all right. They can't do anything without me, so I'm sure Jared will go home for his anniversary, and my guess is Malcolm will join him while I'm recovering."

Tom moved to where Malcolm had been standing. "You're right on target. They're leaving in about two hours. That leaves us with what to do with you until you're able to return to court."

Wyatt glanced at Tom before informing them, "You'll be staying with me. My place is secure. I'm just worried about getting you in and out."

"She'll need to see me next week," Al cut in before they could discuss transportation issues. "Thursday evening would work best. I'll come to you if getting to the office is a logistical problem."

"That would be a better option as it would be a nightmare to get her there and back again," Tom admitted. "She has some major threats against her. We'll have guards around her while she's here. We'll also need a list of anyone who will need to enter her room, the medications she's to take, if any, and it needs to be in sealed packets with manufacturer information."

Al didn't indicate surprise at Tom's revelations. "No medication unless she needs something for pain. While I have your attention, Jill, keep that sling on until Saturday. Once it comes off, you can shower, but that arm is to be kept below shoulder height for the next two weeks. No lifting, period. If you notice your heart racing or missing beats, call Mark. He can check the pacemaker and rhythm. My goal is to not see you here for at least six to ten years."

"Is this one of the MRI-safe pacemakers?" Tom questioned.

"Yes. Microwave-proof also. Bob will check you in a few minutes to make sure it's working correctly before they move you to the floor." He rotated his head to check for the pacemaker representative. Bob was standing outside the door, held in place by the agents who were checking his credentials. "He's okay. We need him to run a test," Al informed the men who let Bob into the recovery room.

Bob glanced back at the guards. "Never ran into that before," he stated while plugging in his equipment. He put a heavy circular thing attached to wires on her chest, then ran two strips and gave them to Al, who studied them.

"Doing good, Jill. Bob will recheck it in the morning. I'll see you then. If everything is good, you can go home.

You should be going to your room in a few minutes."

When he and the rep left, she waited for Wyatt to scold her for not taking her medication. It wasn't that she didn't deserve it this time after scaring everyone half to death.

"Jill, you had better never fucking scare me like this again," he growled, glaring at her.

"I'm sorry," she told him, afraid of what he would do if she screwed up again.

Tom bent over and gave her a kiss. "You were partially taken off the hook. Mark said the meds had been slowly decreasing in effectiveness and the pacemaker was going to have to be done soon anyway. You just speeded it up with not taking the medication, which was pretty stupid on your part."

Okay, so Wyatt wasn't going to scold her. He was leaving it to Tom. "I know. I didn't think anything about it until I passed out the first time, but I recovered and didn't think it would hurt for a few more days," she informed him, nervously picking at the blanket covering her.

He lifted her chin, turning her face toward his. His face was stern. His eyes held hers. "Jill, this was serious. Almost deadly serious. This was an emergency surgery, and they had to keep your heart going with external pacing. It's not something you can ignore. You wouldn't be here talking to us if Jared had believed you when you told him you were okay. Do you understand?"

Lowering her eyelids, she answered, "Yes."

He sat on the edge of the stretcher. "Jill, I know a lot has been going on, but there are some things you can't ignore. I'm glad Jared didn't believe you."

She worried her bottom lip before saying, "He knew I wasn't okay. He was monitoring my pulse. I thought it would go back to normal. It always has in the past."

"I also knew you weren't doing well. You had me worried when you passed out the first time. Your heart was racing then. I was about to call for an ambulance when it finally went back into a normal rhythm. From here on out, you will make all those office visits and checkups, and you will take the medication that's ordered as prescribed. No excuses. I want you around for a long time."

"Tom," she started then stopped.

"What?" His gaze hadn't left hers. His face was stern, but held concern.

A tear ran down her cheek. She lowered her lids as she admitted, "I'm terrified of doctors and have been for as long as I can remember. After what they did to me, I panic at every appointment. Brad had to hold me to keep me from running out of the office not long ago. I almost lost it in the operating room. Mark knew what was happening. He made it so I kept it together. Also, I can't be in a white room for very long without becoming a total nutcase."

She peeked up at him, afraid he would negate her fears. Her hope was for him to understand the unreasonable and unfounded fear she had experienced from the time she was small. It had only been intensified with her experiences in captivity.

Tom cupped her cheek in his hand with a tenderness she hadn't expected. "I understand. Luckily, there are solutions for all those problems except for surgery. You have a lot of people who care for you—a whole lot. Now you need to do your part and keep yourself healthy."

Her eyes went to her grandfather. He had remained quiet. Tom had said everything he would have said to her in a much nicer way. Wyatt shook his head, mouth grim before adding, "Jill, you came within a hair of not making it today. Mark said God was with you in that Al and the pacemaker guy was already here with what he needed. That panic attack wasn't really a panic attack. Your heart went into a dangerous rhythm. Al saved your life by getting that wire in place and getting the pacemaker connected. I lost your grandmother to the same problem when she refused to acknowledge she had a heart condition. I don't want to lose you too."

Tears rolled down her cheeks, fully understanding what she had done to him. She now knew why he had been afraid when she had first been diagnosed with the problem. It was the reason why he had always made sure she had her medication and kept the appointments he made. His simple heartfelt speech told her just how afraid he was for her. She lowered her eyelids, not stopping the tears, ashamed of not taking care of herself.

Her contrite, "I won't do it again. Promise," was meant. It was up to her to take care of herself. This episode had scared her and everyone around her. Wyatt's and Tom's words brought home how stupid she had been.

The nurse interrupted them. "You're ready to go. Let me remove these leads so we can get you to your room."

Tom moved so the nurse could raise the side rail and connect a portable monitor. The guards surrounded the stretcher as Tom and Wyatt followed, keeping watch for the unusual.

They were waiting on the elevator when a man in a suit came around the corner, a gun in his hand. The guard closest to the gunman threw a cup of hot coffee, hitting him in the face. A second agent jumped forward and used his taser. The man dropped to the floor, unable to move, his gun sliding against the wall with a clatter. The guards had him in handcuffs before the nurse had time to react to the threat.

The elevator door opened. Wyatt commanded, "Let's go! Move it!" She was pushed into the safety of the elevator by Wyatt and Tom. Two agents joined them. With a shaking hand, the nurse pushed the button for the fourth floor. Tom gave her a reassuring smile.

They made it to the room without any more problems. Tom and Wyatt moved her to the bed. The nurse made a hasty exit from the room after connecting her to the monitor mounted on the wall above the bed. Jill remained quiet, guilt filling her at how she had put all those she loved in jeopardy by not admitting she had a heart condition.

Mark ambled into the room a few minutes later. "Jill, you scared the hell out of me earlier, now the nurse is out there saying a man with a gun was trying to undo all the work Al just did."

Wyatt grumped, "Fucking asshole. Should've known we'd have fucking guards around her."

"I take it you have a person or two who would be perfectly happy if you hadn't survived?" Mark questioned, watching her with raised brows.

"Yeah," she admitted. "It's the reason for all the security. They aren't local either, if you get my drift."

"I sort of figured that. I won't need to see you tomorrow, so, as soon as Al says it's all right, you can leave. I want to see you in six weeks. No excuses, Jill."

"Yes, sir," she meekly told him.

Tom added, "I'll make sure she shows up, even if I have to get help to get her there."

Keeping her head down, she admitted, "And he can get a lot of help, too."

Mark chortled, "Like the guards and family."

"More if needed. I'll be there."

Mark sobered. "Jill, I'm sure you were told how close it was today. There's no reason to have it happen again. I'm not sure I could handle the stress for one thing. The next time, you might not be so lucky.

"You're going to be pacemaker-dependent. That means more frequent battery changes. They're quick, and you can go home the same day. We're going to need to monitor the pacemaker closely to make sure your battery doesn't run out of power. You're to get a medic alert and wear it. On the medic alert, it needs to say pacemaker dependent. They can't stop that pacemaker for any reason. There's a card you'll need to carry with you stating the type of pacemaker you have. The nurse will give it to you with your discharge papers. These things are very important, young lady."

"I understand. I've used up three of my nine lives. I need to keep the rest in reserve."

"Right. I'll see you in six weeks, earlier if you have any problems or concerns. Call me for any questions. You have my cell number, and don't say you don't."

He winked at Tom and left. Tom sat on the bed, face serious and eyes boring into hers.

"What do you need to do when you get out of here?"

"Make an appointment for six weeks and order the medic alert thingy."

She scooted down in the bed. Talk about screwing up royally. Tom wiped away the couple of tears she couldn't hold in check. Shame at her stupidity made her want to hide from him.

"Jill, it's over. Please don't cry."

"I screwed up big time. Scared everyone half to death.

Delayed a major trial and put more lives than mine on the line. Wonder what else I can mess up in the next few days." Her voice was filled with disgust at causing so many problems.

"Hmm, not sure. I can think of a few things, but let's not try for those," Tom joked.

A person from food service came in and asked, "Last name, please?"

"Potter," Jill replied. The lady left the meal for her and returned with two more for Tom and Wyatt. Jill lifted the cover over her plate and frowned.

"Eat, Jill," Wyatt commanded.

She took a small bite of the mashed sweet potatoes. The rest of the meal looked disgusting. Poking at the meat, she refused to even try it, unable to recognize what it was. She took a bite of the mixed vegetables and spit it back out, her face scrunched up in disgust. After eating the Jell-O and a bite of the cake, she gave up. They had given her margarine, so she couldn't even enjoy having bread and butter. There was no salt either. Hopefully, she would have a decent breakfast.

Wyatt watched, an amused grin on his face, as Tom spread her bread with real butter and handed it to her. She ate it and drank the water from her pitcher, refusing to even consider the coffee, aware it was decaf. She hated anything decaf and would drink herbal teas instead. It was hell when you were hungry and didn't have any decent food to eat.

Accepting there was no way to sate her hunger until morning, she attempted to get comfortable. Her shoulder was hurting, but she didn't want to take any medication. She sighed, resigned to an uncomfortable hospital bed, pain, hunger, and the lack of Tom's arms around her. Yeah, it was going to be a really lousy night.

Tom put the trays on the table outside the door when he and Wyatt had finished eating. There were two guards in the room and two outside the door. Wyatt made himself comfortable on the couch. Tom surprised her when he reclined next to her on the narrow bed. She happily curled into him until she remembered how her stupidity had hurt him.

Raising her face to his, she told him, "I'm sorry, Tom. I really am. You can't fix stupid, and I was stupid."

"It's over. You aren't going to do it again. I'll chalk it up to fear and denial of the severity of the problem, along with avoiding an uncomfortable situation."

"Mostly fear. Fear of the doctor and of what I can't control. I'm not good at facing physical problems. I expect them to go away. Like I said, stupid."

"Go to sleep. It'll be better in the morning."

She lowered her head before timidly asking, "Are you angry with me?"

"No. Mostly concerned that my fairy seems to be a bit self-destructive. I need her to see that she has to help herself to be able to fly again. Like a motorized toy, you'll need to change that battery at regular intervals to keep you working. Don't forget that."

"I won't. I found my prince and I want to go dancing in the moonlight with him, and I almost messed it up big time."

"Yeah. I'm still trying to get myself out of fear mode. You gave us all a big scare."

Okay. He was still recovering from her scaring him half to death, let alone her brother and grandfather. It was time to grow up and take care of herself and stop avoiding the things she needed to do. If she wanted to keep him, she had to become an adult and take responsibility for herself.

Chapter 24

CHANGES

It took her a long time to fall asleep. Tom's arms and

steady heartbeat finally lulled her into a restless slumber. A hand on her shoulder woke her. Still half asleep, she turned to discover what the person wanted. Her mind didn't comprehend what she was seeing. A heavyset woman in a nurse's uniform had a gun pointed at her. The woman's grin was more of a grimace.

Jill stared at the large black hole of the pistol pointed at her head, her body refusing to move. The gun suddenly tilted up and fired into the ceiling. Wyatt held the woman, an arm around her neck, holding the woman's arm with the gun in the air. Tom easily removed the gun from the woman's hand before the guards moved, surrounding them.

She attempted to calm herself as several people ran into the room to investigate the gunshot. The lights came on before Fred ambled over, shaking his head, tsking as he observed the woman whom Tom had handcuffed.

"Callie, I would have thought you had learned from the last time. This time, you'll spend more than five years and it'll be a federal lockup. Attempted murder on a federal witness will get you up to fifty years."

"What do you mean federal?" Callie snapped.

"Oh, they didn't tell you? Our little lady here is a federal witness. You really do need to ask questions before you take a contract," Fred informed her.

Several agents entered the room to take her into custody. One read her the required rights while she glared at Fred.

With a nod, she acknowledged that she understood her rights before saying, "You had better do a lot better in protecting her. Rob Roy is coming after her. He won't give up easily. He got a good down payment and wants the rest."

Fred quirked an eyebrow. "He can try, but he won't make it. See you in a few weeks, Callie."

Wyatt shook his head, letting out a big breath. "Looks like the fuckers still can't see that they aren't going to fucking walk away this time."

Tom glanced at her then back at Wyatt. "She knows something, and they know she has the information. I don't believe she's even aware of what they want to keep her from telling."

"What the fuck does that mean?" Wyatt growled, a scowl on his face.

"Jill has some information they don't want shared and they're doing everything they can to make sure that that information isn't extracted. I'm not sure she even knows she has the information or what it really means."

"Hey, guys, I'm here and awake," she grumped, not in the best of moods at being awakened after having difficulty going to sleep.

The men turned to her and Wyatt snapped, "In that fucking case, go back over all the fucking crap and find out what the fuck they're after."

She shifted in the bed, uncomfortable with being unable to lie on her left side along with the pain from the surgery. "I know what they're after," she informed them, voice even and gaze direct as the two men stared at her.

"What?" Wyatt snapped.

Tom, brows drawn together, questioned, "What do you have on them that's so important?"

"Not telling because then you two will be in big trouble like me. I'm just waiting for Malcolm or Shaun to ask the right questions."

"So, you make us fucking crazy trying to keep you fucking safe," Wyatt grumped before giving her a kiss.

"I love you, too, Grandpa," she told him, understanding what he wasn't saying.

"Yeah. Right. Tom, you sure you really want this sprite? She'll drive you fucking nuts."

Tom grinned, "Hey, it won't be boring, that much I know."

Wyatt laughed. Tom was right. It wouldn't be boring. He sat on the edge of the bed with a grin. Her hand went to his.

She had a crooked grin as she stated, "You seem to be okay with me not being the normal female."

"Honey, any normal sane female won't give me the time of day with the type of job I do."

"And that job is?" she probed.

He glanced at Wyatt. "For the time being, your pay

grade and security clearance aren't quite high enough for that information."

"You know I'll find out eventually," she informed him with confidence.

His soft lips brushed hers before he stated, "I'm sure you will. For now, it's best that you don't know. Like you, I have a few secrets which need to be kept until the right time."

"Al said I could go home today." She watched as he glanced at Wyatt, not sure of what the two men had planned. She knew being here wasn't exactly the safest place to be. Readjusting herself in the bed, she put her hand on her chest before softly saying, "Have them call Al. I think there's a problem."

Her calmness belied the fear coursing through her. Wyatt didn't even bother with the nurses, placing the call himself. She waited, hoping the surgeon wasn't far away.

"He'll be here in a couple of minutes," Wyatt informed her. He and Tom stayed close, eyes on the monitor above her head.

Al burst through the door to her room. "The OR is being set up. The lead I was concerned about moved. It's just a matter of readjusting it, but I couldn't do it earlier due to your rhythm. If everything stays like it is now, I'll have the time to get it placed in a better spot. Depending on how comfortable I am with where the lead is placed will determine whether you'll have that hated sling or not."

Less than ten minutes later, two orderlies with a stretcher entered the room. "Your chariot is here. Let's get this show on the road," Al stated, giving her hand a gentle squeeze.

Wyatt and Tom moved her to the stretcher. The anesthetist connected her to the portable monitor then injected some medication into her IV. It wasn't until the stretcher moved the panic hit her. Tom stopped them and gave her a kiss.

"Jill, go to where Mark sent you yesterday. I'll be right here with you until you go into the OR. They won't let me go in with you."

His hand kept her from going from panic to terror. She closed her eyes, starting the routine Mark had taught her. It would help if she stayed calm, but how do you keep an unreasonable panic from rising up and making you do things you normally wouldn't. Even her therapist hadn't discovered why she panicked with certain things and not others. For now, she just needed to get it under control.

As she kept her breathing deep and regular, Tom's hand gave her the security she needed to relax. The movement stopped. Wyatt was speaking, and Tom answered, but she didn't attend to what they were saying. Pulling herself back to what she needed to do, she let them talk. At the edge of her consciousness, she was aware when the stretcher stopped a second time. Then, her hair was covered with a cap. When Tom's hand left hers, her eyes popped open, panic sweeping over her. She gasped, eyes wild in her search for Tom.

"Tom, put on a bunny suit and rules be damned. Go back to where you were, Jill. Tom will stay with you. Give him a second to get dressed," Al stated with authority.

Her wide eyes went to Tom for confirmation. He winked at her as he started to pull on an overall-type white paper coverall. An older lady stalked toward them, mouth in a grim line.

The lady stated, "I'm sorry, but it's against our policy to allow anyone without prior approval into the operating suites. You will . . ."

Tom cut her off. "Lady, you have no authority to stop me. This young lady's life is on the line right now and she's in federal custody. Our orders are to not leave her side unless someone with appropriate clearance is with her. Unless you can produce level eight or higher federal security clearance within the next ten seconds, I'm following orders from Washington, D.C., which, I do believe, will override your policies. If you have any concerns, you may contact my superior." He handed her a card.

Al barked, "Ruth, do what you want, but he's going back, I don't have time to stand here and argue with you, so take out that pen and start writing. Let's go."

The stretcher started moving with Tom beside her, holding her hand. With an impish grin, he stated, "I can hardly wait for her to really look at the card I gave her."

"Why?" she asked.

"Let's just say, she may want to think twice about calling. If you think Wyatt is bad, you should call my boss over something he thinks is ridiculous. He'll let her know, in words not exactly meant for ladies, how she had better not interfere, and if she does, she'll end up with federal charges of obstruction. He'll then call me and ream me out for not keeping him up to date."

Al commented, "I take it that boss is one most of us would know not to bother for access to an OR."

"Yeah, you could say that," he chortled as he expertly tied on a mask while Al went to scrub.

Tom helped to push the stretcher into the operating room. She noticed he was comfortable with the sterile room. He, the two orderlies, and the anesthetist lifted her to the OR table. Once the stretcher was moved, he came to her right side and held her hand.

"Now, go back to where you were before the evil witch made you come back here."

She giggled, "Thanks for pulling rank for me."

"Anytime. Now, go back to that nice sunny scene where you see all those pretty flowers and bright colors. I'll be right here beside you."

She closed her eyes again, her hand in his while she went back to her fantasy. Tom's voice informed her of what was to come next, allowing her to stay calm. He asked her,

"What music will go with where you are?"

"Enigma or Enya," she answered.

Her answer hadn't pulled her from where she had gone in her mind. Those were the songs she was imagining in her head. She relaxed, the music surrounded her with Tom's hand connecting her to him, keeping the panic at bay. The anesthetist gave her medication to take the edge off the local being injected. The wince and tighter grip on his hand were the only indications she was aware of what was happening.

In her meditation, the sun was warming her when Tom's "He just needs to put the battery back. He's almost done," elicited a squeeze to his hand to show she had heard. The light touch of his hand on her face had her smiling. She had imagined him beside her on the steps of the villa. The soft breeze in the early-morning light brought the scent of the saltwater, overlaid by the sweet fragrances of various flowers to them. His hand and closeness almost made it real.

Opening her eyes, she stared at the man who cared enough to pull rank and stay with her. He brushed his lips across hers, love in his eyes as he made sure she wasn't going to have a meltdown. No matter what else happened, she wanted him to be with her for a very long time. This time, she wasn't going to mess it up by being stupid.

Al's voice pulled her from her thoughts. "We're done. I don't believe you'll have a problem this time. I want you to wear the sling for another day though. You'll have that same feeling you had earlier if the lead moves again. This will only keep you here for a couple of more hours."

The voice of Bob, the rep, stated, "Looking real good. Much better pattern this time, and the numbers are better."

A hand pulled back the drape that was hiding her from the doctor. His head popped into view.

"Goes to prove we just needed slightly more time to do it right. No more unplanned crap, got it?"

"Got it," she told him with a grin.

It wasn't but a few minutes later before she was in the recovery room. When Al had finished his charting, he took a seat on the edge of the stretcher, lifting her hand in his.

"Jill, you're going to need an ablation procedure to keep your chaotic heartbeat from interfering with the pacemaker. It can wait a few weeks, but you need to make plans to have it done. Mark really wanted to do it while you were here, but I nixed it. I want those leads to be held in place nice and tight, so plan on returning in six to eight weeks to go to the specials area for the procedure. It'll only mean a few hours' stay. You already have the pacemaker which is overriding the nodes."

She twisted her mouth, resigned to what she would need to do. "I know. He explained everything after all the testing was done. I refused to have it done because the guy who was to do it gave me the creeps."

"Well, you'll be able to meet who will be doing it. If you don't like him, we'll go to the next one, their ego be damned. You need to be comfortable with them, because like here, you'll be in a twilight sleep and aware of what's going on in the room."

She glanced at Tom and asked, "Will Tom be able to pull rank and be there with me?"

"Of course. The director didn't talk to his boss, but she did make that call. Let's see, her words were, 'The receptionist gave me the information I needed when she answered the phone. I apologize for the inconvenience,' before going and finding something else to do."

"What card did you give her?" she asked as Tom and Al exchanged a merry look.

Tom handed her the card he seldom used. She looked at it and handed it back to him. "You could have used a less important 'boss' to pull rank," she expressed.

"True, but she'll tell them to leave me alone when we show up again. Besides, he really is my boss."

It was a toss-up as to whether to believe him or not. The card did have his supposedly superior's name on it and his phone number. Like the operating room director, she most likely would have backed off and not disturbed the man whose name was listed on the card.

Malcolm had alluded to his being in charge and not normally working regular cases. It made her wonder what had made him so involved on this particular case and specifically with her. Maybe she would learn the why sooner or later. This wasn't the time or place to ask questions.

The stay in recovery was short. Back in the room, Tom made sure she was comfortable before asking Wyatt, "What level of security do you have?"

"Enough to play footsie with the fucking prick on that card," Wyatt revealed.

Tom looked down at her. "What about you?"

"I don't know. I can stand in for Wyatt when sending reports and taking orders and accessing information. The only place I can't access is his personal files, just like he can't access mine."

Her grandfather didn't shy away when Tom stated, "I certainly hope she was cleared, Wyatt."

Wyatt sat back and crossed his arms. "Oh, she was fucking cleared right to the top. Why, I don't know, but she's on your fucking level, Tom. I'm the low-level guy here. I believe it has something to do with her fucking memory and all the fucking information she has stashed in that fucking brain. What I do know is, the fucking Feds have kept close tabs on her ever since she began working for me."

The next question from Tom had her wondering what he knew about her.

"What about before that time?"

Her gaze switched to Wyatt, curious as to what he

would say.

"Enough that she could run the fucking agency without me and get all the fucking reports to the appropriate people without raising any fucking alarms."

"How did you get that clearance for her?"

"It was when she was working for me as a teenager. One of your fucking guys attempted to get information from her without any success. His fucking comment was to the effect that her innocence and pleasantly telling him she couldn't divulge any information without fucking authorization from a higher source stymied him. She was unaware that he really was the fucking higher source in fucking person. I was out of the office, and she fucking refused to let him past the reception area to wait on me. She even made him go to the fucking hall bathroom until I returned."

Tom's eyebrows went up as he rotated, so he was facing her. "I'm surprised he didn't pop a gasket at having to wait in the waiting area."

Her eyes went between him and Wyatt, who was having fun with her not knowing who the man was at the time. Tom needed an explanation of what had happened.

"Grandpa, you can't blame me if you didn't give me the okay to let him wait in your office. He didn't give me any way of verifying who he was. I was told to allow no one in the offices without being able to check them out and verify who they were. You also told me to trust no one where security was concerned. I didn't know him, and he wasn't going past that area without you telling me it was okay, and you didn't answer your phone."

Wyatt snickered, "Tell him what he did when you wouldn't let him past you."

"He threatened me with the loss of my job and promised I would never work for law enforcement again."

"And what did you do?"

"I stood in front of the door and told him if he laid a hand on me, I would have him charged with assault. I had my orders, and I wasn't going to get in trouble on account of him. He could wait where I told him to wait until Wyatt came back or he could return later, but he wasn't going into the inner office without the appropriate clearances. He never gave me what I needed to verify who he was, so he waited in the waiting area with me."

"Where was Sam? He could have told you who he was," Tom questioned, eyes twinkling at her run-in with a district supervisor of what she now knew was his agency.

"He was with Wyatt. I was the only one there at that time. Everyone else was out on cases. He only had to wait for thirty minutes, and it isn't like the furniture was all that uncomfortable."

"I bet you got an earful when you got back," Tom chuckled.

"Actually, no. In fact, he was fucking impressed when she didn't give in to his fucking demands. He couldn't believe that she was only fucking fifteen. No matter what he fucking tried, he got absolutely no fucking information other than we were a private investigation agency and he would have to fucking talk to me to determine if he wanted to hire the agency."

"I take it she didn't ask why he wanted to talk to you."

"Well, he wasn't on my fucking appointments, so she treated him as a fucking walk-in customer. If Sam would have been there, she would have fucking deferred to him. Even today, she's still the best fucking one on the front desk. What's funny is, how he recognized her fucking name from some files she had sent for me. Her fucking name is under mine when she's the one doing the actual work."

"I take it he attempted to get information from her."

"Fucking A, he did. Didn't work. She just kept repeating, 'I'm sorry, sir, but I'm not at liberty to discuss issues which may or may not be related to the agency. I'm sure Wyatt or Sam will be able to address any questions or concerns when they return.' She didn't even fucking look up as she repeated it over and over again to all the questions he fucking asked. When he tried discussing the fucking weather, she looked out the fucking window and stated, 'It's sunny,' and went back to work."

Tom laughed at how she had thwarted one of the bosses because the man didn't give her the means to verify his identity. She really didn't care who he was at the time. Not only wasn't he getting into the main office, he wasn't getting any information from her. Period.

Al entered the room, pulling her attention to him. "Ready to leave?" he asked.

"Yes," she stated hopefully.

"I'll make arrangements to see you in seven to ten days. Keep that arm down and use it as little as possible. No lifting, pushing, or pulling. I'll bring Bob with me to check the pacemaker again just to verify it's still doing a good job. If anything feels funny or different, call me or Mark."

"Will do. No more ignoring things."

"Better not," he warned before leaving.

Her gaze went to Tom. He just lifted an eyebrow and didn't say what she was expecting. Okay, it was up to her to take care of herself or pay the price. He wasn't her keeper. Wyatt left, leaving Tom to help her dress. To her surprise, he avoided exposing her as much as possible. He was gentle and considerate in his assistance.

When she was fully dressed, he stood before her and ran a hand through his hair. "Jill, I have access to this really great plastics guy. I'd like him to take a look at your back. He may be able to fix some of the damage without major reconstruction."

She lowered her gaze. "It would be great, but not right now. Let me get through all this crap first. I still need that ablation in six weeks or so and to get through this trial. After that, then maybe. Doctors aren't my favorite people even though I like Mark and Al."

"Just throwing it out there for you to consider. You'd

like him, too. He's really funny and he'll tell you the truth about what he can and can't do."

He didn't say anything more when Wyatt and the nurse entered the room. She signed the discharge papers then handed the copies to Wyatt to keep for her. He took the copies and made a call.

When he hung up, he stated, "Sam will have the SUV at the front door by the time we get down there. I'm sure some fucking people are going to wonder at the fucking coverage we have for her, but I don't fucking care. Her getting home safe is more fucking important than inconveniencing a few fucking people."

She was put in a wheelchair, surrounded by Fred and his guards, as the nurse pushed her to the elevator. She was stopped in the hall until the men had secured the area. It was much the same when they got to the bottom floor. The men surrounded her and the nurse as they made their way to where Sam was waiting on them. A corridor of guards formed a path for them. Once she was in the vehicle, they waited for Tom and Wyatt to join her, as Fred took the passenger seat. The others went to several cars to lead or follow them.

She sniggered, "I get more security than the president."

Sam came back with, "That's because you're more important than he is."

"That and the fucker doesn't have an active fucking contract on him," Wyatt snapped.

It didn't take long for them to reach the tall building on the ocean where Wyatt had a penthouse condo. They pulled into the parking garage and waited until it was cleared, and the elevator was waiting on them. She was surrounded as they headed to the elevator. Once inside, Wyatt used a key to access the panel where he placed his right then left hand. The panel slid shut, and the elevator moved without stopping to the top floor. He was the only tenant to have access to his floor on this elevator since he owned the two condos on this side of the building, living in one and the other was used for important guests to the area. The other two penthouse owners used the elevator on the other side of the building. Like Wyatt, they had keys and used a hand print for access to the top floor from the garage.

The men left the elevator first and went through the rooms of the two condos. They followed as the men cleared rooms and the exits were secured. She noticed Tom watching the men, most of whom were Wyatt's, verifying no one had managed to breach the security. She went to her favorite spot on the couch and waited. Wyatt checked the security system before he picked up a communicator.

"Jim, take four and check the roof. Someone was there about forty-five minutes ago. They didn't make it through the door, but they may still be there, so, code red."

When she turned to where Tom had been standing, he had disappeared. She hadn't seen him leave, but he was gone. Wyatt watched on the screen as the men followed the protocol for searching the roof. They knew all the nooks and crannies where someone could hide.

She had done several practice searches with them as the quarry and learned quickly where the good hiding places were. One time, it had taken them almost an hour to find her, and Wyatt was furious. She knew that their weekly exercises with her hiding had made them aware of various places they wouldn't have thought of before, such as on top of the AC units, the vent pipe, and other places they hadn't been checking.

She noticed the small helicopter on the pad. "Make sure they search the chopper thoroughly. There's a place behind the backseats where someone could hide."

He relayed her information to the men. She watched Tom approach the chopper from the rear with one of his men. They slipped in the rear doors and pulled someone from behind the seats. Another man was found curled up in the cargo area. The men were handcuffed and escorted into the condo.

When they were standing before Wyatt, Jill intoned in a bored voice while checking her nails, "Boys, neither one of you are the brightest bulbs in the box if you expected to get in here that easy. You really need to stick to dealing drugs." She examined the two young men. "Doggy, Squiggles, not bright at all taking this job, and you know it. You might want to roll to keep from being charged with attempted breaking and entering. With your rap sheets, it'll be prison for sure. This time, you made a big mistake. You see, I'm a federal witness and that means federal charges. Just throwing it out there, boys. Not my concern."

The two men blanched. They knew what it meant when she said federal prison. She expected them to sing like divas to keep out of a federal lockup. They were good at breaking and entering with normal security. They had been her snitches to stay out of jail for past infractions. Yeah, she knew them well.

Tom and his men took the two men to the bottom floor via the stairs. Wyatt stared at her after the men were escorted out of the condo.

"Jill, how the fuck do you know those two cocksuckers and what made you suggest the fucking chopper as a hiding place?" he inquired, watching her.

"They're a couple of snitches I didn't turn in when I could have. The helicopter normally isn't there, so it was the only option when they weren't found elsewhere."

He shook his head. "You do have some fucking unusual acquaintances."

"Comes with the job, and you know it. They're minor dealers. The big one was taken in, and they had to find another supplier. It was related to a case I was working."

"Maybe I should fucking rethink you working fucking cases like that."

Her head pivoted to him. "Wyatt, I like what I do."

"That may be, but it may be fucking time for a fucking change once this is all over."

"And if I don't want to?" she probed, not sure why he was considering pulling her out of the field.

"Jill, I know you can run the fucking agency. I believe it's time for me to fucking step back and let you do more of that type of work. You're fucking good at it, and I won't fucking have to panic every fucking time the phone rings."

It was easy to see where he was coming from. He was worried about her, more than ever with her medical condition having become serious. She didn't want to leave the field because she enjoyed working cases, but he was right. She could run the agency, only she didn't want to. It was his agency, not hers.

"Wyatt, give me the real reason you want me out of the field."

"Your fucking medical problems."

"You've known about them forever. What's the difference now?"

"I almost fucking lost you, and I want your fucking ass close to me."

Okay, she had scared him more than she thought she had, and it was now time to pay for her stupidity.

"I understand. I'll agree to it as long as I'm not given busy work just to keep me here. I have a brain and I expect it to be used for something other than filing and answering the fucking phones."

Wyatt joined her on the couch. "No fucking phones or busy work. Full partnership, and you get to handle half the fucking cases. You'll work with the fucking Feds. They like you, and you're fucking good on those cases."

"You don't have to make me a partner. Just let me handle part of the business."

"I want you as a partner. The fucking agency will be yours when I finally fucking retire," he informed her. "It's fucking time for me to relax some, and you're the only fucking one I trust to work it like me."

This wasn't what she had expected. He was giving her a good reason to move to the office. She could still do some things in the field, but she would be handling half of the business. It was easy to understand his reasoning on all levels. Leaning over, she put her one arm around him and kissed his cheek.

"I didn't mean to scare you so much. It won't happen again. Working in the office will just be a different way of doing things," she stated as he held her close to him.

"It made me realize how fucking much you mean to me. I've been fucking avoiding giving you the partnership due to being in fucking control for so long. It's fucking time I backed off some."

"You mean a lot to me, too. This episode showed me how much I really needed to grow up and take responsibility for myself. I've let you and Brad take care of me since I was a child, so I've never needed to become an adult. I think it's time.

"I'll make that appointment for Mark. If I'm kept at the courthouse, I'll arrange for Al to go there. No more being the kid and hiding from things. I'm not invincible, and that was brought home to me in no uncertain terms this time. I'll follow up in six to eight weeks for the ablation. Tom can pull rank and be there with me. I know I'll need someone with me, so I don't go nutso on them."

"That's fucking music to my ears. I guess I didn't fucking help as I liked my little girl and didn't want her to fucking leave me."

"If Tom wants to marry me, I don't know where I'll end up yet."

Wyatt kissed her cheek. "Here. He lives in the area and promised not to take you far away except for a few trips when he has to be in D.C."

Tom returned from handing over the two men to the local police. He sat on the arm of the couch beside her.

"Well, they were singing before the officers showed. The man who paid them should be in custody shortly. They'll get a trespassing charge and a slap on the wrist in return for their testimony. If they renege, they'll end up in a fed lockup."

Wyatt kept her in his embrace as he told Tom, "She agreed to the fucking partnership and keeping mostly to the office. She'll be the fucking liaison for you guys."

"I like that idea. She'll be damn good at it."

"Just don't expect me to swear all the time," she seriously intoned with twinkling eyes as her grandfather laughed.

Tom ran his hand through her hair. "No swearing expected unless we piss you off. Like Wyatt, I'll be a bit more comfortable with you doing the boss stuff."

"You say that now, but you may change your mind when you find out I can be a real bitch when I'm not getting results."

Both men laughed, remembering her being at the helm while Wyatt had been sick. She expected results or a good reason as to why not. They also knew she expected the same quality of work she had done.

Wyatt's "Tom, you sharing a room with Jill or taking one of your own?" had her rotating so she could see his face. He chuckled, "Honey, I'm not a fucking prude. I know he's fucking slept with you ever since you were in hiding. I also know you've only awakened once with a fucking nightmare during that time."

She turned back to Tom. "Up to you," she told him.

"Not really," he answered.

The ball was back in her court. "He'll stay with me. At least, I'll sleep instead of spending most of the night awake."

The maid entered the room and announced supper. Tom put his arm around her as they walked to the dining room.

"Glad you decided to keep me with you. Saves me from sleeping on the floor outside your door," he told her.

"I can see it now. Me getting up in the middle of the night and falling over you."

He chuckled. She knew he would have joined her when she awakened screaming. Wyatt was right. She hadn't had but one bad dream since he'd been with her.

They were halfway through their meal when Brad walked in with Shaun and their sister, Belinda. She wore a dress which accented her voluptuous figure. Overall, she was a beautiful woman. The problem was, she was six-foot-tall and not exactly thin, but next to Shaun and Brad, she looked normal. Meanwhile, Jill knew she appeared to be a child when with her family.

"How're you doing, Jill?" Shaun inquired after kissing her cheek.

"Better. I'll be okay for Monday." She turned to her sister. "Belinda, this is Tom, Shaun's brother. Like me, he's the runt of the family."

Belinda gave a merry laugh and shook his hand. "Nice to meet you."

"Same here. Sorry about stealing your sister away from her vacation."

"Not a problem. Daddy was thrilled when he was asked to help. He does a lot of the grunt work for Wyatt." She turned to Jill. "You okay, sis?"

"For now. I have to take it easy for a while."

Tom glared at her. "For six to eight weeks, for sure."

"That's a while. It isn't like it's forever."

Wyatt stopped them by saying, "True but for the next fucking six to eight weeks, you're on fucking paid medical leave, and don't give me a fucking argument."

Brad grinned. "Great. I'll have time to do that formal portrait I've been wanting to do."

She wasn't going to argue with Wyatt. There was no way she was going to do much of anything until after the ablation other than testify. After the trial was over, she was willing to take a vacation, forced or not. It was time for her to put her life totally back together and the downtime would be a good time to do it.

Letting the conversation drift around her, she let the tension, which had been with her while in the hospital, go. Tom tugged on her hair. She smiled at him. There was no way she could imagine being away from him for an extended period of time. He gave her a quick kiss.

"You're looking like you're tired," he said.

"I probably should have taken a nap this afternoon. I'll go and crash early."

He gave her a quick hug.

Brad added, "Sis, take it easy. There's nothing major you need to do until Monday."

"Planning on it. I promised I would take care of myself and I'm going to keep that promise."

Belinda queried, "I take it you had a problem with

your heart?"

"You could say that." Her eyes begged Wyatt not to tell.

It was Tom who spoke, telling Belinda, "Yes. A major one, and she needs to take it easy. She's going to be all right, but it's going to take some time."

"Jillian, you neglected to let Daddy and Momma know," Belinda scolded.

"Please don't tell them. If they were to start arguing in front of me, I'm not sure I could take it right now. Wyatt, Brad, and Tom will make sure I'm taken care of until I'm better."

"Let me know if you need anything. I know I haven't been the best sister around, but I do care about you."

"Thanks. I will. You can stop by after the trial and keep me company, so I'm not bored out of my skull."

Belinda quickly agreed. "Sounds like a plan. I only work three days a week, so I'll plan on spending my days off with you. You'll have to get Brad to come over on the other days."

Brad glanced at Tom. "We'll play it by ear. Just plan on sitting for that portrait during your recovery."

"In Aruba?" she questioned with hope.

Brad grinned, aware of her love of the villa in Aruba. "Depends on if you'll be allowed to travel. Check with Mark and let me know."

Shaun stated, "No fair. Paid time off and a trip to

Aruba. Not fair at all."

Wyatt sat back, watching her. "You all can go if you want. The house is big enough for a crowd. Just make sure the offer won't get you in trouble with your boss."

Shaun grinned. "Wouldn't if I did it on my own time, there were no strings to it, and it was because I wanted to spend some time with a lovely lady I happen to like."

Belinda blushed as the men laughed.

"It's okay, Belinda. They love to see me blush, too. It's a male thing," Jill informed her sister.

When she finished eating, Tom conveyed by his demeanor she needed to go and rest.

"If you all will excuse me, it's been a long day and I'm overly tired. Enjoy the rest of your evening and don't leave on my account."

She left the room with Tom beside her. He helped her to undress and put on her night clothes, so she wasn't moving her arm. When she reentered the bedroom from the bath, he had the bed turned down. She lay down and he covered her up.

"I'll be back in a little while. I need to talk to Shaun and Wyatt."

She made herself comfortable. He gave her a kiss, making her want him to stay and not leave. He left the bedside lamp on low and closed the door. She drifted off to sleep. The tiredness from the busy day and the recent surgery had taken its toll on her.

Her shrill screams an hour later had everyone running into the room. She was sitting up drenched in sweat. Tears were streaming over her face as she looked around in terror, not sure what was real and what wasn't. Tom's arms came around her before she broke into sobs. It had been so real. So very real.

She didn't notice when Wyatt and the rest of them left her and Tom alone. Clinging to him, she attempted to forget what she had seen in her dream. The coppery scent of blood was still with her as the scene replayed again in her mind. The panic from the remembered dream had her crying harder. It was just a dream. It couldn't come true...could it?

"Jill, it was only a nightmare. I'm right here."

Struggling to tamp down the panic, she begged, "Don't leave me. Please."

"I'm not going to leave you." He held her for a few seconds before saying, "Tell me about the dream."

The words tumbled out of her mouth before she could stop them, relating what had made her scream.

"We were coming out of court. There was a man with an assault rifle who started firing at us, killing everyone around me. He left me standing. When he spotted you, he turned into Franko, who laughed as he killed you. He grinned at me as I stood there among the dead bodies. There was blood everywhere.

"Then Franko started laughing at me. He said, 'Welcome to your living hell, my dear,' as they put him on the penitentiary bus. None of the people paid any attention to the dead bodies. They just walked around us as if it was a normal occurrence, ignoring the blood, bodies, and me. Everyone I cared about was there bleeding, mangled, and dead. Wyatt, Brad, Sam, Cletus, you, Billy. . . everyone."

Tom pulled her closer to him. "Jill, it was a nightmare. I know you're afraid of this trial destroying everything you love. He can't do it unless you let him. There's no way your grandfather and brother will walk away from you. I'm certainly not going anywhere. Think about what prompted the dream."

The panic began to recede at his words. He was right. Her fears had caused it.

"I'm scared," she whispered, hanging on to him.

"I'm sure you are. You have a lot going on to deal with at this time, but none of us are going to let you hang out there all alone." He gave her a kiss before saying, "Let me go and reassure your very scared grandfather that you're all right, then I'll be right back. Okay?"

She loosened her grip on his shirt. He gently laid her back on the pillows before leaving. Voices drifted in the open door. He returned, quickly changed, and lay down beside her. She was still shaking from the dream. Needing his protection, she moved as close as she could to him. The fear eased, leaving an extreme tiredness in its wake.

Pushing the nightmare away, into a box to be dealt with later, she remained in the safety of his arms, enabling her to return to sleep.

Chapter 25

HANGING ON BY A THREAD

Friday and Saturday, Jill attempted to get rid of the vestiges left by the nightmare. By Sunday morning, she was slowly drifting into a state of terror, ready to believe the dream was a prophecy of things to come. She hadn't been this frightened since her recovery. There was no real reason for it other than the nightmare remaining with her.

Tom went out for the day with Shaun and Brad, so it was just her and Wyatt. She was sitting on the couch, attempting to read, but her mind kept going back to where she was standing among the dead. Her silence had Wyatt worried and she knew it, but the unreasonable fear wouldn't go away, and she didn't believe he would understand.

"Jillian, talk to me," Wyatt commanded, pulling her from her morbid thoughts.

She sat for a few seconds before getting up and sitting in his lap, needing to be that little girl again where all her fears could be solved by him. His arms around her comforted her, but didn't dispel the last vestiges of the dream.

"The nightmare I had just won't go away. I'm so scared. I can't seem to get rid of it no matter what I do."

"Tell me about it," he gently requested as he held her against him, his deep voice reverberating in his chest.

She repeated what she told Tom, crying over losing everyone she loved. He now knew her deepest fear. It was being left alone with no one who cared about her. He hugged her close and kissed the top of her head. His arms made her feel safe, but the fear was there, lurking inside of her.

"Girl, we aren't going anywhere. I was wondering if confronting your fucking past wouldn't dredge up all those fucking fears. Franko will win if you let him. He can't take you away from us. It's your fucking choice as to whether to stay with us or not."

He paused, hugging her closer to him. "Remember what Quinn told you before he left. Only you can determine where you fucking end up. That means only you can make that fucking dream come true. Not Franko. You will have to fucking decide to stay with us or go back to where you fucking went when we brought you home. The choice is fucking up to you, Jill. We're here, but we can't fucking keep you here if you don't want to stay."

Sitting calmly in his arms, his words brought the realization that this was the crossroads Quinn, her therapist, had talked about. She could choose to go back to a world filled with a living hell of things from the past or she could stay here with them and live her life. Wyatt was right. This was a choice only she could make.

Yes, facing Franko, as he was the one who had hurt her, not Billings, had dredged up all the things she had refused to face. It was him who had made sure she knew that she had no control over her life. It was him who wanted her to return to the hell he had made her live while in captivity. It was him who wanted her dead, so she couldn't tell his secrets.

It was now time to face the past and put it to rest. She couldn't change the past, but she could change the future. It was the future she wanted along with the man who loved her and wanted her with him. There really wasn't a choice. It was live life or return to the crazy hell Quinn had pulled her from.

The overwhelming terror disintegrated as she decided what she was going to do. No more craziness for her. It was time to stop hanging by a thread and mend the rope to sanity.

Once she had her plan finalized, she sat up and smiled at Wyatt. "Thanks, Grandpa. Quinn was right. It's my choice, and I'm not going to let Franko win. I know what I want, and it isn't a padded room. I've had enough of that crap. I'm just not sure what set this all off, unless it was the fear of not living up to everyone's expectations."

"Jillian, you can be such a fucking dunce sometimes," Wyatt scolded as he pulled her back to him. "You just need to live up to your fucking expectations, no one else's. Stop sabotaging yourself. The only fucking expectation any of us have of you is for you to love us and live your life to the fucking fullest."

She played with her hands as she admitted, "Which I haven't been doing because I'm afraid of what others will think of me. Yet, I get up in a crowded courtroom and tell it to the world. Then, I have a meltdown when I can't seem to integrate how I have a man who loves me and doesn't care about what happened to me. On top of all of that, I've refused to grow up, because if I did, I would need to acknowledge the past. It was easy being a teenager and allowing you and Brad to take care of me. So, I guess I need to get out of denial mode and take responsibility for myself and my future."

"We get it, honey. A fucking lot has happened in a short period of time. So, what are you going to do?"

Jill let herself be that little girl for a few more minutes before sighing and telling him her plan.

"First, get through this trial while making sure Franko doesn't win. Get that ablation done and make sure I'm okay physically. Get back to work. Then see where it goes with my very patient Thomas."

She sat up and turned to face Wyatt. "Grandpa, I just hope I can keep it together. I don't want to go back to that crazy time. I understand the dream was part of the craziness. For whatever reason, I just can't seem to get rid of it, no matter how hard I try."

"Honey, you have come a long fucking way from that time. It may hang around, but you're getting past it, and Tom is helping you a lot. I had a long talk with him about what you fucking went through when you came back home. What you fucking need to do is to let loose of those fucking fears, which are keeping you where you are. Until you fucking do that, you're going to keep having those fucking nightmares."

Sighing, she admitted, "I think my decision to grow up had a bit to do with it. I'm afraid of not being that little girl who didn't have a past. If I grow up, I have to accept the past and integrate it into who I am."

Wyatt examined her face before saying, "That analysis would make Quinn proud. I believe you've got it fucking correct. Now, it's up to you to be that fucking adult you want to be. You can still be the little girl, but she fucking needs to be a part of the adult woman who's this fucking fantastic person. Just ask Tom. He'll fucking tell you that in a heartbeat."

She giggled briefly. "He loves me, so of course he'd say that, just like you. I now have to make it true."

Wyatt pulled her back to him and gave her a kiss before setting her on her feet. She kissed his cheek. It was so easy, yet so very hard. She would use the trial to exorcise the past and move on to the future. Like the men who had abused her, she would put the past in jail where it belonged. She had nothing to be ashamed of, now or in the future. What happened in the future was going to be her choice, not someone else's.

A calmness she hadn't experienced before swept through her at the decision she had just made. There was nothing to fear. Quinn and Wyatt were right. She was the one in control. Not Franko.

Going to her room, she opened her closet and chose the outfit she would be wearing tomorrow. It would make a statement, and she knew it. No more fear. No more hiding. It was her life and she was going to live it, and Franko could go to the hell he had made for himself.

She rejoined Wyatt in the library and read until she got sleepy. Putting her book up, she went over and kissed his cheek. "I'm going to go to bed. I don't need to be half asleep in the morning. You need to get some rest too, Grandpa."

"I will. I love you, Jill. See you in the morning."

Chapter 26

A SLIGHTLY USED FAIRY

Jill had fallen asleep soon after going to bed. Tom didn't come in until late. She woke up and sleepily greeted him with a kiss when he joined her. She snuggled close to him and returned to sleep. When she started to dream. It wasn't a nightmare. Instead, it was a dream where she knew the meaning.

This time, she was standing before a cliff with three caves, a donkey with a saddle on it beside her. She got on the donkey and let it choose its way to the cave on the left. When the donkey stopped, she dismounted and went into the cave.

It was dark, so she used the walls of the tunnel to find

her way to a large room. In the room, she turned and was face-to-face with Franko. He waved a hand. The room changed to grays and blacks with scenes of her time in captivity playing like videos on the walls while he laughed at her. She watched some of the horrendous things from her time in captivity. It was in the past and she didn't want to stay here. It would only give her pain and that wasn't what she was looking for, having experienced enough pain caused by him. She trudged back to the donkey, who returned to where they had started.

The donkey stopped, standing for a few seconds before heading to the cave on the right. As before, she dismounted and entered the mouth of the cave, into another dark tunnel. At various points in the tunnel, things from her past were revealed, but for the most part, there was only black with occasional patches of gray.

As in the first cave, she entered a large room. It was empty other than a chair in the center facing a large blank wall. Perching on the chair, she watched as scenes from her childhood were flashed on the wall. The bleak images depicted all the fears and problems she had growing up. As the fears took hold of her, she fought them. If she stayed, she would become lost in those things she had overcome as a child, never finding what she really wanted.

Returning to the donkey, they went back to the starting point. This time, the donkey stood still as she stared at the middle cave, afraid of what it might hold. Gathering her courage, she rode the donkey to the last cave.

She dismounted, took a deep breath, and headed into the opening. It couldn't be any worse than the other two, but it might contain what she was looking for in the other caves.

Upon entering the tunnel, there was a difference. She could see a faint light shining in the distance. As she walked, the light became brighter, drawing her forward. Rounding a bend, she saw what she had been searching for all along.

It was a beautiful place filled with light, color, and all the people she loved. Running into the meadow, she was greeted by everyone she passed, welcoming her into the beautiful place. They danced through the flowers and moved toward the place where the light was brighter, until they came upon a path.

Those around her motioned for her to follow the path. She happily ambled along, picking flowers which she wove into a circlet. Placing the circle of flowers on her head, she pirouetted and the clothes she wore turned into a beautiful violet gauzy gown. Gliding along the lovely path, she admired the colors and beauty, not attending to where she was headed, but confident it would be somewhere wonderful.

A soft, deep, musical voice had her turning to find the speaker as he happily stated, "I'm so glad you decided to join us. I've been waiting for you."

It was Tom and he was happy she was there. Running to him, he took her in his arms and started a joyous dance with her in the light as the others joined them. Wings appeared on her back. She flew around the group but kept returning to the happy man who laughed as she returned to his arms after each flight. This was where she was going to stay.

Tom's kiss had her sleepily returning it. The dream faded into reality. His smile when she opened her eyes told her she had found the beautiful place where she wanted to stay.

"I don't know what happened yesterday while I was gone, but l love the results," he declared as he examined her face.

She honestly told him, "I just needed to decide where I wanted to live. It really was a no-brainer, but I couldn't see it until Wyatt reminded me how it was up to me to make the choice."

She curled into him, face hidden as she continued speaking. "Quinn had told me before he left I would hit a crossroad where I would have to choose the path I wanted to take. I decided to go with life."

Tom examined her with pursed lips before questioning, "And just what brought all this on?"

"The nightmare, which was triggered by my decision to grow up. It brought out all these fears I've kept hidden. I was letting those fears control me. The result was a tenacious grip on my sanity.

"I had chosen the dark hell I went into when I was rescued, until Quinn showed me how to get out of it. But he told me, I still hadn't really made the choice to live my life. He said I would hit a crisis point where only I could choose the path I wanted to travel. I hit that crisis point, and I almost let the fear push me into a place where my past would control my future."

Tom kissed her again. "Welcome to life, Jill. I was so afraid when I came back last night that I would have lost you. Wyatt told me you were hanging on by a thread and to let him see if he could reach you. If he hadn't succeeded, Quinn was on speed dial and ready to come back. Your grandfather is willing to do anything for his little fairy."

Jill lowered her eyelids, plucking at the T-shirt he had worn to bed. "I know. He knew I was still in teenage mode, afraid to face life as an adult. My struggle with all the crap was easy for him to see. By simply jogging my memory as to what Quinn had told me, it reminded me it was my choice. I could remain a little girl and never grow up, go back to the insanity, or grow up and have a life. Like I said, it really was a no-brainer, but I couldn't see it. I was letting the past pull me back into the darkness, the fear and panic."

She faced him. "I knew I would lose you if I chose any other path. I want my prince who loves me enough to let me fly, then welcomes me back when I return with laughter and love."

"Well, the happy prince needs to let the lovely fairy know she needs to get up, and get ready to put the nasty evil men in their rightful places."

Jill giggled before giving him a quick kiss. She told him as she left the bed, "I'm going to need your help in the shower. I need to wash my hair and can't raise my arm to that level."

His eyes rounded as he stared at her. "Uh, Jill, you sure you want to go there?"

Pivoting to face him, she shook her head, "Tom, it's you or my grandfather. Now, who do you think I would prefer? Besides, you seem to plan on sticking around, so what difference does it make if you see me naked and in the shower?"

Tom stared at her before he took a deep breath and let it out. "I'm not immune to you, Jill."

She laid out the clothes she planned on wearing before turning back to him. "I know you aren't, just like I'm not immune to you. As much as I'd like to keep things chaste, I need help. If you have another solution, let me know, but for now, I don't have one."

He left the bed and followed her to the bath as she turned on the shower and started to undress. Helping her with her top, she let him deal with what he was finally seeing. She stepped into the shower and let the water run over her as he undressed and joined her.

It was evident he wasn't immune to her when he

entered the shower. She remained still, ignoring his erection as he stood close to her while he made sure her hair was wet. His gentle hands applied the shampoo and worked it through her hair. When he turned her to rinse the soap from her hair, she closed her eyes. His gentle hands moving over her head sent spikes of need shooting through her. No, she wasn't immune to him.

Moving her from the running water, he applied the conditioner and worked it through the curly strands. His kiss had her arms going around him. Reaching around her, he added soap to the sponge and started to wash her. His eyes followed his hands as he lovingly soaped her body.

When done, he moved her back under the spray, rinsing the soap from her skin, while his hands ran through her hair, removing the excess conditioner. When done, he took her in his arms, his swollen member against her stomach. The kiss they shared informed her of what he needed. Her hand cupped his scrotum as he closed his eyes, sucking in air as she massaged him.

She knew he wanted to wait, but he needed a release like she did. His kisses were passionate as they gave each other the relief they needed without progressing to intercourse. She faced him after their needs were sated.

"Like you, I'm not immune to you, but I also want to wait." Her eyes examined his face, hoping she hadn't made a mistake.

"Glad you understand, but I wasn't expecting this to

happen," Tom stated, a crooked grin on his face.

She gave him a quick kiss. "I refuse to leave you frustrated because of me. It works and will make things less tense for now."

Tom's passionate kiss stirred a need within her he had just satisfied. When he raised his head, he moved away.

"Give me a minute to wash," he stated, exchanging places with her, indicating he wasn't going to allow things to progress.

She exited the shower with him joining her before she had finished drying the areas she could reach. He wrapped a towel around her hair then dried her back before handing her back her towel. She finished drying herself while he toweled off the water from his shower.

Her eyes ran over him in admiration. He was lean with muscles which bunched as he moved. There were several scars on his torso and left shoulder. She loved the look of the light hair on his chest, arms, and legs. Turning from him, she could imagine touching him in ways she hadn't considered touching a man before now.

She left him shaving, and started to dress. He donned underwear and slacks before assisting her with her bra, then to slip into the dress she had chosen. Returning to the bath, she applied the minimal makeup she wore for court. Other than combing her hair, she was ready. Pulling the towel from her head and hanging it up, she picked up her brush and returned to the bedroom.

Tom was dressed in a suit and tie, turning him into a business man. He took the brush from her and had her sit at the vanity. She watched in the mirror as he ran the brush through her hair until all the tangles were gone. After putting the brush down, he fluffed her hair so soft curls would form. Her eyes met his in the mirror. Turning to him, she pulled him down for a kiss.

He ran a finger over her cheek. "I see how life with you will be full of surprises. I can hardly wait for this trial to end."

Grinning, she told him, "You've only scratched the surface. Just wait until I get it all together."

His laughter showed he had gotten her meaning. This was only the start for her, and he had just had a taste of where she was headed. Yes, he was in for the ride of a lifetime, and she was going to make sure they both enjoyed it.

Wyatt was just sitting down when they entered the dining room to join him for breakfast. Jill noticed his eyes following her as she came toward him. Giving him the kiss he was expecting, she ignored his scrutiny. His quick glance to Tom wasn't missed as she sat beside him, while Tom took the chair across from her.

Wyatt glanced at Tom again before observing, "You seem to be in a good mood this morning."

Meeting his gaze, she told him, "I am. Our little talk last night made a difference. I made my choice. I'm going to join the adult world and enjoy every minute of it."

When his eyes narrowed, she glared at him. "Get your mind out of the gutter. We're waiting to go there. What you see is the result of my decision. I know I'll have a few hiccups along the way, but I'll get there. My reward will be the wonderful man who loves me, and a family who'll enjoy not having to support me at every little turn. We all get to have our lives back."

A voice she knew quite well intoned, "Welcome to the real world, Jillian." The grinning middle-aged man, who could pass for a corporate CEO, walked over and kissed her cheek. "Wyatt called me a couple of days ago, not sure if I would be needed. I couldn't get here until today."

"Quinn! You're the last person I expected to see this morning," she exclaimed happily as he took the chair beside her. Quinn had been her therapist and had pulled her back when she had withdrawn into her little world, taking all the garbage from her time in captivity with her.

"Well, Wyatt told me you were in trouble and wanted me close by, just in case you had that meltdown you seemed to be headed for at the time he called. I see you managed to get it under control."

Lowering her gaze to the table, she told him, "Yes. You were right. Only I could choose my path, and it was up to me where I wanted to be." Glancing at Tom, then facing Quinn as he sat beside her, she added, "I didn't want to be that little girl any longer, and the other path wasn't one where I wanted to be, so I took the option to grow up and live my life. Wyatt just reminded me that it was up to me where I'd end up."

Quinn's smile was bright. "Glad to hear that. I really didn't want to pull you back again. That very intelligent girl made me work extremely hard to get past her defenses. My guess is this trial, the scare of your near miss with that heart condition, and the man who is watching me like a hawk, had a lot to do with this decision."

Laughing, she hugged him. "Yes. Everything was crashing in on me and caused a minor meltdown after a very realistic nightmare wouldn't turn me loose. Tom and Wyatt both told me it was up to me whether that nightmare became a reality, or remained a dream."

With a glance at Tom, Quinn stated, "I take it you didn't want to live in that nightmare."

"No, but I now know I was letting my fears push me there. Your words, which Wyatt reminded me of, made me see it was showing me only one path. I had a choice to live the nightmare or make it just a passing thing." She paused before relating her last dream and her choice as to which cave she wanted to live in for the rest of her life."

When she finished, Quinn chuckled, "Well, it looks like you've graduated to life after all. I was worried you wouldn't see the crossroads and let the past rule your life." He grinned in Wyatt's direction. "You can take me off speed dial. She's going to make it." He then turned to Tom.

"I know you know my name. I'm her therapist and took care of her for six months. She made it back to the teenage stage, but I couldn't get her past that. You're going to be one lucky man."

Tom grinned at him. "I'm very aware of that. Like Wyatt, I was worried she would slip away from me. You did a great job of preparing her for adulthood."

Quinn turned back to her. "She did all the work. I just gave her some guidance. Through it all, she would let that lovely lady peek out, then she would go into hiding again, afraid of what would happen if she moved into adulthood. I take it you discovered all that fear was of your own making, and not real."

"Some of it was real and I'll have to deal with it, but yes, most of it was of my own making based on what happened. I can't let Franko control my life with what he did."

Sobering, Quinn stated, "Jill, you'll need to let them know what he did to totally get rid of it. Once it's in the open, it'll turn you lose."

"It'll become public within the next couple of days. I'll wait until then. I don't want to repeat it but once more." She lowered her head, unable to stop the spike of fear from hitting her. It was the one thing which might make Tom leave her.

Quinn gently lifted her head with his fingers so she was facing him. "Are you sure that's the way you want them to learn about it?"

"It's the only way I can tell it. I can't hide the details under oath. I know I would try to hide a lot of it otherwise."

Without looking away from her, Quinn imparted, "She has one thing she hasn't revealed. You two need to listen to every word of what she will confess. Once she has revealed what she has kept secret, you'll understand why she was so afraid of facing life. Your reaction when she's done will determine if that nightmare comes true or not."

His next words were for her. "I'll be there. If you need help, let me know. Malcolm and Shaun will use me if needed."

Tears ran down her face as she listened to him. She wiped them away and let it go, not commenting on what he had said. There was no way she could repeat it twice. It had been hard enough when she had told Quinn, then Brad when she had developed some problems and needed his assistance.

Her hope was that it would be today. It was the one thing that could destroy her, and had been the reason for her going back to that little girl. She was aware of what would happen if they rejected her after learning the rest of what she had endured before they had rescued her. Quinn would be there if that happened.

Tom watched her as she ate and talked to Quinn and Wyatt. He remained quiet. Jill was aware Quinn was assessing him and his attachment to her. She tamped down the emotions swirling around inside her, remaining calm on the surface, not wanting to face those emotions until after her testimony. Until then, she would do what she must and let the fallout go where it would.

When they went to go to the parking garage, she moved next to Tom. His arm came around her as he gave her a quick kiss. She peered up at him, confident he would understand what she still had to reveal. It would show how used she was and explain the severity of the damage done to her.

Yes, it had been easier to be the little girl who had no knowledge of the depravity of men. She wanted to put it in the past, but until they knew the rest of her story, she couldn't. Hopefully, today would put the past to rest. If not, she would need Quinn to help put all the little pieces back together again. Only, there would be a big hole if Tom left her. One which would never go away.

There were federal agents in the condo garage waiting for them. Tom scanned them before walking her to the armored SUV. He took a seat next to her while Quinn and Wyatt squeezed into the seat facing them with Fred taking the front passenger seat. Sam was the designated driver simply because he was the best. Like her, he had taken the stunt driving course and could handle the various vehicles as well as she could.

Again, they entered the courthouse through the prisoner entrance. They were met by the agents who were to take her to the courtroom. She turned in Tom's embrace and took the kiss she wanted before joining the guards. They held her at the door until the other doors were closed and Llewellyn was on the bench. She was escorted to the witness box, then reminded that she was still under oath.

Shaun was asking the questions today. Her eyes went to Franko. He was sitting back and leering at her. He was going to prison, but what he didn't know yet was how he would never be free again. He was going to pay for more than just her.

Shaun recapped where they were in her testimony. He verified several pieces of information before he started on the track taking them to what she had kept hidden. She didn't cry this time as he reviewed her past testimony. He acquired more information needed for the record. He then asked the question she had been waiting for since the start of the trial.

"Jill, did you ever witness any of the defendants commit murder?"

"Yes," she answered, looking directly at Franko. He sat forward. There was fear on his face, his eyes wide with disbelief.

"Would you please tell the court what you observed?"

"Mr. Franko was doing a sex movie, and I was forced to participate. I was raped by Leroy and Rico while tied to a pole as they filmed what was happening. He brought in Rita and tied her to the pole beside me. The two men did to Rita what they had done to me. They kept filming what they were doing, but stayed away from our faces so we couldn't be identified.

"Mr. Franko came to me and laughed as he raped me. He was extremely rough and hurt me, but I didn't cry or scream like Rita. He then used this hard thing. He pushed it into me until I started to scream in pain. Not stopping, he kept pushing harder until I felt something pop inside of me and I began to bleed. When he noticed the blood, he stopped and removed it. He said, 'Me bad,' then laughed, enjoying how he had finally hurt me enough to have me scream."

She stopped and took a deep breath, steeling herself for what was yet to come. She glanced at Shaun, then Franko before continuing.

"Franko put on a mask and went to Rita. He did things I'd never imagined anyone doing to another person while she screamed in pain. Paul told me to watch closely because it was going to be my fate. Mr. Franko kept doing all these things to her as she cried or screamed. He then started to have anal sex with her. As he was climaxing, he strangled her until she stopped breathing as they continued to film everything."

Jill didn't know when the tears had started, but she couldn't stop now. There was more.

"They brought in another girl. Wendy was about my age. Mr. Franko told me she was my substitute for this film. He took her to the bed and tied her hands above her head. Rico, Leroy, and Paul forced her to do all these things with them. It seemed to go on forever before Mr. Franko started to have sex with her.

"He was rough, but she gave the appearance of enjoying what he was doing until he put his hands around her throat. He again climaxed as she died. They were all laughing as Rico, Leroy, and Paul masturbated and ejaculated on her dead body. Marvin had remained with me to ensure I watched what they were doing. No one seemed to care that I was still bleeding.

"They finally untied me and dragged me to this other room. Dr. Torres was there. He examined me and told them they had done some damage, but I would heal. He put some stuff inside of me and left me there covered in blood, in pain, and naked. Roselyn came in and threw water on me and mopped up the blood but left me in the wet bed with nothing to use to cover myself.

"I don't know how long I was there, but Dr. Torres came back. He removed the stuff from inside of me, and put more in because I was still bleeding. I was left alone again. It was long enough that I was hungry and thirsty. They hadn't fed me or given me water for a long time. When Dr. Torres returned, he left the stuff out, but told Roselyn I needed to be left alone for at least four weeks, but I could still dance."

Jill stopped. The tears continued to run down her face, but she wasn't going to fall apart. Franko stared at her, his mouth open, working as if he wanted to say something. He had thought she wouldn't ever tell what he had done.

Before Shaun could ask another question, she started talking again. "He threatened to kill me if I ever told anyone about what he had done. You see, he wasn't supposed to harm me on orders from Russia. I was supposed to be sent there undamaged. He had damaged me and knew it, so he now had to plan my death. It was to be two days after I was rescued, during another film.

"What he had done was his way of making sure I knew my fate. He showed me exactly what he was going to do to me and how I would die. He even told me that if I did anything wrong before then, he would have me whipped so I would feel every thrust he gave me. It was so I would be reminded of denying him what he wanted from me." She paused before saying, "I got the whipping, but for a different reason."

Stopping again, she finally lowered her gaze to her hands and softly said, "He destroyed me and made it so the likelihood of my ever having a child is almost nil, and he enjoyed doing it."

Shaun handed her a tissue. She lifted her eyes to his. He was crying. He hadn't known what he was asking her to reveal. Giving him a tight wry grin, she told him, "It's all right. I can accept what he did now, because I know he won't ever be able to hurt me or anyone else again."

There was dead silence in the courtroom until Malcolm stated, "We would like to amend the charges on Josef Franko to premeditated murder and felonious assault with permanent bodily harm. On Marvin Peterson, Rico Gomez, Leroy Tibbet, and Paul Connelly, we request additional charges of felony murder one, rape with bodily harm, and desecration of a body."

Jared stated, "So noted."

Jill's gaze went to the defense table when there had been no objection to her last statement. Franko was talking to his lawyer, who had pulled away from him. The lawyer shook his head no to whatever Franko had been wanting him to do.

The questioning moved on to other areas they needed to explore. Shaun hadn't lied. He was a bulldog, and didn't quit until he had all the information she had to give them. By the end of the day, her testimony was close to being completed. It would be the defense's turn tomorrow after Shaun mopped up some details. She wasn't worried, because she knew they couldn't shake what she had told them. The truth would win this time.

When she was taken from the courtroom, Malcolm put his arm around her. "You'll be staying with me until the defense lets you go."

She leaned into the kind man, eyes downcast. "Not a

problem. Mr. Franko didn't think I would ever tell what he had done. He knew about my falling apart. After my testimony last week, he was expecting that woman to show up today, not the one who did."

Malcolm's arm held her close to him. When she glanced up at him, his eyes held admiration. "I don't know what you did over the weekend, but this beautiful woman showed up in court. She wowed everyone with a very clear and concise testimony. What you said to Shaun was heard by the jury and the court reporter. It went on the record with no objection from the defense, which surprised me. I'm positive that one sentence sealed his fate with the jury."

She sighed then shrugged, "I grew up and decided I wanted to live my life and not go back to that crazy place where I was before. I couldn't remain that little girl I'd been for the past seven years. Regardless of what happens now, I know I'll make it." If she kept repeating it enough, she knew it would become her reality. She wanted to be that adult who would have a future with her green-eyed prince.

Tom joined them. He took her from Malcolm and gave her a quick kiss. He wasn't going to run away as she had feared he would.

When they entered Malcolm's rooms, Tom enveloped her in his arms, his head on hers before stating, "I hope to God he becomes someone's bitch in prison, and gets to have the same treatment he gave you."

"Him staying there until he dies is enough for me. The rest would just be the icing on the cake, so to speak," she informed him.

Quinn showed up shortly after they arrived at Malcolm's rooms. She was curled beside Tom on the sofa. He came over and kissed her cheek when she met his gaze. He sat on the arm of the couch where she was sitting, studying her as if he had never seen her before.

"That very strong adult lady showed up in court. The jury was in the palm of your hand, and the defense knows it. Those men and all associated with them will find that they'll be convicted." He glanced at Tom and then told her, "Jill, you need to talk to Bobkin and resolve that one issue. If you don't, it will eat at you and you won't have the total closure you want. Do it before the sentencing, and put in your two cents before he's sentenced."

Studying her hands, she stated, "I was planning on it. They need to have Brad testify. His testimony will show how he tried to help me. If it wasn't for him, I wouldn't have made it out of there. He didn't know what Franko had planned for me, but he was afraid for me after Franko told him I wouldn't ever see Russia."

Tom asked, "Now, how do you know all that?"

"Your man on the inside told me when he let me know Brad was going to get me out. You see, Bobkin was in love with me."

Tom hesitated before saying, "I know. He told me. I was the one who questioned him. He gave us a lot of information. It seems that he wanted to get out, but couldn't and remain alive.

"He explained how he had fallen in love with this young girl named Jill, and how he wanted to take her away from what was going to happen to her. Franko stopped him, but he made sure she was treated as good as possible. When he was watching her dance one night, he noticed her react to a big man at the back of the club.

"He connected Brad to you and sent our man, the only one he trusted, with a note telling Brad how to get you out, and it needed to be as soon as possible or you would disappear. He hoped Brad wasn't someone who would turn him in to Franko, so he could save you. He made it possible for them to get you out by keeping Rosalyn and the others busy when our man told him the day and time."

She thought about what Tom had just said. It appeared she really needed to talk to him. Maybe she could help him like he had helped her. If he had been truthful about getting out, he could have a life. She would have to see once the trial was done. Malcolm would help her.

"I'll have that talk with him. Depending on what he tells me and whether I believe him will determine what I do."

Quinn patted her shoulder. "You'll be open and give him a fair evaluation." He turned to Tom, "So, what are your plans for our little imp?"

She rotated so she could see his face. He grinned and tapped her nose.

"Well, I'm not quite sure. Seems there's this plan of dancing with a fairy in the moonlight in some exotic place, but I guess we'll have to do a bit of talking as to future plans. Been sort of waiting until things were somewhat less stressful to go there. She knows I'm not going anywhere without her, so that sort of tells you my plans."

"Jill?" Quinn questioned.

"He's not going anywhere without me, so I guess that tells you the plan. I'm comfortable with waiting for a less stressful time. So that you know, I'm moving to the office as a partner at the agency. I'll be a boss, not out chasing the bad guys, except occasionally here and there. Not sure if it's a promotion or demotion, but Wyatt won't let me be out in the field all the time now."

Quinn chuckled before telling her, "Sounds like he's finally letting you do what he's trained you to do. You really shouldn't scare the hell out of him like you have recently. I wasn't sure who I was going have to treat when I got here, you or him."

Jill scrunched up her face before admitting, "I guess I've given him more than a few gray hairs over the past few years."

"You know, if I didn't know better, I'd swear he was your father with the way he loves you and has cared for you," Quinn observed.

She studied her hands as she told him, "He's my father in actions only. He took me from my parents when I was a baby. Every time he tried to let them have me back, I couldn't take what was going on in the house.

"I would cry all the time, and my parents couldn't seem to keep me healthy. I wouldn't eat because I was so upset with the constant noise and confusion. Wyatt finally told them he was taking me and keeping me and they would have to deal with it. Brad refused to let him take me without him going too, so Wyatt raised me as his child with Brad to help."

"Why did the noise and confusion upset you?" Quinn questioned, his eyes boring into hers, brows drawn together. He hadn't ever asked her why she was with Wyatt and not her family, so this was all new information for him and Tom.

"It hurt when there was too much noise. I can remember the chest pain and the severe headaches. I was so small I couldn't tell them what was happening. I could feel the tension and it would create all this turmoil inside of me and then the pain.

"I've learned how to deal with the things I feel from others, but severe tension still puts my heart into these rhythms which create pain, and the noise makes my ears and head hurt. When there's so much coming into me, I can't handle it."

He asked a question, which he hadn't ever asked her before, based on what she had just told him. "How did you manage to deal with what was happening to you in captivity?"

"I would go to Aruba and they couldn't reach me there. It was my escape. I would close my eyes and imagine the villa with the flowers and the sunlight. It kept me sane."

Quinn lifted her head so she was facing him. "Jill, do loud noises, confusion, and tension from other people still cause the headaches and pain?"

"Sometimes, if I can't get away. It's the reason I was at the lake when I found Knight. My parents were arguing, and I couldn't take the tension and noise."

"If you couldn't get away, what would you do?"

"Withdraw into this little world where I can't hear or feel them."

He stared at her and shook his head. "Today, you would have been diagnosed with autism. Those are very classic signs. Add to that your remarkable memory and it all fits. It's no wonder I had trouble reaching you. You did the normal autistic thing. You blocked everything from the outside getting to you, going to that living hell inside of you. It explains a lot of what I didn't understand at the time.

"Wyatt didn't share why you were with him rather than your parents, other than them not being able to get you to eat or to stop crying. If I'm not mistaken, Brad kept you from withdrawing, like most autistic children do, so no one ever knew what was going on inside of you."

Jill looked away from him. Her fingers twisted in her lap as she stared at the carpet, tamping down the fear of what the others were thinking about her.

"I figured it out when I was ten," she admitted. "I did a report on autism. I fit the profile, but I didn't want to be classified as different, so I worked on fitting in and making sure no one knew."

She couldn't look at the others in the room. Her last secret was out there now. She was a freak with a diagnosis. Yes, Brad had kept her from withdrawing. It was the reason they were so close. She had told him what she had discovered. He had agreed to help her hide it by learning to react as normally as possible in those situations where she would have withdrawn into her own little world.

Tom's voice had her turning to him. "Jill, if you've handled it all these years, I don't see why things should change. Brad will be close if you need him, and I'll help. No one other than those of us in this room need ever know."

"Thanks. I've been afraid someone other than Brad would find out. and essentially lock me into this label, then treat me like a freak."

Quinn laughed, "Jill, you are a freak. A unique one who has all these abilities no one else does. One who fits into society, so they can't even come close to guessing what is under that cute innocent exterior. I knew there was something I was missing, and you just gave it to me. It goes to show that there are ways of treating the problem where the person turns out normal. Before you say it, you were very normal prior to being kidnapped other than that memory, which you hid quite well until you were on the stand and testifying. I don't think Wyatt even guessed some of the things you could do until this trial."

She grinned at him. "I guess that paper you're going to do on me will topple some beliefs about people like me."

He chuckled merrily, "I'm going to have to go back and do some major revisions. I'll have to do some follow-up from here, but yes, it will topple some long-held beliefs about autism. We'll need to have some talks because I'll need more information on your early childhood from you, Wyatt, Brad, and your parents. I'll also be following how you progress from this point. Somehow, I believe it'll end up being a book about this really remarkable girl who overcomes a lot of things, to end up with a wonderfully full life."

Malcolm stated, "Quinn, I'd love to read it when you're done. It would give me a lot of insight as to how she got to where she is now. This little session has explained a lot about our girl."

"Tom, don't take her to Vegas. She'll win at cards as she'll remember all the cards and make bets accordingly," Shaun warned with a chuckle.

She stuck her tongue out at him, making the others

laugh.

"Jill, is that true?" Tom questioned with a grin.

"Of course, it is. I've been there and I'm very careful not to get into trouble. I usually do well at blackjack and any type of poker. I can also figure the odds for roulette and generally win on it. You really don't want me playing any type of card game though."

"Can we say savant?" Quinn stated.

"Well, there goes my plan. I can't get into trouble in a casino," Tom told her with twinkling eyes.

"You wouldn't. Like I said, I know what not to do. I read people pretty good along with the cards. I've been known to fold a winning hand just so I don't get targeted. I'll walk away a winner though, as I hate losing money. Just not a big winner. Before you ask, no, I wouldn't help you. You'd have to win on your own."

They all laughed. They were aware she was too honest to cheat. She wasn't going to tell them she spent most of her time on the slots and only resorted to the card tables when she was low on cash.

Their supper arrived, and she ate and talked while leaning against Tom. Once she had finished eating, her eyes drifted shut as the men continued to talk, comfortable with Tom holding her.

Quinn woke her. "Jill, we're leaving. I'll be hanging around for a few days. I want to be here for the rest of the cross-examination. I'll see you tomorrow."

"Quinn, thanks. You've been great. At least I know I didn't have it wrong."

"No, you didn't, but it doesn't change one thing other than how you deal with some issues. I believe your man has gotten a better understanding of what makes you tick."

"Probably, though he had a pretty good handle on me before this."

"I know. Night," he told her as he gave her a kiss on her forehead before he and Shaun left.

"Time for bed," Malcolm stated. "I'll see you two in the morning." He left the room, leaving them to prepare for sleep.

Chapter 27

A TRUTH REVEALED

Shaun finished the rest of his questions for her by noon, having pulled out a few more pieces of information on some of the minor characters. He also verified some of the events which took place after the arrest of Franko. It would be the defense's turn starting in the afternoon.

This was the part of a trial she enjoyed. It was fun to see what tactics they would use to try and negate her testimony. The defense attorneys learned to hate her when she quoted what was said word for word from her previous testimony.

She had noticed Franko talking to the lead attorney, so she could just imagine what they were planning. It would be a personal attack this time, and she knew it. They would attempt to make her into a psychotic person who imagined everything happened to her, instead of a victim who actually endured his abuses.

The afternoon was spent with the attorney attempting to prove she was a liar. When that didn't work, she was targeting Franko because she had a vendetta against him. No matter what route he took, she kept to the facts. Every track he took, she negated by repeating what she had testified to before, relying on the proven facts of the case.

The defense lawyer did his best to upset her with having her repeat various things he knew were painful for her. The problem with that line of questioning, was how she added the extra details she had left out in the first telling, but were supported by testimony she hadn't heard. It didn't help his case at all.

He next attempted to negate Franko's involvement with

her. She had to stifle a grin when he stated, "You actually never saw Mr. Franko undressed, did you?"

Okay, he was going to try to make her out to be a liar. Keeping her eyes locked with Franko, she calmly imparted, "Yes, I did. He has a mole on his right side, which is approximately two inches tall by one-inch wide. He has a scar on his right lower abdomen, which is right around four inches long, a circular hole on the front and back of his left shoulder. Would you like me to go on or is that enough? You might want to have him show the jury the shoulder scars or the mole to verify I'm not making things up."

The glare Franko sent in her direction, told her and the jury he would do no such thing. His attitude was turning the jury against him and his lawyer, but he didn't see what he was doing. He was so intent on discrediting her that he didn't care what the jury thought. That was a major mistake on his part.

The defense lawyer spent the rest of the afternoon attempting to locate a hole in her testimony. She wondered how intelligent the man was with the almost childish efforts to discredit her. It wasn't until late in the afternoon she realized it was Franko controlling his lawyer's questioning tactics. The attorney knew she had caught on when her eyes went from Franko to him before quirking an eyebrow.

Franko should have let him do his job. She had been cross-examined by him before, and this was quite lame compared to his performance during that trial. Then again, he was probably playing along with Franko, letting him dig his own hole into prison after what she had revealed concerning what he had done to her, and the other two women, during what she now knew was a snuff film. She had seen how he had pulled back from Franko after she had detailed the abuse and cold-blooded murders he had committed.

Jared finally stopped him, and recessed the court until the next morning. She could feel his frustration at the wasted time, but he would allow the man to finish his questioning without interruption, letting him seal his clients' fates. Malcolm waited until they were in his rooms before talking, shaking his head in disgust.

"I don't know what in the hell is going on, but I know Lowenstein, and that wasn't his normal tactics. He's so much better than that."

Jill stopped him when she stated in a matter-of-fact tone, "Franko is telling him what to do. He's letting Franko put himself in prison. If you would have noticed, all his questions pretty much dealt with Franko's dealings with me."

Malcolm pivoted to see her watching him. His slow smile showed he now understood what was happening.

"Malcolm, he'll try to discredit me over my meltdown when I was rescued. He can't, but he'll try. Franko really should have let him do his job. Lowenstein is quite good when left alone."

"I've been worried about them using that period to discredit you."

She let out a sigh, hoping she was correct in what she was about to say. "It won't work. Those months are totally devoid of what happened before or after. It was all about me and my inability to integrate what had happened to me during those three years into my life. Don't stop him unless he doesn't let me answer the questions. Raise an objection to how he is asking questions and not allowing me to answer if I can't do it. Normally, I'm able to get the lawyers to allow me to give a complete answer."

It was the last of their discussion of the trial due to Quinn and Tom joining them. There was no question in her mind from the way the two men interacted, they had talked over lunch. When Tom hadn't joined her at the break, she figured it was at the request of Quinn. Tom's merry eyes confirmed her educated guess. The two of them acted like old friends. It wasn't until Tom was called out of the room that Quinn confirmed her deductions.

"Jill, fate has been quite kind in putting you and Tom together. He is one smart man and showed he has good insight into your recent issues and how to handle the autism and your unique abilities. For a man with a thousand personalities, he has remained totally himself with you, quickly understanding you would see through any shift in character and call him out."

She chuckled before saying, "I caught on he wasn't just another police officer within the first hour or so of talking to him. We understand each other quite well on several levels."

"My best advice is to hang on to him for all it's worth. You won't find another like him."

She patted the hand he had placed on her shoulder. "Advice not needed. I have no intention of letting him get away. It's the reason I decided to grow up. I want to keep him, and that little girl didn't have a prayer in the world of doing so."

"There is something I'm going to request from you. When you're able, I'd like you to write down what was going through your mind during those months you were out of contact with the world. Include the feelings, thoughts, your reasons, etc. Make it complete. It's time for you to understand what happened so you can prevent it from occurring again."

She glanced up as Tom reentered the room, but answered Quinn's request. "I started it already. I had to understand what was going on inside me, and why I took all the crap with me. I stopped as there was a whole area I couldn't face, but I'll be able to complete it once this trial is finished.

"It was sort of a self-therapy thing I started during the last case when I knew I would have to confront Billings. I was avoiding thinking about Franko, my main tormenter.

I've faced him, and he's no longer the threat he was, so I can finish the evaluation of that time."

There was no way she could miss his gaze going to Tom. They all now understood it was Franko who had targeted her, not Billings. Bobkin had only added to her confusion and fear.

Chapter 28

QUESTIONING HER SANITY

The next morning, the defense went to where she expected them to go when she had mentioned her break with reality after being rescued. He started questioning her about that six-month interval.

"Jill, you have mentioned a period of six months where you weren't able to function normally. Kindly explain what occurred during that period."

"I had a meltdown or if you would prefer an interval of shutting down my mind into what you would call insanity. It was a withdrawal from things I couldn't handle at the time."

"So, we're to believe someone who is classified as insane," he immediately commented, missing how she had said it.

"It was temporary and had nothing to do with what happened before or after that period of time. It was a withdrawal from the internal pain I was experiencing."

"Really? According to all the records I've reviewed, once you have a period of insanity, you're likely to have more episodes in the future."

She quoted the studies he had used then stated, "Those arguments are only valid with the types of psychiatric disorders mentioned. I have none of those disorders, so those conclusions aren't valid in my case."

"Yet you freely admit to a period of insanity."

"No, I didn't. I stated it was what *you* would *call* insanity." She stressed the "you" and "call" so he and the jury would understand what she was saying. "As I stated earlier, what actually happened was I withdrew from the world around me."

Her statement caught him off-guard. His puzzled face made her calmly wait for him to integrate what she had revealed.

"You withdrew from the world? That doesn't sound

quite normal."

"Sir, if you went through what I had experienced, you wouldn't react normally to being thrust back into your previous life without having some sort of reaction. Withdrawal is my normal way of handling things when my system is overloaded. For short periods of time, I withdraw from the world to protect me. Only this time, I took the garbage from the three years with me, instead of going to a safe place."

His next question was no surprise. He had picked up on how the withdrawal was a normal reaction for her.

"So, this wasn't the first time for you to withdraw from the world leaving gaps in your memory?"

"No, it wasn't. But. . ."

"Jill, with all those gaps in your memory, how can we believe what you tell us?"

She was ready for his question with the explanation of what he called gaps in her memory. "Because those gaps are only for those specific periods of time. They have nothing to do with anything that happens outside of them."

Lowenstein's gaze was direct as he attempted to get the jury to doubt her testimony. "How can we be sure of that?"

She was aware it was a fine line she was walking. She had to tell the truth or Franko would walk, and she wouldn't be able to testify again and be believed. This was the make-or-break point for this trial and her future.

"Those gaps protect me from situations I'm unable to

handle in any other way. Outside of those periods, I'm able to remember everything happening to me. They have no bearing on anything other than that specific situation and time."

"When did you start creating these periods of withdrawal or gaps in your memory?"

She turned to Quinn as fear coursed through her, hoping for some idea of what to say. He didn't give her any indication of what to do, so she answered with the truth.

"As a child."

The attorney stopped, pivoted, and stared at her, mouth slightly open before asking, "So, you've had periods of insanity since you were a child?"

"You're using the wrong term. They are not periods of insanity. They are periods of withdrawal from a world, which is overloading my system. If you remember, I stated you would call it insanity, because most normal people, including many psychiatrists, don't understand the withdrawal or what causes it."

"Now, why would you need to escape from the world?"

"I told you. An overload to my system in certain situations."

"So, you're prone to things overwhelming you, so you withdraw, creating gaps in your memory."

"Only in certain situations and for those specific periods of time."

He stood for a few seconds, trying to figure out how to

use this information to discredit her.

"Your Honor, the defense would like to defer further cross-examination of this witness. We would like to ask an expert witness to explain these gaps in the witness's memory."

Shaun stood and stated, "The prosecution has no objection as long as we're permitted to produce our own expert concerning this issue."

"The defense has no objection," Lowenstein stated, believing he had found a way to discredit all her testimony.

She was excused. Malcolm had her sit with him at the prosecution table. It looked like Quinn would be taking the stand after all. So much for keeping her autism out of the public arena.

The defense witness was a doctor she knew quite well. He had seen her before, but had missed the real diagnosis. He gave a good case for her being mentally unstable. When Shaun took his turn in cross-examination, he tore the doctor's testimony to shreds before lunch. She recognized there was still doubt as to her sanity hanging out there. It needed to be dispelled or her career was over.

Quinn joined them for lunch. He talked to Shaun, explaining how to get the relevant information into the record, and protect her confidentiality. She listened as they went over his proposed testimony.

"Quinn," she intoned, when there was a lull in the planning, to get his attention.

"Yes?"

She was aware he was trying to protect her in the way they were planning his testimony. "If you need to give the diagnosis, do so. I'm sure Shaun will allow you to explain how I'm different from the normal autistic person."

"I'm not going to do that if possible. I believe I can get the point across by explaining the overload theory by relating it to what normal people do when in difficult situations."

He had her permission to use all the information at his disposal, but she understood he wouldn't unless forced into a corner. There was no way he wanted to put her career in jeopardy. His hug showed he was still protective of her.

The afternoon started off with Shaun calling Dr. Quinn Richards to the stand. She wanted to shut down but didn't. This was going to make or break her testimony and would affect her career.

Shaun started with her childhood. Quinn answered his questions fully, explaining in plain English her specific problems and the reasons for her withdrawal. She glanced back at the defense expert witness. He stared at her. From what Quinn was saying, he now understood her real diagnosis. He went back to listening to the testimony, interested in learning more about her coping mechanisms.

Quinn's concise explanations debunked the idea of her periods of withdrawal affecting the other parts of her life, or that they were in any way associated with any type of psychiatric disorder. She was totally normal when her system wasn't being overloaded. Shaun went one step further and had Quinn explain her meltdown from a medical standpoint. He had chuckled when Shaun had asked if that period had any effect on her ability to remember things accurately.

"No. It was a total shutdown into a world of her own making. It was due to the trauma of her three years in captivity. Everything from before and after is totally intact. Only during that particular time was she out of contact with the real world. Even if she wanted to, she isn't able to erase what is in her memory."

"If that is so, then why these gaps?"

"If you were to ask her, you would find that she remembers what transpired in those gaps, but it is all internal. It may not make much sense to you and me because those periods don't correlate to what is going on around her, but it is a safe place for her. These gaps are only in her interaction with the world at that specific time. The withdrawal is caused by being unable to process what is occurring around her. Excess noise, emotions, and confusion from others will trigger a need for her to withdraw if she can't leave the situation. When not in withdrawal, she's totally normal and able to relate to everything just as you and I would, except with more detail due to her memory."

"Thank you, Dr. Richards. You may cross-examine the

witness," Shaun stated with a wink at her as he returned to his seat at the table.

Lowenstein did everything he could to shake Quinn's testimony. It didn't work. He hadn't given her diagnosis, but she knew anyone with medical knowledge of childhood problems would be able to fit her into the mold of autism. The defense's ploy hadn't worked.

Court was adjourned until the next morning when Quinn's testimony ended. She would be back on the stand when court reconvened.

Jared commented as he followed them, "Quinn, I loved the way you danced around the diagnosis. Lowenstein still doesn't get it. I wonder if he'll ask his expert his opinion of your testimony."

He didn't say anything more. His comment revealed how closely he was listening to the testimony.

Chapter 29

BOBKIN

The next morning, the defense continued with cross-examining her. Lowenstein didn't ask any more questions about the gaps in her life. Finally, he turned into the great defense lawyer he was, attempting to pick apart various areas of her testimony. Apparently, he, and maybe Billings and Bobkin, had overridden Franko's defense plan.

No matter what he tried, he couldn't negate or create doubt in her previous testimony. By the end of the day, she was excused. It was over except for a few minor details to be taken care of, and the summations.

The case was given to the jury on Friday morning. She was surprised when the jury returned within four hours with a verdict. On all charges for the three men, the jury returned a guilty verdict. She was sitting between Quinn and Tom, their arms around her, afraid until the last verdict was read. Jared stated sentencing would be on Monday. It meant she needed to talk to Bobkin today and get her request to Jared before Monday.

When court was adjourned, she requested for Malcolm to arrange a private meeting between her and Bobkin before he was taken back to jail. Lowenstein didn't object to the meeting. Tom and Malcolm walked with her as the guards guided them to the secure room where Bobkin was being held.

Before she entered the room, Tom rotated her so they were facing. "Jill, do what you think is best. I understand the relationship between you two."

"Do you really?" she inquired.

He chuckled and shook his head, "More than you may think. I know you're coming to me as a whole person. He fell in love with the innocent child you were at the time. Show him the woman you've become, who understands what happened and why. It's all right to still care for him."

As hard as it was to believe, he really did understand. She kissed him before entering the room for the private meeting with the convicted man who had saved her life. Bobkin stood and smiled when she entered the room and closed the door.

In the years she had known him, the tall, thin, dark haired man hadn't changed. His light gray eyes showed his love. The smile was one she had come to look forward to seeing, even after she had been moved from the special room. Even now, she wanted to protect the gentle man who had saved her life.

"Ivan, I hope you don't mind talking to me privately," she stated with uncertainty.

He shrugged, continuing to smile at her. "Not at all. You were so marvelous on the stand. I knew you were special. I just didn't realize how extraordinarily special you were."

"Well, my specialness is putting you in prison."

He lowered his gaze to his folded hands on the table. His shoulders slumped forward and the smile left, leaving his face a mask, hiding his thoughts and feelings. "I really don't mind. It's one way of getting out of the mess I got myself into."

"Explain to me how you got into this mess," she requested.

He twisted his mouth and shrugged again. He sucked in a breath and slowly let it out before speaking, his head down, focusing on his folded hands.

"It wasn't all that hard. I'm an accountant. A very good one. I needed a job, but wanted one which would take me out of Russia. I didn't verify if it was a legitimate business, only that I would be sent overseas to another country."

"Why?"

"If I hadn't left, I would have been relegated to a life of drudgery and poverty. I wanted more than an existence of quiet desperation. It wasn't until I had been here for several months I discovered what I had gotten into. I realized very quickly that there was no way out without returning to Russia or certain death. I had traded one prison for another. It was a much nicer one, but one I wouldn't ever be able to leave."

"How long had you been with them before meeting me?"

"Five years. I'm very good at what I do, and it kept them able to do their thing. I really didn't do anything but the books. I explained that to the agent who interviewed me."

"So, you really weren't in charge of the drug portion of

the business?"

"No. Franko ran the businesses. I did the books and passed messages for him."

"Before me, did you take advantage of any of the others they held in the special room?"

"Only one. She looked much like you, but I couldn't reach her. I've been looking for a fairy like her or you to make my life more pleasant. Franko knew my preference for the tiny fragile-looking girls, but he also knew I normally wouldn't interact with those they would bring in. You and Susan were different."

"So, you went to Susan?"

"Yes. I tried to talk to her. She was very angry and refused to talk to me. I wanted to help her, but I couldn't. Her anger didn't let her see how I would have taken her out of the mix. I did what I could for her, but she never knew it was me."

"What about me?"

Bobkin glanced up at her but immediately dropped his gaze back to his hands. His eyes filled with tears, which ran down his cheeks unchecked.

"When I went into that room, there was this innocent fragile girl who was so terrified. She was very beautiful. There was something inside her which enhanced her physical beauty.

"Those lovely eyes were so full of fear. When I sat on that bed, I wanted to take away the fear. As we talked, this totally innocent girl peeked out. I couldn't hurt her.

"When you took my hand, it sent this jolt through me. I had to protect what I sensed in you. You were different, and I knew it. Franko never recognized what he had in you, or he would have put you to work in another capacity outside of the brothel."

"How did you know I was different from one touch?"

"I can't put it into words. It was like you had this ability to connect most others don't have. It's something I understand but can't explain."

"Why did you keep coming back to me?"

"Because I couldn't stay away. I had fallen in love with the fairy. That beautiful innocent fairy who totally bewitched me with a smile, a hug, and a kiss."

He used the palm of his hand to wipe away his tears. "I did my best to get you away from them. I wanted to put you in a gilded cage where the only pain you had would be from being in the cage. Franko refused. He only saw you in dollars and cents, and a possible recall if you went to Russia and made his boss happy. He hated it here and wanted to return to Russia. He also wanted to hurt me because he hated me. I was the one he had to answer to when the accounts didn't add up, stopping him from skimming from the club."

"What did you do to help me over the time I was there?"

"I had the only person I trusted to get you to dance, so

you were treated better. I made sure you didn't stay in the hole for very long. Little things like that."

"Did you help get me out?"

Ivan lowered his eyes to his hands again.

"Yes. I was watching you that night. It was easy to see the change when you noticed the big man at the back of the room. I knew you recognized him and were ashamed of what you were doing as he watched you dance. I took a chance and sent a note to him, telling him how to get you out. It had a time and day on it. If I was wrong—well, I wouldn't be here right now. Franko would have killed me."

"That isn't the whole truth," Jill stated, eyes boring into his. She wanted the whole truth.

Ivan blinked back tears before speaking. "I knew Franko had hurt you. I threatened him. If anything happened to you, I would kill him. He started to laugh, but when he noticed I was serious, he stated I wouldn't have the nerve to carry through on it. He was wrong. I would have killed him. I had been informed of his plan. It was the reason I took the chance with the big man. I couldn't let him kill you."

His explanation gave credence to his being in love with her. He had put his life on the line to get her out of the club, saving her life in the process.

She watched Ivan as she told him, "That big man was my brother. I don't know how he found me, but by contacting him, you saved my life."

Ivan glanced up at her before admitting, "I have some outside contacts. I let them know that the club wasn't as it seemed, and they needed to check it out."

From what she had discovered about her rescue, he was telling the truth. The love he had for her made him do things which put him in jeopardy to protect her and get her away from Franko.

"Ivan, what would you really like to do with your life if you weren't going to prison?"

"Have a job in some small legitimate company where I could earn a decent income, and live a quiet life. I'd like to find the fairy meant for me to keep and love."

"Would you be willing to change your identity and do that upon getting out of prison?"

He sighed, keeping his head down, "The likelihood of me surviving prison is slim at best. I know that. Franko will have me killed. He now knows I was the one who got you out. I made my choice, and I would do it again to save you."

"What if you were sent to a prison where you would be protected from that threat?"

"They can't stop him. He has a very long reach. There's still a contract out on you, and he won't call it off. He wants revenge. It's okay. I know how these things work. I knew when we were arrested, I wouldn't survive."

"Don't give up yet. I have an in with some very powerful people who'll jump through hoops to keep me working with them. I'm going to give you a card. It gives you how to keep in contact with me. I'll call in those markers I hold to help you if you're sentenced to prison. I'm hoping to keep you out and make you disappear for helping bring Franko down."

"Why would you do that for me?" he questioned, watching her with a frown.

"Because your kindness and love kept me sane. You showed me that not all men are pigs. That locket gave me hope. Those simple words were a talisman for me. I also know you left those letters for me, along with the ledger on Madeline's desk. You made sure I had the time to read the other ledger. You knew I had a photographic memory after you gave me the locket, because after I looked at it, you asked me what it said, and I repeated the poem word for word."

Smiling at her, he admitted, "Yes. I knew. I have the same ability. I made sure no one else knew. If your friends need more information before I'm taken to prison, I can give it to them. It might help them get rid of a couple of the other groups. Thomas never asked what other information I had outside of the group here."

Stunned, she stared at him her mouth open, unable to comprehend his words for a few seconds. Pulling herself together, she happily stated, "I believe you just got a free pass out of prison, Ivan. Once Tom gets what information you have, he can make you disappear. No one will ever find you and you'll have a totally new identity. He's really good at it."

Ivan pursed his lips, studying her before leaning against the back of his chair with a smile. "You're in love with him, aren't you?"

"Yes, and he loves me."

"I'm glad you came back to life. I was scared you wouldn't make it when you collapsed. I'm happy you found the man who will love you the way you deserve to be loved."

"Thank you. I'll notify him you have a lot of information to help them in breaking the Russian mafia enterprises. He'll take it from there."

She stood to leave. Bobkin put a hand on her arm, holding her in place. Facing him, she wondered what he wanted.

"I have one personal thing to ask of you. You have the option of refusing."

"What?"

"One kiss from the woman you have become."

There was no way she could refuse his request. It was because of him she had escaped from Franko and the death he had planned for her. Moving into his embrace, she gave him the kiss he wanted. When he raised his head, he chuckled, "Jill, your man is getting more than he realizes. Be happy."

Tom and Malcolm were waiting outside the door. She

left it open as she told Tom, "Dear, you'll want to spend some time picking Ivan's brain. He can help you in bringing down more cells. Like me, he remembers things after he sees them. Malcolm, you'll need to keep him alive while the Feds can extract all the information he has collected, which means he needs to be handed over to them before sentencing. If you send him to prison, you'll lose everything he knows because they'll kill him."

Tom glanced at the man behind her, then at Malcolm. "I believe we need to send Jill back to the rooms while we verify some recently obtained information."

She rotated her head to Ivan and winked. He bowed his head in her direction, a grin on his lips. He had wanted out alive to give them the information he had gotten over the years. She had just saved his life like he had saved hers. The kindness and love he had shown her was now coming back to him. She couldn't imagine leaving him to a fate he didn't deserve.

Malcolm and Tom stayed to talk to the gentle man who had, unknowingly, gotten in over his head while trying to escape from an existence which would have killed him. She knew they would discover he was telling her the truth when he said he had the information they needed. Hopefully, she would see him one more time before he disappeared into another life.

It was late evening when Malcolm and Tom joined her,

Shaun, and Quinn. The two men weren't smiling. A flash of fear went through her as she studied their faces, not sure what the grim faces meant for Ivan.

Tom sat beside her. "We have him in federal custody and have moved him to an undisclosed location. Jared has been notified that he has been removed from the current case, pending further investigation and that his life is in extreme danger. Jill, how did you find out he had all this information?"

"He told me when I verified he knew I had a photographic memory. He said he was like me and let it drop that you hadn't ask him about what else he knew of the cells here."

"Damn, girl. That man is a wellspring of information. Like you, he's been gathering information on the off chance he could get out alive and bring them down. You know what the kicker is? He's willing to risk his life to give us this information because they hurt you," Malcolm informed her in a voice showing he still couldn't believe their luck.

"We fairies have a way of keeping our subjects loyal," she told them with a grin, well aware of Ivan's penchant for women like her.

Tom lifted a brow, eyes meeting hers. "He admitted the woman the child had become was definitely more than he had ever expected she would be. He also said he would do whatever it took to fulfill that woman's trust in him."

Shrugging, she avoided his gaze. "He still loves me and knows I care for him. He also knows I've found the man I love as a woman." She peeked up at him, afraid he wouldn't understand her kissing Ivan.

"How does he know about the woman you are?" Tom questioned, head tilted, and eyebrows raised.

"Leave it alone, Tom. I just told him thank you and goodbye."

Drawing her into his arms, she could feel him laughing before he said, "Honey, if one kiss produces that type of loyalty, I guess I'm in for some surprises."

"Not really. He just wasn't expecting the woman. Hopefully, he'll find his fairy someday. He's partial to us."

Malcolm growled, "We have to keep him alive first. Tom, that's your department. We need the rest of the information he has tucked away inside that head of his."

"Already in progress. He should be on his way to a new location as we speak. I'm not about to let her protector get killed for helping her stay alive. Besides, I happen to like the man."

Pulling back from him, she stared into his eyes. "You like him?"

"Yes, I like him. He's this honest man who got himself into a situation he couldn't find a way out of once he got here. He seldom came to the club, not liking what they were doing there. It wasn't until he saw you on one of the security videos he started spending time there. He's a gentle soul and has this great sense of humor. I have a very good place for him to disappear. One where they'll never find him."

"Where?" she asked.

"With me. He'll be working for our department in a very protected environment, right out in plain sight with no trail leading to him."

"Tom, are you sure you want to do that?"

"Very sure. He knows the boundaries and how I'm extremely attached to the woman you've become. In fact, he told me I had better not let you go, because I have a woman most men only dream of having next to them."

Taking a deep breath and letting it out, she shook her head. "I'll never figure you men out."

The men roared with laughter. It was the normal statement they would make about women.

"It isn't hard, Jill. He'll be a good friend to us."

Malcolm, sounding like Tom's father, stated, "Unlike most men, Tom doesn't see Ivan as a threat to your relationship with him. In fact, he sees him as someone who helped you become the remarkable woman you are today. There's no reason for him to keep you apart. He understood the kiss Ivan wanted and knows it won't happen again."

She turned back to Tom. He slyly stated, "It's what I would have requested had I been in his shoes. Knowing you, you would have given him that one last thing for being so kind and caring to you. Look at it as his reward for saving your life and it makes sense."

It made no sense as to how he had gotten there, but he was right. It had been Ivan's reward for saving her life. She was glad he would be safe. It was more than she had expected when she had gone to talk to him.

Chapter 30

WHERE YOU GO, THERE GO I

The sentencing hearing was started on time. Bobkin was missing from the defense table. Lowenstein questioned Llewellyn as to why he wasn't there. Jared stated he had been removed from the case by the prosecution. There was nothing more said about Bobkin.

The charges and the verdicts were read for Billings and Franko. Jared asked if there was anyone who wanted to make a statement prior to the sentencing. Jill stood from where she was seated behind the prosecution table.

"I would like to speak," she stated, all eyes in the courtroom on her.

Jared stared at her before stating, "Please be brief."

She moved so she was looking directly at Franko. Her words were for him.

"Mr. Franko, of all the people I encountered during the three years I was in captivity, you were the cruelest and most depraved. You thought of nothing but your twisted, sick, wants and needs, not caring that it was another human you were hurting or killing. You showed no remorse when you killed Rita and Wendy. In fact, you enjoyed what you were doing, encouraging the others who were participating in your sick scenario, to be as depraved as you.

"When you told me their fate was to be mine, except you would make it more painful, should tell everyone here you aren't human. You're an animal of the worst kind. An animal who kills for pleasure. I'll not hide my hatred and anger toward you. You put it there with everything you did to me and every other person you contaminated with your depravity who hurt me. There's no way I'll ever be able to forgive you for what you did. Again, you're not human. You're a vicious, sick animal."

She took a breath and let it out before continuing.

"I would love to have you experience what you did to

me and the others. On second thought, you would probably enjoy it due to your twisted sense of pleasure. My one desire where you are concerned is for you to be caged, like any dangerous animal, at the mercy of those who are like you, until the day you die." Her voice held the anger and pain she had kept bottled up inside of her. There was nothing more for her to do now. It was officially over.

She pivoted away from the defense table and stalked out of the courtroom, not caring what sentence Jared gave him. Her words had told Franko what she thought and felt about him. That was the purpose of her speech. It was her way of ridding herself of the last remnants of pain, fear, and hatred from those three years.

The guards took her to a secure room to wait for the others. The tears had come as she grieved for what Franko had done to her and for the others who had suffered and died because of him. By the time Tom and Malcolm joined her, the tears were gone. She was at peace with her past. Malcolm stared at her for a few seconds before he moved into the room, leaving Tom at the door.

"You should have stayed. You would have loved Jared's comments before he handed down the sentences. Franko got the death penalty, but he'll not be kept on death row. He'll be in the general population until his appeals are done. He'll be in a maximum-security federal prison. It was that last part of the sentence which surprised me, and I quote, 'Sir, I hope you enjoy your accommodations until your appeals are completed. You'll be among men just like you.'"

She couldn't believe it! Jared had made her wish come true. He would experience what she had, and he had no chance of ever being let out on parole. It would be wonderful if he kept the appeals going for twenty or so years. He had his cage, and a very good chance of finding out what rape felt like while you're held down and forced to do as commanded. Sighing, she lowered her eyes, not sure she had done the right thing. It had been something she had needed to do to totally close off that part of her life.

"I know it was wrong of me, but his smirk during the trial and what he did, not just to me, but all the others, made it so I couldn't stop myself from expressing my thoughts and feelings. I really didn't expect it to have any effect. It was just my way of getting the last piece of anger out, letting me close off that part of my life and allow it to have a peaceful death in some small box inside of me."

Jared came to the door and leaned against the frame. "Well, Jill, I have to say it was a job well done. I loved that speech. It made it very easy to hand down that sentence. I figured you'd like it. You are correct. He is an animal."

She stood when he entered the room. He put his arm around her, guiding her to the door. "I also want to thank you for sending us Ivan. The man is amazing. He was counting on you speaking to him before he was sentenced.

He wanted to let you know he would help the man you love to catch more of the Russian mafia in this country. I'm looking forward to working with him. Like you, he's so precise and organized. What little we have gotten so far has been right on the money."

She chuckled before peering up at the kindly judge, "He's like me in a lot of respects. His being put in a situation where he had no out, went against the grain for him. He's actually an honest man who just wanted a job that would allow him to live a quiet life while he looked for a fairy to make his life complete. Like me, he gathered information in the hope he could use it to stop them, not sure if he would ever get the chance to give it to the ones who needed it."

Jared grinned down at her. "My dear, he's going to get that chance. He will be a big part of shutting them down while keeping me and Shaun very busy. He's an extremely intelligent, kind gentleman, and will be a big asset to our team. Thank you for being that wonderful woman who gave him a chance to be the man he really wants to be." He chuckled and added, "I think I know a fairy who would love to meet a man like him."

They were slowly ambling toward the rooms, in no big hurry. She thought about Ivan and what he had told her. He would do well if given half a chance.

She quietly told Jared, "I couldn't see letting him pay for something he didn't know about until it was too late. He took the job in order to get out of an existence—and these are his words, not mine—of quiet desperation."

Jared let out a breath before saying, "Hmm. That explains a lot. I agree. He shouldn't be punished for that, and with what help we get from him, he may actually find himself where he really wanted to be—in a life that means something."

"If so, then my debt to him will be paid," she admitted, unable to meet his gaze.

"Jill, it was paid when you gave him that kiss," he stated with a laugh as she blushed. How in the hell did everyone know about the kiss she had given him?

Wyatt and Shaun were waiting on them in Malcolm's rooms when Jared walked her into the suite. She stopped, observing Ivan sitting in a chair with a big grin on his face. She rotated back to Jared who was also grinning.

"He's going back with me, Malcolm, and Tom, who you'll have to do without for about a week. Wyatt will keep up the security around you with the help of Fred and his men. Shaun gets to stay here and do the mop-up under the local judges for the rest of the group. He'll be using the transcript of your testimony from this trial under my orders, due to the ongoing threats against you.

"I figured a celebration was in order with several animals put in the cages they deserved. I get a good man to work with, and you get to start planning for a future right after you get your medical things completed."

Ivan happily exclaimed, "I couldn't have dreamed of a better ending. You're alive and have the man you deserve. I get a job where I can use all my abilities as soon as I prove my worth, and Franko will get his just rewards for what he did. I just hope he enjoys them."

She gave the happy man a hug. "You had better do a good job. I don't go to bat for many people, and I don't want to be disappointed this time."

"You won't be." He looked over at Tom and winked. She rotated and crossed her arms.

"Okay. I get the feeling I'm missing something here. Out with it," she demanded.

Tom took her hand and pulled her to the divan and had her sit. She scanned the men. They were all smiling. Something was up.

"Jill, I know we really haven't talked about our future, but—will you marry me?"

She looked at the ceiling then back at him and shook her head. It wasn't a romantic proposal, but he wasn't the normal man. "Of course, I'll marry you."

"Now?" he tentatively questioned, his eyes and face hopeful.

She stared at him, having difficulty processing what he was saying. "Now?"

"Yes, now."

Her eyes went to Wyatt. "Honey, don't look at me. It's your fucking choice."

She scanned the men who were waiting for her answer before saying, "Why not? It would be cheaper than a trip to Vegas."

Tom turned to Jared, who chuckled, "Okay. You win. Good thing that special license was approved."

Brad and Belinda entered the room as Malcolm was arranging where they were to stand.

"Did we get here in time?" Brad questioned.

"About fucking time you got here," Wyatt told him with a grin. "Yes, you made it."

This wasn't quite the way she had planned it, but it really didn't matter. The end result would be the same. It meant Tom would be staying with her for a lifetime.

Once everyone had settled, Jared started the ceremony, reciting it from memory. She was surprised when he changed from legal to religious and had them recite their vows. Brad slipped a ring for Tom into her hand. When Tom placed the ring on her finger, she stared at it. Her wide eyes went to his, unable to grasp why he had the ring she had dreamed of having after seeing it in the jewelry store in Tavares. He winked at her. She managed to complete her part of the ceremony before slipping the Celtic ring Brad had given her onto his finger.

Jared's ending was a mix between religious and legal. When he said, "You may kiss the bride," Tom gave her a kiss that elicited a response from her she hadn't expected.

Once all the congratulations were finished, Tom placed

the engagement ring on her finger to complete the set. Before she could ask, he told her, "Yes, I bought the set while you were getting the rest of it. I knew I wasn't going to let you get away, even though I didn't know much about you. I could see this was a set you really wanted by the way you looked at it. You'll just have to wait a bit to dance in the meadow with a flower crown in the country they represent."

She threw her arms around his waist. Going to Ireland and Scotland had been a dream of hers for a long time. He held her close as she cried in happiness while those who loved her surrounded them. Her growing up had made her dreams come true . . . a man who loved her, a family, and a future.

The End, For Now.

Preview of

Montana

He Sent an Angel

by

B. A. Mealer

Chapter 1

Wait till the darkness is over.
Wait, till the tempest is done
Hope, for the sunshine tomorrow
After the darkness is gone.

"Whispering Hope" lyrics by Septimus Winner

Montana had made better time than expected on the gently curved hilly roads. It was still early, but she could use a short day. She was tired. Tired of being a nomad. Tired of struggling. Tired of being poor. Tired of being alone. Tired of trying to stay alive.

The campground was cheap enough and was giving her a discount for staying two nights. She would be able to do a wash in the nearby town of Titusville and to take a shower while here. It is hard when you are on limited funds and couldn't afford anything but the cheapest places.

Even cheap wasn't always affordable for her. She mostly used hidden pull-offs to spend the night, only resorting to campgrounds for one or two nights a week to conserve her very limited funds, allowing her to pay for gas and food. It wasn't unusual for her to do a wash and bathe in a stream. Streams were free, unlike laundromats and campgrounds.

For six of the past seven years, she had lived without electric, a bathroom, or running water. A stream had been her water source, candles or a campfire her light, a hole in the ground her bathroom, and a large pot with heated water her bathtub. Now, she had a home of sorts in the pop-up camper she pulled behind her motorcycle. It took the place of the shelter built of discarded planks of wood and tarps or the small pup tent she had used for a year. She had moved up in the world, but it hadn't changed her life other than becoming nomadic instead of stationary.

The pay from her last job was enough to splurge on the two nights she planned on spending at the campground along with the admission to the park she wanted to visit. She would conserve the rest of her money for expenses as she worked her way northwest toward Sturgis, South Dakota. What she hid was how she didn't have anything to her name but what she carried on her motorcycle and the camper trailer, which was her home. It was a lonely home, but it was paid for and in her name, so no one could take it away from her.

She pulled into the parking area for the campground office. The first thing she noticed was the motorcycle parked near the building. It was packed with bags and a tent, so whoever it belonged to was traveling. The light blue color of the motorcycle reminded her of a clear sky on a summer day. Montana removed her helmet, and grabbed what passed for a purse from the top of the small cooler on her backseat and headed into the office.

Her lowrider looked like the sea beside the blue bike.

Like the other bike, hers stood out. Her bike and trailer were painted a custom pale marine green. The paint shimmered like the sun on deep ocean water. The color had been taken from a picture an acquaintance had taken of the ocean and given to her, not knowing she didn't have a place to hang it. It was one of the few things she had kept and protected while living in the lean-to.

Her bike and trailer had airbrushed artwork. The male angel on the top of the gas tank was the only decoration on the bike itself. She had worked with the artist to ensure the features on the angel were what she wanted. The artwork on the trailer consisted of angels, dragons, and fairies amid various scenes from around the world. The friend who had painted it hadn't charged her. Instead, he had requested she give out cards for advertisement. He got business while she had a bike and trailer she loved.

When she entered the office, there was a man filling out paperwork at the counter. He glanced over at her, then returned to what he was doing. He wasn't someone who would stand out in a crowd. At six feet, give or take an inch or two, with light brown hair and an average body, you would easily pass over him. It was his eyes which caught her attention when they had briefly met hers. They were the color of the bike outside. His rounded face gave her the impression of his being a young boy in a man's body.

Montana picked up a brochure on the park where she was planning on going tomorrow. It was a historical site recommended by a camper who had befriended her during her last sojourn in a campground. This stop was only a couple of hours from her planned route. The ride to here had been over a road with just the right spacing of curves to be fun without being difficult.

Glancing up at the voice of the woman behind the counter, she noted the woman was showing the man where his site was on a map. He took the map and headed for the door. For the time she was in the office, the man hadn't spoken once. His quick nod and slight smile in her direction was the only acknowledgment he gave of her being in the room. Montana moved to the counter, noting the sound of a bike starting. She now had confirmation of who was riding the blue bike.

"I have a reservation. My name is Montana," she stated.

The woman behind the counter flopped a registration form on the counter without looking at her before asking in a tired voice, "What type of site do you need?"

"Something that will handle a pop-up camper pulled by a motorcycle. It'll need to be fairly smooth with electric if possible."

"How many nights?"

"Two."

"Twenty-even fifty a night. Cash or credit?"

"Credit," she stated, completing the registration card before handing it to the woman along with her debit card.

The woman still hadn't looked at her.

After running her card, the receptionist put a pen and the slip to be signed on the counter, then returned her debit card. Placing a map on the counter, the woman marked her campsite and automatically stated, "Your campsite is located here. Have a nice stay," before turning away from the counter, dismissing her.

Montana shook her head. The woman hadn't looked at her for the whole transaction. It had been impersonal and robotic. Returning to her bike, she laid the map on the seat to study as she put on her helmet. She was next to a stream if the map was correct. Her site was the fourth after the first left and was labeled as number thirty.

Site number thirty was a great spot. If nothing else, the woman had understood what she needed. Parking the camper, it took her half an hour to get totally set up and unpacked. She had put up the extra room, seeing as how she would be here for more than one night.

It would give her a place to work so she could complete the job she had started. The pay from the job would give her a cushion just in case she had unforeseen expenses. There was one more job to finish, but she needed more information to complete it. Hopefully, she would get what she needed within the next week. If so, it would pay enough for her to enjoy Sturgis for the three or four days she planned on being there.

There were specific sights she wanted to see around

Sturgis, and a few roads to find, which were a must-ride per some bikers she had met. Of course, there was the requisite shirt to buy to say she had been there. Hopefully, she would be able to do the stay for under five hundred dollars for food and extras over the two hundred a day camping fees. That was her budget for her few days there.

Montana had never met Carl, the person she worked for, but he paid well and was prompt. It gave her enough money to survive without going hungry. The online job of writing informational texts for various companies had come along when she had needed it the most.

She had kept the job during her one sojourn into what she had thought was a normal relationship. That had ended when she had been given a day to move out by Greg, her supposed boyfriend. So much for love and a lasting relationship. She had seen Greg's new girlfriend before she had left. It was easy to understand why he had thrown her out. The girl was a very pretty, tall blonde, not a short brown wren.

Being plain had its disadvantages. At five feet six, she was average height. Her figure was decent, and her face was pleasant, but nothing most men would notice. She was that brown wren with shoulder-length dark brown hair, brown eyes, and skin that was pale with very little color. Like the wren, she could sing, but if not singing, she wasn't ever seen. Being honest with herself, she was probably better off not being noticed.

It was still too early to eat after setting up her camp. She would have time for a walk in the woods. Changing into tennis shoes, she grabbed a bottle of water before heading to where the map showed the start of one of the trails.

The man who had been in the office was two sites away from her. A glance in the direction of his site showed a small tent and fire burning in the fire ring. He was walking ahead of her with a pot in his hand, going toward the water spigot.

As Montana followed the trail into the woods, she let the loneliness, which had been nagging her, out of the box where she normally kept it. Today had been one of those days where she would have loved to have someone to enjoy it with her. What do you do when you have no home, no close friends, and nothing but time on your hands?

She ambled along the path, keeping her head down as the unwanted tears rolled down her cheeks. Why was life so hard for her and so easy for others? What had passed for a family had made it very clear that she wasn't wanted. Even her stepbrother Robert had quit contacting her.

She had a couple of acquaintances who occasionally contacted her online, but they had lives which didn't include her. No one other than Robert and his father had known how she had lived. Not one person she had met after being thrown out of the house had ever asked her about her home or if she needed anything from the time she was seventeen.

Through it all, she had kept the dream of meeting a special man who would love her and share a real home with her at the forefront of her thoughts. So far, it was still a dream. Today was one of those days when she needed to allow the loneliness out and deal with the sadness inside of her.

Other than Carl, her boss, no one would even notice if she dropped out of life. He would only find someone else to do what she did, thinking she had found better work. How can you live for twenty-four years without anyone caring if you were alive or not? If she disappeared, no one would notice or care. That was her reality.

She had gone a good distance into the woods before she was drawn to a group of large rocks a short way off the wooded path to her left. The large rocks were in a rough circle with a small open area in the center where a low rounded rock poked up from the ground, inviting someone to sit on it. The circle of rocks was surrounded by large maples and oaks, their leafy branches filtering the light, giving the impression of being in a dim cathedral.

Proceeding to the rock in the center, she took a seat on it and let the intense sadness wash over her. This was one of the rare occasions where she let the feelings bring her down, preferring to be positive rather than negative in her life. She started humming "Wayfaring Stranger" and was soon singing it, letting her feelings infuse the words with emotion as she sang. Her feelings determined the songs she sang as she continued her concert in the woods, knowing she would feel better by letting the emotions she was feeling out in the only way she could. The tears stopped as she sang. The sadness left as hope took its place.

Her last song was "Whispering Hope." It was all she had. Hope. The picture of that wonderful man who would love her, the house they would have, along with the friends surrounding them, was there in her mind as she sat on the stone. Releasing the tension with a cleansing breath, she stood, a smile lit her face before turning to where she had entered the rock formation. Things happened in time. For now, all she could do was to imagine what life would be like when she had someone who loved her, hoping it would be sooner rather than later. She didn't know how much more she could take of the darkness which had been part of her reality from her first memories.

With bowed head, she moved from the rock where she had been sitting. When she raised her head, her eyes met those of the man who had been in the office. He was leaning against a tree watching her, a twig in his fingers. She could only imagine what he was thinking of her impromptu concert.

When he didn't act like he was leaving, she dropped her gaze to her feet, moving out of the rock circle. When she neared where he was standing, she glanced at him. His eyes dropped to the twig he was twirling between his fingers. His soft shy voice held her in place.

"You have a beautiful voice. It showed what you were feeling." He gave her a quick glance before lowering his eyes back to his twig. It was like he was afraid to look at her. She could almost feel the shyness he was exhibiting with his difficulty in looking at her.

She gave him a smile, not that he saw it. "Thank you," she stated in response to his observation.

He stood, eyes down, tenseness in his hands as he gripped the twig. She could see he was trying to get up the nerve to speak again. She understood his difficulty in talking. Her stepbrother Robert was much the same.

He finally asked, keeping his head down and not looking at her while twirling the twig in his fingers, "You headed back to the campground?"

"Yes. I think I've disturbed the inhabitants of the woods enough for one day."

He flashed her a shy smile. "Mind if I walk with you?"

"No, I don't mind," she told him, her voice calm, comfortable with his shyness.

He walked beside her as she slowly made her way back to the path, giving him time to talk. She had guessed he was like Robert and needed time to find the words.

"Name's Shane," he said with a quick glance at her.

"Mine's Montana. Pleasure to meet you, Shane," she said, trying not to stress him.

They were on the path before he asked, "You staying here for a while or passing through?"

"I'm passing through. I stopped to see Drake Well Park in Titusville. I was told it was different and had a lot of historical information on the oil industry in this area."

Shane didn't say anything for a few more steps. "Where are you headed from here?"

She peered over at him, her eyes meeting his before he refocused on the ground in front of him. She could almost feel him withdraw, afraid he had asked a question he shouldn't have.

Turning to watch where she was going, she answered his question. "I'm planning on ending up in Sturgis for now. Just taking my time getting there."

His tension was palpable. He worried his bottom lip before giving her a quick glance. More than anything, she wanted to tell him she understood and to relax. But not knowing him, she held her peace. He would get it out eventually.

Robert, who was four years older than her, had told her to give him time, then he could say what he wanted without feeling stupid. She had learned from him how hard it was for a shy person to talk, even to their own family. Their parents hadn't understood his shyness and the stuttering it had caused. She had understood because she had her own speech problems.

He was the only one in the family who would have anything to do with her while she lived there. His father had intervened with her mother occasionally, but mostly ignored her and how she was treated. When they had thrown her out, Robert had stopped her as she was walking away from the house. He had cried when she told him she wasn't to contact anyone in the family because she no longer existed for them.

Robert would occasionally send her instant messages if he found her online, or he would e-mail her when he was at a friend's house using their e-mail. He would let her know it was him by putting his name in the subject line. She hadn't heard from him for almost six months now. Her guess was that he had finally joined the rest of her so-called family in ignoring her existence.

Shane finally imparted, "I'm on my way there, too. Just taking my time on some back roads." He hesitated before asking, "Ever been there?"

"No. Figured I'd see what all the hoopla was about."

"You the one on the lowrider?"

She smiled. He had figured out what he wanted to say. "Yes. I take it you're on the dresser?"

"Yes." Again, he hesitated after another quick peek in her direction. "I'm going up around the lakes. I wouldn't be averse to having another rider along. That is if you're going that way."

Smiling, she loved the way he had gotten out of asking her outright to join him on his trip around the lakes. It was a beautifully worded invitation to ride with him. As they walked, she considered his offer. She had the time. He would be pleasant company who wouldn't be making innuendos every other sentence. Plus, it would be nice to have someone around, even if he didn't talk much.

"I take it you're following the lakeshore for most of the trip?" she inquired, wanting to know if it was going to be a blah route or the one she had planned on doing at some later point in time.

He smiled, watching the path. "Yes. The worst part is getting around the cities. I'm planning on following the lakes up into Canada, then coming back down Route 85 to Sturgis."

It was the most he had said without hesitating. His voice was pleasant and almost musical. What the hell. If he turned out to be a creep, she could always go back to riding on her own like she was now.

"Sounds better than my planned way of getting there. It'll be nice to have company."

She gave him a smile with her acceptance. His was brilliant, before he looked away from her. He didn't say anything further on the walk back. He had relaxed some, but he still couldn't talk. It didn't matter to her. She enjoyed his company without all the talking.

When they arrived back at her camp, he finally spoke again. "I was going to the park tomorrow. Want to go together?"

It was an easy question to answer. "Sure. It doesn't open until ten, so, want to leave about nine thirty?"

"Okay." He flashed a shy smile in her direction. "See you then."

She watched him walk toward his camp. It wouldn't be hard to spend time in his company. It would be like being with Robert. Maybe for a few days, she wouldn't feel so alone. She didn't care if he couldn't talk to her. Just having someone around who noticed you existed, even if it was for a short period of time, was better than what she had been feeling earlier.

Fate had again intervened. She had been sent an angel when she needed him most. A few days was all she was wanting. A few days of company. A few days of someone who noticed she was alive.

If you would like to receive updates on new books by B. A. Mealer, please visit:

http://www.bamealer.com

or

http://www.facebook.com/bamealer

Other titles by B. A. Mealer

Abilene   https://www.amazon.com/Abilene-B-Mealer-ebook/dp/B01N5AFLIP

www.ingramcontent.com/pod-product-compliance
Lightning Source LLC
Chambersburg PA
CBHW030536020726
47494CB00005B/1391